The Memphis Kingmaker

A Novel

Cecilia Hallman

Cecilia A. Hallman and L. Douglass Brown

The Memphis Kingmaker

Copyright © Cecilia A. Hallman and L. Douglass Brown, 2006

First printing by IRG Press, April 2006

IRG Press
262 Eastgate Dr. #345
Aiken, SC 29803

ISBN 0-977-8930-0-6

SAN: 850-4504

Library of Congress Control Number: 2006922881

Printed in Canada

Publisher's and authors' note:
The Memphis Kingmaker is a work of fiction. While some names, places and incidents that are portrayed in the book are used fictitiously, the entire book is the product of the authors' imaginations. Any resemblance to any persons, living or dead, business establishments, events or locales is entirely coincidental.

www.thekingmaker.net

To Dennis and Jo Ann...

We miss you.

Acknowledgements

The authors would like to acknowledge their appreciation of the advice, assistance and depth of knowledge provided by Tom Wolfe and Doris O'Donnell, two great authors, journalists and friends. This is a much better book because of you both.

Chapter One

Cadet John Henry Thompson

Cadet John Henry Thompson, Class of 1946, was a not-too-tall, thin young man when he entered West Point. He had never been this far from home, much less in a very foreign land, Yankee territory, just up the Hudson River from that metropolis of New York City – at The United States Military Academy, West Point, just 'The Point' to him and the other cadets.

To John, the Hudson River Valley was not unlike the Tennessee Valley near back home, rolling hills and lots of fresh water. But there were stately mansions there, a definite sense of being out of his world. Sure, there were old plantation homes back home, but none like these. It seemed that everyone lived this way up there, definitely upscale, 'landed gentry' he would call them.

He didn't have to worry. He would rarely see the outside of the gates that were the confines of The Point for his stay. Summers were spent doing extra work and earning money, most of which he sent home to his parents to help out during his absence.

John had met businessmen from New York City while at The Peabody Hotel in Memphis and had dreamed of one day seeing their world for himself. He knew that he would. It was never an impossible dream.

✤ ✤ ✤

John was never expected to get into West Point. He was from that wide spot in the road called simply, 'Slabtown', a nowhere Tennessee community just outside Memphis. He never would have made it if not for the help of one of Slabtown, Tennessee's finest, Fred Hadley.

Sergeant Fred Hadley was in World War I, the 'Great War' he called it, the war to end all wars. But outside his bravado, his telling and re-telling of his escapades in France in 1918, he knew deep down that his country was headed toward the mother of all wars, World War II. A product of Slabtown, Fred was a local icon and held the distinguished post of Army recruiter in Memphis, at least the position of senior enlisted man.

A Master Sergeant who stayed in the Army after the War, when John Henry Thompson approached him on a trip to the city one day in 1941 he knew of John and about him. First in his class at Slabtown may have not meant much to someone from Memphis, but to a man like Sergeant Fred it meant an opportunity for a hometown boy like John to 'make good' – and to him, that meant becoming an officer in the United States Army.

Sergeant Fred knew what it meant to be at the bottom end of the food chain. He left Slabtown in 1917 to join up with old General John Joseph 'Black Jack' Pershing and fight the Kaiser in Europe. He got his fill of serving his country in wartime, of being gassed – and of saying 'yes sir' and 'no sir' to the elitist officers, most of them Yankees from New England. Just boys themselves, they had one thing that Fred would never have – a college education. Some even had graduated from that venerated institution called the United States Military Academy at West Point. That's where he wanted to see young John Henry Thompson land as an officer and a gentleman.

John knew of West Point, that General John J. Pershing had

led the Allies in defeating the Kaiser's Germany and that John's grandfather had served in another war with him, the Spanish-American War in 1898. He also knew that what separated his grandfather from Pershing was the fact that Pershing was a West Pointer. To him, that was the great barrier, the divide that would always keep him from achieving greatness. At least in the case of John Henry Thompson, he would have a leg up on getting out of Slabtown and into West Point.

When John entered the Army Recruiting Center on Union Avenue, just down the street from the Peabody Hotel in Memphis that November day in 1941, he immediately knew Sergeant Fred. Lantern-jawed and upright as he was when he took the field in the Great War, Fred knew John too, although not on sight. He was Fred's dream come true, a chance to be all that he could be, all that he never was – through John.

What John didn't know was that Fred's father had actually served under General Pershing too, chasing Poncho Villa in northern Mexico. Even more important to his future was the fact that Fred knew Pershing personally from his service in World War I. It somehow comforted John when he learned that Pershing was the son a railroad foreman in nearby Laclede, Missouri.

Over the next year and a half Sergeant Fred would ask the only favor he had asked of The General in his life. Please help this one young man, a special man from his hometown, achieve the dream of his life, Fred's dream. It would be the support he needed to get in, to change his life forever, to put him on the road to being one of the wealthiest men in the world – a kingmaker. And the war was on.

⚜ ⚜ ⚜

John had never known a Yankee boy, but Harmon Vance had known many young men like John. His father owned a string of appliance stores, many located in Southern cities like Memphis. Harmon was a shoo-in for The Point. His father had served in the 328th Infantry in France during World War I and had fought with Alvin York, the war hero and Medal of Honor winner.

"So you're from Tennessee. My dad's best friend in the Great War was Alvin York!" would be all the words John needed to hear from a Yankee boy to form a bond that would last a lifetime.

Alvin York was a folk hero to Tennessee boys coming up with stories of the Great War. Sergeant Fred had even met him once. York returned to Tennessee after the War and opened a mill. The state of Tennessee had given him a white frame home up on the Kentucky line and he made a go of it. But in the end, the mill didn't make it. The state even stepped in to lend a hand, but they just ended up taking over some of the property to help out. Tennessee kids from all over the state eventually attended a school built there. John would send flowers to York's funeral in 1964.

"I am and I'm proud of it!" would be a common, proud Tennessee refrain John would proclaim for years, many times defensive, other times provocative, urging on his would-be detractors. He would use this prejudice, not unlike the racial strife he had seen in the rural South to his advantage.

Harmon Vance knew he had a live one on his hands. Puzzled as to how a backwoods boy had made it to West Point, Harmon never had a chance against John. After his obligated service in the Army after The Point, Harmon would have known John well enough by then to serve as his lifelong assistant, a life that Harmon would have never dreamed of that first day at The United States Military Academy.

"Boy, is this the first time you've ever had on shoes?!" screamed the first real cadet John ever met, Cadet Sergeant Mark Davis, a grisly man for his young years as a senior cadet from Brooklyn. Harmon couldn't help himself. He laughed out loud and thus suffered the same consequences as John – thirty pushups, twenty of which were completed.

Down the line were future comrades who wondered what in the hell they had gotten themselves into. A special few would be friends, close friends of John. They would need his help in scaling great heights in politics while another, the dictator of his own banana republic. John would know them for life, control them all and have more money and power than all of them combined. He would enable them too, helping them climb their ladders of success – quite a Class of 1946.

Lessons were learned – leadership, strategy, cunning and a desire to win. It was in a business sense that John would carry this West Point education with him always, to succeed at all costs. World War II, a war that would dwarf Sergeant Fred's Great War, was in full throttle now making York-like heroes in every American town, most of them coming home in flag-draped coffins.

While John was initially inspired to join the Army as a private, Sergeant Fred and John's own ambition to get the best education the United States government could give him kept his eye on the prize of a West Point diploma. Immediately there were real problems.

Being up at 5:00 AM was no problem for John. Working until 8:00 PM studying was a cinch, lights out at 10:00 PM was a relief. He ate well, gained a healthy 25 pounds and grew an inch, but there were problems indeed.

"I can't hit those targets," John would repeat as others cursed and damned the rifle range. As a Tennessee farm boy, everyone expected John to be a crack shot just like Alvin York who grew up shooting the eyes out of turkeys, then Germans at 300 yards.

"It's these books, Harmon. I'm spending so much time, all my efforts in getting through these books!" he would explain to his now best and most trusted friend, Harmon Vance.

"Listen. You get me through calculus and I'll handle your range qualification," Harmon would continue to assure John, even though John knew what Harmon had on their tormentor Sergeant Davis, and he didn't like it.

It seemed that Davis' father had a Vance appliance franchise, one of the few profitable ones left in Brooklyn. Sergeant Davis didn't know that Harmon Vance was one of *those* Vances from Chicago. But he was about to learn the hard way.

Range time was dirty, windy and hell for John, but not physically. Fitted with prescription glasses by now, John became almost mentally ill when the corps marched to the fields near the Hudson River. John was used to the outdoors. The hell of it was that he could not seem to make a qualifying score, a result that could end his dream of graduation.

Enter the business of politics, power and influence. Sergeant Davis was riding everyone hard. John and Harmon thought that surely Davis would have a stroke - they had never seen a jugular vein bulge so much.

"Thompson, you fool! What are you going to do when a Jap charges you, drawl him to death? You hayseed bumpkin, fire your rifle and hit that bull's eye!" Davis would scream, over and over again.

It killed Davis's soul that Harmon Vance was a crack shot. There was something he didn't like about Vance, something beyond the fact that he was a good student and almost unbreakable in the hazing, the continual heaping of pressure poured on the best and worst students in an effort to cull the weak, the unfit from the Corps of Cadets. Davis was merely a tool in the Academy's molding of future officers, making sure the cadets would graduate into the best military officers in the world.

"And you Vance, I'm going to make it my personal goal that you take your sorry ass back to…where the hell do they make such shit like you?" he baited Harmon at the range.

"Chicago, Illinois, Sergeant Davis, home of Vance Industries, Sergeant!" Harmon blasted back to Davis.

John saw the look on Davis' face; he knew what it meant, more prophetically what it meant for him, his future that would include owning, making or breaking men like Sergeant Davis.

Davis was no fool. Somewhat limited in his intellectual pursuits, he was nevertheless Army all the way and he couldn't wait to get into the shit. In just six months he would get his chance as a platoon leader in the Gilbert Islands where his physical acumen and West Point training would keep him and as many of his platoon as he could alive. But he was first and foremost a survivor, and he wanted to be an officer in the United States Army for the rest of his life.

As Cadet Harmon Vance proceeded to drill the center out of *John's* target with shots from *his* rifle, Davis said nothing. Davis even steered the range officers away as he knew he was being part and parcel to John's fraudulent qualifying rounds. John knew what was going on, that Davis realized he was jeopardizing his gold Lieutenant's bar by harassing the scion of Vance Industries, and by extension his best friend John Henry Thompson.

John would be humbled, even offended that he had allowed the deception, the fraud to take place – but he needed Harmon Vance then, and would depend on him for his entire life – but Harmon Vance would be compensated far beyond anything that Vance Industries could ever hope to provide. John had learned a basic tenant of human behavior that day; money is power, and he would use it well. Might does make right – damned right, John thought.

⚜ ⚜ ⚜

World War II ended a year before John or Harmon could take part in saving the Free World, of ridding the world of Hitler and the Evil Empire that was Japan. Cadet Sergeant Davis had gotten his glory and by the end of the War his major's-rank oak leaf on his collar, a career in the Army that suited him.

John was finishing a respectful place in his class, Harmon just below him at graduation. But there the paths would diverge, Harmon off for his full service obligation of five years, off to a boring post-war occupation force duty serving among hardened veterans of the War, of an inflated wartime officers' corps that would be quickly thinned. 'Reduction in force' they called it.

John was shocked and saddened to learn that his problems at the firing range wouldn't be the last time his vision would plague him. But it would be a fortuitous event that kept him from the Army. Being disqualified from service for poor vision, vision that amazingly, to the Army, allowed him to graduate from the Academy, opened the door for John to enter the business world via his brother Gordon.

Gordon Thompson, John's older brother, had done well after college in Tennessee, better than John had known. Gordon didn't write much while John was at The Point and John didn't have much time to write him either. Gordon was making the trip up for the graduation ceremonies, their parents both being ill, a fact that they left out of their letters to John. It was left up to Gordon to let John know, to give their love and admiration for what would be their second son, in fact the second person from Slabtown to ever graduate from college, any college, much less the United States Military Academy.

"I'm out Gordon. They won't let me in the Army. After all this, after General Pershing, qualifying on the range, everything it took to graduate. You will never know how hard this has been," he confessed to Gordon with more than one tear in his eye.

The United States Army had conducted its own health examination of the graduating cadets and found that John's vision would keep him from service. Even though John had been fitted with glasses, ones that didn't help him on the range, he didn't pass their physical tests. It was strange, but true.

"John, we're so proud of you. Mom and Dad wanted to be here more than you know, but they're sick John. They're both having heart trouble. But they'll be okay, they're strong," Gordon told him, oddly thinking that it might cheer him up.

John, until now slumped on his bunk, sat up straight at the news. Somehow now all the disappointment in not being allowed in the Army was insignificant, a remote thought that strangely made him wonder why he ever should want such a thing.

"What's wrong? Tell me everything and all that you want me to do. I'm coming home Gordon. After all this, the Army doesn't want me and I don't want them."

It was from West Point on that John and Gordon never looked back. Gordon had the beginnings of a fortune being made on the bustling Mississippi River at Memphis. He had seen the prospects of turning unused, discarded riverfront land near the river bridge into what would be the Tennessee boys' 'bird's nest on the ground' as they called it.

Their father's cotton and everyone else's, all the soybeans and rice that everyone grew from a hundred miles around now went through the port of Memphis – and Gordon had a foothold that included grain dryers he was building and a deepwater port where the new barge traffic could anchor. A one-stop shop - power, synergy, money – influence.

"You're not just coming home with me, you're going into business with me, John. Memphis will respect a man from a small

Tennessee town that's been up here, done all this and is willing to come back home to work among them like common folk," Gordon said in an admirable tone.

"Hell, Gordon, I am common folk. Let's go home."

✤ ✤ ✤

With their hats tossed into the air, the Class of 1946 was off to conquer the world. John was only one of two that would not go through their service obligation with the United States Army. Before leaving, fellow cadets, now graduates, Ramon Hernandez, Jerry Slater, Truman Forsythe and Danny Carson almost prophetically wished John the best. John would stay in touch and they would be elated.

While Ramon would head back to Nicaragua to work for his brother, already the strongman ruler of the country and be the heir-apparent, Jerry and Truman looked forward to serving their country and then returning home to make their fortunes and enter politics. It was their plan since childhood - run for public office, start low, maybe a House seat at the state level and then a meteoric rise to, who knows, maybe even the White House - cold, calculated, power-hungry.

Ramon had been trouble at The Academy. He was only at The Point because of his older brother. The US government was trying to pacify his brother by letting Ramon in, but he defied the authority exerted by the senior cadets and detested the constant drilling. The government figured that they would rather have a US-trained ruler in Nicaragua one day than one trained by the Soviets. It couldn't hurt, they thought.

Jerry Slater was a Missouri boy through and through, his hero being the old US Senator Thomas Hart Benton. He had a plan, but would need some help. Everyone needed some sort of help in those days. His would come from a source that was surprising to him. No one figured John Henry Thompson for a kingmaker back then.

Truman Forsythe was a bookworm and loved the law. He thought he was destined to go to law school some day, if he could ever make it through the Army. He didn't know it at graduation, but he would be one of the most honored of the cadets as he made his way from the Army into the new branch of the service called the US Air Force.

But although John knew these young men had it in them, he also knew that one man really had what he thought it took to grab that brass ring, the shiniest of all. This man didn't want to be a House member or even a Governor, although he knew he couldn't get there overnight. Cadet Danny Ray Carson wanted it all.

Danny was first in his class, a leader, straight-laced and good-looking. He had it all planned out, didn't make any secret of it – and John would help Danny and all the rest reach their goals - for a price. This is their story, the Class of 1946.

Chapter Two

Bright Lights, Big City

Memphis had been a home away from home for John in many respects. Working at the Peabody Hotel as a young man was his refuge from Slabtown for many years. The hotel was a grand landmark of the South, ornate and elegant, an icon standing less than a mile from the mighty Mississippi River. With its detailed woodwork and giant central fountain in the middle of the ground floor lounge, it was a palace to John in his youth. But now he was returning a grown man who could stride into the magnificent lobby of the South's most grand hotel, brother Gordon at his side, and take a place at the finest table.

Gordon had done well, but John wasn't prepared for the reception Gordon and he received as they drove up in Gordon's shiny new 1946 Cadillac.

"Good morning, Mr. Gordon," came a voice from the past. Old Rufus Muggs, a black man of seemingly endless age had been a fixture as the head porter at The Peabody Hotel as long as anyone could remember. John was now part of what some Southerners would call 'bottom rail on top now', meaning newly acquired social upward mobility, especially since he was the newest West Point graduate from Tennessee.

"Mr. John, is that you?" Rufus asked as he knew John's face only because he was with Gordon, and because everyone knew a hometown boy was returning, one that had made good, one who would now call Memphis, not Slabtown, his home.

"Rufus, I'm home now and one good thing about that is I get to be back here at The Peabody. Have you held down the fort for me?"

"Sure enough, Mr. John. You got a whole lot of catchin up to do!" Rufus said, meaning every word.

"Yes, I do and I'm sure I will. I plan on catching up with everyone," John replied prophetically.

Memphis, Tennessee was, and is, a Southern town first and foremost. Gordon had a large home downtown, one of the old antebellum houses saved from the destruction that was becoming the high-rise skyline of the new Memphis. He had made room for his brother at his home, but John would have none of it.

"I'll just take a space down near Beale Street, Gordon. I know some people down there from The Peabody and I don't need much except for work. Just show me where the office is," John told him.

Where that office would be was the first of many 'Thompson Building' locations, an old warehouse down on the river near where Gordon had set up his barge and grain drying operations. Gordon had bought it for a song, with a little help, since no one had ideas of making anything out of it beyond a parking lot. Built with thick timbers and brick walls, it was structurally sound if not a bit plain in appearance. Gordon told John that someday this whole riverfront would be booming, and John believed him.

"Your office is right down the hall from mine, John," Gordon said as he pointed to a small, yet comfortable space overlooking the Mississippi.

The untamed river was just as John had remembered, swirling with whirlpools that would take anyone dumb enough to swim in it as far down as Helena, Arkansas before she would let you see daylight again.

"When did they build that bridge?" John asked as he pointed to a newly constructed span that linked Memphis, and Gordon's grain dryers and barges, with the rich farmland of Arkansas.

"Senator Moore built that bridge, at least he got the money from Washington, DC for it. Would you like to meet him?"

John was about to be swiftly introduced to the Memphis political and business power players Gordon had become involved with during John's absence. Senator Hugo Moore was chief among the local politicos that dominated the Memphis political scene. Shrewd, fat and rich, he subscribed to the 'three Bs' of being a success in Southern politics; that is Booze, Blondes and Beef. Just get the right people boozed, bred and fed and you'll get what you want in this town, hell even in DC, he thought.

This was new news to John. Still reeling from the regimentation of West Point, his head spun after the first shot of Jack Daniels at Senator Moore's estate just south of Memphis. Old Hugo Moore owned everything south of Memphis from the Shelby County line all the way damned near to Greenville, Mississippi. Although he had the Southern drawl, the gut and plantation hat that marked him as Old South, in truth his family were carpetbaggers down from the North after the 'War of Northern Aggression' as Memphians called the everything-but *Civil* War.

Gordon and John had arrived at Moore's estate that Saturday afternoon for a little 'garden party' as Hugo would call them. Thinly disguised as fundraisers for his ever-present and ongoing campaigns, even though no one had the balls to run against him, the events were really mixers where potential highway, defense and other contractors came to curry favor with the single most powerful Senator in the United States.

The soiree was styled after something out of F. Scott Fitzgerald.

Hugo spared no expense, especially since everything was donated. Cabanas were set up on the lawn to accommodate the expected three hundred people who were invited from all over the United States.

John was quickly separated from Gordon who gravitated to the familiar faces of the Peabody Hotel Bar, people he had made fast friends with while building up his properties just two blocks away on the riverfront. John had decided he would try the only familiar drink he found, Black Jack, like General Pershing's nickname. That's Jack Daniels whiskey, to the uninitiated.

"Boy, you gonna be alright or do I have to send my man out for a doctor?" boomed Senator Hugo Moore, as he always boomed and implied his authority in every sentence. He always had a 'man', or a 'boy' or someone at his beck and call to do his bidding. A 'step and fetch' man as John would call them.

"No sir, I'm just getting used to being back home. I think I'm still on West Point time," John sighed, as Hugo's eyes became the size of shot glasses.

Big Hugo Moore had always been a fat-ass. To be sure, he was the scion of the General Horatio Moore family and fortune, that's Union General Horatio Moore from Pennsylvania. But Hugo was never allowed in the service, any service, Army or Navy since he was a momma's boy, expected to hang around the plantation and be the heir to the family fortune of politics and cotton.

"You're not Gordon Thompson's brother are you?" Hugo demanded as he pressed his whiskeyed face nearly to John's.

"Yes sir, I am," is all John could muster as he vicariously had another Black Jack just from Hugo's breath.

"West Point! West Point! That's where my grandfather Horatio Moore graduated! Any Point man is welcome in my home! We need more real men like you around this goddamned place!" Hugo declared, booming again as just about everyone fell silent.

Everyone but Gordon.

"Hey brother, where have you been? Senator, I want you to meet my brother John," Gordon sheepishly announced as if everyone didn't know by now.

John saw an expression on Gordon's face he had never seen before, one of awkwardness and contrition. Gordon was afraid of this man while at the same time seeking his approval.

John felt like a show pony at the county fair. Gordon had brought him there to show off for the Senator, to curry favor, a human bargaining chip. John hadn't been back home long enough to see his parents and already his questions he had for them about how Gordon had made so much money were being answered.

"Yep, John's coming to work for me Senator! He's a real go-getter, a West Point man!" Gordon squealed as he looked as if he might just piss in his pants if he couldn't kiss Hugo on the mouth right then and there.

"John, is it? Well why in the hell would you want to work with little Gordon when you can work for me?" Hugo bellowed, seemingly genuinely incredulous. "And where in the hell is your ring?"

John didn't have the stomach to wear his class ring, something almost everyone wore through their senior year at West Point. He was upset with the Army for denying him his service obligation and the ring would be a constant reminder. In an act of silent protest, he had left it on his bunk at The Point. Anyway, he had never before owned a ring and thought them a little sissy looking. And, he didn't want any questions as to why he wasn't in the Army now, especially since he had just graduated.

"Just didn't take the time to buy one Senator. I was in too big a hurry to get back here and get to work in Tennessee. Just wanted to get to work," he said quite matter-of-factly and believably.

It didn't even dawn on Hugo to ask why John wasn't away somewhere doing boring post-war duty like Harmon Vance, or how John received a million-dollar education and didn't have to serve his country in the field. It would only be many years later that John would not worry that someone might ask that question.

"Charles, get his ring size and call up there tomorrow and tell the Point that if they want their goddamned appropriation to go through, to get this young man a ring down here. I want him looking right when he's working for me!" Hugo ordered his nearest underling, now shouting as if leading a cavalry charge.

A flurry of thoughts ran through John's head. He owed Gordon so much, he thought, but was he being used? To assume that, John felt he would have to have a pretty high opinion of himself, one that he didn't possess as he sat on his bunk at The Point when Gordon offered him a job. But here was a big-time US Senator offering him a job with him, no, a life in the fast lane and power that was Old South politics, a life he knew really nothing about.

You could have heard the proverbial pin drop when John responded calmly, "I'll think about it Senator".

Senator Hugo Moore was not accustomed to hearing 'no', or 'maybe', certainly not in taking either for an answer. He didn't know how to react although his immediate inclination was to rise to anger, indignation and hurt. But he didn't. Somewhere deep down Hugo knew that in John he had not just another follower, a flunkie nor a dope.

He thought John Henry Thompson to be a rising star, the kind he wanted under his control. But he knew he would have to take a more subtle route. No more manhandling, controlling a man's life and spirit through brute force. He would have to play a game of carrot and stick with John. He was much more shrewd, tougher than his brother Gordon. After all, John was a West Point man.

"That's fine son, just fine," was Hugo's only public response, a line that elicited an audible sigh from the small crowd of Hugo's entourage.

Hugo had finally found a man, a real man, and he would be determined to see him succeed, a success that is, as defined according to Hugo Moore.

"Why in the hell didn't you tell me that you worked for Senator Hugo Moore?" John demanded, more than asked of Gordon as they negotiated their way out of the estate in the shiny Cadillac, somehow not so shiny as the rest he had seen at the compound.

"John, *everyone* works for Hugo Moore! He not only owns most of the real estate in Shelby County, he owns most of the people too," Gordon gasped, not even taking a breath to exhale the smoke from the Cuban cigar Hugo had pressed into service with Gordon and all the other followers.

As Gordon coughed, John took his cigar, his first bribe from the Big Man, the political boss of the South and struck a match. He had never smoked; he had needed the air at West Point. He had been health conscious without a second thought all his life. But he inhaled the thick smoke like a pro. As he exhaled he said in a tone that Gordon would remember, "Gordon, some day *I'm* going to own *that* man!"

Gordon just drove. Somehow he believed John – and in him.

⚜ ⚜ ⚜

John came back down to earth as soon as he was dropped off a block from Beale Street at the Union Hotel where Gordon had secured a room for him. The Union was not fit to be a cloak room for The Peabody Hotel, but it was clean and dignified, a place where many of the men returning from the war hung their hats while they boozed it up on Beale Street, catching up on the opposite sex just two blocks off Union Avenue.

"John, you know you don't have to stay down here. Hell, there's nothing but a bunch of drunks and whores running all over the place. I've been trying to get the city to condemn this damned place. Beale Street and all, well it just doesn't look good for The Peabody," Gordon whined, not realizing the gold mine that was the Memphis jazzy Blues music, the tourism, and the real estate that Beale Street rested on.

John thought it was ironic that Gordon, a man that had made his money, so far, on reclaiming land that had been discarded, overlooked and neglected, would turn a blind eye to this prime property. John was wondering more and more about Gordon, his plans and his acumen.

"John Henry Thompson," a voice known to John from his childhood rang out like a rifle shot ricocheting off the marble walls and floors of the Union Hotel lobby. It was Lamont Boone, Jr., childhood friend and right-hand man to John and Gordon's father at the farm. Now a strapping black man, not so fresh off the farm, Lamont had been eking out a living doing odd jobs in Memphis, one of which was doing the maintenance at The Union Hotel.

"Lamont, how are you? You look well, and what in the hell are you doing here?" John asked with a ring of suspicion.

"Mr. Gordon brought me up from Slabtown about a year ago and put me up here at The Union. He told me you needed a room and I got you the best one in this little hotel. If you look real hard hanging out the window, you can just see the Mississippi!" a ringing endorsement in Lamont's mind.

"Thanks, Lamont. Say, where are you working anyway and how are your parents?" John asked without remembering that

Gordon had told him of their 'passing' as his family called their deaths.

"They're gone, Mr. John", Lamont said with a resignation that cast his eyes to the marble floor, a floor sparkling clean and awash in patterns that Lamont's eyes kept searching as if he was looking for something he had dropped.

Lamont's parents had meant everything to him. With his brothers off to Chicago and Gordon and John's parents no longer able to farm, Lamont reluctantly moved to the city the minute Gordon offered him the job at The Union.

"When Mr. Gordon bought…I mean when he took over this place I was glad to get this job, and I been doin' well for myself. Heck, I even got a part time job at the Bumbles Pool Hall!" Lamont declared, insisting that he was okay, much more than okay. He was businessman himself.

"Do you mean to tell me Gordon *owns* The Union?" John asked incredulously. He knew about the 'Thompson Building' where he would hang his business hat, but now Gordon owns the hotel where he would live?

"I got to get back to work, Mr. John. It's good to see you," Lamont called as he tossed John the key to Room 404. "Call me down in the lobby if you need anything!"

As Lamont turned, John threw in, "No more *Mr.* John, Lamont. It's just John."

It now figured that Gordon would be trying to control John, or so he thought, after the experience at Senator Moore's. But why didn't Gordon tell him about owning The Union? It wasn't a dump or a palace either, but nothing to be ashamed of owning, unless there was something wrong with how Gordon had acquired it.

As John hung out the window of Room 404 to see the Mississippi River, he still had that taste in his mouth, of fine Cuban cigars, of Black Jack Daniels – and power. Not so suddenly John realized that he had something these people didn't – discipline, and a drive that couldn't be suppressed. Hell, these people think that graduating from West Point makes you better than everyone else. Maybe here, in this town, being a West Point graduate would be just what a man needed to get a leg up on everyone else.

Like a ringing in John's ear, the rejection by the Army was still fresh, gnawing at him like an itch he couldn't scratch. In that moment, with the music of Beale Street beating out a melody that only could be made in Memphis, John Henry Thompson made up his mind to conquer this town. He had learned tactics well at The Point. The conquests of Alexander the Great, Julius Caesar, Sun Tzu and Napoleon were fresh lessons learned. With Gordon's business experience and help from people like Senator Moore, he could pull it off, building alliances, making friends, all the while steeling himself to acquire the strength and power he would need – like that power Harmon Vance had over Sergeant Davis at The Point. Power, synergy – it just might work.

Chapter Three

Business

"The business of America is business", or so President Calvin Coolidge supposedly was quoted as saying, the only quote most people could remember from him. But John was a quick study of powerful people, having read Thomas Carlyle and his writing on heroes and hero worship at The Point.

He remembered the entire Coolidge quote was "The business of the American *people* is business". *People* being the key word. He even knew the corollary remark was "Of course the accumulation of wealth cannot be justified as the chief end of existence". That was John's philosophy. He wanted power, to make a name for himself and to achieve, to show the US Army what he was made of, to show Memphis, the world that he could do great things not only for himself but for other people.

Gordon Thompson's desk had a grand view of the Mississippi, of the barges lashed together as they headed down toward the Port of New Orleans. Except for the land on the Arkansas side of the river, from Gordon's vantage point, he literally owned all he surveyed from his perch on the sixth floor of the converted warehouse.

"Get in here, John. We've got a lot of work to do. I've got some of my University of Tennessee buddies coming in here after a while to talk about some grain contracts. These UT boys are great contacts," Gordon boomed as if doing his best Hugo Moore impression, cigar and all.

John, still dressed in the sport coat Gordon had loaned him for the Senator Moore bash, fell into the leather chair, one of three that ringed Gordon's desk.

"Gordon, I need to get some clothes. I can't keep wearing these cadet khakis. And when can we go and see Mom and Dad?" he asked, realizing he had been in town two full days without Gordon even offering to take him back to Slabtown.

"We'll get down there, it's not like they're going anywhere. Anyway, you're right, we've got to get you some new clothes," Gordon said as he grabbed his coat, tapping John on the shoulder as he headed out the door.

"Irene, we'll be back after lunch," he commanded.

Irene was a fiftyish school marm of a woman who Gordon trusted explicitly. She had been with him from day one – and was also a friend of Senator Moore's. John didn't know what to think of her, or her of him. She knew that John had been at West Point and that Gordon had taken him into the business, but she was wary. She wondered how long it would take John to figure out what was really going on there.

Marx's Men Store was a fixture on the square blocks radiating from The Peabody, the core of downtown Memphis. Hiram Marx was the clothier to Memphis's best-dressed men.

"Come in my friend," Hiram invited Gordon, as he looked straight at John, wondering if he had a new client. "We have the newest double-breasted suits straight in from New York. And I will make them better!" was always his refrain, even though Gordon had his clothes custom tailored by Hiram and his tailors in the shop.

"This is my brother John, Mr. Marx. Let's get him fitted for three new suits and five shirts. I'll pick out the ties," ordered Gordon as Marx scurried about John with the tape measure he had yanked from his neck.

John was seeing Gordon in a way he had never seen him before. First, Gordon introduces him to a political boss, a kingpin of Southern politics, a man to whom Gordon was clearly beholden. The he sees Gordon emulating the man's actions, his bravado making weak attempts to style himself, literally, after a man who John did not immediately trust. John was worried that he may not be the sort to follow his lead, to blindly submit to whatever plans and lifestyle Gordon and others had in store for him. But he was shrewd enough not to reject out of hand what they had to offer.

"Mr. Thompson, you have a great build for the fine suits I make. What weight of cloth would you like?" Marx asked a quizzical John.

"Well, ah," spoke John who never had a custom-made suit and had never heard the word 'weight' used in that way.

"Make'em just like mine, Hiram. Nothing makes a man feel better than a new suit," Gordon said as if he'd said it a thousand times before.

John did feel good. He enjoyed the Senator's attention, the notoriety he had earned and the new suit, his first since becoming a man. Hiram threw one on John off the rack just to get him out the door and around town until his tailor-made ones would be ready. Then it was off to the landmark, the nexus of power and Old South hospitality, The Peabody Hotel.

❖ ❖ ❖

Thursday nights were reserved for rooftop parties at The Peabody. Everyone who was anyone gathered there – lawyers, doctors, insurance agents, plantation owners, even the nouveau-riche Yankees that had come down to buy up the cheap land with ideas of getting rich in the cotton trade. But the centers of attention were always the politicians, who conversely centered their attention on where they could get the next campaign donation before dispensing a favor.

After watching the famous Peabody ducks, mallards and hens that had famously been swimming in the fountain pool in the lobby for years, being led into an elevator for their return to the rooftop pen, Gordon and John along with a too-packed elevator emerged onto the rooftop. Moonlight, stars and cocktail bars, all right there in River City. The Mississippi was a ribbon on the edge of town to the west, the lights of the ever-growing skyline all around them.

John had only been to the roof when he worked at The Peabody to feed the ducks and had never seen the view quite like this. Twinkling lights rimmed the railing as cocktail waitresses flitted from group to group occasionally getting a little pinch for a tip. John ordered his now-familiar Black Jack Daniels whiskey, as did Gordon who tugged at John's arm to drag him from politico to businessman. This was an almost exclusively male group even though many of the men at the soiree were backed by their wives' money. Women were not welcome when it came to the cigar chomping, wheeling and dealing that took place on The Peabody rooftop.

And there he was, almost luminescent in his big-daddy white suit. Senator Moore flung his suitors from him as he recognized John, making his way diagonally across the rooftop, parting the sea of people with the grace of a freight train.

"I got that ring coming for you young man. I want you down at my house next weekend to get it. I'm having one of my small parties for a group of up and comers. We're goin' fishin' too," boomed the Senator with everyone hanging on every word. This was as big an endorsement as John would ever need to get started.

John was ready. He had made up his mind what to say if ever

offered the chance again to ingratiate himself with the Senator.

"Yes sir, I'll be there," was all he knew he needed to say.

For a big man, the Senator turned on his heel adroitly and almost darted back to his circle to hold court, so quickly that Gordon was visibly left with his mouth open, ready to respond to what he thought would surely be his invitation as well.

"John, you know you're going to need a ride to The Moores. Unless you think you can drive yourself way down there," was all Gordon could say.

"I appreciate the offer Gordon. I'd better go by myself, sink or swim; I do still know how to drive. I've been at West Point, not in jail for four years."

The rest of the night was downhill for John, a miserable face-saving ordeal for Gordon. He had been purposefully excluded from this enclave, this party, meeting at Moore's estate and the understood endorsement from the Senator. John was courted by everyone on the roof, on top of the world of Memphis, Tennessee, quite literally since this was the tallest structure for 300 miles around.

"Let's get the hell out of here, John. These people are insufferable pricks. All they want is to suck up to the Boss," Gordon whined, visibly upset at the attention John was receiving.

"Okay, but only if I get to choose where we go," John said throwing a bone to Gordon. He didn't want to heap any more grief on his big brother, even though he knew by now that Gordon's plan to use him as a show pony had gone horribly wrong.

Gordon snatched his hat from the hatcheck girl and gave in with a, "Where to?"

"My favorite place in Memphis besides here, Gordon," said John. "Beale Street".

✣ ✣ ✣

Beale Street, Memphis, Tennessee. W. C. Handy, a black trumpet player cracked open what became the Blues, 'Memphis Blues' to be exact, a mixture of Gospel and Jazz - and Beale has never been the same ever since. In John and Gordon's time, another black man named Riley King was making his mark. He would become known as the 'Blues Boy' King, and later just as B. B. King.

Beale Street had pretty much seen its high-water mark, figuratively as well as literally since it was two blocks off Front Street on the Mississippi where Gordon's Thompson Building stood.

Gordon hated it. It was full of the blacks that had come to town, from the countrified life that Gordon was trying to forget. The days of W. C. Handy were gone; the Depression had wreaked havoc on what was once a bustling street full of music, clubs and open-air concerts.

But there were a couple of clubs, 'joints' as Gordon would call them, where you could get a beer, a whiskey and even a woman if you wanted one.

"I'll see you in the morning, John. I haven't lost anything down here. You be careful." Gordon had seen all he wanted to see of Beale Street. Beale was actually on the wrong side of the tracks from the Thompson Building, the Missouri Pacific Railroad tracks and racial, cultural tracks he had laid down for himself in building his infant empire. But John loved it.

The Boogie Woogie Café was a landmark that also had seen more profitable days and it lay smack in the middle of Beale. John knew that Lamont Boone would be there enjoying a respite from The Union Hotel. Almost ramshackle by now, the 'Boogie' was home to whites and blacks alike, no one caring about the segregation of the races. It was pure Blues music, the beginnings of what would be rock and roll, booze and sex.

John's entry didn't cause anyone's head to turn, in their world, a world yet only two blocks away from The Peabody. Lamont was at the back slugging down some kind of home brew he and his friends would make at home and smuggle into the club through the back door. Lamont was part of a regular group of black men that called the Boogie Woogie their home away from home.

"John Thompson! What in the good name of all that is holy are you doing in here?" Lamont shouted as no one noticed.

"I need some Black Jack. Do they still have some in here?" John would almost plead as he scanned the room from floor to ceiling. "Get yourself one too, on me, Lamont."

Lamont snapped his fingers at an obese pretty young thing who couldn't have been more than 18 years old. She had heard the order and was already on her way to the bar; two flat oak boards over two 50-gallon drums, a makeshift bar, but it worked for them.

"John, you're takin' a big chance bein' here now. This ain't the same Beale Street from when you worked at The Peabody. This place's goin' downhill fast," warned Lamont.

Lamont forgot for just a few minutes about John's West Point training and that he never was afraid to go anywhere in Memphis, day or night.

"Thanks, but I'm fine. Let's take a walk. I have something I want to talk with you about. I need your help Lamont," John said sternly, looking Lamont straight in the eye, a look Lamont knew well from their childhood days together.

In the 1940's you took a drink right out of the club, they even sold it on the street, cheaper than in the clubs. Lamont led John out the back way, the way he came in with his bootleg hooch making their way out the back alley and onto Beale Street. With most of the street lamps broken or burned out, the street itself had the look of an alley instead of the grand street it once was.

"What's my brother up to, Lamont? What's going on with this Senator? I'm afraid I'm getting in over my head. I'm a good swimmer, but damn, this seems like deep Mississippi mud to me," John said while trying to see Lamont's expression in the dim light.

"John, your brother has done well here in Memphis. When he graduated college over in Nashville he brought me up here after Momma and Daddy died. I owe him a lot," Lamont added as he strained to see how John would take his disclaimer.

"I know that, Lamont. But you've been a good friend to me all these years. I know you'll tell me the truth. I just want to know what's going on here so I can know where I'm going. I've been away for four years. I'm asking you as one of the best friends I've ever known – tell me."

Lamont Boone, Jr. was no fool. Even though he owed his minor position in life, his rescue from Slabtown to Gordon, he knew John Thompson was a force to contend with. As boys, Lamont knew that John would succeed, that he would extend his reach far beyond the confines of the cotton fields of Shelby County. When John left for West Point, one of the last people he saw at the train station was Lamont.

But Lamont never felt abandoned. He knew someday John would be back and that they would always be friends. He made a fateful decision that day to lay it all out for John.

"John Thompson, you're gonna get me killed or fired and I don't know which one would be worse!" Lamont said giving in. "But you are my friend, you want the truth and the truth's what you'll get."

"Gordon came back over here from Nashville with a couple of his buddies, one named Billy Moore, and don't ever speak that name again," Lamont pleaded.

"Why, who is he. Is he related to the Senator?"

33

"He was until he died in a car crash, drowned in the Mississippi when his car ran off the old bridge between here and Arkansas. He was the Senator's nephew, his dead sister's boy," Lamont said in a reverent tone.

Now the pieces were coming together for John. Gordon's 'in' was the Senator's nephew. That's how he got close to the old man. That's how the bridge got built, sort of a memorial to his nephew, a new span, wide enough for all the traffic, with high rails, just at the right spot to drop by Gordon's operation too.

"But John, I don't know that you ought to talk with Gordon about all this. See, Gordon gets business from Senator Moore. And I think it's more than just because of Billy. See, lots of people don't like the way all this land has been bought up. When Beale Street got hit hard after the depression all our folks, you know us blacks got moved off. That's the reason all this has gone down hill like it is," Lamont said as he looked up and down what was left of the street.

"Folks like Gordon done bought it up, not Beale, but all the good stuff. Some folks think all that ain't right, John. Heck, it ain't right! The Senator's doin' it through folks like Gordon. They're a hundred people like him. Gordon don't even own all that house and building he likes to call 'The Thompson Building'. They call themselves 'straw men', I've heard'em tell it", Lamont confessed, wondering if he'd already said too much.

'Straw men', stand-ins for others, a human facade through which the Senator could own damned near everything east of the Mississippi without the appearance of any impropriety. But how would Lamont know all this? A young black man with no education, who lived at The Union, a man who had never been on the rooftop at The Peabody, much less in the Thompson Building on the sixth floor. Could it be true?

John had heard enough. After swearing himself to silence in

34

front of Lamont who was clearly petrified that he had even opened his mouth, John and Lamont walked back to The Union Hotel. They didn't say much to each other. In that day, the fact that a black man and a white man were walking the streets of Memphis late at night together said it all. They were two lifelong friends and they had just shared a big secret, one that would cement the bond between them forever.

Chapter Four

Big Daddy's Calling

John hadn't noticed the big sign on his first visit into the Senator Hugo Moore estate. 'The Moores' it read. Sounded appropriate enough until he heard everyone at the gathering, the enclave, refer to it as if it were something of a 'moors' from Sherlock Holmes' *Hounds of the Baskervilles*. "Good to have you here at 'The Moores'". Or even, "We're going fishing out on 'The Moores'". John thought it appropriate that Senator Hugo was almost identical to Hugo Baskerville of the novel, a debaucherous, shadowy character, and full of aristocratic excess.

'The Moores' was about 4,000 acres of prime Shelby County farm land and woodlands with three large oxbow, or old river channel lakes, a stable and river frontage that seemed to run for miles.

John was feeling a little guilty having rejected Gordon's offer to drive him down to the mansion. But with all the unanswered questions John had yet to ask Gordon, the issues of the land grabbing and being one of Senator Moore's 'straw men', questions that were eating at John's insides so much that he quickly overcame any remorse he might have held.

Grandfather, patriarch and General, Hugo's grandfather Horatio Moore had cut a swath across Tennessee with the Union Army's 3rd Pennsylvania and got accustomed to the sweltering heat of the Tennessee summers. A bachelor, he also found himself enamored with the beautiful Southern Belles with their mint juleps and hoop skirts. After he mustered out of service in 1865, he shocked his blue-blood family and took the first train back to Memphis, talked a disaffected Southern girl into marrying him and quickly became a conduit and contact for all the carpetbaggers who flooded down from the North after the war.

General Moore started gobbling up as much of the land with the attendant former slave laborers as he could. Although he expressed a disdain for slavery, he effectively sustained its existence in Shelby County for many years by insisting that poor blacks and their descendants only sharecrop the land with no real hope of ever really owning any for themselves.

Active in Reconstruction politics, he knew future President Andrew Johnson when Johnson served as military Governor of Tennessee. Later, when Johnson was impeached and Tennessee had refused to ratify the 14th amendment that guaranteed civil rights to freed slaves, Moore cut Johnson from his circle of friends. Always the manipulator and capitalist, Moore helped Johnson get elected to the US Senate from Tennessee in 1875 shortly before Moore died.

The apple didn't fall far from the tree in the Moore family. Horatio, Jr. occupied the Senate seat after Johnson and passed it on, a right of passage, to Hugo Moore who was never challenged. The Moores were a dynasty, but there was no heir, by blood or otherwise, since Hugo's nephew Billy had died.

"I had this shipped by airplane my young man. I hope it fits. Hell, if it doesn't, we'll bring my jeweler in and make it fit," boomed Senator Hugo Moore as everyone looked on with considerable envy, an all-male group who watched in a jealous silence.

The ring was beautiful. Set with a red stone with the US Army crest on one side and John's West Point class seal on the other, John slipped it neatly onto his ring finger – a perfect fit.

John caught a glimpse of Hugo smiling, puffing on his cigar and nodding approvingly. In Hugo's mind, this was a major bonding experience.

"Thank you sir," was all John had to say.

"Call me Senator, just Senator from here on out," an admonition John would remember always.

The Moores was an awesome sight. A colonial revival antebellum mansion the General had liberated for a song from the widow of a 1st Tennessee General killed in the war, the thick colonnades of the front portico gave it the look of Tara from *Gone With the Wind*. John had seen only the back lawn where the garden party had been held on his visit with Gordon. Many people saw only that side if they just attended a party or if they were making one of the many deliveries of supplies needed to keep the estate and farm operation going.

The mansion itself faced the mighty Mississippi with a boat dock big enough to land the largest paddle wheeler, the *Delta Queen*. Hugo would often charter the *Queen* for a private cruise for his entourage, a guided tour up river to Memphis and back down with Hugo as the master of ceremonies, lording over the event, pointing out all the places his grandfather had crossed and re-crossed the river chasing after Rebel stragglers. No one dared to have the guts to show their disdain for anyone in Yankee blue, much less for a Yankee General from a war many on board were still trying to fight or at best forget. At one dramatic point in the tour Hugo would show everyone where he believed Hernando de Soto had crossed the river in the 1500's.

From the instant after the ring ceremony Hugo led John around the mansion showing him family heirlooms including his grandfather's General's sword in its gold presentation scabbard.

"I'll bet a few of you Rebs were run through with this,"

exclaimed Hugo, forgetting that he too was a born and bred Southerner, or was he? Hugo was first a Moore, a greedy fat cat Moore who had lived off not the land his grandfather had seized, but the people of Tennessee, a bloodsucker feeding on the lives of the disenfranchised and poor.

"Yes Senator, I can see that happening," John admitted.

Eight bedrooms and a formal dining room later, John was ushered into the library, a massive tome-filled cavern filled with the big game trophies Hugo had rescued from the far corners of the earth. It seemed that Hugo liked to keep wild animal trophies as well as the human ones around to compensate for his inadequacies and reinforce his belief that he was all-powerful and in control.

Interspersed between the buffalo, zebra heads and Mississippi whitetails were the beastly portraits of Hugo's ancestors. One portrait was strategically placed among all others. It was undoubtedly of the equally plump General Moore clad in Yankee blue with the same sword Hugo had brandished earlier. He appeared to be still alive, his eyes following John everywhere he went in the room. It was as if the old General was still keeping an eye on the place, making sure Hugo was carrying on the family tradition.

John knew no one there. Nine other young men, nicely dressed and to a man, each smoking a cigar, were standing near the walk-in fireplace, one so big it looked like a separate room.

"Gentleman, I want you to meet John Henry Thompson, my friend."

Many of the men had seen John at the rooftop Peabody Hotel love-in and all had witnessed the ring ceremony earlier in the day. In fact, they had all been waiting impatiently while Hugo gave John the grand tour. Each took their turn in shaking John's hand and introducing themselves. John recognized none of them, but each seemed to know him. What was this fraternity, if that's what it was?

It was a curious, almost West Point-like initiation but without the hazing.

But why were they all there? Clearly no one among them knew, each looking at the other searching for a clue in these unfamiliar faces. The Senator's political race, if ever he had an opponent, was two years away. Was this just an exercise in Hugo massaging his masculinity, a show of power and control? It was much more nefarious and self-serving than that. Hugo Moore was looking for an heir, or at least an heir-apparent.

"Gentleman, I have called you all here for one reason and one reason alone. To give you all a chance to be millionaires!" Hugo said catching everyone in mid-puff.

Three men were so visibly shaken that they fell into the nearest chair, fortunately for them, ass first. John didn't blink – and Hugo was looking directly at him when he spoke those words.

"I don't mean just a millionaire, hell they're made every day when some old bastard like me kicks the bucket. I mean seed money gentleman, $100,000 cash. A start from which I expect you to make a fortune, just like the one I've made. One you earn!" Hugo boomed.

A curious but profitable proposition indeed, one maybe only a crazy man would make. Hell, old Hugo didn't have any family to speak of, Billy Moore ended that when he died in the car crash. The only folks Hugo had were stragglers, third and fourth cousins who had been given all the money they were going to get, and they had already pissed it all away on fast cars and women.

But what was the catch? What would they have to do? Hugo's announcement was followed by an awkward silence as he scanned the room for the reactions of the other nine men. Having taken in John's emotionless stare, Hugo's eyes darted from face to face, counting the beads of sweat, the wrinkles in the brows, and he never

40

lost count.

Hugo may have been a fat blowhard, but he didn't get to where he was by someone just giving him an inheritance. That was it! Hugo wanted to see who could build an empire, who could be his rightful, deserving heir!

"If given a chance, with a little luck, and money, any man can make a fortune, build an empire – if he has the right work ethic and horse sense," Hugo declared as if he were Henry Ford and Calvin Coolidge all rolled into one, which given the size of his waist, they could have fit in there with him.

But there must be something else. Even though Hugo had $100 million, and that was just what everyone knew about, he was about to give away a total of $1 million in ten $100,000 increments to, if Hugo didn't know any of the other men any better than John, almost total strangers. Then he dropped the bombshell on them.

"But you can't just sit on this money, gentlemen – you must invest it, here in Shelby County only, spend it on business projects, whatever; but you must *make* money with it! And at the end of one year, whoever has accumulated the most wealth, I'll give him $1 million!"

This was truly Hugo Moore's finest hour. Although he pulled so many strings on innumerable puppets he controlled from coast to coast every day, here he could openly, almost sadistically manipulate ten young men's lives for one whole year, or at least in this one fine moment.

Each man kept inching forward, looking for something to sign, where to join up for the giveaway - everyone except John. He quickly was left at the back of the room as Hugo held his arms wide open as if to embrace his new flock. Hugo noticed John at the back of the crowd and his gaping, cigar-accented smile turned slowly upside down.

"John, you got a question do you?" Hugo demanded more than asked.

"Senator Moore, what happens to the losers? Do they get to keep what they made?" John asked as he looked at the creeping crowd who quickly froze in mid-stalk.

Hugo's smile immediately returned and suddenly frightened the other nine men.

"As a matter of fact son, no, they don't. All the investments, monies made, interest, will revert to me, 100 per cent!" Hugo bellowed as the group backtracked, suddenly taking stock, their minds racing as if it was the first instance of taking the proposition seriously, something other than a gift.

It was clear to everyone now, not that the point was ever missed by John, that old Hugo had a self-serving motive in getting these young 'go-getters', as he liked to call them, on their feet and out into the business world, clearly to make him money. He had carefully selected them, culled them from all his soirees at The Moores to make him money, to further sink his claws into the Memphis business world. He knew everyone would kick ass and take names to build their original $100,000 into the biggest bankroll within the year in order to win the enormous prize of a million dollars of cold hard cash – and to keep what they had made.

They were his posse to be let loose on the unsuspecting Memphians – and he would get more back than he would pay out, a sort of race with only one survivor, winner takes all with Hugo still on top. Hugo would then place the best performers in some part of his operation, pat the rest of the lot on the back and go back to making more money. There wasn't anything illegal about the 'experiment', it just stunk to high heaven.

Just as everyone was beginning to come to grips with what they had just heard, that their lives would be changed forever, a tiny, bespectacled bald man emerged from what John thought was a closet. With a sheaf of papers under each arm, he looked like he needed help. But no one approached him as he surprised everyone almost as if he was the man behind the curtain in *The Wizard of Oz*, the guy who had been pulling all the levers that controlled the smoke and mirrors that was the Wizard. But Hugo was no Wizard, and this sure as hell wasn't Oz - this was for real.

"This is Mr. Koonce, gentlemen. He'll monitor every dime you spend, so don't go getting any bright ideas about giving all this money to your poor mammy and pappy. He has an agreement drafted for each and every one of you. It details the terms and conditions of your seed money, its distribution, use and subsequent return to me of all assets you acquire exactly one year from today – *if* you are not the clear dollar winner in this exercise," Hugo stated flatly.

"Your contract also contains a strict secrecy clause, which, if violated, will cause you to forfeit everything you have been given or have accumulated. There can be no collusion, no pooling of funds, no sharing in any business plans. You are to each operate separately and apart," Hugo continued, now in his big business voice.

That's the way John would want it. He had learned to survive on his own, except for that little problem he had on the firing range where he desperately needed Harmon Vance's help, his influence, his power.

"Sign your agreements now and you will have $100,000 wired to Union Planters Bank of Memphis today in an account already set up in your name as the sole signatory - decline and I will bid you good day and good luck. It's a cold, hard world out there. I told you boys we were goin' to do a little fishin' today. It's time to fish or cut bait boys, to be a little fish in a big sea, or be a winner, a go-getter."

Everyone knew that there was no option but to sign and take part in the experiment. Senator Hugo Moore was the most powerful man in the South, hell, one of the most powerful in the country. For God's sake, he had known FDR personally and lunched often with Harry Truman. Each of them knew that if they didn't sign they would be ruined. This was typical Hugo Moore – you play or pay.

While the others were stunned, boyishly absorbing the facts, although apparent, real in every sense, unavoidable, standing there still recoiling from the little man with their futures in his papers, now neatly aligned in ten stacks, John was making his way to the front of the room. He found his name quickly, the last of the stacks that had been all arranged alphabetically by the meticulous Mr. Koonce.

A quick study and reader due to the rigors of The Point, John had read every word and signed on the bottom of the last page before any other man had stepped forward. Hugo Moore smiled and lit another cigar. As Sherlock Holmes might tell Watson in the *Baskervilles*, "The game is on".

Chapter Five

Stealth and Strength in Numbers

John didn't even have a bank account and he certainly didn't want to let Gordon know he had this one. As far as he knew all the other men had taken Hugo up on the offer, what else could they do? Hugo's final admonition was that none of the men could contact each other, combine forces, pool money or otherwise communicate for any reason. They barely knew each other's name and most had forgotten them anyway, not to say that Memphis was a big city, a big business environment so as to ensure that they would not bump into each other. Many had seen John at The Peabody earlier. In fact, each would see each other, in person and in deed as they tried to manipulate their seed money into the biggest fortune they could muster before the 365 days would pass.

The Union Planters Bank was an imposing building right in the middle of downtown Memphis. John had made deposits for The Peabody there many times but never knew anyone who had an account there, but he was sure Gordon must have one since Planters was the most prestigious bank in town.

The tiny Mr. Koonce at The Moores had instructed him to see Fred Simms, the bank manager, to sign the paperwork necessary for John to make withdrawals, transfer money and to order checks. John only hoped as he met with Simms that he would not recognize the Thompson name and worse, mention the account and its balance to Gordon.

"Mr. Thompson," Simms said recognizing the name and

apparent significance of the account that Koonce had set up. "Step right in. Mr. Koonce has told me of your inheritance and we're proud to have you here in Memphis. You may be assured of our complete discretion. I understand you will be moving some money around. Please contact me directly."

The Senator had thought of everything. There would be no loose lips here. John, and presumably all the others had direct access and were dealing with the top man at the bank. No one would ever know. With his signature and a few blank drafts in hand, John headed for the door. As he neared the revolving brass doors, doors so fine they had been shipped from Tiffany's in New York, John caught a glimpse of Royce, John couldn't remember his last name at first, the red-haired young man who looked as if he'd seem some action in the war, the guy that stood near the back with John in the library at Hugo Moore's. Royce Phelan.

Phelan barely noticed John as they whirled past each other, John having just become $100,000 richer, maybe if only temporarily, and Phelan about five minutes away from it. But Phelan did recognize him. John saw the look on his face and recognized it for what it was – anger, pure and deep. The last time he had seen that look was on the face of Cadet Sergeant Mark Davis, and he knew what it meant. Phelan would be a formidable foe, a competitor that might have to be dealt with severely as was Davis, to be hit above and below the belt, whatever it took to remove him from competition, or at least to beat him.

But John knew the problem inherent in the 'experiment' was that no one would know what sort of progress, or lack of it, each other was making, even though many actions on the parts of the participants would be speaking for themselves, the buying of land, the construction of a building or the opening of a business. His West Point training would come in handy, serve him like he never anticipated – it would help him stealth his moves.

There was no time to waste. Phelan had that hungry look John had seen before, like young men at The Point on the verge of being kicked out. Some had feared the firing range like John, others academics; others who just couldn't take the pressure had the 'look', a sort of thousand-yard stare you get when you know you are in a live-or-die situation.

In the weeks to come, John would see concrete evidence, hallmarks of the work of Phelan and the others. Small businesses in downtown Memphis would spring up, a vacant lot developed here and there as houses were going up everywhere, what with the war heroes returning home. And John had kept his eye on the revolving door at the Union Planters Bank for faces he remembered from The Moores. Business intelligence gathering would always be a concern and strength of John Henry Thompson.

But John knew that he had to see his Mom and Dad back on the farm before all this got started, got out of hand, before it started to consume him.

✤ ✤ ✤

Gordon did everything he could to get John to tell him what had happened at The Moores. He even offered to buy John a new, well, used car to get him back and forth to the country to see the folks. John just said he wouldn't know where to put it, after all, he said, you could walk anywhere in downtown Memphis. Any place anyone might want to go was within a mile radius of The Peabody Hotel.

"No, just let me borrow your car and we'll talk when I get back tonight," was John's escape line, giving hope to Gordon that he might learn what all the fuss was about, why he had been excluded from the meeting at The Moores.

John took Highway 61 right out of Memphis, a straight shot to the Slabtown farm that had never changed. His father and mother almost didn't recognize him, but they knew the Cadillac.

"John Henry Thompson! Is that you?" old man Thompson and his wife sang almost simultaneously, amazed what West Point had done to their youngest, the prodigal son returning to do who knows what. After all, they didn't even know Gordon and John had returned from West Point

"I'm okay Mom and Dad. I'm here in Memphis for good, and I'm going to make a name for myself. I owe it to you both and to myself to make good after all this at West Point," John declared as both of his parents touched his hand and the West Point ring as if it were the Holy Grail, a symbol of their dream come true.

Both boys, college graduates, moved out of Slabtown, doing well. Effie, just 'Sister' to John and Gordon, would take care of their parents on the old cotton farm until the end of their days. But for the Thompsons, all was well and good. Their boy was home and not in the Army. They didn't even ask how or why.

⚜ ⚜ ⚜

"You want to what!?" Lamont Boone, Jr. cried out loud enough for everyone in their corner of the Boogie Woogie Café to hear. "You want to buy Beale Street? Yeah and I'm goin' to be a Negro aviator!" Lamont announced as John held his side laughing. He loved this guy like a brother, trusted him as Lamont had trusted John in revealing Gordon's business arrangement with the Senator.

It took John a full half an hour to convince Lamont that he was serious.

"What could you want with this run-down street, John? Ain't nothin' but trash down here, white and black!" Lamont cried.

"I want to bring it back, Lamont. I can do it, but I can't do it without you, without the *people*," John said as Lamont for the first time saw that he was serious, dead serious on making Beale Street into what it used to be, a showcase of music, dancing, good times, the Mid-South's version of Bourbon Street.

Lamont was all for it, but he couldn't understand how, in terms of plans, method, much less of money that John could pull it off. And why? After all, Lamont was right. Beale had turned into a mockery of its old self. If there was any building code enforcement to speak of in Memphis the whole place would have been condemned, but fortunately there wasn't. Memphis needed all the revenue it could generate through whatever means, and Beale Street did sell whiskey and beer, heavily taxed, even back then.

"How you gonna do it, John? Where you gonna get the money, I mean, this whole street ain't worth a lot I know, but…"

"Let's go, Lamont. Let's head over to The Union. I have a plan."

A plan well constructed. John knew that he would have to operate in secret to give himself an advantage over the others. He figured that everyone else would spend time, even money trying to monitor the others' activities, trying to take stock on where they were in the great race to be Memphis's newest millionaire. He didn't know any of the young men beyond sharing the same confined air space with Royce Phelan in the revolving door at the Union Planters Bank, but he knew human behavior. There was a lot at stake here for people who must be somewhat like himself financially, struggling, coming from a relative nothing compared to the wealth and influence, the power player like Senator Moore.

Harmon Vance had taught John Henry Thompson one lesson at West Point he would never forget, if it's all about winning – that might makes right, and when it comes to winning for a noble cause, to better one's self and others, whether getting through The Point or making a nest egg to help his parents, himself and the people - almost anything goes. At least that's what John believed for now, what would work.

The black population of Memphis, especially in the Beale Street section was demoralized, downtrodden, in ruin. Many had fled north to Chicago, Detroit, Cleveland, anywhere but the life, the legacy left to them by their slave ancestors and the lifestyles perpetuated by men like Senator Hugo Moore and his straw men. John knew now that his brother Gordon had been part and parcel to the gobbling up of Memphis properties, mostly from poor or struggling blacks who were forced to sell their land and buildings because they were unable to pay property taxes.

Lamont would reveal the sordid details in the sessions at The Union. When monetary pressures didn't work, some of the straw men would resort to terror tactics, a quasi-Klan of robber barons who would use physical intimidation to get what they wanted. At the end of the day, the blacks lost their property, bottom line.

"We're going to turn Beale Street around, Lamont. Hell, we're sitting two blocks from The Peabody, two blocks from that old baseball stadium. We're smack dab in the middle of what should be the most prime pieces of property in all Memphis!" John shouted, almost unable to contain his enthusiasm of thought that had been running through his mind ever since he first sat at The Boogie with Lamont that first night back in town.

All this was not lost on Lamont. What he lacked in book smarts he more than made up for with his street education, a savvy learned from living these streets, an intellect that John needed.

"And when I've done well, Lamont, I'll take care of you for the rest of your life."

John and Lamont both held back a tear, of excitement, joy and anticipation of the things, the hard work and accomplishments that they both believed were to come. They held it as long as two men might. Then they just shook hands and retreated to their rooms at The Union.

⚜ ⚜ ⚜

Old man Streeter was a black man who owned two buildings and a vacant lot all in a row on Beale Street. His family had passed down the properties ever since the War, the one that created the opportunity for his Boston family to join up with the 54th Massachusetts and help liberate enslaved blacks. His grandfather saw opportunity and returned with the carpetbaggers to Memphis buying up land in what was then a suburb of Memphis.

Beale Street of the 1920's was long gone. W. C. Handy's era was now a distant memory. Removed to Harlem, Handy had fallen in a subway accident a few years earlier and was totally blind. Beale was separated from its glory, but not its legacy or future which John would build.

"What in the *hell* you want with these old buildings, boy!? There ain't nothin' down here no more 'cept broken dreams," Streeter told John who didn't blink an eye.

"But there are still dreams here aren't there? I can help rebuild this street, this dream that has never gone away. Listen Mr. Streeter, hear that trumpet?" John almost pleaded.

"That's old fool Tom at the Boogie Woogie Café. He's there every day, all night, playing that horn. He knew Handy. He could've been somebody, but he's still hanging out on Beale," Streeter told John.

"That's my point exactly. There will always be people on Beale Street. You own The Boogie, Bumbles Billiards and this lot here don't you?" asked John, already having been briefed by Lamont who knew every owner of every parcel by name and reputation.

"And? I'm gonna lose them before I die. This shit ain't worth nothing to nobody 'cept my kids. They think it's *history*!" Streeter said in a subdued voice, his eyes surveying the two ramshackle buildings, the lot strewn with trash, as if looking for some, any, redeeming quality in the land.

It was as if Beale Street had not just been neglected after the Depression after Handy left, it was as if it had been forgotten. Gordon hated it, others just ignored it. But Streeter's kids were right. It *was* history. And it was a viable commodity, it was affordable on a Hugo Moore $100,000 budget and it was marketable. John knew it. He knew people. He believed with literally a new coat of paint, not a whitewash, that Beale Street could boom again with the sound of trumpets, white and black. And that the people would come.

John had done his research. There were no comparable properties to establish a price, a real value. It was the perceived price and return that John knew he would have to offer. He didn't want to steal the property, make Streeter subservient, an adversary as so many others had been made by people like Gordon and the straw men. He wanted a partner.

"You gonna give me $10,000 for this shit!? Boy either you ain't got money like that, or you ain't right – you 'touched'", was Streeter's way of saying John was crazy.

"Not only that, but I will give your family 10% ownership in the properties and profits we make. But I run the show. And there's only one catch, no one can ever know I own all this," John told him.

Streeter was now just staring at Lamont, a young black man he knew, and one he could read to see if there was any sign of newly acquired insanity. After all, he was a man who obviously was in on this escapade.

"He ain't jokin', Mr. Streeter," Lamont assured him.

John and Streeter met at the Union Planters Bank the next day. Mr. Simms closed the window blinds in the office keeping one eye on Streeter. He had been instructed to assist the ten participants in any way they asked. Only if Simms suspected one of them of trying to withdraw the funds to flee, or defraud the Senator of the money was he to alert Mr. Koonce, otherwise Koonce would check in once a week to see what actions had been taken.

John explained that this was a simple property transaction, an investment with a potential for exponential growth. Streeter had his title and deed from the Shelby County Clerk's office in hand. Both were ready to close the deal. They only needed Simms to draft the paperwork and give Streeter his money. John was watching Simms closely. Simms's only physical betrayal of his objectivity was an ever-so-slightly raised eyebrow as John explained the proposed transaction. Nevertheless, he left the room with a polite, "As you wish".

Streeter still couldn't believe it. The sidebar agreement had been prepared giving his children the 10% John had promised, the bank draft was good, as was Streeter's word to keep silent about the arrangement. He had even agreed to serve as John's first 'straw man', continuing to run the club, the pool hall and to stand outside and oversee the next phase of 'John Henry Thompson's Beale Street Revival' – an investment in Memphis and its people.

Chapter Six

A Study in Human Behavior

If anything, John Henry Thompson knew people. John loved people too, respecting them as human beings. He respected Senator Hugo Moore, but he never loved him. Many years later he would recall how he had really become a protégé of Senator Hugo Moore.

"What in the hell are you doing boy!? I want you to know I'm going against my instincts bringing you down here to The Moores while my experiment is going on, but Mr. Koonce told me you bought some property on *Beale Street*!" Hugo boomed, incredulous that his fair-haired boy had made such an apparent misstep.

Hugo at once felt shocked, disappointed, and yet curious. He had summoned John to the estate the minute Mr. Koonce had relayed his reports on the young men's activities. He looked for a reaction in John, one he wouldn't get, at least not one he could detect. He was used to sparking sweat from a person's brow, panic, and a visible reaction to his pressure tactics. They didn't work on John.

"Senator, this place is a gold mine. Sooner or later what's going on with the straw men taking these people's land from them will not stand. I know what people like my brother are doing. I don't think it's bad, illegal or unprofitable – for now. But in the long term, by not partnering, sharing, these ends will be undone by the means," John firmly explained to the Senator. "May I have a cigar, Senator?"

Senator Hugo Moore may never have been speechless in

his entire life. His last lesson given to him was at Harvard and he didn't know how to react. He was used to telling and not being told, surrounded by 'yes men' and 'straw men', of being tutor and not being the subject of a tutorial. But he wasn't stupid. His only reaction was to open the humidor and take out a Cubano. He hesitated a millisecond, and then he handed it John.

"Proceed," was the only remark John had to hear. John began to lay out his plan, or just enough of it to whet Hugo's appetite, to convince him that he was on to something, that he hadn't made a mistake, that both of them were on to the biggest development in Memphis for the last thirty years.

John held back all the details, but he convinced Hugo that his vision would become a reality – and that no one, not Royce Phelan with his housing boom plan to become a real estate developer cum baron, not any of the others with restaurants or automobile dealership dreams, not one would come close to building a legacy, a profitable one. John knew that even though Hugo had purportedly given the men free reign, outside of fraud or lack of confidentiality, that Hugo could pull the plug any time he wanted.

Hugo didn't pull it. If anything he admonished John to keep him informed. Hugo saw political as well as financial opportunity in the venture. He had never been able to tap into the black vote, only to suppress it through a poll tax that most blacks couldn't afford to pay in order to be able to vote. Hugo saw that at the end of the experiment as planned, in John he would have the sort of return he expected. He would own the operation if John wasn't the clear winner. He would own the homes Royce Phelan had developed, even though he may have a few unprofitable restaurants he might have to close with the other men.

"You're a go-getter, John. Be careful down there. This $100,000 may get you in the door. But remember, you have to be the clear winner at end of 365, now 345 days to collect the prize. Keep your eye on it. A million dollars can make you for life, a bad investment could break you," Hugo almost whispered as he leaned into John's cigar smoke. Good advice, John thought. He wouldn't forget it.

As John turned to walk out, the Senator had a gift, one of protection, even though it violated what he had hoped would be his neutrality while the ten men were working.

"I believe in you, boy. I'm going to go against my better judgment and help you out on this one. I'm going to keep people, my people, off your ass. If they see that your project is making money, they will try and take it away from you".

"Thank you, Senator. That's all the endorsement I need. You won't be sorry."

✠ ✠ ✠

As soon as he got back to Memphis John knew he would have to deal with Gordon. John had been making excuses for his absences from the Thompson Building, excuses that were becoming pretty transparent to his brother.

"Come in here and sit down, John. It's time we had a heart-to-heart boy," Gordon would ask more than command, now with a more respectful tone to his voice. He had come to be skeptical of John, of his loyalty, certainly of his allegiance to him. After all, he had rescued John from the great unknown of being essentially discharged from the Army after The Point.

John had given plenty of thought as to what his cover story would be, one that would pacify Gordon, remove him from the mix that would be his project on Beale Street.

"Gordon, I'm not going be at the Thompson Building anymore. I don't know what your plans are for me here, but my heart's not into working for someone else. Hell, I've been taking orders for four years. I'm going to sink or swim on my own," John said to a stunned, silent Gordon.

As he delivered the last word he pushed three, crisp $100 bills across Gordon's desk as payment for the new suits. Gordon didn't want to touch them, he feared in doing so that he would lose any sort of control he had over John. Although he had been playing the fool for Senator Moore for a few years now, he knew something was up. And John wasn't leaving until Gordon took the money.

Gordon smelled a rat - a big, fat, cigar-chomping rat. With that, Gordon also knew that he couldn't fight whatever John may be up to, especially if it was sanctioned by Hugo Moore. He had no choice but to play along, indeed to be whatever accomplice he needed to be. He was, after all, a straw man – and he took the money.

Then and there, the two were still brothers, but more than that, silent partners, silent to each other. Their bond was more than blood but now business, Memphis business and politics. John and Gordon had drifted apart, John to The Point, Gordon to UT and his political and business cronies he had made. Senator Moore would have approached John with or without Gordon and John knew it now. John hadn't gone unnoticed. He had been on the Senator's radar screen all along. He wouldn't hold it against Gordon that he had tried to capitalize on John being his brother. John would learn from it. After all, might makes right.

"Fine John. I'll always respect your wishes." Gordon would have to – that's the way it would be from now on.

✠ ✠ ✠

Old man Streeter just stood in the middle of Beale Street and smiled. The new roof, the hardwood floors cut from the timber over in Arkansas, were a dream come true. He never imagined a real neon sign would grace the front of his, or John's Boogie Woogie Café and bar. But there it was.

John knew he couldn't tear down, that he had to rebuild Beale Street. He would have to build upon the legacy, the history, the people that were the heart and soul of Beale.

John figured all that Beale needed besides a facelift, some great marketing and networking was a fantastic one-of-a kind restaurant. Memphis was known for its ribs and barbeque. The city was dotted with little Mom and Pop cafés that served up hot food with the baked beans and slaw that went best with Southern comfort food. But there was no landmark, no iconic restaurant where it was hip to eat and be seen.

That foundation would be laid at John's new restaurant, Porky's Barbeque, a homage to the cartoon character pig, right across from the Boogie Woogie Café. John took care to not make it a new-looking flashy joint, but to blend in with the casual, down-home rustic and Bluesy facades of the Boogie and of Bumble's Billiards down the street.

John had spent another $10,000 just on renovation by the time all was said and done, the new pool tables in Bumbles, the new flooring, roofing and real oak bars brought in from St. Louis to the Boogie. The curious onlookers from the top of the Peabody every Thursday wondered what all the hubbub was about. What was happening over on Beale Street? Oh, well, they didn't go over there anyway, or not yet.

The black community of Beale Street and its environs had seen the renewal, the excitement that Beale was coming back. All they knew for sure was that old man Streeter had been pumping money into those old buildings and was building a nice restaurant. Two black property owners approached Streeter offering to sell. Streeter made a beeline to John who made the same offer of partnership, a 10% ownership interest with them working as John's straw men if John put up the money.

John now had an entire block, basically the guts of Beale Street under his name, stealthed from everyone but *his* straw men and Lamont, but under his control and all within two months. Now, he figured it was time to visit The Peabody and buy Gordon a drink.

✤ ✤ ✤

Gordon had been staying out of John's business, whatever it was. He had his own fish to fry at the Thompson Building. Business was good. The soybeans were coming in and the grain drying operation was in full swing. He was busy making money. The only thing that got him up to The Peabody rooftop was his curiosity about what John had been doing these two months.

It was just as John had remembered that first day back in Memphis. The lights twinkled, the Mississippi glistened in the distance and cigars provided the rest of the light needed to illuminate the evening. Booze, blondes and beef – some things never change.

"John, you're looking tired little brother. How about a Jack Daniels?" offered Gordon as he introduced his UT buddy; John thought his name was Daniel, a Nashville native who had come over to trade cotton.

"I believe I will. I need one."

John maneuvered the pair around to the south side of the rooftop where he could keep an eye on what was happening on Beale Street. Work was continuing night and day on Porky's Barbeque, the skeleton of the roof now covered with the bright tin John had specifically ordered to ensure its rustic appearance.

John purposefully kept the group camped out the whole night in that spot on the roof. As each Memphian came and went, conversation centered on Beale, what was going on, the construction, old man Streeter and speculation about what is was all about.

To a man, each thought about the old days of Beale Street, the stories of W. C. Handy, this new guy named B. B. King whose cousin, Bukka White, already famous as a Blues man, was trotting out to play the Blues. There was music in the air again. It was all still a curiosity to them.

When the rooftop party broke up, John had gathered his intelligence well. People were interested in Beale. They would come back.

✤ ✤ ✤

Old man Streeter was earning every penny he was paid. He was even smoking cigars now, looking every bit like a black Hugo Moore with his pocket watch and wide grin. He was a great actor, the king of Beale Street, the great urban renewer, and he loved it.

John had made a good and profitable alliance. The Boogie Woogie Café and Bumbles Billiards were making more money than ever. John instituted new rules on operations, kept meticulous books and made sure nothing was coming in or out of the back door. Lamont was the key to that success. If anyone knew how that was done, it was him.

John knew he needed an icebreaker, a hook that would start a real flow of business. To be sure, whites were now coming into the businesses with many asking when Porky's Barbeque would be open. Old man Streeter would come through with not just an icebreaker, but an iceberg breaker.

Streeter had known W. C. Handy for years. Since his accident and blindness, Handy had not been back to Memphis and was still in Harlem when Streeter made a telephone call that would change everything. Handy would take a train to make his first visit to Memphis since Beale Street had declined. He was excited that Streeter had saved Beale from ruin and Handy would do all he could. Streeter was a friend, someone from the old days. Loyalty was everything, he just needed a heads-up on when to be there.

But John had a lot of money left to invest, maybe just enough to put him over the top. He had put $10,000 more into the two newly acquired properties, a steak house and a theatre/playhouse that needed some renovation. After an additional $5,000 both were up and running a month later. But John knew he couldn't just sit back and hope they would remain profitable. Porky's was about ready to open and he needed more publicity, a new draw. He needed something he could bank on – America's pastime, baseball.

The Tennessee Blues baseball team had long since been disbanded, a casualty of World War II. The major leagues had trouble enough fielding players during the war and the farm clubs like the Blues all but went away when the talent left for the Pacific and European theaters of war. But there was a resurgence in baseball now. The stadium sat two blocks away from The Peabody, unused except for the pickup games every Sunday afternoon.

Mr. Simms and the Union Planters Bank held the title to the land and it had been for sale for years, just waiting to be bought and torn down. As John made his way through the revolving door he had negotiated so well for the last three months, Simms wondered what he had in mind now. He never imagined that John would be gambling what would be nearly the remainder of his seed money on a vacant lot with some rundown stands. John would have just enough money to buy the land and the facility with money left over to run the Beale Street operation and pay taxes and other essentials until he was ready to make his next move. It didn't hurt that Senator Moore was on the board of the bank.

Free press exposure, 'earned media' as it was called, was all that was needed for what came to be known as 'The Beale Street Revival'. The *Memphis Commercial Appeal*, a daily newspaper founded in 1841 and a Memphis institution in itself, had survived the Civil War by fleeing Memphis with its presses when old General Horatio Moore and his troops took over. They published from all over the South sending smuggled copies into Memphis just to let the people know they were still around, and loyal to the cause.

The *Appeal* had won a Pulitzer Prize in the 1920's for their editorial opposition to the Klan. It made sense that they would heap coverage on the Beale Street Revival along with the resurgence of 'The New Ball Park at Memphis' as John called the old stadium he had just bought.

Just six months into the 365 days Senator Moore had given the ten young men, John Henry Thompson's project, with a 10% ownership by old man Streeter and the others, was ready for prime time. *The Commercial Appeal* went to press with the headline, "W. C. Handy To Make His Return At The New Ball Park at Memphis". The subtitle read, "He Reopens Beale Street To The World". John couldn't buy press like that.

As the rumor mill swirled so did the activity on Beale. The rooftop party at the Peabody became a prelude to the gatherings afterward on Beale Street. The Boogie Woogie Café couldn't be hotter. Lamont Boone was taking names for seating at Porky's that now had a waiting list for ribs and barbeque, "the hottest barbeque in the South" proclaimed the *Appeal*.

John Henry Thompson had studied his people well. He

knew what they wanted; a new Memphis – and he had again been summoned to The Moores.

Chapter Seven

The New Memphis, John Henry Thompson Style

"Money's good, right young man?" asked Senator Moore. "I've been following you like none of the rest. I hope you're making good money down there because according to Mr. Koonce, you're just about out of your seed money. I haven't asked him what you're pulling down there in revenue, but I just wanted you to know I personally approved you buying the ballpark," he flatly told John as he handed him a Cubano cigar at The Moores.

John sensed an almost eerie camaraderie with the Senator now, a feeling of a calm fraternalism. John knew the Senator was pleased, yet at the same time almost jealous.

"I'm giving it my best, Senator. I don't know exactly what the others are doing, but I hope in six months you'll be writing me that big check," John smiled, perhaps for the first time at the Senator.

"And do you know what you're going to do when they, the blacks, want more? When they want their neighborhood and businesses back? What will you do when they demand their share?" Hugo demanded, again back in his superlative tone.

"I have a contract Senator, one that makes *them*, as you put it, a partner. If, when I succeed, they succeed. Isn't that what your experiment is all about? It hasn't been lost on me that you come out a winner in this exercise, no matter how it turns out."

John was as bold as he dared. Hugo was silent, examining the ash on his cigar as if to make sure it burned as commanded, evenly, white and long.

"You'll win, young man. Just keep doing what you're doing. You didn't forget your roots. Now don't you ever forget who got you your start!" Hugo now boomed with an enthusiastic laser-like stare at John's West Point ring. "I am a man of my word, but I want to be in on this. I don't want you getting too big for your britches. I'm going to go halves with you on this ball team of yours. You *do* want to be partners, don't you?"

John couldn't believe what he was hearing. The old man wanted to muscle in on the project, not all of it, just the ball team. He at once was mad as hell, although he didn't dare show it, and at the same time relieved, relieved since he thought this meeting might be bad news.

But John didn't have a choice. He should have known that the Senator's favor at the bank, his private meeting with him and none of the other guys, were all a part of the Senator winning even bigger when all was said and done. But John had one bold card to play. He knew if he didn't play it now, he might eventually lose control to the Senator.

"Sure Senator, I'm flattered that you want to be a partner. If you fund the baseball team, build up the roster from scratch, construct new seating, refurbish the field and fund the first season, I'll make you a 49% partner. You'll make your money back in a year or I'll pay you back your investment," John offered flatly, almost as if this was the only proposal he was to make.

The silence was stunning to John. In what seemed like an eternity, what looked like three inches of Hugo's cigar being burned in one puff, Senator Hugo Moore found himself in a quandary. After all, he had never been a junior partner in anything. The last person that talked to him like this was his daddy. But Hugo Moore sucked it up, realized that this was just a product of what he had seen all along in John – and accepted the deal.

"Boy, you *are* a go-getter! I accept, like the man I am, the man that gave you your start. Just you don't forget it!"

How could John forget? Years later John would tell the story, the story up to this point a hundred times – in Vegas, Miami, at the World Series and on the jets when he would give the occasional odd celebrity, some Hollywood vacuous otherwise-nobody a free ride to whatever far corner John desired.

And 'the ring' as the old Senator would so often call it? John wore it until the day the old man died, which was exactly one year after John bought the Senator's interest in the ball team back, then took it off, never to wear it again. It reminded him too much of the old days when he was beholden to people such as the Senator. Without it, he was his own man, off on his own journey with money of his own.

✣ ✣ ✣

John Henry Thompson's 'New Memphis' took off the day W. C. Handy stepped off the train and played his horn at The New Ball Park at Memphis. The blind Handy was then the first person to "see" the bronze statue of himself that John had commissioned – the one that still stands on Beale Street today.

The minor league Memphis Blues had been recruited from top-notch ball players who had come back from the war. As the team was a hit with the people, Senator Moore struggled being the silent partner in the Ballpark, not used to being in the background – to being a straw man. People flocked to the Park with its new seating and manicured field. It was akin to Fenway Park in Boston, retaining its 'Green Monster' outfield wall and homey look and feel and fit right in the folksy downtown Memphis. And all roads led to Beale Street.

The Boogie Woogie, Porky's Barbeque and Bumbles Billiards had record sales that night. W. C. Handy gave an impromptu concert after the game and the streets were filled with revelers as The Memphis Blues, still in uniform, mixed among the people.

"The *people*. Damned right," John said to himself as he took it all in. It was all about the people, and the rooftop at The Peabody was empty.

⚜ ⚜ ⚜

To say that John Henry Thompson invested his million dollars well would be a classic understatement. By the 1980's The Beale Street Revival and The New Ball Park at Memphis, home of the now *Major League* Memphis Blues, bordered the 'Thompson Group's Peabody Hotel at Memphis'. Old Senator Hugo Moore died back in 1965, being forever amazed at John's foresight.

None of the other young men ever had a chance. John had done his homework, learning that there was a property re-assessment coming in Shelby County before the year of the experiment was done. The Beale Street properties he had snapped up and renewed, the ballpark and its refurbishment; all were reassessed at 100 times their previous values. John was a millionaire in his own right before the exercise was over. The million-dollar check from the Senator was icing on the cake.

Royce Phelan and the others who took part in the competition surrendered their comparatively miniscule properties to the Senator who literally smiled all the way to the Union Planters Bank. Some said Phelan committed suicide two years later, never really able to come to grips with losing out to John. Every other participant went to work for Senator Moore and made him more money than ever before.

It turned out that the Senator had all his straw men come up with the ten men for the project, even though the straw men like Gordon didn't know the full details of the experiment. The old Senator said only that he was looking for 'new talent' and that they were to bring their best new employees around so that the Senator could see how his straw men were recruiting, whether or not they were advancing his interests.

John was Gordon's prospect, a fact that John learned directly from the Senator himself. It was a scar on the relationship between he and his brother that really never healed.

Gordon had died a wealthy man, but never anywhere near the net worth John had accumulated. The grain drying and barge business remained profitable, but Gordon was content to stay with what he knew. He was never really his own man. The Senator had a piece of him until the day Gordon died in 1975. John bought everything from Gordon and turned the operations into a really profitable business extending it all up and down the length of the Mississippi, with extensive holdings in St. Louis and New Orleans.

While John still allowed rooftop parties since he bought The Peabody Hotel, he now had fully one-half of the top floor as his penthouse for use when he was in Memphis dodging his miserable son Marvin and Henrietta, Marvin's harpie wife, 'Hennie', as John loved to call her. Marvin had taken over as general manager, CEO of the baseball team under John's directorship two years before in 1983.

John's oldest son, Hank had enough of Marvin and Hennie in 1977 and went out on his own, making his own way developing commercial properties throughout the South. John was very proud of Hank, his children and the course he had taken in life.

John wondered if Marvin and Hennie felt about him as he thought of the old Senator back in the 1940's. He knew they despised him, begrudged his longevity and continuance of control, effective control anyway, of the family money. While Marvin was a disappointment as a son, Hennie was an embarrassment.

The Memphis Blues were in continual competition for not just the playoffs but for the World Series. They had taken the place of the perennial New York Yankees as the team to beat.

John was no team owner like George Steinbrenner at the Yankees. He paid a fair wage, fair according to major league baseball standards, but he wouldn't load up on individual players of superstar caliber. He spread out his money, making a well-rounded team, a team family that wanted to be there because of the atmosphere and continual success – and the players loved him. In time, John had made hundreds of millions of dollars from the team alone. By the time he was fifty he was a billionaire.

Every day, it was looking like the Atlanta Braves would be The Memphis Blues' next opponent in The Series. John loved to attend the games, sit in his owner's box and watch the pretty girls who flocked in from all over the mid-South to what was not just a baseball game, but a major event, a party that extended from the deluxe rooms at the Thompson Peabody Hotel to Beale Street and back to The Park.

Since John's divorce from Marvin and Hank's mother, he had filled the void with a series of women Lamont would recruit for him at the games. The last one cost him a house he had built for her out in Whitehaven, then still a nice bedroom community just outside Memphis.

John was married now to a former beauty queen, Roberta,

whom he trusted, as he would say later, "about as far as I can throw her". Roberta was about Marvin's age - and Marvin mistrusted her more than John did. After all, he and Hennie were convinced she was after only one thing – money. Marvin and Hennie had what John called a 'conniption fit' when he married her, even though their mother was a Memphis Belle right off of the beauty pageant runway too. John never was a genius with women, but he knew what he wanted.

It was John's element of insanity, as he readily admitted. He always paraphrased Einstein's comment of insanity being defined as someone doing something over and over again while expecting different results. John knew what he was getting with these women, something different on the surface every time, but at the end of the day, he always lost money over them. After Roberta, he would have his insanity cured and never marry again.

But John had plenty of money, he had so much that he sometimes wasn't quite clear how much. His first wife had not taken too much, about ten million. She deserved it and needed it raising Marvin. Marvin saw his father infrequently growing up, returning to Memphis only when he saw an opportunity to muscle in on John's fortune.

Marvin was delighted when his brother Hank moved out on his own. Hennie loved it. From then on, Marvin and Hennie became caricatures of Memphis socialites, dorky misfits who were despised and never quite trusted. The only people who associated with them did so for business reasons, holding their noses and breathing sighs of relief when they were able to escape their company.

Marvin tried to make all the arrangements for his father's travel, but John would always trump any rigorous schedule opting for a more "let's go" or "let's hit it" approach. John, already 60 years old now, knew everything, and everyone he owned.

Everyone did their best to keep up with him, but John was always a hands-on man, someone who wanted to know where his money was, something the old Senator had taught him years ago.

✤ ✤ ✤

The West Point class of 1946 had done well for themselves. Jerry Slater had made it as far as Governor of Missouri, right next door. John had used his mid-South synergy in company holdings, fund raising ability and his way with people to convince enough Missourians to vote for him. Even if Jerry wasn't as attractive a candidate as Danny Carson over in Georgia, John liked him, a harmless enough sort of guy who was useful at times.

They sat together whenever the Blues played the St. Louis Cardinals at Busch Stadium. After all, Missouri tax breaks made it easy for John to effectively control damned near the entire Mississippi river traffic, partly thanks to John's buyout of Gordon's holdings twenty years ago when Gordon moved away, concerned that the truth about Billy Moore's death may come out someday.

Truman Forsythe captured a bigger prize. He was effectively king of California, a four-term Governor and war hero of Korea, a fighter pilot after he joined the Army Air Corps, later the US Air Force after The Point.

Both had come directly to John, made a beeline after they had served six years each in the Army. Jerry, not two days behind Truman, had ideas of developing the dilapidated riverfront in St. Louis in 1953, patterning himself after John's success in Memphis. It was such a good idea John was amazed that he hadn't thought of it himself. He could steal the idea, make Jerry a junior partner like old man Streeter, and have the prize for himself.

But Jerry only wanted to be a politician. Business success was only a means toward an end for him, a way of raising capital. And St. Louis didn't have the hook, the music of Beale, the Bourbon Street look and feel. Hell, after all, St. Louis was in the Midwest. John would settle for being the Streeter character in that project. John gave him the money. Jerry was honest and a hard worker and it would return dividends.

Anyway, Truman had taken a bigger bite out of the apple. He had a reputation that preceded him. Fresh out of the Air Force he was a fighter jock, kicking ass over Korea shooting down MiGs left and right, and he looked good too, movie star good looks. He was the only guy John had ever known at The Point that knew how to surf.

Truman approached John after he had heard about the renewal of downtown Memphis, after John had emerged from the shadows of Streeter's straw man cover. Truman had the law and politics in his sight since The Point. California's Governor Earl Warren had just been appointed Chief Justice of the Supreme Court back then. Truman was from Los Angeles, actually the beaches of Laguna Beach and wanted to attend law school and follow in Warren's footsteps.

Truman had never forgotten that in the year they graduated from The Point, Warren had taken advantage of a quirk in California law that allowed a person to run in any primary election they wanted. Warren entered the Republican, Democratic *and* Progressive party primaries, all at the same time. He won all three and thus ran unopposed for Governor going on to be the first California Governor to be re-elected twice. Now that was power.

John didn't particularly like California at the time. He had never liked the Hollywood film made on W. C. Handy, felt it too patronizing, never capturing the essence of the man and the Blues movement. But he knew there was influence there, maybe style

72

over substance, but a source of power.

The Veteran's Administration was not as kind to the soldiers of Korea, not like they had been to the heroes of World War II, the soldiers and their wives who had pumped money into the successful Memphis revival orchestrated by John Thompson. John knew that Truman would be a hot commodity, much more than just a Point graduate like him straight off the train in Memphis, fortunate enough to have a benefactor and admirer like Senator Moore.

John sent Truman away with a promise that he would see him through law school, help him get a foothold in California politics and support him, as long as Truman 'stayed straight'. John knew he could count on his Point friends. They were a tight fraternity, men of honor, of commitment, men of their word.

That's the real reason Harmon Vance had been brought in by John just two years into his service obligation from occupation duty in Germany. Harmon's father had bankrupted Vance Industries leaving not only Cadet Sergeant, then-Major Davis's father out in the cold, but effectively making a career out of the Army for Harmon, a career he never planned. He submitted a request to resign his commission and, with John and Senator Moore's help, it was accepted and he was on his way to Memphis.

Harmon was a people person like John. He knew power, had used his leverage on Sergeant Davis back at The Point and John owed him. Harmon had forgotten more about people than John's wimpy son Marvin would ever know. As much as Marvin and Hennie hated it, Harmon really ran the show at The Thompson Group and The Memphis Blues.

"John, we need to get to the airport", Harmon would so often repeat, urging John to meet some fictitious schedule, one he never intended to set or meet. John would make his own timetable. At 60, he could dictate when and where he should be on any given day.

73

That's just part of what irked Marvin and Hennie. They wanted John to make more magic, to build up that pie that would be his fortune carved up on his deathbed, hopefully without trophy wife Roberta taking too much with her.

✤ ✤ ✤

Danny Carson had waited patiently. He didn't ask his old West Point buddy John for help as he crept up the political ladder of Georgia politics, but John had given it. John knew Danny had the right stuff, what it took to make it all the way to the top. He knew it that day they tossed their hats into the air at graduation. John had admired his political acumen from afar, contributing large sums of money but never taking part in the celebrations of Danny's wins at the Georgia statehouse or when he won the US Senate race in 1980. Danny Carson wanted one more thing – the White House.

"Let's take the Citation, Harmon. I *know* those bars are stocked on that jet. Lamont is getting low on Black Jack on all the others. I don't know why he doesn't want me to drink. I've earned a shot now and then. And tell him not to let Roberta know we're leaving," John shot across the penthouse, knowing full well that Lamont was standing within earshot.

Lamont Boone had become John's caretaker, his confidant, obedient servant and confessor and had been there since boyhood, since Beale Street. Lamont knew all, or almost all about John's private life; the affairs, the booze, the dinners where lives were made or broken. Hell, Lamont knew that nothing much had changed in Memphis, it was still about booze, blondes and beef – and power, just on a much larger scale now.

Senator Danny Carson had asked for a meeting, a formal one.

To be sure the two had met since The Point, just not in a formal meeting, one where the Senator would ask a favor.

"Get that, Harmon. Hell, *he's* asking *me* for a favor! Who the hell does he think he is?" as John almost finished the sentence with 'The President of the United States?'

John thought how he had come full circle, that the tables had turned since he became involved with Senator Hugo Moore. It was 'bottom rail on top now' for sure. This time a Senator needed him, but it would be a hard favor to grant, and the cost would be enormous.

The old man, Senator Moore had ended up donating most of his money to charity. Funny how he had become philanthropic in his old age. It happens to many people like him when they feel the devil biting them on the ass. John knew he was a long way from that. He had lots of work to do yet.

John had benefited from old Hugo's charity. The Senator's sitting on the bank board, his influence in getting the sale of the baseball field to go through and his partnership were just the start of Hugo's teaming up with John. As John and Harmon soared toward Atlanta on one of seven jets he now owned, John's mind drifted back to the time the Senator and John went partners on setting up the first real civil aviation hangar at Memphis International Airport. John even brought in a surplus Saber jet to do an aerial show at the grand opening, piloted by none other than Truman Forsythe, war hero and by then, Attorney General of California. John smiled as he remembered old Hugo Moore's last words, "I sure wish I had another 75 years, boy. We could have done some real damage!"

The both of them had really 'done some damage' already. Although John's net worth had greatly surpassed the Senator's by the time of Hugo's death, John and the Senator were a lot alike in one disappointing way. Indeed, while John had a family in sons Marvin and Hank, he never had the family life he grew up with. Harmon, Lamont and the ball team were his real family now. Although Effie, 'Sister', was still alive, he saw her on the occasion of when he felt nostalgic about Slabtown, sometimes when dedicating one of the school buildings he would build for the community from time to time.

John's parents lived only three years into his millionaire days, with John spending most of his time on growing his businesses. Effie had made their parents' lives hers, nursing them to their deaths just three months apart. John would always take care of Effie, build her a new home and visit when he could. She never really liked Memphis much and John necessarily made the trips back to Slabtown and to her home on his Mom and Dad's land. They even fished together in the same ponds they frequented back when they were young.

Effie never tore down the old homestead, instead keeping it as sort of a memorial to her parents and their roots. John could never bring himself to set foot back inside the home. He didn't like the emotion of guilt, never dealt with it well and preferred to avoid situations that may generate it.

Now, with Marvin trying to run his life as he accumulated wealth through John, driven by the wretch Hennie, and with Hank giving his family space from the Thompson operation and lifestyle, John was pretty much alone. Harmon had a wife and children, a stable life when not occupied by John's hectic schedule. Lamont had a family now too. John had paid both of them well, Harmon earning a portion of the business while Lamont had realized his dream of owning The Union, the hotel where it all started just off of Beale Street. He kept Room 404 in the same condition it was when he and John lived there. Guests could rent it at a premium price since it was where it all started that fateful night he and John left the Boogie Woogie to plan John's empire.

Roberta had become John's show pony, seemed like he needed one. After all, the old Senator had John for one all those years. She still had her brunette beauty queen good looks and dressed to kill. She and John had not had a real marriage for many years and John basically just tolerated her.

As John closed his eyes he mumbled the corollary that Calvin Coolidge had spoken so many years ago. "Of course the accumulation of wealth cannot be justified as the chief end of existence," Coolidge added. Damned right. John Henry Thompson was, above all else, a lonely man.

Chapter Eight

The Kingmaker Emerges

John awoke at the Atlanta airport as the Cessna Citation touched down. Harmon and Lamont were still asleep, John thought they slept too much as he seemed to forever be awake when everyone else was asleep, always thinking more, planning, with more on his mind, maybe more memories to sort out. He would make a memory today that the whole world would never forget.

The jet had barely come to a stop at the private terminal when Danny Carson made his appearance at the stairway. Lamont was off first, then Harmon as Carson waited for John to make his appearance.

"Hats in the air, Class of '46," was John's somewhat Black Jack Daniels-induced cry as he made his way to Danny's outstretched hand. "It's good to see you, Senator," was John's salutation, one he remembered from long ago.

"John, you look swell," Senator Carson threw to John even though John knew he looked the worse for wear.

Senator Danny Carson had done well. John knew at The Point that Danny was the one who could go all the way. Danny had kept his distance from John, as much as John would let him. While never in the same room for more than an hour for the last forty years, Danny was in a way, a money way, in the sense of power and being beholden to John, very much in John's back pocket.

The ride in the Senator's limousine to his downtown Atlanta office was marked with pleasantries, the usual chitchat of 'how's the weather' and the insistences that John was looking well. Lamont and Harmon rode in the back with John, something he insisted on wherever they traveled, unless there was intensely private business to be discussed. He wanted them there by his side, an inconvenience and disruptive fact to some, but it didn't matter to John. They were with him all the way. But John knew there would be a time with Danny Carson when they would have to leave the room. After all, he knew why Danny Carson had called this meeting. He knew the favor he was about to ask, one that would cause Danny to owe John *the* big favor.

As the group ascended the private elevator in Atlanta's Marietta Tower, a glassy skyscraper on the skyline for just ten years at that time, John kept noticing how Carson kept the same exact smile on his face – all the time. He even smiled as he was talking to you, as if he had it surgically implanted. Carson was campaigning, kissing someone's ass continuously. Funny how things had changed since Senator Moore's days on his throne, John thought, arrogance was out, style over substance now.

Carson was in Atlanta just about as much as he was in DC, big on constituent services and mingling with the people every chance he could. John felt like he needed another Black Jack if he was going to have to deal, really make a deal with Danny. After all, Danny never was the kind of guy you'd knock one back with on Beale Street, sort of tight, squeaky clean with that Pepsodent grin. It reminded John of what he used to call the Brylcreem and Pepsodent boys, they looked good on the outside, he'd say, but full of shit on the inside.

Danny Carson had major hurdles to leap now that he wanted to run for the highest office in the land, in the world. He was Chairman of the Senate Foreign Relations Committee and things were not well. A major conflict in Nicaragua was brewing, near the boiling point in Danny's mind. Human rights violations were rife with the nation's military allegedly murdering people right and left. Danny wanted something done about it and sought to ride his foreign relations skills into the White House. He also knew John Henry Thompson could help do just that.

Ramon Hernandez graduated with Danny and John in Class of 1946 at The Point. John had more than stayed in touch, especially since he became wealthy and had invested in banana and tobacco plantations in Nicaragua. Ramon had returned to the country to be his brother's trusted assistant, that is until his brother was assassinated, some thought with Ramon's and/or John's help, in 1980. Ever since, things had gone from bad to worse under Ramon's leadership with American interests in jeopardy. All but John Henry Thompson's interests.

Danny knew that John had made an awful lot of money in Nicaragua but Danny had avoided Ramon like the plague. He held his nose at the thought that John had helped Ramon come to power, that John seemed secure in his investments there while other Americans were fleeing the country. Wealthy Americans were sick of losing money due to Ramon's strong-arming of the populace, the human rights advocates were raising immortal hell along with the UN, and as much as Danny hated to openly ask John for help, it was the only place he could turn.

After all, everyone in the Senate knew that Danny and John were classmates and that John had supported Danny since the beginning of his political career. But only John had been smart enough to maintain relations with Ramon, to give him kickbacks for what had become essentially a tax haven for John's businesses there.

"John, Ramon is embarrassing you down there. You've either got to sever your ties with him or get him to change," Danny dared to demand, all the while watching for John to deviate from the attention he was paying to lighting his cigar.

"Danny, I've given you lots of money, helped you get to where you are today, am I right?" John muttered as he puffed on his Cuban cigar, his *Cubano*.

"Right, John, and by the way this is a no-smoking building, but…" was all Danny could get out before John had leaped to his feet, uncharacteristically puffing hard on the Cubano and gesturing for Harmon and Lamont to leave the room.

"You don't dare pretend to order me around like some step-and-fetch porter at The Peabody you toothy son-of-a-bitch! I know what you're after. You want that brass ring you've wanted ever since we graduated from The Point! And I'll buy this goddamned building if I have to, but I'm going to smoke!" John bellowed, recalling his best Senator Hugo Moore.

"I can handle Ramon, I can make him set for the rest of his life or break him in half. I just don't want those damned Communists to take over that country. Would you have them in our back yard, just like in Cuba?" John demanded more than asked.

Danny by this time had sat down, retreated almost across the top of the desk to his executive chair near the window. Danny knew that John was as concerned about his businesses there as much as anything, but also that John was an ardent anti-Communist, refusing to do business with the Soviets no matter what money was to be made.

Danny felt like he was back on the wrestling mat at The Point with John on top pounding his ass. John was the 900-pound gorilla and Danny was his banana in his hand squeezing his balls like a vise. He wished his staff were there. He had the genuine look of fear on his face.

"John, I understand your concerns. But Ramon may have to go," Danny whined.

"What do I get out of it, Danny? What do I get for betraying one of the best and oldest friends I have made over these forty years? What can you promise me after you hog all the glory on Capitol Hill? Hell man, you can't even replace the Cubanos he supplies me with," John asked, knowing that Danny was prepared, knew what he was willing to give up in return for being able to claim credit for ending a political, hemispherical nightmare.

"John, you have my word that, now, and especially if elected President of the United States, you will have my undying gratitude and promise of any favors I might be able to grant," was Danny's carefully worded answer.

"Bullshit, Danny, make that *any* favor I might ask and you've got it. Otherwise, Ramon Hernandez may just invite the Soviets in tomorrow for a look around! Now hurry up, I never have liked farting around with politicians. Play or pay!" John ordered. More familiar words had never been spoken.

Danny Carson was shocked, dismayed, but, he knew, beaten.

"Okay, John. You get this done and I will owe you."

"Consider it done. Just read the news," was all John had to say as he turned on his heel for the door, reminiscent of Hugo Moore parting the sea of people on the rooftop of The Peabody Hotel.

"John, I don't want to know any details."

"You leave that up to me, Danny. If I'm anything, I'm a detail man," John said, managing a smile while never breaking stride.

Lamont and Harmon knew what that smile meant. They had seen it hundreds of times, during the wins, big and little, successful meetings, acquisitions and mergers. It was *the* look of John Henry Thompson. And this was one of the biggest wins of all. Making a king.

✤ ✤ ✤

"Harmon, just like you told me years ago would come to pass, Ramon has become a problem. Make sure his replacement is ready. Ramon has to go. It's a shame. I always liked him from the first day I met him at The Point," John said in a flat voice, knowing full well that Harmon Vance would start in motion a chain of events, that when started, could not be halted.

John loved Nicaragua and had taken the country, or what he owned of it, on as his pet project. He was determined to make it a better place – for the people. With John, it was always about the people.

Ramon Hernandez had become a rich man, a veritable king in his own banana republic just like his brother before him. John had pumped money into his regime and made incredible amounts of money in return. He had built a ranch in the mountains of an island called Ometepe, grown his own coffee and tobacco, some pretty good Nicaraguan cigars at that.

But John had not visited in several years due to the 'troubles' in the countryside, content to allow his estate manager, Julio Fuentes, and the locals to run the show. John practiced putting distance between his straw men and himself. He had learned almost forty years ago to micromanage from afar, just like the Senator, come up for air, show yourself only when necessary.

Ramon Hernandez died in his sleep less than two weeks later. Just of what causes or cause, no one knew for sure at the time. Harmon had made one telephone call, had relayed the news that John was upset with Ramon and didn't know if he could support his presidency any longer. The message was clear, and Ramon's political nemesis, Hector Gonzalez, had waited years for that call. One telephone call, that's all it took. Might makes right. Power is good, power is money and sometimes the exercise of it is not pretty.

John was eerily reminded of Billy Moore, nephew of Senator Hugo Moore, and his death many years ago, a death that opened doors for many people in Memphis, Tennessee, the thresholds of which John Henry Thompson crossed and never looked back. The payoff here had the potential to be much greater. Danny Carson would be shocked to hear of Ramon's death, but in all his sanctimony he knew Ramon's removal would be swift, if not deadly.

Senator Danny Carson, now the second Great Emancipator, claimed credit for the installation of Hector Gonzalez, the centrist leader of the former opposition party in Nicaragua, thus stabilizing the country and securing the properties and interests held by so many wealthy Americans, while at the same time averting the fear of Soviet intervention. In the weeks leading up to Ramon's death Danny had assured all on Capitol Hill that Ramon was on his way out.

To be sure, the political unrest subsided and the threat of Soviet influence was eliminated, might made right due to swift, decisive action, John Henry Thompson style. But it was all only temporary. John hadn't done anything he already wasn't pre-disposed to do anyway. But Danny didn't know that.

John knew that he should not ever meet personally with Danny Carson again, at least not while Danny was running for the White House. He would have to stealth his every move. Harmon would have to be careful too. All eyes would be on 'the candidate' as he inched ever slowly toward the upcoming campaign.

To be sure, John would contribute heavily, sponsor fundraisers and make in-kind contributions such as the use of his corporate jets, but the stakes were so high now that John would necessarily have to use surrogates, the old 'straw man' tactics to shepherd Danny through his Presidential bid – and for that, he needed a new straw man. Ophelia Hartwell would be just such a person.

✤ ✤ ✤

Ophelia Hartwell's appointment with destiny, or rather with Thompson Properties, Atlanta Division was supposed to be just another meeting, one that she would make to secure a strategic partnership in her career as a commercial real estate broker.

She had left Franklin, Georgia behind years ago for the big city environs of Atlanta. She had broken free of her own Slabtown, Tennessee equivalent by working hard, saving her money and literally buying her way out, out of the seclusion and desperation of the small town economy, social life and politics.

Ophelia was a people person too. She had attended all the right events, all those that were of a social/political nature, functions where she could maximize her time spent, making all the connections she could, while she could.

Georgia politics was funny, parochial, kind of clannish and it was hard for an 'outsider' to break into the fold. Her statuesque, blonde, buxom good looks didn't hurt either. But her strength lay in her personality, a witty charm that disarmed even the most hardened politico, even though she had just celebrated only her thirtieth birthday.

John was now making more and more trips to Atlanta to keep watch on his contender, to get reports from his straw men who were now on the inside of Danny Carson's all-but-declared campaign for the White House. Real estate was always a passion for John, ever since the days of the Beale Street Revival, The New Ball Park at Memphis and the St. Louis revival that set the stage for the successful Missouri statehouse run of Jerry Slater.

After all, John thought many times, when a man has a piece of property, he really has something concrete, something he can develop, can pass on to others. He would use his property holdings as an excuse to stay close to the action of Carson's campaign while still hoping The Memphis Blues would ultimately play the Atlanta

Braves in that year's World Series. In that event, John could set up camp for a while in Atlanta with no other excuse needed for his presence.

The Marietta Tower was the center of activity now. Not only was there a nexus with the Carson offices and campaign headquarters, the Thompson Commercial Realty offices were there too. John had been instrumental in funding the rebirth of Atlanta's downtown, especially the section known as 'Underground Atlanta', the underbelly of downtown Atlanta that was left after the streets were elevated in the 1920's.

John saw it as another opportunity to recreate his Beale Street miracle - and it happened. He masterminded the saving of the old ornate storefronts of the Underground and gave birth to a five-block area that was teeming with shops, restaurants, and new life. John had made his mark in Atlanta but preferred to stay close to home in his revered Memphis, his first true love.

Ophelia was in awe of what had been done in Atlanta's downtown. She knew of John Henry Thompson, pretty much anyone in commercial real estate knew of him, of what he had done for Memphis and Atlanta. Some even knew of his connection to the St. Louis revival, usually people within the political circle of friends, the Class of 1946 and those who benefited from knowing John, and subsequently owing him.

Ophelia had fought the decline of the Underground Atlanta too. After the rapid transit system called MARTA had been built, the Underground had fallen into decline. She watched as John worked his magic bringing the Underground back, and she was determined to emulate his success.

From everything she had read about John, she knew he was a rags-to-riches success story. Like him, she too had come from nowhere with nothing. She had made it to the City, but not the corporate boardrooms or jets of that rarified air John Henry Thompson breathed. Her first breath of that air was to be a memorable one.

✠ ✠ ✠

Harmon Vance saw her first. Ophelia was introduced as being a representative of Charles Waller's commercial real estate firm, one of the companies involved in the Underground Atlanta renewal project. Years later Ophelia could not remember who she met first. After all, she had only seen photographs of John, dated ones at that.

"Miss Hartwell, I'd like for you to meet John Henry Thompson, my boss," Harmon introduced a somewhat bored John.

John's eyes lit up when he saw Ophelia. In what had been a lame excuse to be in Atlanta for political reasons, for more power, money, he now had met someone really interesting, someone with a radiant smile that drew John in, mesmerizing him almost in an instant.

"Why I'm proud to meet you, my dear. Where have you been keeping her Harmon? Does she work for me?" John almost demanded, certain that she did and all the while thinking of the possibilities.

"No. Mr. Thompson, I work for Mr. Waller, although I do believe we share the same goal, you know, sort of pulling on the same rope," Ophelia joked, a folksy phrase that instantly hooked John.

Here he had a real people person, one that knew how to turn a phrase. And, it helped that he knew she was right. That's what it was all about, synergy, and power, getting things done. In Ophelia he had found his own 'go-getter' as old Senator Hugo Moore would have said.

John was all of a sudden interested in this meeting, demanding now to know more. As Ophelia made her presentation that consisted of a proposal to sell Thompson Properties a $400,000 lot, one very near John's holding in the five block area of the Underground, John let it be known very quickly that he was interested, not just interested, sold!

"Let's buy it, Harmon. I like the idea of buying up everything we can down here. It's not Beale Street, but we can sure make it a reasonable facsimile with the help of Miss Hartwell. It's a done deal!" John bellowed, putting on his best show for Ophelia.

And Ophelia was duly impressed. She knew there was to be a fundraiser for Danny Carson that night and hoped she would see John there. She fully intended to pattern herself, as best she knew she could, after John's legendary success and would love to see him at the event.

"I'm not into politics my dear. Just don't have the stomach to sit around and watch politicians try to impress everyone. I'd rather be on the bench just watching the game," John said, using one of his baseball metaphors he loved to employ when he was trying to make a real-life, but important and even coy point.

"Maybe I'll see you some other time," he said as he elbowed Harmon, the elbow move that Harmon knew so well, one that meant Harmon was not to let her get away. But there was time for that later, much more time.

Chapter Nine

The Memphis Blues

In that brief encounter with Ophelia Hartwell at Atlanta, John had seen something in Ophelia that he trusted. Back in Memphis, he actually wished he had attended the Carson fundraiser. But he knew that his presence would have fueled speculation about Ramon's death. Everyone knew the connections he had in Nicaragua. John didn't need to change his methods now, methods that had taken him this far, with a long way to go before he was done.

Anyway, John was a busy man. The Memphis Blues were in first place in the American League East, the playoffs were coming up and he wouldn't miss a game. Harmon and Lamont would be there with him for all the festivities, the parties that John threw at The Peabody and the drinking sessions afterward at his private room at the old Boogie Woogie, now teeming with visitors from all over the world. Elvis had come and gone, but B. B. King was now a fixture on Beale Street with his own Blues joint hopping every night. It was Bourbon Street in Memphis, only more tight-knit, casually more comfortable and friendly.

John hated the hangers-on. Every playoff season, certainly every World Series there would be the glad-handers who wanted tickets. John had an ample share and delegated the requests to Harmon and Lamont. John personally had to approve the people who would attend his private parties in his owner's box and on Beale Street. He had worked too hard and too long to suffer through the inanities of idle conversation or by being harassed by people who wanted nothing except money from him. Life was too short for that.

John's son Marvin hated it when John came back home. He and Hennie loved running the show while he was gone, or at least thinking they were. John had Harmon place loyal troops in key positions to ensure that Marvin and Hennie wouldn't get too bold with the business while John was otherwise occupying himself in Atlanta or anywhere else in the world.

John had already suffered the casualty of seeing his son Hank flee the chaos and treachery that Marvin and Hennie pulled down over the business like a pall. But John was content that Hank had prospered on his own, raising a family outside the Thompson umbrella. Anyway, John would always take care of Hank.

Back in Atlanta, Ophelia was still reeling from the whirlwind real estate deal, the easiest one she had ever closed. It was a very straightforward deal. It was only a vacant lot, but a strategically placed one right in the middle of the Thompson Underground Atlanta. Although she had no idea as to what John was planning for the site, if what she had seen in her visits to Memphis were any clues, she knew he had something up his sleeve.

It was all very simple to John. Synergy, pure synergy. He already had Harmon working on a contingency plan in case The Memphis Blues and Atlanta Braves would face each other in The Series. John had contacts in all the television networks and had a plan to use them well if and when The Series were to shake out that way.

Live remotes from Beale Street on the days The Blues played at home and the same from The Underground when the Braves hosted. Earned media, free advertising, just like back in the good old days with the Memphis *Commercial Appeal.*

It was in that business sense that John arranged the next meeting with Ophelia. He had done his homework on her. Money can buy a lot of information in the business world and John put Harmon and his network to task finding out all about her, who she was, where she came from, whether or not she could be trusted.

John sat on the rooftop, his now private rooftop at The Peabody in Memphis and read the dossier on Ophelia. It read almost like his early biography, as if she were a second generation 'go-getter' as the old Senator might have said. Hell, if the Senator had allowed women into his circle, in that time, Ophelia would have been there. If John were to bet, she probably even smoked cigars.

As he read on, it was apparent that Franklin, Georgia was most obviously a lot like Slabtown, Tennessee, John thought. At thirty, she was in an early stage of her real estate career having made her way out of Franklin, saving money for college at Auburn University, making a few money-making deals on her own and then on to Atlanta to make it big in the booming market there while working for Charles Waller.

She had shunned the thought of getting married too early, afraid that she would succumb to the fate of her classmates at Franklin High. Most girls just got married, before or after high school, and raised a family hoping to keep it together in poor, rough rural Georgia, in many ways not unlike John's Slabtown, Tennessee. The men she had met in Atlanta either moved away with no offer of marriage or just didn't work out. Ophelia had tried marriage once, marrying an older man with the baggage of selfish older children that fueled the ruination of the marriage.

The Thompson Underground Atlanta lot was her latest project

put together on her own initiative, based apparently on the same mindset as John's, opportunity, foresight, synergy. She didn't own the property, but sought the owners out through a painstaking search of property records, ultimately finding that the lot had been tied up in a trust, something John's people had missed. Imagine that, a go-getter finding something that John had missed and then putting together the deal on her own, right in his backyard.

"Hell, Harmon, she's even active in old Danny's campaign, a real political animal!" John proclaimed.

He knew then and there he had to have her on his team.

✤ ✤ ✤

Ophelia didn't think it unusual when the buyer of a property wanted to close the deal so soon. She didn't know just how John wanted to do it, that is, bring *her* to *him*. It wasn't a long flight to Memphis from Atlanta by commercial air anyway. But to have a private jet sent for her was a first. With the Thompson presence in Atlanta, it was easy for John to get a limo to take her to the Atlanta airport and to one of his corporate jets.

Lamont was in the limo when Ophelia was picked up at her downtown office not far from the Marietta Tower.

"Miss Hartwell, I'm Lamont Boone, Mr. Thompson's assistant."

Ophelia hadn't missed Lamont at the meeting. She knew the way she saw John signal to, address and otherwise include Lamont in his business that he was an integral component of John Henry Thompson's affairs.

"I'm very pleased to meet you Mr. Boone. Will Mr. Thompson be joining us? I have all the paperwork right here," she asked, assuming they would be whisked to the Marietta Tower.

"If you don't mind terribly, Miss Hartwell, Mr. Thompson would like for you to just come on up to Memphis. It's October, and he likes to take lunch up on the deck at The Peabody Hotel."

Ophelia was, which was not often to happen, at a loss for words. She wasn't about to say no, even as she thought for a second that it was not such a short drive to Memphis from Atlanta.

"It'll just take us a few minutes to get to his jet. I'll have you back by three o'clock," Lamont told her.

"Sure, why not?" was all she could say as she slumped back into the plush leather. This was not to be her average real estate closing.

❖ ❖ ❖

John and Harmon were waiting at Memphis when John's favorite jet touched down. John had christened it the 'Room 404', a reference to his old room at The Union hotel where his Memphis miracle all started. He had Harmon make sure Marvin and Hennie hadn't commandeered it for one of their junkets.

"John, you like this girl, don't you? I mean, why else fly her up here? I could have handled this for you," Harmon said, for once not able to guess where John was going with this relationship.

"I'm just thinking ahead, Harmon. You know how we want to hit a home run if, sorry, *when* we get to The Series? Well, I think it's going to be against Atlanta, in the middle of Danny's campaign, and all of the press will be swarming around Beale Street and then The Underground. This girl can be an asset. She looks good, is articulate and is political. She's a go-getter," he said to Harmon whose eyebrows arched higher on every word.

Prophetically John added, "And she just might like the plantation in Nicaragua."

Harmon knew John was probably right. After all, he had read Ophelia's dossier. He too was reminded of John's journey from Slabtown to Memphis, to the world. He smiled as he thought John must be reminiscing of his old days, how he came up from nothing to all this. John was always one to spot talent, to reward initiative and capitalize on new ideas. This girl obviously had some of all of that. And she could be a real asset in his plans – in *the* plan.

Harmon didn't worry about any 'hanky-panky' as John called it. Sure, Ophelia was a 'doll', but Harmon could tell when John was being all business. Anyway, Roberta was all John could handle for now.

"Miss Hartwell, I'm John Henry Thompson, we met in Atlanta some time ago," John said in an earnest tone.

"Of course Mr. Thompson, how could I forget? Thank you for the first-class transportation. Mr. Boone has been so kind," Ophelia said in her Southern, charming Georgia accent, one that was sincere, not overdrawn or syrupy; one that was genuinely 'Southern', attractive.

"You know that jet you were on, it's my favorite. I call it Room 404. You want to know why?" John related, sure that Ophelia could appreciate the story he was about to tell.

As they rode in the limo on their way to The Peabody, John told his story, one that he did not tell often, and for her, it was her first time to hear it. As he recounted the nights at The Boogie Woogie Café, the acquisition of property, even of old Senator Moore, the looks on the face of Lamont Boone did not go unnoticed by Ophelia.

Lamont was grinning from ear to ear. He absolutely reveled in the fact that he was there when it all began. Even more important to him was the fact that John actually included him in the story, that

John started it at the first day he returned to Memphis from The Point, not after it all took off, the story that the media knew.

It was about then that John realized that he rarely told the story – *the* story, all of it, not anymore. To be sure Lamont knew, had lived it and Harmon knew almost all of it. Roberta never cared, she didn't know John back then and couldn't relate to John, never could. She still had her head up in the clouds of her beauty pageant days.

It occurred to John that he was telling this story to someone he trusted not to tell it again, at least not to tell it to just anyone, at a cocktail party prefaced with some inanity like, "Guess whose limo I was in today?" like some name-dropping gold-digger. No, John's people skills, an almost radar-like skill he had honed from his early days, had kicked in. He knew somehow that Ophelia was special.

The limo, big enough for eight, drove them from Memphis International and the flight operations that housed the Thompson jets, through the growing suburbs of Memphis, but still only a ten minute drive to downtown and The Peabody. Unavoidably they passed through the heart of Beale Street, down the riverfront and up to the portico of the hotel. Now that the story was over, Ophelia, John, everyone remained silent, John watching Ophelia crane to see the sites, the Boogie Woogie, The New Ball Park at Memphis. He could see her visualizing the story he had just told as each landmark passed. John just smiled as Harmon and Lamont watched approvingly.

"This is a nice town you've built Mr. Thompson. I wish Atlanta looked like this," she said, and Ophelia meant it.

"In good time, my dear. In good time," and John meant it as well.

Ophelia had stayed at The Peabody once on a trip to see Beale Street, taking a trip on the *Delta Queen* riverboat and seeing Graceland, the home of Elvis Presley. She had never been to the rooftop or seen anything like the parties that were held there when John made his fortune under the wing of Senator Moore.

The ducks were swimming in the lobby fountain pool, marble floors and columns dominating the ground floor. Nothing much had changed here in almost a hundred years. Even the old black man, Rufus Muggs's presence was still being felt. John had given the late head porter's son, David, a job there as head of security for the hotel. John trusted him completely.

The elevators were still slow, making the ride to the top seem like an eternity for Ophelia. The rear door of the elevator, instead of the front, opened revealing an opulent office-style setting. Rita, a woman at the first desk looked up at the group. She closely resembled brother Gordon's secretary back at the old Thompson Building down on the river, a place John had expanded with a view for his Mud Island amusement park development. Rita was John's reminder of those days at the Thompson Building and in fact was the daughter of Gordon's old secretary. She kept secrets too, mostly from John's wife Roberta. It ran in her family.

And there was Roberta, waiting, wondering "where in the hell", at least in her mind, never vocalizing, John had been. But she didn't even speak. Instead, she turned, walked past them into the elevator and pushed the down button. Ophelia wondered, as she would relate to John *much* later, "Who died?" It was that sort of look.

As if on cue, Marvin met John and the group just after Roberta made her exit. He gave a stinky look Ophelia's way. In Ophelia's mind it didn't make a damn if you didn't like someone or if you had all the money in the world, you didn't treat people like shit on your shoes. She threw the look right back, not ever thinking that this would be John's son.

Marvin didn't even speak. Instead, when he saw an unfamiliar

96

face in the inner sanctum, he knew his father was up to something. He already knew from his spies at the aircraft hangar that John had used the Lear jet, the '404', to ferry someone he didn't know to Memphis. He had only come up to John's office and townhouse in order to get a glimpse. What pissed off John was that he brought his wife Hennie with him.

Hennie only showed her face from behind Rita's desk. She showed it long enough to give the entire group a 'go to hell' look.

"That insufferable bitch! What is she doing here Harmon? I'm not dead yet and already she's up here looking for the combination to the safe!" John yelled as they walked into John's office, his penthouse.

Ophelia couldn't suppress her very Southern giggle – and John liked it.

John's office in many ways was like Gordon's at the old Thompson Building forty years ago. From his perch he could see his beloved Mighty Mississippi and Beale Street. The view of The New Ball Park at Memphis replete with the one 'World Series Champions' banner waving proudly above the field was his most prized addition to the skyline that Gordon never got to see.

John kept his penthouse there as well, a sanctuary where he could be alone, away from Marvin, Hennie and even Roberta who stayed at the estate he had built near the old Senator's many years ago, at least when she wasn't doing the social scene or playing politics raising money for one of John's political cronies. Roberta loved that sort of thing, just standing around looking pretty, socializing and spending John's money.

"Choose your chair, Miss Hartwell," John waved at the sofa, leather chairs and ballpark stadium seats from the original park. Lamont and Harmon were already scurrying about to fill John's favorite crystal highball glass with Black Jack and securing a

97

Cubano from the wall-sized humidor. John was in his environment, surrounded by the wood paneling, massive desk, and all just steps from the four bedrooms and massive library of his penthouse.

"How about a drink?" John asked, never knowing that this woman was the only one he would know that could keep up with him in that regard.

"You know, I believe I will," offered Ophelia as she made her way to the ballpark seats. "Somehow, I like these seats the best". John smiled that smile of inevitability – she was a baseball fan at that.

After lunch on the balcony of the penthouse, one of John's favorite haunts, papers were signed and small conversation ensued as John felt his way around just who Ophelia Hartwell was, seeing if she had the right stuff to be a team leader in Atlanta. He wanted to find out if she was someone who could pull off the next phase of the great Thompson marketing strategy he hoped would materialize; if The Series came the way of The Blues and the Braves.

Ophelia, for her part, thought that just maybe this was a one-time deal. But in the back of her mind she hoped John had brought her there for something bigger. This may be her big break.

"Miss Hartwell, I hope to see you again soon. This property would be a great fit for my Underground Atlanta. I may want you to do some more work for me – if you're interested. You don't have any problems with Danny Carson do you?" John threw out almost like bait.

"I just might be interested. Let me know what you have in mind," Ophelia responded, immediately reminding John of his first real encounter with Senator Moore, playing it cool, not overanxious.

"And no, Senator Carson, other than being a politician, Danny's alright by me. As long as he doesn't get too big for his britches,"

Ophelia quipped as John allowed an approving, agreeing smile to creep across his face.

"Fine. Then I want to get back with you in about one week. As you know, I have offices in Atlanta and I hope I'm going to be busy winning another World Series banner for that stadium," John said as he pointed to The Park.

"I'd like to see that too. I can't stand the Braves' owner," Ophelia remarked as she quickly grabbed her mouth, not sure whether or not he may be a friend of John's.

"Hell, that's alright by me. Why do you think I want to kick his ass?" he assured her.

John liked her candor. She was straightforward and a little rough around the edges, just like him. After all, they were products of the rugged South; no matter how far either one had come. He liked someone who didn't change, was the same person they were when they had nothing, deep down that is. He couldn't bear people who put on a front. Those were the kind of people you couldn't trust, people like Danny Carson - for that matter, Marvin and Hennie.

Harmon and Lamont escorted Ophelia down the elevator and into the limousine. They left her to ride alone back to the Memphis airport as if to let her collect her thoughts, absorb all that she had just seen and heard. Ophelia had been in the company of wealthy people before. After all, Atlanta was a big city and she had been involved in her share of real estate transactions since putting down roots there. She was back in Atlanta by three o'clock, just as Lamont had promised.

Ophelia felt much as John did when he got up off his bunk at The Point, the time when Gordon offered him a place in Memphis. She later would tell John that she knew then that her whole life would change, that it was headed in the right direction with the right people.

She did not hear from John for a week. During that time John busied himself with The Blues while they made their way to the World Series. Ophelia kept up with The Blues and the Atlanta Braves as she naturally would. The match between the two was cemented by the Braves' win over the Houston Astros giving John his synergistic match up of all time in The Series.

She naturally immersed herself in the politics of Danny Carson as well. She knew that John had something in mind when he asked her if she had any problem with Carson.

Since his offices were at the Marietta Tower, as were the Thompson operations in Atlanta, Ophelia could drop in on both while there. Carson had not announced his intentions formally, but his coordinators were looking for good people in Atlanta to raise money and staff the campaign.

Ophelia talked to the right people while she was there, letting them know that she was in the Thompson loop. It would prove to be a wise move on her part since John needed all the trusted surrogates he could get in order to exert his influence over Carson, to keep tabs on his operation.

Ophelia was ready for the call that came from Harmon in the interlude between the playoffs and The Series. She knew she could handle the proposition of being the 'go-to' person for John's media calls, ticket requests and promotion of Beale Street and Underground Atlanta as the places to be before, during and after The Series. She had never before encountered a movable fortress of a man, a business empire maker like John Henry Thompson, 'Mr. Thompson' as she would always call him. And she would be one of the last people to see him in full force.

She would also be one of the few to stay with him thereafter. The Series was going to be John Henry Thompson's last great ride, and Ophelia would be there with him. She also had a deal in the making, one of her own that would confirm her relationship with John.

Chapter Ten

The Big Shows

To be sure, just getting to the major leagues, the 'big show', is a serious accomplishment. Ophelia couldn't grasp how it felt to own a major league team much less one that had made it to the World Series, to win it once and to go back again. But that's where she was going with John and his crew.

John loved to watch politicians jockey for position like the show ponies of the old days. To him, politics was much like baseball. You could buy a good baseball team, stock it with best players in the league. But politicians were a motley group, interested only in power and themselves, not in being a team player like the ones John had hired when he built The Blues from scratch, that is, he and old Hugo Moore. Besides, politicians could be bought a lot cheaper and were much easier to maintain than a good baseball player, he thought.

Ophelia had been directed to meet John at his penthouse at the Ritz-Carlton, an extravagant hotel built just a few years before in downtown Atlanta near the Marietta Tower and John's Atlanta offices. Ophelia had been there many times for fundraisers, social events and drinks at the popular nightspot housed within the hotel. John had taken The Ritz as his Atlanta residence ever since the hotel was built in 1983. He liked the staff who gave him the service he demanded, much as it was at The Peabody.

Lamont met Ophelia downstairs and escorted her up to the penthouse.

"What'd you think of The Peabody, Miss Ophelia?" Lamont asked as he kept his eye on the floor numbers in the elevator.

"I loved it! I can tell Mr. Thompson loves being there. How does he like it here at The Ritz?"

"He would much rather be in Memphis. He doesn't like this town as much. Course he's got a lot of memories there," answered Lamont as they reached the penthouse floor.

John's digs were much more modern at the Ritz. Everything from the building itself to the furnishings was new, not rugged and used with the attendant character of the leather furniture he loved so much at The Peabody. The living room was spacious with a balcony that provided John with a sensational view of downtown Atlanta.

With four bedrooms, John liked for Lamont to stay at the penthouse. Harmon took a room of his own and was always available for John. This would be their base of operations and Ophelia would be there often.

They both met in the middle of the living room and hugged followed by what Ophelia would call a 'sister kiss', one of those shared between two people who loved each other but not in a romantic way. Harmon was on the balcony surveying the skyline.

"Come right in, Ophelia. Are you ready to go to work?" John asked, hoping that Ophelia had made up her mind to join his operation.

"Yes sir, I believe you can put me on the roster. I want to be on the team."

They both laughed realizing that they often used baseball metaphors now, something John adored about Ophelia.

"I have another property for you, Mr. Thompson. It's near the Atlanta Underground and the lot I sold you. I thought you might be interested."

Ophelia proceeded to explain how she had heard of plans by the venerable Atlanta-based Coca-Cola Company to build a museum in downtown Atlanta. It was to be dedicated to the history of the world-renowned products they had produced since the 1800's, with their origination right there in Atlanta.

"Coca-Cola, you say? Where's the property?"

Ophelia explained that the land was between the state capitol and the Underground, had great potential, and, after all, she had a contact at Coca-Cola she had met at one of Danny Carson's fundraisers. She knew they were seeking a property near Underground Atlanta for the museum but had no firm plans yet.

"Harmon, get in here. Sounds like we've got some more land to buy over here," John yelled toward the window, somehow this time in his own command form devoid of the old Hugo Moore tone Ophelia had heard before.

"Harmon, get with Ophelia and work out this Coke deal," John said to a quizzical Harmon who was not sure if John was talking about a cocaine deal or just what. That would indeed be a first.

John hadn't expected Ophelia to come to him with another moneymaker, especially when she could have done this one on her own. But Ophelia knew that if she were to sign on to John's team, he would have to have her full attention – and loyalty.

Over the next month John would watch the project be completed smoothly. He bought the land and flipped it nicely to the Coca-Cola people, properly stealthed, all at a hefty markup. But in the interim, John had chores for Ophelia.

"We've got this World Series coming up, Ophelia. We're going to be back and forth from here to Memphis a lot. Are you up to it?" he asked, knowing full well what answer he would get.

"Mr. Thompson, you can count on me. I'll get the job done no matter what."

That was really all John needed to hear. If there were any questions about Ophelia's loyalty they were answered when she brought forward the Coke deal.

"Well, first of all. Tell me what's been going on with my friend Danny Carson."

"I've been attending all his fundraisers here in Atlanta, the cocktail gatherings as well as the big events. I must tell you, I think he's going to win. I think he'll be the next President. I think he's got what it takes," Ophelia said as she waited for John's reaction, one that seemed to take an eternity to reach his face.

John had thought the same thing as Danny and he, along with all the others bid farewell to West Point.

"I think you're right, Ophelia. And let me tell you why."

John told Ophelia everything, everything that is, except for Ramon and his timely death in Nicaragua. He would never tell her such things in their entirety. He wanted Ophelia to always have respect, admiration for him with her never seeing the underbelly of the business and political moves John had to sometimes make. Making kings, after all, was sometimes a dirty business.

But there was The Series first. John necessarily explained the relationship between his son Marvin, and Hennie, such as it was. They were leeches, opportunists first, not unlike what she had already seen in politics and business. And they were the worst pains in the ass at The Series. But Ophelia would have to deal with them often.

Hennie, for her part, lived for the parties and wanted all the tickets she could get her hands on. Marvin loved to play the owner, the pseudo-big-daddy owner, and he played it clumsily. Compared to John's laid back, earned, sophisticated demeanor, Marvin seemed to operate from a Halloween costume when trying to assert authority.

Everyone knew he was a sad joke and wondered why John allowed it all. John just wanted to enjoy life. After all, he had Harmon really running the Big Shows of The Thompson Group and The Memphis Blues.

But, Ophelia would have to make the obligatory appearance before Marvin and Hennie. There was no doubt that John loved his son in spite of his faults, particularly the harpie he had married and attached to his hip.

When they both arrived in Atlanta for the first games of The Series, the time for Ophelia to meet them had finally come.

"Ophelia, I want you to meet one of my two sons, Marvin," was always how John referred to Marvin, as Marvin was aghast to hear, ever-reminded of the price he paid as being the supposedly favored, while still the most distrusted son.

"I am so pleased to meet you. Mr. Thompson has told me so much about you!" Ophelia offered in her most sincere, disarming Georgia accent.

"I look forward to seeing more of you," she added for effect.

Marvin for his part didn't know just who Ophelia was and made his usual bad first impression. He hated anyone who even appeared to exert any influence on John. This attitude would do Marvin a disservice in business, politics and in his personal life.

'Paranoia will destroy you', were Ophelia's thoughts as she shook Marvin's clammy hands, hands that she knew had never done a decent day's work in their lives.

"Well, we'll see," was Marvin's only response.

Ophelia knew she had made an enemy for life. However unjustifiable and uncaring toward his father, it would be one of Marvin Thompson's little petty goals in life to separate her from John.

Ophelia thought that little people like Marvin Thompson had a little black book in their heads. In it, they would jot down people's names, people they wanted to avoid, even destroy. Marvin was one of these people who lived by it, referring to the book before making the more grave decisions in life.

Sad, she thought. John didn't deserve it.

John's penthouses at The Ritz and back at The Peabody in Memphis would be the headquarters for The Series, the one John wanted to win even more than the first. He despised Ted Turner who had bought the Braves back in 1976, never even hiring a groundskeeper for the field. Instead, an Atlanta city street crew tended the grounds.

Ophelia had been charged with screening the people who wanted tickets from John and her contact was Harmon, when it was not John himself. Harmon and Ophelia liked each other immediately, for Harmon's part, because of the same things John saw in her.

Ophelia respected Harmon for who he was and what he meant to John. She had learned early on to trust whomever Mr. Thompson trusted. That was always good enough for her.

Ophelia was swimming in a deep sea now, and there were sharks everywhere. World Series tickets and the people that would do anything to get them could be big trouble – for John, and by extension for her if she didn't know whom to exclude.

Everyone John had ever known suddenly appeared from out of the woodwork claiming that he had invited them personally to The Series. It was bad enough during the regular season, but now, it was almost overwhelming trying to sort out fact from fantasy. It was a big draw to say the least.

"Mr. Vance," as she similarly addressed Harmon, "do we know who these people are?" as she showed Harmon a request for first-day tickets.

John had realized that by vetting all requests for the new Series he would be re-examining his connections, or rather the ones Marvin and Hennie had made and planted. Many of the people who were getting in did not belong to John's circle of friends. Harmon, through Ophelia, would be able to clean up much of the mess that Marvin and Hennie had made, keeping people away from John he didn't want to see, ones that he didn't want to benefit from his success. Not real people, John thought.

"Ophelia, you have a good eye. John would have a cow if he knew these people were getting into The Series on his tickets. Keep running them by me," Harmon would tell her over and over. Harmon recognized that this girl had organizational skills as well as good looks and a real personality.

Marvin knew what was going on with Ophelia but wisely remained silent. He had made the mistake of crossing his dad before with tragic results. During the last Series Marvin brought in a friend of his mother, John's ex-wife, to John's owner's box without having asked John first. John had the locks to the owner's skybox changed and told the guards not to let Marvin in for the next game. Marvin never said a word – he had gotten the message.

But Ophelia had not encountered Hennie yet. That is, until the day Ophelia turned down a ticket request from Hennie's 'office', a made-up status Marvin had given her at her demand. It was overall an effort to legitimize her position in the family business.

'From the Office of Henrietta C. Thompson', the memorandum started. Addressed to Harmon Vance it was immediately referred to Ophelia for handling in due course, right along with the rest of the general inquiries and requests regarding The Series. John had already told Harmon not to give Marvin or Hennie any special privileges. Just refer them to Ophelia Hartwell.

"Miss Hartwell, this is Henrietta Thompson, *John's* daughter-in-law," was Hennie's first salutation ever to Ophelia, this time over the telephone.

Hennie was always one to avoid conflict in person, preferring memos or, at worst, telephone conversations when dealing with the 'underlings' as she would call John's assistants.

"Good to finally talk with you, Mrs. Thompson. What can I do for you?" was the best Ophelia could do, given what she had already been told about Hennie.

"I want to know where the tickets are for David Sadler and his wife. I've had the letter in for two days now and The Series starts tomorrow!" Hennie demanded, obviously spoiling for a fight.

Ophelia did not lose her cool. Although she knew John despised this woman, in deference to her position, who she was, the wife of John's son, she would have to handle this with kid gloves. John knew this would be a hurdle for Ophelia. If she could handle this witch, she could do anything.

"Mrs. Thompson, I'm new to all this. I run these by Harmon Vance, but I will check with Mr. Thompson personally. I'm sure if he wants them to have the tickets, they will get to them," Ophelia said firmly with no hint of retreat. "I'll get back to you."

Hennie for her part would have none of it. She slammed the telephone down so hard that it bounced back off the receiver so quickly as to not cut off the call.

Ophelia could hear what she thought was a banshee scream and the distinct sound of breaking glass. Hennie Thompson was having one of her 'conniption fits' as John would call it, or sometimes a 'Class A' fit.

Hennie liked to grab the nearest breakable object she could find and smash it. It was her way of handling the stress and rejection she knew she deserved.

"Ophelia, I gave you this job so that I would not have to deal with these people. Hennie is a two-faced, snake-eyed witch with the personality of a salt shaker, minus one," John stated flatly, in the business voice he used for serious conversation. Ophelia took notice.

"Sadler is President of the Memphis Chamber of Commerce and an insufferable bore. Write Hennie a memo and quote me on that – at least on the Sadler part, and be done with it," John said firmly, in so many ways letting Ophelia know he would stand behind her.

"And watch her," John added. "She's a man-eater!"

Ophelia Hartwell was no dummy. She drafted a memorandum to Hennie that would become legendary. She still has it and reads it often. It read:

Memorandum

From: Ophelia Hartwell
*   Offices of John Henry Thompson*
*   The Memphis Blues*

To: Mrs. Henrietta C. Thompson
*   Memphis, Tennessee*

Mrs. Thompson,

Please be advised that Mr. Thompson has acknowledged your request for the two tickets for tomorrow night's game between The Memphis Blues and the Atlanta Braves. Unfortunately, Mr. and Mrs. Sadler's names do not appear on any list, except the one Mr. Thompson says he has for " insufferable bores". According to Mr. Thompson, there shall be no "insufferable bores" seating areas at Fulton County Stadium, nor at The New Ballpark at Memphis, especially in general proximity to himself.

Please advise me if there may be any other names and I will check the lists for their inclusion.

X - original signed
Ophelia Hartwell
Special Assistant to Mr. Thompson

Hennie was furious. Right then and there, in the millisecond after she read the last word of that memorandum, she made up her mind that Ophelia Hartwell would be history, out of John Henry Thompson's life, sooner or later. She would use all her influence, her continual harping with Marvin to be rid of her. She knew she couldn't change John's mind about her, but she sure as hell could, would, kill the messenger, the straw man, the agent of change that was Ophelia. But it would take her some time and be literally over John's dead body.

Hennie knew she had to use Marvin as her agent, her straw man. Unfortunately John Henry Thompson had forgotten more than Hennie would ever know about straw men. He had the best teacher in the world, early on, in old Senator Hugo Moore. Hennie never realized she was never in John's league when it came to interpersonal communications.

"Marvin, I swear to God I will divorce you if you do not get rid of that Ophelia woman!" Hennie demanded. "I know she's fucking us out of our money!" she slipped in as Marvin showed a rare sign of anger.

But Marvin was a girly man; 'pussy-whipped' John would call it. His anger quickly subsided and he did as he always did, just

110

walked out of the room. No one could figure out why he put up with Hennie. 'Must be some great stuff' people would say. They couldn't be more wrong.

John's owner's box at The New Ballpark at Memphis made the seating at the aging Fulton County Stadium in Atlanta look like the cheap seats, not that any seat was cheap at The Series. Harmon and Lamont accompanied John to the first game. Marvin, minus Hennie, was there too in the second row on the Blues' side of the field.

Although Ophelia could have been there, she knew that a hornet's nest had been stirred up over the memo to Hennie. She wisely stayed out of the limelight even though John wanted her there with him, especially when he was out in the open, in a hostile environment in Atlanta.

Keeping up with the ticket requests turned into a fulltime job for Ophelia, what with the people wanting into the parties that went right along with The Series. John kept his base of operations at The Ritz. He liked it there as opposed to all the craziness at the Underground Atlanta where his idea of after-game partying was coming to fruition.

Ophelia had used her media contacts in Atlanta well, setting the stage for the blowout in Memphis. She handled only the requests for comments from the home office, the one John owned. The players and coaches were outside the scope of her job, and that's the way she liked it. Protecting John was her first priority.

While the parties continued at the Underground, John spoke with the media people at the Ritz, that is, the ones Ophelia had screened for him. John was never a media man, not one to be up front, but this business was different. He was obliged, to a degree, to give interviews on the success and failure of the team, of new player acquisitions and especially on the big party coming up as The

Series traveled to Memphis.

It had been a long playoff season already with the league going to a best-of-seven format just like The Series. The Blues split the first two at Atlanta and were heading back to Memphis with a win under their belt hoping to sweep the Braves in the three home games.

In between the games John loved to go down to the locker rooms of The Blues and encourage the players, make them feel more at ease even though The Series was tied. He would reward them well if they put another World Champion banner on The New Ballpark at Memphis.

Ophelia was quickly learning that life with John Henry Thompson was tiring. The Series and the campaign, the two big shows going on at the same time, were the perfect synergy for John and by extension Ophelia as she connected with the power brokers of business and Danny Carson's campaign all at once.

In doing so, she put in long nights at the Underground in Atlanta and at The Ritz. She had always loved to socialize, dance and, as John now knew, could keep up with the best drinkers in town, while always keeping her senses about her, making connections for John, the team and the campaign. 'Synergy', John thought. This girl was a go-getter all right.

John was tired too. He had not told Ophelia of his problems with Roberta back in Memphis, but Ophelia knew John well enough by now to know something was wrong.

As they enjoyed the smooth ride back to Memphis on Room 404, the Lear jet was not in the air long when Lamont and Harmon fell asleep. John was well on his way, enjoying a Black Jack Daniels before drifting off to sleep himself. Ophelia took a chance and broke the silence.

"Mr. Thompson, are you feeling okay? It seems like this

baseball really takes it toll on you."

John sipped the last of his drink, pausing just long enough to make Ophelia wonder if she might have asked too much, too soon.

"Ophelia, this team is like a child to me. Not like the children I have, although they might not believe it, the children I love very much," John started, surprising Ophelia with the depth of his story.

"But, girl, let me tell you; there's a big difference with this baby called The Memphis Blues. This team is a reminder to me that I set out to do something good for myself, my family and for Memphis. You know the story. This is the only true, good *thing*, not friends like Harmon and Lamont, that I have from my past, something that has stayed with me all these years. The one thing that everyone would love to have, but they know can never be taken away from me."

"They can't take away my friendship with you, my gratitude to you, Mr. Thompson. I'll always appreciate what you've given me, your trust and confidence in a girl from little old Franklin, Georgia," Ophelia said with a slight cracking in her low voice.

"I know, girl. I know."

Chapter Eleven

Politics and Strange Bedfellows

Unfortunately, Ophelia had to try and keep up with the Danny Carson campaign as she did her best with the people problems of The Series. Politics and baseball, Ophelia thought, strange bedfellows indeed. John would point out that both were as American as apple pie and went hand in hand, especially when a candidate could make use of a well-timed appearance, taking the opportunity to style himself as 'one of the guys'.

Ophelia would make sure Danny Carson had tickets, but John did not want to have anything to do with it. Danny didn't want to see John either. To have them together in the owner's box would be mutually detrimental. It was time for one of Danny's straw men to surface.

"Ophelia, there's a man named Corky Benedict. He's Danny Carson's Chief of Staff. He sort of runs Danny's life, as I understand it. I want you to arrange a meeting between him and me. Have you met him yet?" John asked.

"I certainly have. I made my way to the top people the first time I attended one of the campaign events. I received all the solicitations, you know all the things in the mail wanting me to contribute to Danny's campaign. But I waited until I could get the best 'bang for the buck' and contribute when I knew all the right people would be there. You know what I mean, Mr. Thompson?" Ophelia explained as John grinned that approving grin he wore when he was pleased with the execution of a well-laid plan, and at Ophelia's wise use of money.

"Ophelia, you are a gem! That's just the way you play it. No use spreading your money out too thinly. But don't you spend another dime of your money. Between you and me, I've been stuffing old Danny's pockets for many years now. From now on, I'll have tickets for you at those events, the best ones, at the table with old Danny or his straw men every time the door's open – or the hand's out!"

Ophelia knew what a straw man was, she'd seen people all over Atlanta that didn't want to be in the limelight, preferring to stay in the shadows and be the man behind the curtain. She figured that she was about to be one herself.

"Is that what I'm going to be, Mr. Thompson, your straw man with Danny Carson?"

"You're my employee first, then you're my friend. I trust you Ophelia. I can do a lot for you, I can promise you that."

As Harmon and Lamont smiled, Ophelia felt that John had just tapped her shoulder with a sword, knighting her into the realm of confidants, or in her case, confidante for life. Ophelia was about to be introduced into the confidence that was the inner circle of John Henry Thompson's business and personal world.

"How will Corky know that he needs to make this meeting, that I have the authority to arrange it?" she asked.

John turned to Harmon and gave him the nod, the nod that always meant 'take care of it', whether it was a Ramon problem or something like this.

"He'll know," was all John had to say. Ophelia had learned by now not to question him.

Corky Benedict did not like being Danny Carson's straw man, or campaign chief at that. An impish, rich boy from Florida, he came from one of the landed gentry families that both John and Ophelia distrusted. He never knew what it meant to live in near-poverty. His interest in politics was self-glorification with a foolish eye toward one day running for public office himself.

Ophelia didn't like him in the beginning. But she had an innate sense of how to deal with pricks like Corky – blow smoke up their ass until they couldn't see that they were the ones being played.

"Mr. Benedict, I believe we met at the Ritz during that last fundraiser," Ophelia cooed as Corky definitely remembered this woman. In fact, Corky had made a special note on his list of attendees that she was articulate, good looking and interested in working in the campaign.

"Of course, of course," Corky said as he was prone to repeat himself, "Senator Carson is excited about your participation!"

What Corky didn't know was that he couldn't bullshit a bullshitter like Ophelia. In her he had met his match. Where Corky was an opportunist who reeked of insincerity, Ophelia came across as a genuine Carsonite, a believer in Danny Carson's dream of changing America, even though she thought his smile was so wide it made him look like he had sixty teeth in his mouth.

"The Senator would like for you to make as many events as you can. I understand you have extensive contacts in the real estate community. We really need some support there. They can be great contributors!" Corky chirped.

Corky was all about the money. In it, he saw media buys, campaign expenses being footed by people who had no idea where the money went, how it was being spent and where. It would take many millions to get Danny all the way, to reach the highest and shiniest brass ring of all, just like John knew he could do from The

Point on.

But Ophelia knew her chore was not only to raise money, hell, there was plenty of that to go around. She was to be John's eyes and ears on the trail. Harmon had gone into enough detail for her to know that. John didn't have to tell her. By now, she knew when Harmon spoke it was with John's voice.

"You're right, Corky. Let's go and get it. After all, we're pulling on the same rope, right? Here are two tickets to the three games here in Memphis. Also, Mr. Thompson would like to meet with you."

Corky Benedict didn't have any idea why John Henry Thompson, *the* John Henry Thompson would want to meet with him. Why not go straight to the top and see Danny himself? His first response was to call Danny Carson immediately. He caught up with Danny while he was en route to Memphis for the games.

"What's John Henry Thompson want with me, Senator? I mean, why didn't he call you directly?" Corky squealed as if a schoolyard bully had pulled him up by the scruff of the neck.

"Settle down, Corky. He just wants to make sure you grant him access to the campaign. That girl of his, that Ophelia, I know she does most of that for him, but John is a hands-on sort of guy, always has been," Danny did his best in calming Corky.

"But be secure in this, John Henry Thompson and I are good friends – ever since West Point. Just remember, he's no fool. Shoot straight with him. He's all about winning, Corky," Danny admonished.

Absolutely, damned right. It was all about winning, for different reasons, of course. Corky wanted power; Ophelia and John wanted to win, to increase John's existing power and security. 'Synergy' John always called it. Politicians may be public servants first, but they were a means toward an end for John, people who must be dealt

117

with in order to seal deals, get things done – for the plan.

John's theory was that the government had its nose into everything and politicians, elected politicians, at least in theory, ran the show. In John's mind it was a lot easier to make a politician than break one, at least at the highest levels of government.

While John footed the bill Ophelia did the footwork, the political dance of fundraising and travel during the following months as the race heated up. It would go far beyond the confines of Atlanta and Georgia. 'Room 404' would take her there, a Lear jet being what was called an 'in-kind' contribution, skirting the campaign finance laws that carefully tracked the monetary contributions John would funnel to Carson's campaign.

Danny Carson didn't like Ophelia, someone he felt to be, knew to be, an interloper on the campaign trail. He knew that reports were going back to John and he didn't like it. He should have known better. How could he really think that the meeting at the Marietta Tower would have been the last he would see of John until he was ready to cash in that chip, that piece of Danny Carson John now held in his pocket? Danny knew that the meeting with Corky was a prelude to that event.

Harmon and Rita met Corky at John's office. They gave him what amounted to a visual 'patting down' before Rita called into John letting him know Corky was there.

"Mr. Thompson, a great pleasure and honor sir," was Corky's rehearsed line and it sounded like it.

"Have a seat, Mr. Benedict. I'll get straight to the point. I just wanted you and Danny to know that Ophelia Hartwell has my utmost confidence. Danny knows I have always supported him and I want that to continue. He's been a good friend to me. But I won't be seeing him while he's here in Memphis. It may actually hurt Danny more than help him. But, I would like for you to ask him to call me from time to time. Fair enough?" John said firmly, leaving no doubt that this was the only message he had for Danny.

"Why, yes sir, why of course, yes sir!" was all Corky could repeat.

John rose from his seat and offered his hand to Corky. Corky sprang from his chair and clasped John's hand as he was led to door.

"Now, be sure and ask Danny to call me, okay Mr. Benedict?"

"Absolutely, absolutely!" the poor Corky bleated, by now being led into the elevator by Harmon.

Corky couldn't wait until he got back to his hotel room to call Danny.

"What's he mean, what's he mean?" Corky whined, almost unable to control himself.

"Hell, Corky, he means just what he said. From now on, when you talk to that girl, just act like you were talking to John. I'll call him later on this week," Danny responded, feigning his best-disinterested voice. And he would avoid making that call at all costs.

Danny knew he would have heard from John sooner or later. After all, here he was coming into John's hometown to watch John's baseball team play the pride of Danny's home state, the Atlanta Braves. Maybe it was just a courtesy call. Maybe John didn't like what Ophelia had seen on the campaign trail.

While Ophelia was jetting around the country and handling the details for The Series, John had his hands full in Memphis with Roberta, Marvin and Hennie. Things were not well. Roberta wanted to take part in The Series and the campaign, the formal balls and events in Memphis, Nashville and Washington, DC, especially the ones in DC.

"I want to know exactly what is going on John. Why won't you let me get on the campaign trail and go to the games? And what is going on with this Ophelia woman?" Roberta demanded as she barged into John's office.

Roberta was the only person who came into John's office unannounced, or so she thought. Secretary Rita, that trusted vestige from the old Thompson building, Gordon's secretary's daughter, not much to look at with her 60's hair in a bun, had a system of alerting John to Roberta's presence. She simply pressed a button under her desk, which would buzz John in his office. Any conversations, or anything else going on, would be terminated before Roberta had time to get to John's door, much less inside the office.

"Let's see, my dear Roberta," John said as opened his locked file drawer. "Just this month you have spent over $76,000 on your jaunts. Now, I don't ask you what you've been spending that money on, and you damned sure are not going to propose to ask me how I make my money or what I do with it – or are you?" John asked, clearly taking Roberta by surprise.

Roberta had been used to spending as she wished, but now there was a catch. If she were to start making demands, so would John. There would be attached accountability now that the stakes were higher. John didn't need Roberta in his Danny Carson business and he sure as hell didn't need any monkey business from Roberta right now.

"I feel like a fool when you don't show up at these things, when I can't be involved up front as your wife. It's insulting John," Roberta almost demanded, careful not to push John too far.

Roberta was, after all, John now realized, a gold-digger, even though he originally thought her to be a well meaning and loving one. She had spent millions on decorating the mansion south of Memphis, a place John shunned, preferring to stay at his Peabody penthouse. She had given John several good years, he thought, but she clearly was operating far outside any reach of John's control, except for the money. Besides, she hated baseball.

"Honey, you *will* do as I say on this campaign! You can be the social butterfly all you want, but in *this*, the campaign, from now on you are to clear your schedule with me. I have told Harmon so, and therefore, that's the way it shall be."

Shocked, dismayed and hurt, Roberta left as fast as she came in. Harmon Vance was standing just outside. Alerted by Rita that Roberta had made another invasion of John's office, Harmon gave her his look of dread. He had never liked the woman.

"You haven't seen the last of me Harmon Vance," Roberta whispered, never looking Harmon in the eye. Instead her pinpoint pupils were fixed on the West Point ring Harmon wore. She knew she could never break that bond between John and Harmon – and that her days were numbered.

Ophelia would always stop in Memphis to give John updates on the campaign when not being there for the home stand of The Series. Short luncheons on the balcony of John's office were filled with the details of Carson's meetings throughout the country as he built upon the networks he had cultivated while serving in the Senate. Ophelia was a constant reminder to Carson that no matter which supporters or groups he courted, he owed John Henry Thompson above all others.

John, for his part, would make commentary or send messages to Danny whenever he felt appropriate, which was not often. Ophelia was doing her job. That was enough for John. He felt comfortable with her as his surrogate, his straw man on the campaign. And he would make his demand when the time was right.

John was increasingly sharing with Ophelia his stories of the days with Senator Hugo Moore. They would both laugh at the similarities, and at the same time, the differences in what had happened in John's life and what was going on with Ophelia now. While Danny was a much more appealing, polished candidate, he still was as conniving as old Hugo Moore ever was, willing to compromise himself for the sake of power. Might still makes right, they thought. It was working out as planned.

Many years later, Ophelia would wonder just how she managed to deal with the Corky Benedicts and Hennie Thompsons of the world and still manage to be the go-to person for John Henry Thompson during that World Series in Atlanta and Memphis. The two games in Atlanta were hectic enough, but the events planned for Memphis were a different story.

Those three October days in Memphis were like New Year's Eve and Mardi Gras rolled into one. Wrap that in America's favorite pastime, baseball, and one might get a sense of what it was like. The sights and smells of Beale Street were in full bloom, even though the nights were crisp, the days still warm. The Boogie Woogie Café, Bumbles Billiards and Porky's Barbeque were filled to overflowing. So were the streets.

Ophelia had arranged for live remote shots in one of the three venues for all three of the network television affiliates. The networks themselves had all their big name on-air celebrities there, and they all stayed at The Peabody. John knew how to put on a good show, and how to show everyone a good time.

'Blondes, booze and beef', John often thought. Things had not changed at all.

Memphis was ready for the crowds of revelers; John and Ophelia had made sure of it. The old *Commercial Appeal*, still going strong, was running front-page stories of The Blues, of Beale and of its favorite son, John Henry Thompson, the boy from Slabtown who made it big – and put Memphis on the map.

Ophelia coordinated the few interviews John gave and the story, not all of it, was told to a handpicked few. The story, John told them, was of the people, the Memphians who rebuilt the city, with a little help from him. He owed the people, he would say. And he did his best to give back.

John even had the novel idea of building high temporary bleachers outside the stadium so the real people, the Memphians who loved the team, could see the games. He gave away the seats through a lottery system where visitors to Beale Street could simply sign up for the give-away seats. Beale Street during those days turned into a street party that extended all the way down to the river, almost a mile away. It was simply amazing - and he had just thought the whole thing up.

As Danny Carson sat at his Memphis hotel near the airport he wondered who was running for President – him or John? He groaned as *The Commercial Appeal* actually banner-headlined an issue during The Series with "John Henry Thompson For President!" only slightly tongue-in-cheek, and definitely a jab at the Senator, and Braves fan, from Georgia.

He thought it was time to give John a telephone call. As he dialed the number, John's private number at the penthouse, he felt a sinking feeling, one of all the power and glory being drained from his body, ceded to the real power broker and kingmaker that John had become to him.

"John, its Danny. How's The Series going for you?" Danny asked, realizing too late that a one to one game count was not a good score for someone like John who wanted to win at all costs.

"Danny, we'll win because we have the best team. They're motivated Danny, just like you, just like you've always been. How's your campaign for the other 'Big Show'?" John asked, inserting the obligatory baseball metaphor.

"It's early, John. We've got a full year to go yet. I don't know how it's going to shake out, but I'm working really hard."

"You just let me know what I can do to help, Danny. You'll be good for this country. Stay in touch," John said with an almost command forming in his voice.

"Call me if you need me," Danny answered, almost forgetting that it didn't need to be said. He knew he would get that call sooner or later.

"You know I will, Danny. You know I will."

✣ ✣ ✣

Danny squirmed in his seat as The Memphis Blues tore into the Atlanta Braves. With every base hit The Blues made Danny could just see John smiling, even though he couldn't really see past the dark tinted glass of John's sky box high over the field. Danny felt more trapped than ever, beholden to a man he knew would call in the favor when he needed it most, and when Danny would be most likely not to want to grant it.

A three-game sweep ensured John's immortality as the greatest man ever to live in Memphis, Tennessee. The Memphis Blues had won The Series four games to one.

John met with the ball team in the clubhouse after The Series win and rewarded them with the free use of one of those 'private islands' the cruise lines have for their passengers. He had found a cruise ship company that was going bankrupt and just bought the entire Caribbean island. The team and their families were to be flown down any time they wanted, as long as they were on the team.

John may not have paid the highest baseball salaries, but he sure had good fringe benefits. A $50,000 bonus per team member along with a Presidential Rolex went a long way too.

Ophelia, John, Harmon and Lamont celebrated with a weeklong trip to Las Vegas in a fabulous penthouse at Caesar's Palace. For Danny Carson, it was back to the campaign. Marvin and Hennie stayed in Memphis and groaned - they had been shut out.

It was the high water mark for Memphis – and John Henry Thompson.

Chapter Twelve

A New Day Dawns

John had everything most men would kill for – all the money he could ever spend, security for his family and the people who cared about him. But he wasn't happy. He was tired and, at just over sixty now, he was ready to take it a little easier, a little slower.

Harmon and Lamont had always done what they could to ease the burden of owning a major league baseball team, help John acquire more property and in general help him build his empire. But they could only do so much. John had always been that way, a hands-on man, and a go-getter ever since the days of old Hugo Moore. That's the only way he knew how to live his life. It was his path to success.

It was unfortunate that Ophelia did not come along sooner. She might have extended John's more productive years by ten or more. But the years had taken their toll on John. And so had the Black Jack Daniels, the Cubanos, the late nights, Marvin and Hennie - those tortured souls that never comforted or consoled John. And then there was Roberta.

Back in Memphis Roberta was fuming that John had taken his 'gang' as she called Harmon and Lamont, now Ophelia, to Vegas without her. To be sure, John had told her to come along, have fun, and celebrate. But he knew all she would want is to spend time at the shows, buy jewelry and otherwise spend John's money. All John wanted to do was relax and have a good time, something Roberta knew nothing about.

Harmon and Lamont were tired as well. They had been along for the ride, Lamont for all of it, from Slabtown to Beale Street, to The Series. Both had made money beyond their wildest dreams. But John could not have done it without them. They were not only trusted friends, they both helped John's empire flourish. Harmon's sound advice and Lamont's common sense were indispensable.

John had helped make the kingdoms of California and Missouri; such as they were for Truman Forsythe and Jerry Slater. They would always owe John for their success in the Governors' offices. But Danny Carson was still the big prize. He had a shot to win it all, the White House.

Now, Ophelia was part of the team, firmly affixed to the hip of Danny Carson and his campaign. It was John's last, great quest. To finish his last grand plan. To make a king of all political kings.

Ophelia was new to the game, at least at this level. Even at thirty, she eventually got tired too, but she enjoyed making the campaign events, still being John's eyes and ears as to what Danny Carson was doing, who he was seeing and what he was promising for his brave new world, the White House according to Danny Carson.

Danny had become quick to make promises to people, even ones he never intended on keeping. Sometimes he would forget what he had promised, where and when. People like Corky Benedict were not good at keeping him straight either. They eventually had to resort to taping all of his appearances, big or small, and transcribe what he had said. That's how bad it became.

Ophelia's reports to John were pretty much non-eventful. Danny was doing the usual glad-handing, baby kissing, fund raising and making promises for a new America that all politicians made. The only thing that caught Ophelia's attention was the recurring questions about the death of Ramon Hernandez in Nicaragua. The press was curious and Ophelia didn't know why. It could be the fact that Ramon's son Miguel was making news in exile in Venezuela, calling Danny Carson an enemy of Nicaragua and by extension of all Central America.

Neither John nor Harmon had ever wanted Ophelia to know what had happened between John and Ramon, how they were West Point classmates with Danny Carson. To be sure, Ophelia knew about Danny and John's connections, it was in Danny and John's bios she had circulated. Ramon's death was not on her radar screen at the time he died. Although she passed on the media inquiries about Ramon she witnessed on the campaign, John never showed any concerns. For all she knew, it was Danny Carson's activities on the Senate Foreign Relations Committee that bothered Miguel Hernandez. She wouldn't learn the whole truth for some time.

That's not to say that Ophelia wasn't becoming more curious about the Hernandez situation. At a campaign event at the Biltmore Hotel in Coral Gables, Florida, Ophelia was approached by a Latino-looking man who passed her a note. Before she could even look at it, Corky Benedict told Ophelia he would 'handle' it.

Ophelia didn't think anything about it and gave the note to Benedict. A minute or so later she saw the Latino man being led away by police. She didn't know that the man was actually Miguel Hernandez. His eyes met hers as he was being escorted from the hotel. She would remember that look when she saw him again much later. There was a story there, she thought.

⚜ ⚜ ⚜

Whenever Ophelia was back in Memphis for campaign meetings with John, Marvin and Hennie ignored her. It always amazed Ophelia that Marvin, Hennie and Roberta despised Harmon and Lamont so much. Did they never realize how important the two were to John? But why her? Did they think that she was having an affair with John, that she would take some of his beloved money from him, leaving them with only a few hundred million?

It was all about the money for them. For a while it was for John too. All that was about to change.

Roberta, deep down, really didn't want a separation, much less a divorce. She wanted to continue her flights of fancy, the trips on the campaign trail and appearances at fundraisers where she could be John Henry Thompson's wife, at least in name only.

But John didn't mind that she eventually did ask for a divorce. He didn't know if she was fooling around or not, but it didn't matter. It was an exercise in superficial nonsense to remain married to this woman and he was done with such transparencies.

Harmon would take care of it all. He always did. Roberta would be satisfied as well, John thought. She knew John had resigned himself to the fact that she had her hooks into him, deeply and forever.

Marvin and Hennie worried themselves sick that Roberta would take all of John's money. But John had not been stupid. In what was an early form of a pre-nuptial agreement, Roberta got a fixed amount, no more, no less. She had two wonderful children from one of her earlier marriages that John thought she didn't deserve. He would see them still, no matter what happened between Roberta and him.

Ophelia had gone back to Atlanta to ready herself for the campaign activity she was charged with by John. Danny Carson had left town the minute The Blues had cemented The Series win with that third game in Memphis. Danny knew he was a winner either way. If Atlanta won, they were his team, his home team. If Memphis won, whatever, the owner was one of his best friends from The Point.

The Coca-Cola deal at Underground Atlanta had gone smoothly for Ophelia, making a name of sorts for her in the Atlanta real estate community. Anyway, she was getting some rest from the campaign trips when Harmon called.

"Ophelia, I knew you would want to know," was how Harmon started the blindside of the news.

"John has had a heart attack, and he's not doing well. I'll send the '404' for you right now. Lamont will pick you up at your office."

✠ ✠ ✠

Baptist Memorial Hospital in downtown Memphis was one of John's favorite charities. So was St. Jude Hospital, the world-renowned children's hospital that called Memphis its home. They had even called over to offer their services for John.

But John, ever the Baptist he had been from childhood, had always told everyone, everyone that mattered, that if he needed hospitalization he wanted to be at Baptist Memorial, the place started in 1912 by a group of Baptist visionaries. After all, the hospital was just in sight of The Peabody, due east from the hotel.

To be sure, they were taking good care of him as Ophelia landed in Memphis on the '404' Lear jet.

"He ain't too good, Ophelia," Lamont said, crying like a small child.

"That damned Roberta, Marvin and Hennie, they ain't even up

there. And they caused all this!"

Ophelia had never heard Lamont curse, so she was prepared for the worst. And she hoped that Harmon was there with John.

It had been a good eight hours since John had suffered what the doctors were telling Harmon Vance was a near-fatal heart attack and stroke. They had no idea whether or not he would even survive.

"We were just sitting in his office, Ophelia. He just slumped over. Nothing like you see in the movies, no grasping of the chest. None of that. He just collapsed onto the desk," Harmon told Ophelia, choking back tears.

Ophelia wasn't prepared for what she would see next. John was lying helpless, unconscious and unresponsive in a hospital suite unlike any other she had seen before. The room was so elaborate and plush, it was like it was being reserved for John, so exquisite that it made Ophelia wonder who in Memphis could possibly occupy it except for John, a man who was as close as Memphis ever had to a king since the death of Elvis ten years earlier.

David Muggs, head of Peabody security was the only one in the room. She remembered him from the hotel, the black man that was old Rufus Muggs's son from years ago. Ophelia thought it was curious he was there and not a grieving family member. Was there something nefarious going on here, she wondered?

John was on a ventilator and surely knew no one was there, but his hand moved as Ophelia spoke. She just slumped into a chair next to him. Until now, she hadn't noticed that David Muggs was crying. She started to cry too. But she had to go; Marvin and Hennie were on the way.

Marvin Thompson had made sure he didn't run into his brother at the hospital. Marvin hadn't seen Hank in about a year, even though they lived in the same city and shared a father that loved them both very much. He envied Hank, to be sure, solely because Hank had gone his own way, out into the world on a track that, although greased by his father, was separate and apart from the family business. And that was all right by Marvin, more for him, he thought.

The family had been to the hospital soon after it had happened. Hank had been there first. They were the ones Harmon called after the heart attack. Hank's children had come along too. They would jump at the chance to see their grandfather in whatever physical state he may be in.

John didn't seem to be any better or worse to Marvin and Hennie, just 'non-responsive', as they told others. As they looked at John their minds were racing with thoughts, questions of what would happen next. Would he survive, die – today, tomorrow? And just how much money *would* Roberta get?

Roberta, for her part, could not bring herself to visit more than once. Actually concerned that her tirades and demands of divorce had brought on the attack, she holed herself up in the estate south of Memphis. Roberta preferred instead to 'receive' guests; the socialites that did not even know the John Henry Thompson that Ophelia, Harmon and Lamont knew and loved.

"What in the *hell* are *you* doing here Muggs? Get your black ass back down to The Peabody! What? Do you think my father is in danger down here?" Marvin demanded, screaming at the top of his voice the second he entered John's room.

Just at that instant Harmon Vance calmly entered the room and slapped Marvin so hard that it sounded like a gunshot, sending snot and drool down the side of Marvin's mouth, slamming him to the tile floor.

Hennie screamed as Muggs grabbed her, ushering her from the room.

"You silly bitch-man! I'll throw your ass out this window if you raise your voice one more time around this man. This man who is my friend and who, while I am living, will not be disgraced by the piece of shit son like you! Get out of here and let this man be in peace or I swear to God I'll kill you right here and have Muggs throw your sorry ass to the catfish at the bottom of the Mississippi!" Harmon said in a slow, metered voice.

Marvin did not say a word. He simply struggled from the floor, seeking to clear his double vision, wipe his mouth and sulk out of the room, hoping and praying to God that David Muggs would never reveal what had just happened. He never looked Harmon Vance in the eye again.

⚜ ⚜ ⚜

Harmon made sure Ophelia was comfortable at her suite at The Peabody. She had stayed at the hospital as long as Harmon would let her, knowing that she needed to leave as soon as Marvin, Hennie or Roberta came up to see John. He had not regained consciousness yet, but the doctors had warned everyone that John would not be the same man. He had apparently suffered a partially debilitating stroke along with the heart attack.

It was three days before he regained consciousness – and he was not the same. His speech was impaired and he was weak, too weak to see Ophelia although he did ask Harmon if she knew, knew all that had happened to him and that if she knew he wanted to see her – but not like this.

Harmon thought it was time to have a talk with Ophelia. He knew that she was vulnerable now that Marvin and Hennie knew she was there and that he had bitch-slapped Marvin in front of Muggs. It didn't help matters that Roberta had by now filed for a divorce.

"Lamont will take you back to Atlanta, Ophelia. I promise you that I will keep you informed – I promise. John wants it this way, at least for now. He has a lot of work to do before he's back on his feet," Harmon told a not-so-convinced Ophelia.

"He's one of the strongest people I've ever known. He'll come back. And I know he will want you there. Please hang on for him," Harmon said, almost pleading a case now with Ophelia.

"I will. Tell him to call me whenever he's able, please."

Harmon had one last word, one final admonition for Ophelia.

"And watch Marvin and Hennie. I just left an imprint of this West Point ring on his face. It's us and them from now on."

Chapter Thirteen

Enjoying Life

Marvin and Hennie Thompson had thrown themselves into high gear. Marvin though, for his part, would now concern himself with taking control, complete control of The Thompson Group. That necessarily involved the immediate firing of Lamont Boone, David Muggs as chief of security and seeing that Harmon Vance knew he was finished – that is, as long as John Henry Thompson was not running things now.

But, for now, that fact was anything but certain. John was out of danger of death, and he was far from being removed from effective control of the businesses. Harmon did not have the heart to tell John how Marvin and Hennie had acted at the hospital before he regained consciousness. Harmon figured John knew his son well enough to know what he and Hennie would have been like in that situation. It didn't make sense to Harmon to remind him.

And Marvin would not have dared tell his father about the bitch-slap episode. It would only have served to confirm what an insensitive ass Marvin had been.

No, Marvin would depend on the fact his father would obviously not be well enough, in his mind, to run the business from now on, at least not in the hands-on way he had in the past.

Lamont Boone had enough of Marvin and Hennie Thompson the day they came back to Memphis. He was financially secure now and would prefer to be a friend to John, although he would do anything John asked. Neither Harmon nor Lamont wanted to end up like him.

Ophelia was still waiting to hear from John. Harmon had kept her abreast of his progress and although he was out of the woods with the heart attack, the stroke was to have the lasting effects of speech problems and numbness on one side of his body.

John yearned to be better, to get back to his life, a new life, one that would not include the stress of making money anymore – just spending it. That was a fact that would cause immense distress for Marvin and Hennie.

Marvin had been upset since the day John demanded to be moved back to The Peabody.

"Dad, you *can't* leave the hospital now!" Marvin would urge John over and over again. "It's just too dangerous!"

"Boy, you'd better get me my goddamned car, Lamont Boone and my doctor, all in that order, or I'm going to disinherit your ass immediately!"

Marvin Thompson had never moved so fast. Within fifteen minutes he had rehired Lamont Boone with a $10,000 bonus, had the limousine downstairs at Baptist Memorial and every doctor that had ever seen John Henry Thompson inside his room.

"Dad, I'll make sure we get a hospital bed set up in your penthouse at The Peabody, a doctor and nurse there 24 hours a day and your speech therapist as well. We don't want anything to happen Dad," Marvin crowed with a pseudo-sense of sincerity.

Lamont would have done it for free. The first thing he did after getting John into the limousine was to call Ophelia for him.

"I love you girl," was all Ophelia needed to hear. It was something John had never told her. He meant it in a platonic way, she knew. But in hearing those three words she knew he would make it, if at least for only a while longer.

"I love you too, Mr. Thompson. I can't wait to see you. Are you okay?" Ophelia gushed.

"No, but I will be girl. I'll call you soon."

"Lamont, get me Marvin on the telephone. I want you and Harmon to meet with us at The Peabody tonight," commanded John, this time with the tone of an employer.

"Yes sir," Lamont answered with a smile. Lamont knew that John, not the same 100% John, but just the same John Henry Thompson was coming back.

⚜ ⚜ ⚜

"Marvin, sit down son. I want to get one thing straight, crystal clear," John said, all the while with Marvin looking at Harmon's West Point ring, remembering its sting.

"I am not dead. At the same time I will not be the same man I was before this illness," John said as he struggled to form the words, still reeling from the effects of the stroke.

"Having said that, I am not going to be running this ball team anymore. Harmon Vance will be, if he wants the job. Failing that, you will be," John said as Marvin's eyes met John's.

"John, I'm getting too old for a job like that. I think Marvin is up to it, with a little supervision which I don't mind giving though," Harmon said as his eyes drifted to Marvin, almost challenging Marvin to look at him.

"How about it son? Are you up to it?" asked John, knowing Marvin would say yes, if he was even a part of the man John hoped he was.

"It would be an honor, sir. And I hope Lamont will stay on as

137

well," Marvin threw in for good measure.

"Then it's settled. Now listen, I'm going to try and get well for a while, rest up and get my strength back. And I don't want to hear of *any* problems. Do you understand?" John asked leaning toward Marvin.

"I understand," Marvin said as his eyes drifted back toward Harmon, this time making it to shoelace level.

In less than five minutes John had made clear that he would not relinquish real control until they put him in the ground. Harmon Vance or whomever he appointed would run The Thompson Group and The Blues and report to John. Marvin was humiliated and disappointed but contrite. He knew he was beaten, for now.

As Marvin started to leave the room John threw out a parting shot.

"And where's David Muggs? You don't want anything to happen to me – do you?"

"Now get that speech therapist in here," John commanded. "I've got to start getting well."

Not much was going to slip past John Henry Thompson, even in this state of health.

✤ ✤ ✤

The Peabody was the scene for melodrama every day, and not just in John's penthouse. Big business deals were still the order of the day. People were still making big money in Memphis and tourism was at its peak, what with the ball team and Beale Street bigger than ever. And even though John was in a recuperative mode for a while, events at The Peabody would not slow down. John had to depend on his straw men to hold down the fort for now.

One of John's key straw men, David Muggs, had an important job at The Peabody as chief of security. He would do anything John Henry Thompson told him to do. He was old school in that way, a sort of inheritance from his father who John revered as an institution at The Peabody from his days as a young boy working there, the days before The Point.

David Muggs was the man who kept the secrets for John. The son of old man Rufus Muggs, the black head porter at The Peabody back in the old days, Rufus had shared a few secrets of his own. That is, he shared them when rich old men wouldn't pay him the hush money he wanted when Rufus found out that they were seeing their mistresses at The Peabody.

The apple didn't fall far from the tree with his son David. Although educated and more refined, David gathered secrets for John at The Peabody, especially the ones that Marvin and Hennie kept. John thought it was time he used a little leverage on Marvin, now that he was obviously getting a little big for his britches and John more frail now.

Marvin Thompson had no real friends, disliked everyone and had a pitiful racist streak, almost sadistic in his disdain for black people like Muggs and Lamont. John always told Ophelia that Marvin reminded him of his brother Gordon years ago. Gordon never did like Beale Street and the poor blacks that inhabited it - the ones that reminded him of their poor shared beginnings back in Slabtown.

But Marvin had needs. Hennie was as frigid as a Frigidaire and that icebox had caused him to necessarily stray like an old tomcat. Marvin in his racist way used to joke that he liked a "little dark meat" – and he didn't mean a chicken wing or a thigh. That's where David came into play.

David knew where all the bodies were buried. He did jobs for

John when John didn't want to involve Harmon or Lamont. David also knew about Marvin's escapades with Lucy Barnes, Henrietta's black personal assistant. Hennie treated Lucy like dirt on her shoes. Hennie instead preferred her gay house servants, decorators and assistants for close company. A beautiful, tall woman, Lucy tolerated Hennie just to be close to Marvin, his money and the power of the Thompson family. Lucy was a player, intent on making big money with the Thompsons.

It wasn't hard for David to plant the audio and video devices in Marvin's office and suite at The Peabody where all the hanky-panky took place. After all, he had total access and all the funding he needed. John knew all about it too. He had told David to plant them.

Marvin was his son, but John knew he might need to have a trump card sooner or later. And he may have to play it soon.

David knew he couldn't get much on old Henrietta. He knew she was an ice queen, a man-eater and straight as a string. But she was insanely jealous. Hennie came from a middle-class family and always wanted the trappings of wealth and all that she thought it could bring her. Marvin was always a means toward that end. She even reluctantly gave him the two children they shared, ones they never intended to share with John. John was a little too 'rough around the edges' Hennie thought – just not the grandfatherly type you wanted your kids around.

But Marvin grossly underestimated David Muggs. He was lying in wait with a plan that would knock Marvin's socks off. And Marvin had pissed off David, and John, just enough for John to order David into action.

It was a well-laid plan many years in the making, not pretty, but effective. Marvin and Lucy always met on Friday nights after Hennie was long gone from The Peabody. Marvin naturally had the run of the huge hotel and could grab a key to any room he wanted, or needed. That was the hell of it, thought David. Instead, Marvin was so simple-minded as to use his own suite for his transgressions. And it was wired for sight and sound.

David had a signed directive from John Henry Thompson allowing him to install audio and video equipment anywhere he wanted on The Peabody property. John always worked in 'nods' like the ones he would give to Harmon or Lamont when he wanted something done. He had given David the 'nod' one day after making a comment about 'wondering who Marvin was doing', certain that Hennie wouldn't be fulfilling his manly needs. After all, John thought, a little video surveillance was good for The Peabody's security.

The very first Friday after John was back at The Peabody from the hospital, David checked his equipment. Everything was functioning properly in Marvin's suite as David was going to get it all on tape that night. David knew that he and John now needed some insurance against any more bold behavior by Marvin. The videotape of Marvin and Lucy in bed should do the trick.

What David didn't count on was the fact that Hennie Thompson was a pretty sharp operator herself. She had both Marvin and her offices at The Peabody swept for bugs two months before, discovering the audio and video equipment in Marvin's office.

Unfortunately for David, the equipment in Marvin's office was not activated 24 hours a day, missing the sweep by Hennie's technicians. Hennie was bribing one of the security guards in David's employ, Gary Henderson, to let her know when and if any tapes of Marvin or her were made.

Hennie thought she would use the fact that John and David were spying against them whenever she thought she could best blackmail them. Since the blowup at the hospital, combined with the humbling of Marvin at the hands of John and his gang, Hennie thought the time was right.

Gary Henderson spit coffee all over the security desk after he viewed the secret tape, having played it from the recorder hidden in a corner of the security office the Saturday after the taping. He checked the taping system every day to see if David was doing any taping on Marvin or Hennie. David hadn't made it in yet to check the tape, secure in what he thought was still a stealthed operation. Henderson wasn't prepared to see Lucy and Marvin rolling on the sofa bed with Marvin clumsily ripping Lucy's blouse trying to get some 'dark meat'. He was hungry indeed.

Gary quickly secured the tape for Hennie and foolishly replaced it with a blank tape before David made it in to the office.

After David showed up and prudently excused Gary, ostensibly to give him a restroom break, he checked the tape recorder and found the blank tape that Gary had left in the machine. He didn't have time to watch it and just stuffed it in his briefcase. He knew what he thought would be on it. He would later find it curiously blank. Henderson had been so stupid as to not let the tape run on a seemingly empty room. David immediately knew their operation had been compromised.

Gary feverishly called Hennie at the number he had been given for such emergencies. He told her he had intercepted a tape David had made, one that she needed to see.

Chapter Fourteen

Self-Destruction

"You want how much money? You little son-of-a-bitch, I'll go straight to John Henry Thompson and tell him you've been spying on him if you don't give me that tape. Your sorry black ass will be hanging off the Mississippi River bridge by midnight," and Hennie meant every word of it.

Gary Henderson wanted $10,000 before he would even tell Hennie what was on the tape, much less where it was. He was an underling on the security staff and his only job was to watch the video monitors and call someone with some sense if he saw anything. But he knew an opportunity to make a quick buck when he saw it.

"What I *will* do is give you $5,000 if you help me do what I want with this tape, no questions asked," she demanded more than asked, knowing she would need help in following up on whatever was on the tape. After all, she had to put a plan into action and she wanted to stealth it as much as she could.

"Okay Mrs. Thompson, okay. Just don't tell Mr. John what I've been doing – please!"

Hennie had her bluff in on Gary Henderson. She knew if there ever was anything taped that Henderson would want more money. What the hell, it was John's money anyway.

Hennie didn't want Gary in the room when she played the tape. She took it back to her and Marvin's estate to make sure no one else saw what might be on it. It was a good thing she did.

Hennie broke a 14th Century Ming vase in the fireplace of her private bedroom as she cursed her "nigger whore underling" as she watched Lucy writhe on top of her miserable wretch of a husband. It was lost on her that Marvin had anything to do with being responsible for the encounter.

All of a sudden, Hennie Thompson had a greater goal in mind. In that tape, John Henry Thompson, she thought, had given her the key to at least half of all that Marvin Thompson would inherit when "that old bastard", as she called John, was to finally die. But she wanted some payback, and she thought she knew just how to get it.

It must have been a full moon that weekend. Gary Henderson saw gold. With his $5,000 in hand he went straight to David Muggs with *his* copy of the tape, the second one he made after discovering it that Saturday morning, the one Hennie didn't know he had made. He knew not to demand any money from David, he thought David would probably shoot him and leave him in a dumpster for the Memphis sanitation crew if he did. He would have been right.

David gave Gary five crisp $100 bills, swore Gary to silence, or otherwise death, and took the tape straight to John in the penthouse. He also told Gary to do anything Hennie asked in setting up whatever plan she had in mind, but to let David know every detail.

"Mr. Thompson, I think we struck gold on the surveillance operation. Unfortunately we've been compromised."

John and David watched the tape twice. John thought about calling in Harmon or Lamont, and didn't when he got to the end of the sordid show when Marvin got sick to his stomach, vomiting all over Lucy at the conclusion of the X-rated scene they had just played out. Marvin had apparently drunk a little too much the night of the rendezvous. Marvin just got sick and passed out. It was quite a pitiful sight.

John was gaining strength every day. His speech therapist had done great work and this was a bit of good news, John thought. But he had to play this carefully. He felt sorry for Marvin, but he quickly was reminded of how Marvin and Hennie acted as soon as they thought he was going to die, something Muggs thought he should know. They had to be taught a lesson.

"Does she know about the taping at their house?" John asked David, generating a smile from them both.

"That's the catch. She doesn't," David said as he could see the wheels turning in John's mind.

And neither did Gary Henderson. Being patently illegal to tape a private residence, David and John held this secret close to the vest. 'Might makes right', John thought. Synergy, power. It sure was working this time.

It was fortunate for Gary Henderson that he came straight to David Muggs that weekend. David had already made arrangements to have Henderson hung from the river bridge by his heels until he told Muggs where the tape was. David knew Hennie had a copy since David had already viewed *his* tape of Hennie watching the Marvin and Lucy show at her house. Hennie wasn't as sharp as she thought. David not only had their offices at The Peabody bugged, but *their house* too.

"I knew Hennie had the tape because I saw her watching it at her house, Mr. Thompson. We can get them now!"

"See to it, David. You're doing a good job. We need to get these two under control as soon as possible. I'm worried that they're on a downward spiral and I don't need any problems like this right now. I don't want them taking this company down with them either."

John wasn't surprised in what he had seen. Marvin and Hennie were racist pigs, users of people who were trying to get ahead at any cost. It would be sweet justice that their failings would be the undoing of them both, something that would get them out of John's hair for good, he thought.

Hennie was a cold and calculating bitch, plain and simple. She also was a formidable adversary and could be vengeful to a fault. She had a plan of her own, one that would provide her with her measure of revenge with a hefty dose of humiliation for Marvin.

Lucy Barnes, the consummate player in the game of getting ahead, was using Marvin as much as he was using her. She disliked the sex, after all, Marvin was clumsy, goofy and altogether not someone a good-looking woman would seek out for companionship or affection.

But Lucy had always banked on Marvin coming to her rescue if Hennie ever tried to fire her. It didn't hurt that Marvin bought her clothes and kept her supplied with all the spending money she needed.

What Lucy didn't know was that Hennie "ruled the roost" as John called it. Hennie would confront Lucy and turn her allegiance, and sexual compliance, away from Marvin and use it to her advantage. Lucy would have no choice but to go along with Hennie's plan as soon as she realized who was the most powerful person in Hennie and Marvin's marriage.

✤ ✤ ✤

For Marvin's part, he never saw it coming. Hennie had called him to their estate early in the morning. It being a Friday, just one week after the taping episode, he didn't have plans to be home that early. It was Friday, hell, he had a date with Lucy that night, his weekly slap and tickle, he thought.

Marvin and Hennie's estate was much more extravagant than

John and Roberta's. Hennie liked to flaunt the wealth, show the trappings of the rich and entertain high-society Memphians whenever she could. She needed it all for the show she put on, 'the airs' John called her silly facade.

Marvin flung open the door to the Georgian main house and curiously saw no 'servants' as he liked to call them, around the first floor.

"Henrietta, where are you. What's all the fuss about?" Marvin called as the house had a ghostly silence, unlike the usual hustle and bustle of Hennie's household chores being carried out by the help.

Marvin thought something was wrong, especially when he heard what he thought was a cry for help from upstairs. He was concerned enough by now to start yelling for Hennie, thoughts flashing through his mind of her being hurt. Or what if it was one of the children? His mind was racing uncontrollably now and his blood pressure was rising to a critical level. Hennie had only told him to get home as soon as he could. Something was terribly wrong.

As Marvin threw open the door to Hennie's private suite he was already wringing wet with sweat. He was sure her room was where he'd heard the cries come from – or were they moans he had heard?

To Marvin's astonishment there lay Hennie and Lucy, bare-ass naked in the bed together watching the video of Lucy and Marvin on an enormous television screen. They were both sipping champagne and eating strawberries, fondling each other's breasts.

Marvin fell to the floor – he had passed out, fainted like a little girl.

John and David Muggs were watching the ordeal play out in John's office via real-time video streaming. It was high comedy at its best. It was a scene for the ages. David was laughing so hard his side hurt while John had a slight drool of laughter due to the stroke.

He killed a Black Jack Daniels, the first since the hospital.

"Ophelia's not going to believe this," John howled. "Get her over here, David. Hell, if I'm well enough to put up with this trash, I'm well enough to have my friends around me to enjoy it too!"

A sight to behold, for sure. Hennie and Lucy laughed until they both rolled off the bed. They got dressed and left a copy of the Lucy and Marvin tape for posterity on Marvin's crumpled body. Lucy went back to work – Hennie made a cup of tea. All was right with the world for them now. Marvin Thompson had been neutralized, cut like a gelding.

Hennie laughing, John thought. How curious. He gave her one thing from then on. She sure knew how to exact revenge. He made sure that within the day that Hennie and Lucy knew that David and he had shared the joke as it played out. No need in letting her think she had one up on anyone. Hennie, Marvin and Lucy were done. Game over. And the video surveillance was promptly removed from their home.

Hell, and these people wanted to run one of the largest companies in the South. 'God help us', John thought. He'd better get Ophelia back to Memphis right away.

⚜ ⚜ ⚜

John thought he'd better call Ophelia first. She had been apprised of his progress, the fact that he had somewhat slurred speech and was weak. She knew he hadn't made it out of The Peabody either. Harmon had told her that he was 'having problems' with Marvin and Hennie, but never the sordid, now laughable details.

"I love you, girl. Why don't you let me send my '404' jet after you and spend some time with me before you get back out on that campaign? I need some company."

"Mr. Thompson, I would love nothing better. I hope you're feeling well enough for me to come over. I don't want to be a burden to you," Ophelia said sincerely.

"You don't worry about that. I'll have David Muggs and Lamont over there today."

John thought that Muggs needed to be there with Lamont. Lamont and Harmon were staying on with him just out of friendship. David would have to take up some slack if one of them decided they'd had enough of the sideshow that Marvin and Hennie had become.

The wheels had clearly come off Marvin and Hennie's ideas of taking control of The Thompson Group. Bad timing, John thought. Marvin was never good at that.

Marvin told his dad that he needed a week off. Hell, just a week, John thought? This boy is stronger than he realized. As traumatized as Marvin had been, John had expected a short hospital stay at best.

Hennie never skipped a beat. She and Lucy were back at her office the next Monday – fully clothed.

Ophelia arrived at The Peabody that same day just as John was about to play the tape again. John was in a wheelchair now, still weak, but in good spirits now that she was there. It had been three weeks since she had seen him.

"Come here, girl. I want you to see the most laughable cinematic moment ever captured on tape. Have you ever seen *Debbie Does Dallas*?" he asked with a twinkle as Ophelia hugged him in his chair.

Ophelia didn't know what to think. She had never seen her 'Mr. Thompson' as a porn voyeur. Was this an after-effect of the stroke? John looked better than she expected, even though it was strange to see him in a wheelchair. His speech was somewhat slurred but he still seemed coherent. John had a surprise. But she wasn't ready for this.

As she pulled one of the stadium seats up to his wheelchair, her eyes widened.

"Girl, I want you to see what buffoons I am surrounded by here."

With the tape rolling, they laughed and both enjoyed a Black Jack Daniels and a Cuban cigar. Life was starting to get better for them both.

Chapter Fifteen

Going Home Again

"When's the last time you've been fishing, Ophelia? I know a place where the crappie jump out of the water before your hook's wet," John boasted, only halfway joking with Ophelia.

"Oh Mr. Thompson, I don't know if I'd remember how to bait a hook. Where is this place?"

Ophelia was about to be introduced to John's roots, those beyond the trappings of Memphis, The Ballpark and Beale Street. Slabtown hadn't changed much since the day John left to make his way to West Point. Sure, his parents were gone, so were Lamont's. But his sister Effie, just 'Sister' to him, was still there holding down the fort and baiting the fishhooks.

Sister still lived on the property their parents had farmed. John had bought up much of the land and had filled it with Hereford cattle, quarter horses and a few hogs, just to remind him of how it used to be. Effie never had to deal with the animals. John had caretakers to handle all that. But she would walk the fields every day as if she was listening for the voices of her father and the boys in the cotton fields.

Highway 61 out of Memphis hadn't changed much either. But, unlike that trip he had taken so many years ago when John drove Gordon's shiny '46 Cadillac, John now had Lamont driving their Range Rover, wheelchair in the back, to show Ophelia around, into the inner sanctum of John's real private life, his roots.

"Sister, let's go fishin'," was all John had to say as he called Effie on the way to the farm.

"I've got someone I want you to meet."

Effie liked Ophelia immediately. With Ophelia being thirty years John's junior, she wondered if there was anything else there besides friendship. It wouldn't take her long to realize that the two were close friends, business associates, but with a deep affection and trust between them. She also saw quickly that Ophelia was one of them, a country girl that could have been raised just down the road.

Ophelia was seeing a completely new John. He left the business side of himself in Memphis and was almost unrecognizable when in Slabtown, on the farm and around Effie. He looked more like the common man on this trip since he would be seen in a wheelchair. You would have never known he had a dime to his name.

Lamont was in his element as well. The four of them had gotten into the Range Rover and headed down Highway 61, the only way in or out of Slabtown. They both had driven it many times. And each time they came or went, they thought of the days long ago when they trudged along behind a mule team tilling the soil, dreaming of what it would be like to leave for good.

"I'm going to show you downtown Slabtown, Ophelia. Now don't blink, or you'll miss it!" John yelled over the sound of the wind rushing through the open windows as Effie and Lamont smiled.

They drove for several miles before Ophelia saw anything, much less anything that looked like a town. Effie's house hadn't really been anything spectacular, a comfortable brick home surrounded by the dormant fields and barns that housed the animals quite comfortably as well. She could get a sense of the isolation that would have been very real when the Thompson's had their farm there.

Finally, a modern school, complete with a football field, a nice one at that, loomed in the distance, fully 300 yards from the highway. 'The Thompson School' is all the sign read. Ophelia didn't ask, she knew John had done things for Slabtown, that he had never forgotten this place or of his promise to make it a better place to live, to raise kids and, if they wanted, for them to move out into the wider world with a good education.

"This reminds me so much of Franklin, Mr. Thompson. My Mom and Dad still live in a place much like this. I wish you could meet them."

"We'll get them over here, girl. This is one of my favorite places on earth. A man can go all over the world and never see a place like this, like home," John declared, surveying the land.

John would point out ponds, streams, and other landmarks of his youth. Ophelia could visualize the stories John would tell, seeing that they were streaming back into his consciousness as vivid as though they just happened yesterday. She could also see the sadness in his eyes, of yearning for those long lost days. You could trust people then. Everyone worked hard and enjoyed life, enjoyed being alive. He missed that.

It was sad for her in a way too. Franklin, Georgia held many fond memories for her, of her sister and brother, her parents who were still living much the same lives they always had. She knew that she shared a special bond with John, of coming up in a country home, from a hard life. But until she actually saw Slabtown, she didn't know how similar their circumstances had been.

The campaign, Danny Carson, even Marvin and Hennie seemed worlds away now. Slabtown would be their refuge when times got too complicated in Memphis or anywhere else. It was clear to Ophelia now that this had been true for John for many years. Whenever the trappings of wealth didn't matter, when the business became too much for him, John and usually Lamont would retreat to Slabtown, good old Slabtown.

"Lamont, have you been to Kesterson's lately? I wonder if they have any chicken and dumplings?" John asked as the Range Rover neared the first building Ophelia saw after the Thompson School complex.

"Not since we were down here last. I'm sure Mrs. Kesterson will make some if she doesn't already have'em though. And some of that cornbread too!" Lamont answered as he turned into a shack of a building just on the roadside.

Kesterson's had been a fixture at Slabtown since John was a boy. Mrs. Kesterson was the only thing keeping the place open, her husband having been dead for ten years. It was a general store, blue-plate special kitchen and hardware store all rolled into one. And John loved it.

A table of old men barely looked up as Lamont, John, Effie and Ophelia came in, Lamont pushing John in his chair. They were too involved in the intense Domino game that had been going on all morning, marking down their scores on the blackboard table top with chalk, yelling at each other when someone scored a point the others didn't think he deserved.

An old woman who looked too old to be still running a store embraced John the minute he entered the building. Lamont and Effie were greeted warmly and Ophelia soon felt like she had been there a hundred times before. She'd been in a store just like this one in Franklin. Every little wide spot in the road in Georgia had one.

'Mrs. Kesterson' as everyone called her, even John, served up the best chicken and dumplings as John told stories of how Gordon, Effie and he would save a nickel to go to Kesterson's store in the old days. Old man Kesterson would just let them reach their tiny hands down into what seemed to be a huge jar and draw out as many hard candies as they could grab. Those were the good old days, everyone at once realized.

Ophelia looked around to see she was in an old building that was almost falling in on itself. Made of vertical split logs called 'slabs', the building was gray, looking like it was made of barn boards. In the old days there were many such buildings made from the vertical boards. The community never having a formal name, it became known as simply 'Slabtown'.

There were fishing supplies, deer heads mounted on the walls and food staples for sale in the old store. There were even old postal cubbyholes leftover from when the store served as a post office.

John clearly loved the place. He would later tell Ophelia that he tried to buy the store many times to shore it up and save it. But Mrs. Kesterson would have none of it. She wanted to pass it on to her grandchildren. It was all she had. People in Slabtown were like that. John felt the same way about the old Thompson farm.

The day couldn't have been long enough for all of them. A stock pond John led them to yielded enough fish for everyone. Ophelia thought she might never fish in an old stock pond again after leaving Franklin, much less be fishing for supper with a billionaire.

Effie cooked the fish at her place in an iron skillet with cornbread muffins and turnip greens on the side. Everyone held their side in a food-induced pain as they sat on the front porch watching Venus chase the crescent moon down to the horizon in the western sky. It was like something out of another place in time. It was, after all, a re-living of their past.

John was almost in visible mental anguish as they made their way back to Memphis on the clear night driving along the Mississippi.

"I don't know why I don't move back down there, girl. I love that place. It's real," John moaned as Lamont nodded vigorously.

Ophelia loved it too.

✤ ✤ ✤

There was still a sting in the memories of Franklin, Georgia for Ophelia. She had only been in Atlanta for ten years, making money and enjoying her new life away from the relative poverty she grew up in. The trip to Slabtown made her think about her meager beginnings in a different way. Franklin was her home, however much she tried to forget or deny it.

She often wondered if John, by taking her to Slabtown, was trying to tell her something, to ease her mind.

"You can't go home again," as Thomas Wolfe put it, Ophelia would later say. You can't really ever recover the past. It's lost forever, she thought. 'Don't tell that to John' would be her refrain. That man never lost his roots.

But John had seemed to be able to find only the parts he loved. There was something almost *Citizen Kane* about it, Ophelia would later tell people, something sad. That is, if you hadn't known the real John Henry Thompson. He loved it. It was his salvation. He was always a country boy at heart, whether it was the country farm at Slabtown or the country estate at old Hugo Moore's.

Marvin and Hennie wanted to know where John had been with his 'gang'. They suspected that he had been down to that 'white nigger ghetto' as Hennie had the audacity to call it. She knew that when Harmon was absent from the gang it probably meant that John was at Slabtown.

Even with the problems Marvin and Hennie had over the last

few weeks, what with the video taping and Marvin's 'vacation', they both still wanted to know where John was and what he was doing. It was an almost vulture-like behavior that would continue until they were sure they could have it all, no matter what they had to go through to get it, humiliation, degradation - anything.

At John's office, Rita would only tell Marvin or Hennie that John was 'unavailable' or 'not reachable', much to the consternation of them both. Rita knew that as soon as John was gone, so was she. Marvin and Hennie hated her with a passion, just another one of John's enablers, they thought.

But Marvin and Hennie had been put in their place with the Lucy episodes. They would have to be content with checking in on John through Rita and the flying service where the jets were housed. They couldn't risk being caught in his gun sights again.

And they hated Ophelia even more, blaming her for 'alienating' whatever affection they thought John might still have for them. It had gotten to the point of an almost juvenile jealousy, one that occupied their thoughts every day.

But as every day passed that Marvin and Hennie became more entrenched in their sordid lives, John became stronger. He was also more determined than ever since the illness to live his life to its fullest. It occurred to him one day that he had not really shared Beale Street with Ophelia. To be sure, Ophelia had seen the Street on the way in from the airport. But John was determined, even though ill, to show Ophelia around his pride and joy.

"Girl, I want to take you down to one of my 'other beginnings'," John was to tell her. "My first real girlfriend – Beale Street, Memphis, Tennessee!"

They had never been there together, even during The Series. Lamont was wondering if John would want to make a trip to Beale Street in his condition. He was worried that John would not want his image to be marred by the fact he needed a wheelchair to get around now, although he was told it would only be temporary.

Lamont should have known by now that nothing could keep John down and out. The trip to Slabtown should have told him that. However, he was pleasantly surprised when he received the call to come to the penthouse for the roll two blocks over to Beale.

Even though it was November the weather was still tolerable. The cool breeze, night chill and smell of barbeque were augmented by the sounds of Beale. Ophelia was to learn that it was an intoxicating mix. The atmosphere was the same as it was when it all took off for John back in the 40's.

Old man Streeter, John's first straw man was gone now. True to their deal, John and Streeter's that is, Streeter's children owned a full 10% of the operation and were active in managing the properties. Bumble's Billiards, The Boogie Woogie Café and Porky's were all in full swing.

"See that barbeque joint? We built that from scratch. All the rest, it's been here a long time. We just got it back on its feet," John said modestly as he waved his hand over Beale Street as if to give it his blessing.

As if on cue, the annual W. C. Handy Birthday Celebration kicked off with a parade coming east down Beale Street from the river. People were pouring out of The Peabody over to Beale. Everyone came out of the clubs and even brought their plates out of Porky's to see the show. It was that Mardi Gras and New Year's Eve feeling all over again.

As Lamont rolled John to the foot of the bronze statue of W. C. Handy that John unveiled so many years ago, Ophelia thought for a brief moment that she saw a tear in John's eye as he took a long look at Handy's image.

"I owe that man a lot girl. I owe this town and these people a lot. This is my town."

Ophelia would make it her town too – for now.

158

Chapter Sixteen

Back to Work

Ophelia loved Memphis. But she had an important job to do keeping up with Danny Carson. It was a curious mission. She knew that John was keenly interested in Danny's campaign, knowing that John had given Danny's campaign an enormous amount of money. But she realized early on that there must be much more to the story.

Rejoining Danny's road trip in Miami, Ophelia met Corky Benedict at the Ritz Carlton South Beach near Miami International Airport. Danny had a quirk about having his base of operations near an airport. Curious, Ophelia thought, or maybe he just wanted to be able to catch a flight as quickly as possible. Whatever, the hotel was a luxurious one, a common trait for Danny's digs no matter where he was.

"Ophelia, Mr. Carson would like to meet you tonight for dinner. It's about time you two spent some time together," Corky said, doing his best to light a cigar, clumsily at that.

Corky had become a quick study of John Henry Thompson. He took Danny's admonition to pay attention to Ophelia and John to heart. He had even taken to smoking Cuban cigars, *Cubanos*, the ones the Cuban exiles gave him in Miami Beach.

Ophelia thought it all comical and transparent. She was wondering when Danny would come calling. John had told her about the meeting with Corky at the penthouse back in Memphis, but only that John had told him that she was to be John's representative on the campaign.

"I'd be delighted. Where shall we meet," she responded as she produced a Dunhill lighter, embarrassed for Corky that he couldn't keep a match lit long enough to get the Cubano going.

Ophelia felt genuinely sorry for Corky. He was in an untenable situation with Danny and John, caught in a crossfire of sorts, she thought. She sat in Corky's suite calming his unease with being the middleman. They smoked the Cubano, had a couple of Black Jacks and talked about the weather, anything but the campaign.

Ophelia could have exerted what Corky may have thought was her inordinate amount of power, been domineering, coming across as a power bitch. There was no need. She was a quick study of power and its prudent use and John knew she would be judicious with it.

"Just lay behind that log, girl. You'll know when to peep out and take a shot," John would often say in his disarming country metaphor.

Corky would be much more useful as a friend than foe, and much more willing to cooperate, give up information if he thought Ophelia would not be a threat. After all, Ophelia could sense that Corky was involved in the campaign for Corky Benedict's well being, not because he was a Carsonite, one of Danny's 'deer in the headlights' believers as John would call them, those folks who would jump off the river bridge at Danny's command.

Corky was somewhat taken aback, while still being at ease with Ophelia's demeanor. A little tipsy by the time their meeting was concluded, Corky had shared quite a bit that was useful to Ophelia and John

"You know Danny's scared shitless of Mr. Thompson," Corky

blurbed, now feeling Ophelia to be every bit his friend instead of foe.

"And by extension, he's *real* apprehensive about meeting with you Ophelia."

Ophelia wasn't surprised. John commanded respect and fear in many quarters, much less among a bunch of politicians, people who pandered to others just for the sake of a campaign contribution or a vote. She had a real distaste for the lot of them, a disgusting bunch who just wanted power, to win, much different from John who decried the style-over-substance shallowness of the politician.

"I'm just an old Southern girl from Franklin, Georgia, Corky. I don't know why he would be worried about someone like me," Ophelia cooed a convincing disclaimer.

"Yeah, right," Corky said as he rolled his eyes. "You don't know Danny like I do."

Corky was right. But, as she was prone to say, by the end of the campaign she would have forgotten more about Danny Carson than Corky Benedict ever would know.

⚜ ⚜ ⚜

For a Southern Baptist Holy-Roller, Danny Carson liked the trappings of wealth and power. Danny was even a lay preacher at the Atlanta Missionary Baptist Church, the huge one downtown, so big it needed three services to tend its flock. But you'd never know it on the campaign. He was focused on one thing – winning the White House. And in that, saving the world, the world according to Danny Carson.

Danny surrounded himself with smart people, policy experts both foreign and domestic, media affairs consultants, and fundraisers.

It was so much about the money. It didn't matter to him if you had all the right stuff, if you didn't have the money to get the message out, to hold rallies, pay for the hotels and travel, all that it took to win.

Danny had everything else. John knew that. Danny had the intellect, the looks, the obligatory pretty wife and kids, a nice sellable package with the funding to boot. But, in John's mind the only exception to his 'might makes right' axiom was when it involved politics.

John had been taught too well by his mentor Senator Hugo Moore that politics *was* all about the money. He believed in politics you could make a silk purse out of a sow's ear if you had enough bucks. Hugo proved that with some good common horse sense, with enough money, you could buy the connections you needed to capture the control of enough people to gain power.

Synergy, John thought. It was as much about the connections you make just like when he built Beale Street, The Ballpark, how he made the careers of people in public office in Missouri and California. None of that had changed.

John didn't have to spell it out for Ophelia. She was a quick study having seen John in action. Harmon and Lamont had filled in all the blanks. She knew that in Danny Carson this was the biggest prize of all. Although she didn't know just how John would benefit from a Carson White House, she believed and trusted John knew what he was doing.

✤ ✤ ✤

Danny Carson's penthouse suite was at worst, in a word, plush. The Presidential Suite at The Ritz South Beach was reserved for, other than The President, foreign heads of state, CEO's of major corporations or anyone who had the money to cover the obscene price tag. It didn't go unnoticed to Ophelia that Danny liked the Ritz penthouses just like John did. John's at The Ritz Carlton Atlanta resembled Danny's in South Beach even though the South Beach location was about thirty years older. Danny's campaign had the money. John had made sure of that. After all, nothing was too good for John's biggest straw man yet.

You couldn't just walk into Danny's penthouse. The US Secret Service protection had been assigned to him as soon as he had raised enough money to qualify as a candidate and he used the Service well. He resented the confining atmosphere the agents imposed but he loved the attention – and the protection it gave him from the unwanted aggressive admirers, the ones that didn't have any money.

Ophelia had actually met Carson in Atlanta and Danny remembered it. He didn't know it at the time, neither did Ophelia, that she would be the emissary of his old West Point buddy, his biggest contributor and the person to whom he would owe the most.

"Ophelia, it's so good to see you again!" Danny chirped as Ophelia was led into the suite.

Curiously there was no one else there, not Corky or any campaign staffer would be present.

"Senator, it's good to see you as well. Mr. Thompson sends his regards," Ophelia said as she glanced around the room.

Ophelia noticed right away that Danny was well staffed in the penthouse, even though there was no evidence that anyone was present in the room. Three desks had been moved in, all with computers and faxes along with reams of papers stacked high on each one that gave evidence there was major work going on there.

He must have cleared the room just for her.

Danny was dressed smartly in a dark blue business suit, red tie, the classic political look, especially for a Republican. He led her to a living room area and offered her something to drink. Black Jack was definitely on the menu.

"How's John? I sent some flowers to the hospital after the heart attack. I know he's tough as nails. You know, he and I go back a long way, all the way to The Point."

"He's recovering well. I just left him in Memphis," Ophelia added, making sure Danny knew John was aware of the meeting. Danny was concise, to the point, making it very clear he knew John was keeping an eye on his campaign.

"I know John is interested in what's going on here, Ophelia. Anytime you have any questions, any input, you just tell Corky you want a meeting. I'm open and accessible. I value John's opinion greatly," Danny said, leaning forward with a sense of believability.

And Ophelia believed him. Whatever bonds Danny and John shared, they must have been solid and well-forged. She would take his words to heart over the next year, ferrying messages between the two whenever the need arose. Often, the content would be mundane suggestions from John about what to say on a particular issue, especially when John thought Danny was lacking in focus.

Many times John would have Ophelia take someone with her to introduce to Danny, people she didn't really know but came to know through John's circle of friends, his sphere of influence in the business world. Ophelia knew there was a reason for everything John did. He was a consummate planner and organizer. She wasn't always sure why John did some of the things he did, only that it was all part of a plan. She was just proud to be part of it.

"If you have any problems, *anything,* you need to talk to me about, just see Corky. He will make sure the Secret Service people let you in," Danny assured Ophelia.

Strange, she thought. Any problems? Ophelia just chalked her uneasiness up to Danny being a politician. They talked in riddles anyway.

The campaign always put Ophelia up in the nicest rooms when on the go with Danny. And The Ritz at South Beach was about as nice as it got on the road. A resort since 1953 it lay smack in the middle of Miami Beach and the famed Art Deco district. The South Beach nightlife was an attractive diversion from the hectic, 'always on' campaign schedule and Ophelia was determined to take advantage of it.

The meeting with Danny Carson was about what Ophelia had expected, a no-nonsense 'how do you do?' with the firm message of Danny's commitment being delivered to Ophelia with the understanding it would be passed on to John. By the end of the day, Ophelia felt reassured with her status as John's straw man.

Sure, she had been involved in politics before. But this was for all the marbles and it worried her that she was starting to like it too much. Just as she was about to begin to relax, the telephone rang.

"Ophelia, this is Corky. I'd like to show you around a bit tonight if you like. South Beach is a hopping place if you know where to go," Corky said, seemingly earnest in his native Floridian invitation.

Ophelia was surprised at the call. She didn't know what motivations lay behind it, whether it was an attempt to watch her, pacify her, or just plain entertain, a sincere gesture made by a bored Corky. Ophelia was a grownup and could take care of herself. She wasn't worried about a little guy like Corky Benedict. She already had plans but she figured it would be worth it just to pick his brain a little more. She'd take Corky with her. John would approve.

"Sure. Why not? I haven't spent much time down here. What time should I meet you?" Ophelia asked.

Corky liked to party. That was evident. He had ideas of taking Ophelia down to The Abbey, a South Beach kick-ass bar for dinner and dancing. His turf being a native Floridian, a South Beach boy, Ophelia thought. What Corky Benedict didn't know was that this was not Ophelia's 'first rodeo' as John would say, something John realized when he found that Ophelia could keep up with him drinking Black Jack.

"Let *me* take *you* somewhere, Corky. Ever heard of a bar called Tobacco Road?"

Hell no. Corky Benedict was too button-downed for that. Ophelia had been there many times before when on real estate business in South Florida. If you were anywhere near Miami, she thought, it was worth the drive down to Tobacco Road.

"You'd better leave that tie here Corky," Ophelia said ominously. "You might get strangled with it down at Tobacco Road."

Corky had begun to wonder what he had gotten himself into. In fact, Danny hadn't sent him to watch over Ophelia or attempt to get information. He honestly thought he might have a friend in Ophelia, someone he could talk to. It didn't hurt that she was attractive, single and appeared to be able to tolerate him.

Corky had clearly been drinking since they left each other earlier. Gin and tonic, Ophelia could smell it a mile away. It was the lubricant that allowed him to make the call to her in the first place.

They grabbed a cab at The Ritz South Beach and headed downtown to Miami Avenue. Ophelia felt more comfortable in her type of drinking establishment, one more 'down to earth'. The Tobacco Road was just that and more. A landmark since the early 1900's it had the dubious distinction of holding the oldest liquor license in Miami-Dade. It was a popular hangout during Prohibition and a favorite of Al Capone and his gang and a problem for the police until just a few years before Ophelia started to frequent it.

Tobacco Road had even been closed down during World War II because the GI's were exhibiting lewd and malicious conduct and the place was raided regularly. The new owners had brought in an old friend of John's, 'Blues Boy' also known as 'B. B.' King, the same Blues man who got his start on John Henry Thompson's Beale Street.

"Don't mind those bikers, Corky. They won't bite," Ophelia told a somewhat bewildered Corky as they got out of the cab. "This place is safe."

The place literally glowed in its pink facade and neon lights, akin to something off the *Miami Vice* television series of the day. Corky grabbed Ophelia's arm, more a security measure he thought instead of a move reminiscent of a Southern gentleman. Ophelia went straight to the front of the line that extended around the corner. John had tickets for her already.

The place was packed and Corky was wide-eyed. John might say, 'I've been to three goat-ropings and two mule-milkings and I've never quite seen anything like this!' - the kind of phraseology he saved when viewing the more remarkable sights one might encounter in life.

They swam their way through the crowd that included Hells Angels types and stockbrokers. A Cuban called Marco, the manager since the new owners came in greeted Ophelia, leading them to a table on a slightly elevated platform that overlooked the stage where B. B. King would soon appear.

Corky, for his part, had not yet started to relax. He didn't ask how they got the preferential treatment. But he started to enjoy himself when the canned Blues music started blaring and 'mojito' Cuban drinks began flowing.

Ophelia had to have a mojito to get the night moving and ordered two. She and Corky had just noticed a familiar face in the crowd, the Latino man she had received the note from that day in Coral Gables, the one Corky took away from her as they escorted the man from the event.

Ophelia saw that Corky was surprised by the look on her face as she stared at the man. He didn't know how she would know him. She didn't ask him who he was. She would find out later.

"What's this?" Corky yelled as he examined the leafy looking beverage she shoved toward him.

"Nectar of the gods, my friend, a mojito! Drink up!"

Ophelia was in her element, Corky thought. She had been here before, that was for sure. The mojito was deceptively sweet to Corky. The rum was cleverly hidden by the shredded mint leaves and sugar. The soda water made it acceptable to Corky's stomach. The mojito was a risky drink already since he had been downing gin at The Ritz South Beach before they left. It was one kickass night and Corky, now properly lubricated, was having a good time.

"B. B. will be out in a minute, Corky. You're going to hear some Memphis Blues, some *real* music."

Corky just went along for the ride. He was amazed. B. B. King came over and gave Ophelia one of those 'sister kisses' like she and John shared. This woman got around – and knew everyone like she owned the place. Well, not exactly. The club was owned by John Henry Thompson – just like the penthouse suite back at The Ritz South Beach where Danny slept so well that night. John was the one that got around.

Chapter Seventeen

Stumping For The Money

Corky was in visible pain. He told Danny that he had a virus. Yeah, right – a 'mojitan' virus. Ophelia thought she even saw some mint leaves still wedged in his front teeth. He had been a gentleman the night before, or as best as he could remember.

The fundraiser at The Ritz South Beach the night after their long night at Tobacco Road was about as glamorous as you could get. It was a formal one at that. Ophelia sat with Corky right in front of the head table where Danny was up on the dais with his beauty queen wife. Danny had married well alright. Unlike John, he had married right after The Point to a pretty and smart girl, one that would stay with him all the way.

Danny kept watching Corky wondering what was wrong with him. Strangely to Danny, Corky kept pushing away his mint-laced iced tea as if it made him sick. It did.

Nothing more miserable than a sweet drink hangover, Ophelia mused.

Danny Carson was introduced by his Miami-Dade campaign coordinator, Sterling Cochran, a millionaire real estate mogul who owned half of Ocean Boulevard in South Beach. To hear him tell it, Danny was a cross between the second coming, Abraham Lincoln and FDR. America's 'next greatest President', whatever in the hell that meant.

Danny made a good speech as far as the rubber chicken circuit goes. He seemed to have that captivating delivery that kept people on the edge of their seats, especially the women. He was forbidden fruit they knew, but damned, he looked and sounded good. He just *had* to win. After all, there hadn't been anyone to swoon over in the White House since John Kennedy, they thought.

At the end of the speech Danny made his usual trek off the dais down to the little rich people for a 'meet and greet', much to the consternation of the Secret Service detail. He made a beeline to Ophelia and showed his mastery of the 'sister kiss'. Damned, thought Ophelia. He *is* good.

As Danny made his way through the crowd of the ballroom at The Ritz South Beach that night, Ophelia realized that he had it all - organization, leadership skills and bullshit. You would have thought JFK himself had risen from the grave. In him, she saw a political John Henry Thompson.

Damned – what did they teach these people at this 'Point' Danny and John had attended? It at once just occurred to her – he was going to win this damned thing.

⚜ ⚜ ⚜

John laughed until his side hurt, causing quite a panic from Rita at the penthouse suite and office in Memphis. Ophelia reveled in sharing what she termed her 'war stories' from the campaign. The '404' jet wasn't even cooled off by the time she had made it to The Peabody and had John belly-laughing.

Ophelia told John about the Tobacco Road incident first, of how Corky had fallen in love with mojitos, then a certain Cuban 'lady of the night'. Ophelia rescued him from a fate worse than death as she got him out of the club and back to the Ritz South Beach. Without her, Corky would have certainly been AWOL from the campaign the next day.

"I'm liking this Corky boy more and more, Ophelia. Where's Danny now?"

Ophelia showed John the campaign schedule for the next thirty days, stops that were always subject to change at the last minute according to the amount of dollars that may be raised at any alternative event that may come up.

"I want you to make this New York event at The Plaza Hotel. Danny and I have a few friends in common there I want you to meet," John told her.

"Will he introduce them to me, Mr. Thompson? I mean, my meeting with him was short and sweet. He told me to contact Corky whenever I need to talk with him."

John told Ophelia that this time she would be contacted by his friends. She was to take a room at The Plaza the day before the event and be prepared for a dinner meeting that night.

Ophelia found it all a little mysterious, but John was that way. He always told her just what she needed to know, nothing more, nothing less.

"Corky was a lot of help, Mr. Thompson. After he got his head into the mojitos, he told me just about everything that's going on inside Danny's campaign. Did you know Danny has a girlfriend?"

John, although still wheelchair-bound, shot up in his seat.

"Are you sure about that?" John shot back, clearly alarmed.

Ophelia suddenly was shocked back into her role of employee, realizing that the information she brought back was not only amusing to John but useful intelligence he depended upon in his dealings with Carson.

"Mr. Thompson, that's what Corky was telling me. He was

drunk, but I believe he was telling the truth."

Ophelia hesitated before she told John anything else. John could see that his reaction had prompted her reticence. He immediately sought to remedy it.

"Girl, I want you to tell me everything. To be sure, it bothers me that Danny would be fooling around on that gorgeous wife of his, but that's not what concerns me. He is taking a big risk, one of destroying his chance to become President, of doing what I need done."

Ophelia could see that this was a serious turn of events. In her employee mindset she realized that she owed John her complete allegiance. He was paying her a good salary, much more than she was making in her Atlanta real estate ventures, but it wasn't about the money. She had become 'comfortable' as she would call it before leaving Atlanta, enough money to take care of her family and have the things she always wanted.

In her friendship, Ophelia had learned that John was a compassionate man, but this was business. She had to ask.

"Mr. Thompson, there's a man I think may be following me. He's Latino, my age, about 30 years old. That's about all I can tell you."

John was calmly alarmed, Ophelia could tell. He wanted to know more, he would know more.

"Where did you see him? What did he do to alarm you Ophelia?" John asked, now leaning forward from his wheelchair.

Ophelia explained that she had first seen him in Coral Gables, the time when the man handed her the note. She also told him that Corky had taken the note from her and never gave her an explanation.

It was the second sighting in Miami that alarmed her. She had Corky drunk as a skunk but somehow she could not get him to tell her anything about the man. He played dumb, more dumb than usual.

John slumped back down into his wheelchair and reached for the intercom button.

"Rita, get David Muggs in here please."

Ophelia began to wonder if she should have said anything about Corky's comment or the suspicious man. She had begun to like the guy and didn't want to get him into trouble with Carson. She thought he was a useful tool in knowing what was going on, someone they didn't need to compromise.

"Mr. Thompson, before David gets here, I think I should tell you that I believe Corky is important to us. He can be a great help in keeping our thumb on Danny."

"Don't worry, girl. I know what I'm doing," John said in his now calm, casual voice he used when he sought to reassure or tutor Ophelia.

"But from now on, Muggs is going to travel with you."

⚜ ⚜ ⚜

Ophelia wished she could spend more time in Memphis with John. Typically she had only two days before the next campaign event and John was having his hands full with Roberta. With Marvin and Hennie still reeling from the Lucy episode, John could now focus on the divorce.

Roberta wanted out – but comfortably. The pre-nuptial agreement gave her a $10 million maximum payout. But she wanted more. She had become fond of the London apartment John kept for their past forays to Europe. John wouldn't budge and a protracted fight would prove expensive, possibly more than the place was worth.

Ophelia felt terrible for him, wishing there was something she could do. Having seen the videos of Marvin, Hennie and Lucy, was it possible that something similar existed with Roberta? She knew it was technically none of her business, but she thought it worth a shot.

David Muggs didn't know the whole story about the details of the divorce. John told him what he needed to know, included him in specific things, but not everything. He trusted David, that was obvious, but John was a careful man, operating through surrogates for stealth and protection for his entire adult life, ever since the days of Hugo Moore. He had been taught well.

Ophelia approached David as he was leaving The Peabody one day. He agreed to talk with her but not anywhere close to the hotel. The riverfront, although just a few blocks away would provide the cover they needed.

David was, despite all his covert capabilities, a good man. He was loyal to John first and Ophelia knew she had to convince David that she was only trying to help.

"David, Mr. Thompson's having trouble with Roberta. She's trying to take the London apartment, something that's not in their pre-marital agreement. It's just not right."

David's mind was put at ease. He liked Ophelia and hoped that she wasn't going to say anything detrimental, something that he would have to report to John.

"Ophelia, you don't know how much I appreciate you coming to me. I was always worried about that woman. She was a gold-digger from day one in my book. I've seen a million of them looking at Mr. Thompson over the years, wanting nothing but his money."

Ophelia felt relieved. She didn't know just how David would react – much less the surprise he had in store.

"If Mr. Thompson knew what I knew, he wouldn't be wanting

to give her the time of day, much less any more of a settlement than she's already going to get. It's been my job to watch out for Mr. Thompson for fifteen years now, be his eyes and ears around The Peabody and anywhere he goes. I know you don't know what I mean, but I've seen things, you know, bad things that involve Mrs. Thompson. That Roberta, she's no good."

A flurry of thoughts passed through Ophelia's mind. She immediately thought of the videos David had secured for John, the ones of Marvin, Hennie and Lucy. Could David have caught something of Roberta? Quick on her feet, she came up with a solution she thought would work. She would be at risk, but it might help John.

"David, I'll tell you what. You know I work for Mr. Thompson as his personal assistant?" she asked as David nodded.

"If you know *anyone* that might have *anything* that might help Mr. Thompson, you need to use it. I can help get it to the right person. I am in Suite 316, but will be out until midnight tonight."

David just smiled and said, "I just might know *someone* who knows *something*."

They sat and watched the barge traffic go down the Mississippi as the sun sat into the Arkansas farmland on the other side of the river. They both loved John Henry Thompson and would do anything they could for him. It wasn't just about the money or the apartment in London. They wanted to protect the man that had been good to them both.

You could say that David and Ophelia felt 'comfortable in their own skin' as John would say of them. They both had their faults, insecurities, and every emotion other people felt. They both had experienced love and hate, the desperation of poverty and loneliness. And they felt okay with doing everything they could for John, no matter what the cost They would be okay with it.

175

Ophelia spent the rest of the night driving all over Memphis. She was moving there, relocating to be near John, to do her job of being his personal assistant and confidante. It was more than just a job. It was a new start for her. She knew she would never be the same, and that she was taking a big chance in getting involved in John's personal affairs, the divorce with Roberta. But Ophelia had a streak of stubbornness that sometimes did not serve her well.

But in this endeavor, since she was always up to a challenge, Ophelia thought that John needed help. She returned to her suite at The Peabody around midnight to find the hotel bar still hopping. The Beale Street Revival had made The Peabody the crash site for party revelers from now on, the bar being the last stop before everyone made their last journey up the ever-slow elevators to their room.

A manila envelope left on her bed held the gift that Ophelia needed. As Ophelia popped the VHS tape into her player in the suite she held her breath. Whatever it was, she hoped it was good, worth sticking her neck out with David.

It was excellent. David, or 'anonymous' as Ophelia would style it, had caught poor clumsy Roberta trying to extract information about John with Marvin – and that wasn't all that she was trying to extract.

An obvious by-product of David's video surveillance at Marvin's suite at The Peabody, Ophelia saw an eye-popping video of Roberta seducing Marvin! She had succeeded in getting Marvin's pants down and was doing her best extraction techniques, both oral in the interrogative sense and sexually. Marvin told all he knew, which wasn't much, trivia about John's holdings Roberta may have not known about, but nothing that any other Jane (or Joe) Blow couldn't have gotten from a careful reading of a Securities Exchange Commission filing.

Roberta left Marvin's suite somewhat frustrated leaving

Marvin obviously relieved. It was a 'short' episode all around, but revealing in many ways – and deadly for Roberta.

Ophelia laughed until the people in the suite next door banged on the walls. She had what she needed.

✠ ✠ ✠

Ophelia was indeed taking a big chance. John could have any range of reactions to what she was about to do, if he ever found out. At the end of the day she thought it couldn't hurt. After all, this woman was reneging on their agreement, one that had been laid out before they got married.

Hell, Roberta was getting more money than she had sense enough to count. That always made Ophelia, and David, wonder if she had her own straw man that was calling the shots, one who was pulling her strings in their marriage and was waiting in the wings to snuggle up with her after she had split from John.

Roberta already didn't like Ophelia. The day she 'met' her coming off the elevator her first day at The Peabody, Roberta never spoke. Ophelia thought that was an omen then and put Roberta on her list for people she should watch out for. So, it came as a big surprise when Roberta saw Ophelia approach her at the Goldsmith's Department store, the place that used to be the lead fashion shop in downtown Memphis.

Ophelia knew just what to say, something that no one else would understand or know, a message only Roberta would get.

Roberta started for the door, trying to get past Ophelia before she could get inside. Ophelia stepped right in front of her. Roberta was taken aback, Ophelia being taller and looking like she was 'heavily pissed', as she would say, had the right of way. As she

177

leaned toward a shocked Roberta, Ophelia delivered her lines.

"Roberta, I've seen the video and I can't imagine what it would be like," she said to a stunned, clueless Roberta.

As Ophelia leaned into Roberta's face, an inch from her mouth she lowered the proverbial bombshell.

"Is that Marvin's dick I smell on your breath?"

Roberta let out a scream that caused the Chanel girl to drop a $100 bottle of perfume. She blazed past Ophelia out onto Union Avenue throwing her bag of goodies she had just bought with John's money.

Ophelia calmly walked outside and back to The Peabody. Roberta had left a trail that included her purse and topcoat she had flung into the street. She was obviously upset, 'panties in a wad', John might say.

⚜ ⚜ ⚜

"Girl, you be careful up in New York now," John told Ophelia as David Muggs helped her onto the '404' jet at the Memphis airport the next day.

"One other thing," John added. "You know that crazy-ass Roberta signed those divorce papers today. She said that she just wanted out and that I could keep that damned London apartment. You just can't ever tell about these women!"

Damned right, thought Ophelia. Damned right.

Chapter Eighteen

New York, New York

The '404' jet carrying David Muggs and Ophelia landed at La Guardia airport just as snow had begun to fall. Ophelia was ready for the cold. Wrapped in her full-length mink she and David made their way to the limo waiting on the tarmac.

She and David had forged a real bond now, even though it was an unspoken one, a deed they never acknowledged they shared a role in, even though both knew it was David who had left the tape on Ophelia's bed that night.

David was aware of everything on Ophelia's agenda. John had confided in him completely. She was to have dinner that night at Peter Luger's Steakhouse in Brooklyn, one of John's favorite places. It was a sure thing that they wouldn't run into Danny Carson there. To be sure, Luger's was one of the best steakhouses in the world, but it wasn't fancy enough for Danny. Besides, he was a Manhattan kind of guy. Brooklyn was beneath him.

Ophelia was to meet Julio Fuentes, John's estate manager in Nicaragua. She thought it was going to be just a casual get-to-know-one-another sort of thing, a mixer of sorts to raise money for Danny in private before the big fundraiser the next night at The Plaza Hotel.

The Plaza Hotel was Ophelia and John's favorite in New York. Just across the street from Central Park, it was the perfect home base for their jaunts in Manhattan, and just a cab ride to Peter Luger's over the river into Brooklyn. And it was comfortable with a penthouse suite just the right size for John, comparable to his digs in Atlanta and Miami at the Ritz properties.

Muggs had taken a room down the hall but helped Ophelia get situated in her suite. He always carried a large hard-sided briefcase but Ophelia never paid any attention to it until he popped it open on the sofa of her suite.

She was surprised, almost shocked, even though Ophelia hardly was ever shocked at anything. What she saw David pull out of the case was an electronic black box with an antenna that resembled the television aerial that still towered over Ophelia's Mom and Pop's house back in Franklin, Georgia.

"What on earth is that?" Ophelia asked crouching to see what may be printed on the box.

"Mr. Thompson wants me to make sure your room is swept. It'll only take a minute, Ophelia," Muggs said as he put on a set of headphones and began to walk around the suite holding the antenna.

'Sweep the room', Ophelia thought. Why would John think the room might be bugged? She assumed Danny Carson would be staying at the hotel before the fundraiser, but not in her room. She would understand much better after dinner.

"You're okay. I'll be just down the hall," Muggs said as he handed Ophelia a walkie-talkie.

"Just call me on this if you need anything."

Ophelia had never been through a room sweep before. It was quick and looked professional. She knew David always carried a gun, but now she wondered what else he had in that case.

The limo picked up David and Ophelia at seven o'clock and headed for Brooklyn. Ophelia had never been to the restaurant and wondered why they would dine across the river. It became apparent when they arrived in front of the small brick facade of the restaurant replete with a black awning that proclaimed the date '1887' at the top.

It was the beginning of the year-long 100th anniversary of what she recognized now as being a landmark in the city across the river. There were banners and a line that extended around the corner that reminded her of Tobacco Road back in Miami, the site of Corky's mojito demise.

They were expected. The doorman rushed to the limo and flung the door open to greet them. People naturally stared, wondering who the rich and/or famous were. They were neither, but they were about to be in the company of such.

Old Sol Forman, already in his 70's in the 1980's, still runs the place these days in his 90's. He was a fixture at Luger's since he bought the place after Peter Luger's death in the early 1940's. He met David and Ophelia at the front door and led them through the small, wood-paneled dining room lined with its simple tables and minimalist decorations.

A back room in this place? Ophelia thought it too small to have one. But even the smallest of pubs and restaurants in New York had a back room, that is, the ones that had been around since before Prohibition.

And there was John, and once again he had surprised her.

"What are you doing here? Why didn't you tell me? Are you all right?" Ophelia cried, almost a real cry as her voice rose with every word. She was alarmed, not upset that John did not tell her he would be meeting her in New York.

It wasn't until they had exchanged their sort of kisses that she noticed the men sitting beside John's wheelchair. One she knew. Corky Benedict sprang from his seat and did his impression of a

181

'sister kiss' with Ophelia. He was all smiles.

Now, clearly perplexed, Ophelia turned her attention to the Latino man sitting beside John. He had been calmly watching the excitement and finally rose from his seat introducing himself as Julio Fuentes, the manager of John's estate in Nicaragua.

'Black Jack's all around' was the command from John. He was holding court now, in his element in the private room of Peter Luger's. Cubanos were passed around much to the chagrin of Corky. He was about to be indoctrinated into another of John and Ophelia's small pleasures, that of the Cuban cigar, smoked like it should be smoked, no clumsy lighting here like in Miami.

"Julio, I hope you don't mind me smoking a Cubano instead of one of our home-grown Nicaraguans. I don't get to smoke that much anymore since the heart attack. The doctors tell me it may be the end of me," John said as Ophelia lit his cigar.

Julio was obviously an educated man, spoke crisp, fluent English and lit up as well.

"Not at all, John. Not at all."

Ophelia thought it curious, Julio calling Mr. Thompson 'John'.

John barely cracked a smile when Ophelia asked Corky if he would like a mojito. Corky, for his part, managed a polite, but curt, 'no, thank you very much'.

There was talk about the snow, the steaks, 'the best in town', John would say. They tasted just like he dreamed they would when he was a boy working at The Peabody, the times when the businessmen from 'The City' would stop in and tell him stories of the big city life. John didn't even get to experience the restaurant back in the 1940's when he was at West Point, just up the Hudson River.

Ophelia had almost forgotten about the obvious questions she had, of why John was there, and how he had gotten there in such a secretive manner, of the room sweeping, and of Corky Benedict. Why in the world would he be here? He worked for Danny Carson.

Corky was getting a fast education courtesy of the Carson campaign and his dealings with John and Ophelia. He had finally figured out who was boss – and who he should be working for. He had come over to the Thompson side of the fence.

"Ophelia, Mr. Fuentes here is a very good friend of mine. He runs my estate down in Nicaragua. He and Corky have had a short meeting and they'll fill you in later on what you need to know – when the time is right," John said to a somewhat still confused Ophelia.

All the while David Muggs was silent, content to be a fly on the wall, never speaking unless spoken to by the group. There was something strange about all this and Ophelia never liked being in the dark. It was one of the few times she felt insecure, left wondering where she stood. The stakes were high in this campaign and the mixture of business and politics left the lines between the two blurry.

Ophelia would not be told what she needed to know that night. Instead, the entire group retreated to the limo waiting outside. Julio Fuentes and Corky said their goodbyes with no mention of a meeting to follow, of instructions for the dinner to be held the next night at The Plaza. The only hint came from Julio who told Ophelia that 'she would be good for his country'.

David Muggs was just putting his black box of de-bugging tricks, the ones Ophelia had seen at The Plaza during the room sweep, into the trunk of the limo. He had obviously been working with them on the limo before the others came outside.

Muggs helped John out of his wheelchair and into the limo with Ophelia following. Muggs took the shotgun seat in the front with the driver. Ophelia could hear Muggs talking with the limo driver as John poured a Black Jack and proceeded to cut another Cubano.

"We need to take a ride girl. I've got a few things I want to explain to you. I hear it was Miguel Hernandez who has been trying to get to you."

Now Ophelia would hear the explanation she had finally been waiting for, the one that might explain why this Latino man had been trying to get to her on the campaign.

"He's trying to blackmail me, Ophelia. He thinks I had something to do with his daddy's death."

It all made sense now to Ophelia. Ramon Hernandez, Danny Carson, John Henry Thompson. All West Point men, all the Class of 1946. Ramon had been a problem for Danny. Ramon was dead.

"You see, Ramon was a good friend of mine. I made him down there, set him up in government so to speak. You know, Ramon died sometime back and now his son is on the warpath."

John went on to answer the question of what was in the note Corky Benedict had intercepted back in Coral Gables at the campaign event.

"That note he tried to pass you was to supposedly tell you to be careful. I don't know what in the hell that meant. He was just trying to get you to listen to him. He obviously knows you are in my inner circle."

Inner circle. Funny, Ophelia had never thought of herself as being in that position. And now, maybe, just maybe because she was, she was in danger.

"You just stay clear of him and let David Muggs know if he tries to contact you."

That was it? Ophelia was puzzled, not knowing whether to follow up and ask questions or just comply. It was the very first time in her relationship with John that she was left wondering what to do.

She chose to remain silent. The only other question beyond that was whether to bail out, abandon ship – on John and the campaign. She thought for a millisecond and decided to ride it out. She had come a long way. She would be in for the long haul.

John puffed heavily on his cigar. Ophelia just nodded when John told her what to do, although he left uncertain as to what she should expect from now on. He was looking for some sign of concern, some reaction. In Ophelia he had found a cool customer. She would show no emotion now.

"You want to take a ride and see where phase two of my life began? You've heard me talk about it so much I figured I'd just show you. To hear these doctors tell it, it'll probably be the last time I'll see it."

"It's your car, Mr. Thompson. It's a beautiful night, and I don't have anywhere else to go," Ophelia said, this time, for the first time since they both met that night, with a little more business-like tone. It was the only indication John would get that she was upset at not being told the whole story.

Fortunately for them both, for John as the storyteller and Ophelia the witness, it was a bold and beautiful moonlit night. It seemed that John had ordered up the whole night, from the dinner to the Miguel Hernandez explanation and now the scenery. The drive up the Hudson River was beautiful, even at night.

"Have you ever been to West Point?"

Just then it occurred to Ophelia. West Point. Somehow in all the times she had been to New York City, she had never been the 50 miles up the river to the United States Military Academy. Most people hadn't, she thought. Most people didn't care, she guessed.

"I've never been there. I had even forgotten it was in New York. How are we going to get inside at this time of night?"

A good question. After all, The Point was an official military installation and it was eleven o'clock by the time their limo arrived at the gates.

Following John's lead, Muggs had arranged it all. General Thomas Taylor was at the front gate to meet the limo, personally waving the car through as John rolled down his window.

"John, it's good to see you. Just pull over up there and I'll be right with you," Taylor said.

"Mr. Thompson, I've seen everything now!" Ophelia whispered.

"Not quite," was John's response.

The limo pulled to the side just long enough for the General, still clad in uniform from the day's work as Commandant of The Point, to crawl inside and sit by John.

"Tom, this is Ophelia Hartwell, a good friend of mine. She's never been to The Point. Let's show her around, where we really grew up."

Ophelia never saw the Army officer that had taken the place of David Muggs in the front seat. He directed the limo through the grounds as John gave the guided tour like he had done it many times. Ophelia saw all the highlights of The Point, the Cadet Chapel, Pershing's Barracks where, appropriately, John had lived; the football field and the old firing range where Harmon Vance had come to John's rescue.

"What do you think, Miss Hartwell?" General Taylor asked Ophelia as they returned to the gate.

"I am duly impressed, General. Do they let women in here?" she asked as John laughed.

"As a matter of fact, Miss Hartwell, our current Captain of the Corps is a young woman from Tennessee."

The General and John smiled. Ophelia knew to just nod her head.

The drive back to the city was nostalgic for John. He told

Ophelia he hadn't been able to see the city as a cadet, he was working the summers or going on Academy sponsored field drills. By the time they reached the Manhattan skyline Ophelia had summoned the nerve to ask how they had been given such a late night visitation privilege.

"I just built them a new baseball stadium girl – and old Tom Taylor was in my class. That opens a lot of doors," John said as he looked at the skyline.

It sure as hell does.

Chapter Nineteen

Loneliness

Ophelia suspected John wasn't in the mood to answer questions about why he had made such a mysterious entrance, now exit into and out of New York. She had seen a side of John she never thought she would see. It was revealing. John had secrets she would never know. She resigned herself to not caring, in trusting his judgment. She had signed on to the 'might makes right' philosophy some time ago.

David Muggs took her back to The Plaza after John was on the jet en route back to Memphis. She thought more than once about asking him what had happened that night, what Julio Fuentes meant about her being good for his country, what *really* had happened. In the end, she knew, trusted, that David would tell John everything she had said on that ride to the hotel. She would give him nothing to report.

The dinner at The Plaza was one of the most grand of the campaign. Movers, shakers, all the monied people of New York were there, having paid $2,000 per plate to wine and dine with the apparent next President of the United States.

Corky was there too, and he wasn't talking – or drinking. Ophelia didn't know what he had been told, but he was a new man now that he was working for John. Danny Carson would have had him hanged if he knew Corky had turned into one of John's straw men, she thought.

Danny Carson made the speech of his life sounding very Presidential and looking the part. He focused on foreign relations, how the world was a very dangerous place these days, as if that was lost on anyone that lived in New York. The highlight of the talk was a self-congratulatory treatise on how the United States had rescued Nicaragua from the threat of Soviet influence. The Ramon story, thought Ophelia. How appropriate.

A standing ovation was Danny's reward, and the continuing gratitude of the Nicaraguan people, he must have thought. Ophelia looked around and wondered if there was anyone in the crowd that had a clue, a clue like the one she had. The inside story of how things really get done. She was all alone in the room in that respect. These were clueless Carsonites. She went up to bed.

⚜ ⚜ ⚜

Ophelia wanted to visit one of her favorite spots in New York before she left the next day. The venerable Tavern on the Green was a famous Central Park restaurant not far from The Plaza Hotel. There was heavy snow falling now and Ophelia really wanted to be alone, even though she knew David Muggs wouldn't ever be far away, not now, not after this trip.

The snow was falling in sheets. It looked like a scene from a calendar, one of those hanging in her Pop's workshop back home, Ophelia thought. She wished John were there. Given what had happened on this trip he might just show up. The Tavern was full of people as it usually was. But that didn't matter to Ophelia. She just wanted to relax, reclaim some of her sanity and calm down after the last two days.

She took a table overlooking the garden filled with the topiary sculpted animals. It was beautiful. It was just then, just at that point where there was that first real lull in her jaunts across the country with Danny Carson or John that she wondered if she would ever have anyone with whom she could share her life. It was such a shame to be there in that wonderful place alone, alone except for all the people who had flocked to be there in that spectacular setting. Perhaps it was the events of the last two days, but for whatever reason, Ophelia began to cry.

David Muggs was watching her, and talking with John on the telephone. John was worried. It was time to bring her back to Memphis.

⚜ ⚜ ⚜

"I want you to move over here for good, girl. And I think we need to get you a new car and a place to stay," John said to Ophelia who for the first time was smiling again.

"You've been working too hard on this campaign. Let's give old Danny and yourself a break."

John realized he had been pushing Ophelia too hard. She was tough, he knew that. But he had just introduced her to what she must realize was the darker side of politics, the underbelly and dirty side of the things that had to be done.

"Let's go down to Miami, girl. Let's go to Tobacco Road!"

⚜ ⚜ ⚜

John had been there many times, had drank his share of Black Jacks and saved the place from being closed down by the Miami-

190

Dade vice cops, bringing in talent like B. B. King and sprucing up the place.

The '404' jet that took them everywhere ferried them back to Miami again. Lamont, Harmon and David Muggs, the entire gang loved it as much as John did. It was their kind of place. Ophelia needed the break from the campaign, and John was going to do his best to make it happen.

John had not told Ophelia that the trip had another purpose. David Muggs was to get a look at Miguel Hernandez if he showed up at Tobacco Road, and to give him some real Memphis-style advice. It was time a message was sent to Hernandez, John thought.

John took his penthouse at The Ritz South Beach now that Danny was out of it and there was plenty of room for everyone. David Muggs had found out that Hernandez was living in South Florida now and was making all the campaign events when Danny Carson was in the state. That was obviously how he first spotted Ophelia back in Coral Gables. He must have followed her to the Tobacco Road from the hotel that night with Corky.

John was worried Hernandez may be dangerous and he didn't know if Miguel knew the truth about his father's death. For that matter, John really didn't know how Ramon had died, just that he made his exit at an opportune time for Danny Carson to benefit from his demise. Harmon had handled it all.

But John wanted to show Ophelia around his 'playground' first. He had a 72-foot long Hatteras yacht docked not far from the hotel on Biscayne Bay. He loved it like a child and had not been able to use it as Roberta had coveted it too, taking it out every time she was in Miami with her friends, some of whom John suspected as being a little too close for comfort, too close for fidelity at that.

John had named it 'The Roberta' but by now he had the name changed.

"Ophelia, I want you to meet the '*Ophelia*'," John said to a wide-eyed and shocked Ophelia Hartwell.

The paint was barely dry as Ophelia squealed that she had never had a boat named for her. Originally a 63-footer, John had the aft deck lengthened years ago. She, like Ophelia, was well-equipped. The main salon had 275 square feet of living space and boasted a crew quarters as well as three spacious suites. It was luxurious.

"Mr. Thompson, this is fabulous," was all Ophelia could say as she watched David Muggs start to work with his black box, sweeping the boat for security.

"It's just a toy, my girl. Just a toy," John said as Lamont and Harmon wheeled him on board.

And it was a toy that John was determined to play with more. Now that he was enjoying life more, even if from a wheelchair, he told Ophelia that they would come there at least once every month, or as often as she wanted. Harmon and Lamont often brought their families in as well and loved to cruise over to Freeport, Bahamas where John had a small oceanfront home. It was paradise found.

Muggs had just completed his electronic sweep as they cruised past South Pointe Park, a beautiful day to be alive, thought John. Ophelia was in the wheelhouse with John and the crew, Lamont and Harmon in the galley making drinks. Muggs was never far away from Ophelia, just like John had ordered.

John wasn't much of a deep-sea fisherman, preferring the lakes and ponds back home. But he indulged Ophelia's request to catch a few fish while they were out. Nothing big, just some snapper and jack. Just like back home, they fried them up in the galley and had a feast replete with a fine wine and after-dinner Black Jacks and cigars.

The crew took them back to the marina just before dark, everyone, especially John, tired and sunburned from the trip, all of them turning in early. They would not try to make the Tobacco Road club tonight. It would take David Muggs a day to make sure the club was safe, and that his trap for Miguel Hernandez was set.

✤ ✤ ✤

Harmon had made sure B. B. King was at the Tobacco Road the next night, even though his next scheduled engagement was two months away. John and Ophelia loved his music and she liked the fact that he and John shared a Beale Street past, coming up during the same time in the 1940's.

B. B. met them at the door and joined them for the first Black Jack at John's table. Harmon and Lamont were going to stay for the first set of the show and then take off for the hotel with John. John told Ophelia he wanted her to stay so B. B. wouldn't be offended that they all had left early. He was still tired from the yacht trip and recovering from the illness. She didn't mind. She loved the place and the music.

David Muggs would stay with her, watch her and hope to see Miguel Hernandez. Muggs had obtained a photograph from Nicaragua from the days when Ramon was friends with John. It was one taken at John's estate on Lake Nicaragua on the occasion of Miguel's birthday, a party that John hosted for the dictator and his son.

Ophelia didn't have a clue that the reason for the visit was to draw Miguel out. It did cross her mind that this was the spot where she had seen the same man she had seen in Coral Gables. But she now had a name for his haunting face, and the alleged reason he was stalking John through her. She knew Muggs was watching and felt safe. John would never let anything happen to her, she thought.

Muggs would stay at a separate table and watch. Ophelia was enjoying the music, watching the diverse crowd dance and cheer B. B. on as they drank and partied. It was just like she remembered when she brought Corky in a few months ago. She wondered where he was now. That mystery was never quite cleared up by John. All she knew was that Corky, unknown to Danny Carson, was on their team now.

Ophelia thought she would go to the bar and order a mojito in honor of Corky. The service wasn't timely since the club was packed as usual. She made a stop at the restroom in the back when she made the discovery that had been missed by Muggs.

Muggs had made a big mistake by not going ahead and violating the fire code and locking the back door, the only one Tobacco Road had. Miguel Hernandez was waiting just outside it. Muggs wasn't far behind Ophelia as she headed for the restroom when he saw the back door was cracked open. It was then that he realized his mistake. But it was too late.

Ophelia already had the note in her hand as she went into the restroom. Muggs wasn't going to risk starting a panic by going in behind her. Whatever was in the note, he would have to answer to John as to how it made it into Ophelia's hands.

Ophelia hadn't seen Miguel's face clearly enough to be frightened when he shoved the note toward her. She dropped it as soon as she saw who it was and had only picked it back up as Muggs made it to the door. She thought twice about even reading it, thinking instead she should give it to Muggs who surely couldn't be far away.

At once, Ophelia felt very afraid, wondering how Miguel had gotten into the club, how Muggs could have let him get that close. Suddenly the rest room was a threatening, dangerous place without Muggs there. Was there someone else in the room?

Ophelia darted back out the door to find Muggs waiting just outside, apparently still trying to decide whether or not he should barge in anyway.

"Did you see what happened, David?" Ophelia asked as Muggs dropped his head, dejected and dismayed he hadn't caught Miguel in time.

"I did. Are you going to tell Mr. Thompson?"

"Not unless you tell him I have this note, David. I haven't read it, but I will. You keep your mouth shut and I will too," she said firmly.

David just nodded his head, resigned to the compromise he would regret making.

Chapter Twenty

Whom Do You Trust?

"You are in danger. I want to help you. I know you can't talk to me in Miami. I will come to Memphis. Just leave instructions in an envelope under your suite door tonight. I will be there," the staccato note read.

Ophelia was conflicted on what to do. Her loyalty and gratitude to John was of paramount importance to her. If she told John what had happened, much less about the note, she would surely never know, and never feel at ease. Besides, she would be smothered with more security, more than she could live with. John wouldn't want her to be miserable.

Ophelia's mind raced as she sought to find an answer. Could this be the work of Marvin and Hennie, an attempt to separate her from John? Or was the threat real? How could she be in danger? Her thoughts kept going back to the night in New York at Peter Luger's Steakhouse when John later told her about Miguel, of his claims that John was responsible for Ramon Hernandez's death, of Julio Fuentes's curious comment about her being 'good' for Nicaragua.

She decided she wanted answers. She would leave the note for Miguel under the door after she was sure everyone was in bed. "Meet me on Thursday at 10:00 PM in the Birmingham, Alabama airport. I will have security watching. I will not meet you without some protection. I have told no one of your note except for my security man. Take it or leave it. These are my terms," was her brief note. Ophelia was always one to get straight to the point.

The security caveat was a bluff. In this encounter, Ophelia could trust no one to know of this meeting. It was a calculated risk, but one she was prepared to take.

Ophelia would be haunted by the thought, the realization that she was doing something behind John's back. She felt like a traitor. But she was always her own woman, not someone who could be bought, sold, or controlled – at worst, lied to by someone she trusted and loved. She had been that way since she was a little girl, never one to be patronized or told what to do.

Since childhood, growing up in Franklin she learned to depend on herself first, to trust her instincts. After all, they had brought her this far. She thought to change now would be foolish. She knew she could not continue in this new life she was making with John Henry Thompson, with Danny Carson and all that life included without knowing more.

The rest of the trip in Miami was clouded with the events of Tobacco Road. Many years later Ophelia would visit the club to just sit and think about what had happened as she and the gang were there that night listening to B. B. King. She remembered how she must have been the only one not waiting for Miguel to appear, of how it was a defining moment in her life, one of those more grave major events, the ones that change your life forever.

"I need to stop by and see my family for a day or two, Mr. Thompson. Then I'll be on to Memphis. I don't think I'll need David in little old Franklin," she told John, for once catching him off guard.

"You take your time, girl. Do you want me to fly you up there in the '404'?"

"No, there's commercial air service into Birmingham. Franklin's only about 60 miles from there and I'll get a rental car. I'd like to surprise them. It's been a while."

John understood that line. He had waited too long to see his family when he was building the empire that started on Beale Street. His parents only lived a few years into his success, only enjoyed the new house John had built them for a short time. It was tragic and John always regretted not spending more time in Slabtown. John would give Ophelia her space. He wanted Ophelia to go.

⚜ ⚜ ⚜

Ophelia made sure no one was following her, as best she could tell, when she departed The Ritz at South Beach for Miami International to catch her flight to Birmingham. Birmingham wasn't an international airport in the 1980's and it wouldn't be hard for Miguel to spot Ophelia or difficult for someone to see she was meeting him either. She had to be careful.

Ophelia saw him immediately as she deplaned in Birmingham. He was bold in showing himself so soon, she thought. His eyes met hers, and she was more nonchalant, moving straight to the baggage claim instead of saying a word, not even acknowledging his presence.

Ophelia was looking for signs of David Muggs, or any Muggs-like characters, anyone that may appear to be interested in her being in Birmingham, much less in whether or not she was meeting someone. Miguel followed her at a discrete distance. He had already done his counter-surveillance and spotted no one of interest, no one suspicious, even though he believed Ophelia's claim of being watched for her own protection. He knew the resources John and

Ophelia had at their disposal. He would take that chance in order to talk with her.

Ophelia claimed the one bag she had brought, the rest being flown on the '404' jet back to Memphis with John and the gang. She made her way to the rental car counter and arranged for a car, a quick process at such a small airport.

Ophelia motioned to Miguel with her eyes, a glance toward the parking lot meaning she wanted him to follow her. She thought it best that they talk outside the terminal giving her one more chance to spot anyone that may follow.

Miguel understood her signal and followed her out the door into the crisp air. It was a beautiful night and Ophelia was immediately reminded of home, a thought that somehow comforted her in what she was doing. She was determined to get to the bottom of this, but at once had a feeling of dread. Had she made a mistake in agreeing to meet this man?

Miguel touched her arm causing Ophelia to stop short of the rental car. It was one of those moments where you don't know whether to run or stand and fight. 'Flight or fight' John would say. She would see this through.

"I think you know who I am. My father is dead because of Danny Carson and John Thompson, your boss," Miguel said with a voice Ophelia thought to be unusually calm, almost a whisper.

Ophelia turned slowly, not knowing what to expect in Miguel's face, his expression, and his eyes. It was as close as she had been to him and she was amazed at the calm she saw. This man was almost regal in his appearance, with the proverbial tall, dark and handsome looks of what she thought a Latino movie star would resemble.

Always straight to the point, Ophelia said calmly, "And *what proof* do you have, sir?"

Miguel, still touching her arm reeled, was caught off-guard,

199

and did not have an answer. It was because he didn't have any solid proof, only the suppositions borne of circumstantial evidence, of rumors gleaned from his father's associates in Nicaragua. He lacked the kind of proof one needs for court, but sufficient to make accusations, to spark a search for the real proof that would answer the questions yet to be answered in his mind, those of how his father really died.

"I don't have any. But they are the only people that wanted him dead, at least the only ones with the power to have it done and get away with it. I know Mr. Thompson put my father in office. I've heard them speak of it all my life. My father did exactly what Mr. Thompson said. No questions asked."

Ophelia somehow sensed grains of truth in what he was saying, even though she knew of the turmoil that existed in his country long before his father's death. But somehow it sounded just like John. She knew Ramon Hernandez and John were right there at The Point together, sharing the barracks John had shown her on their trip up the Hudson River.

But she also knew that Ramon Hernandez's rise to power was mostly a right of passage, an inheritance from his brother, the Nicaraguan strongman before Ramon.

But Ophelia did not believe that John had caused Miguel's father's death. It suddenly dawned on Ophelia to ask the simple question of 'what do you want from me?'

What could she do to answer Miguel's questions and why should she? Above all, why did Miguel think she was in danger?

"Listen, I don't believe Mr. Thompson could harm a fly, much less kill your father. You'll never make me believe any differently," Ophelia told Miguel who took it to heart immediately. In the event he was wrong about John, he still believed to a certainty that Carson was behind it and that John was behind him, that John had made him.

"The only reason I met with you is to find out why you think I am in danger."

"Danny Carson is the real reason my father is dead. I know that," Miguel said knowing he had Ophelia's attention.

"My people tell me that Carson got rid of my father through Mr. Thompson – and I believe that too. I also believe Danny Carson owes a great debt to Mr. Thompson, one he will never be able to repay. I believe Carson will use you to keep Mr. Thompson at bay. And that means you are in a great deal of danger," Miguel warned her.

Ophelia could see this man was sincere in his belief that John had something to do with Ramon's death. He had tears of deep pain, not anger, in his eyes that she could see were evidence of his sincerity. She also knew that it stood to reason that what was good for Danny was good for John, at this point a disturbing fact.

"Get in the car," Ophelia said as Miguel took her bag and put in the back seat. "We're going for a ride."

Miguel started to cry uncontrollably as Ophelia drove out of the airport. He had finally succeeded in getting someone to listen, someone who mattered and had access to the resources he would need to find answers.

He told her his father's body was not autopsied. All they were told was that Ramon 'died in his sleep', code for execution in his country. The family wasn't even allowed to bury the body. The new regime thought it too risky, a possible rallying point for any leftover opposition. But Miguel looked and acted more frustrated than angry.

"I know you are close to Mr. Thompson. If you don't believe him to be the man responsible for my father's death, then please help me in finding who is. My country is in turmoil as much now as it ever was when my father was in power. It will be as big a problem in the future for the United States as it has been in the past," Miguel pleaded.

Ophelia just drove, sensing she should tread carefully with Miguel, more careful than even before. There was no doubt in her mind now that he was on what he thought was a justified crusade to learn the truth. But she had to know why he thought there had been foul play. She also suddenly felt a rush of fear realizing she had just put a strange Nicaraguan man in her car who may now think *she* had something to do with his father's death.

"Are you saying you believe your father was killed? That he did not die a natural death?" Ophelia asked, just now realizing and feeling the full force of the accusation that Ramon Hernandez had been more or less executed to enhance Danny Carson's position in the Senate, in the world's eyes as being the great foreign policy guru, and in the end to further his Presidential bid.

"That's exactly what I've been trying to tell you. Danny Carson is an evil man," Miguel said, fully recovered from his tearful state.

"He had him killed!"

Ophelia stopped the car having made a full circle back to the airport, a fact missed by Miguel. She knew the area well having flown in and out of Birmingham for many years. She wasn't going to stray too far away from the relative safety of the airport. She had heard enough and, tough as she was, she was getting scared. She put on her best, most stern face.

"Now Mr. Hernandez, let me get this straight. Danny Carson wanted your father dead," she began as Miguel nodded vigorously.

"And you think that Mr. Thompson had something to do with it, no, *had* it done?"

"Not only that, Miss Hartwell. I believe Mr. Thompson will

be running this country as soon as Carson is elected."

"I'll tell you this. I'm no genius, but as far as believing Mr. Thompson killed someone, well, as we say around here, you're about as full of shit as a Christmas turkey!" she screamed, hoping nothing would be lost in the translation.

"Get out. Call me at this number, no have someone you trust, someone without your accent call me in one month. I'll have your answer," Ophelia ordered as Miguel opened the door, taking her card with her number at The Peabody.

"But one thing's certain, you'd better go along with the truth that I find, or I swear before God Almighty you won't be long for this earth," she said sternly, turning another Southern phrase on certain death.

With that, Ophelia drove away leaving Miguel staring after her, mouth open. He had gotten her attention, and she had his.

Chapter Twenty-One

You *Can* Go Home Again

Ophelia needed to decompress, that's putting it mildly enough. She was confused, concerned and amazed at the circumstances she had found herself living in now. And she was hurt. John had clearly not told her everything.

She felt a strong need to see her family. Ophelia never thought that returning home to Franklin would feel so good, like someone giving her a big warm hug, embracing her with the familiarity she grew up with. Her tough upbringing suddenly didn't feel so bad. It was comforting.

Franklin was dead center between Atlanta and Birmingham, just over the Alabama line into Georgia, not far from where she attended college at Auburn University. A town of just a few hundred people, Ophelia's parents actually lived up the Chattahoochee River north of town at a little bend in the river called Daniel Shoals.

It was a pretty place, simple and slow in the pace of the lives people lived. Ophelia's memories of Slabtown, Kesterson's store, all of her experience with John flooded back as she realized just how similar the two places were. Small town America, she thought, everywhere and nowhere, a Mayberry of sorts.

She really would be surprising her parents since they hadn't seen her since her odyssey with John Henry Thompson had begun. No one ever came out to the homestead, or what was left of it.

There was no reason. Her mother and father, 'Mom and Pop' to her, stayed on the go all the time. When they weren't fishing in the Chattahoochee they were 'downtown' as they called the three stores and restaurant that were Franklin.

Mom and Pop couldn't imagine who would be pulling up at almost midnight, but it didn't surprise Ophelia that they were still awake. That new satellite dish she had bought them, one of the huge ones that looked like something from outer space, entertained them up into the late night hours.

Pop grabbed his double-barrel 12-gauge shotgun as he stepped onto the porch.

"Stand and deliver," he yelled from the porch as he flipped the light switch. It was Pop's favorite saying from the old country, one Ophelia never could convince him actually was used by highway robbers and not homeowners putting trespassers on notice.

"It's just me, Pop, Ophelia."

Pop propped his gun up against the wall and joined Mom in bear-hugging Ophelia at the car. They could move pretty quickly when they wanted.

"What's wrong, what's wrong? Are you sick? Get in this house and let me take a good look at you!" Mom cried wiping her face with her apron.

It was just as if she had never left. Even at the late hour, the house oozed the smells of cornbread, apple pie and freshly cleaned catfish from the river. Before she could sit down, a plate was made up for her and a tray table set in front of the television. The folks hardly ever ate at the dining table anymore. The 'front parlor' with the satellite television was their home base now.

She was home now and she felt safe. But no one ever saw David Muggs's truck parked in the woods down the road. He wondered what had taken her so long to get there.

⚜ ⚜ ⚜

Ophelia stayed only two days. She visited the family, her sister and brother mostly, just sat around and talked about who was pregnant, where her old school buddies were. But the more Ophelia stayed, the more she remembered why she left. It was as if time had stood still in Franklin, Georgia, like one of those *Twilight Zone* episodes on television. Old Thomas Wolfe did know what he was talking about, all that about not being able to go home again.

She felt trapped in Franklin, suffocated. She had lived this life already and didn't want to go through it all again. Sure, it was great seeing her family, but the more she trod the ground she had walked so many years ago, the more she missed her new life, the one with John.

Even though that life was fraught with uncertainty now, it was the one she had made for herself with the hard work and tenacity she exhibited in Atlanta, in Memphis and on a nationwide campaign for the highest office in the land. She had built upon what she had learned at home, but Franklin could never reclaim her.

Muggs left his post the day after Ophelia arrived. He hadn't dared follow her from the airport the night she made it to Birmingham. Instead, he had come up to Birmingham a day before Ophelia, secure in the knowledge that Ophelia would spend her last day in Miami in the company of John, Lamont and Harmon. He didn't imagine Ophelia had enough time at the airport to get into any trouble.

Besides, David Muggs, a black man, stood out like a sore thumb in rural all-white Franklin, Georgia and it was time for him to leave. John had told him only to make sure she got to Franklin okay and then break off his surveillance. John was just worried, that's all. He knew Ophelia was tired.

John had sent the '404' jet for Ophelia to Birmingham. He wanted her back as soon as possible as Marvin and Hennie were amazingly giving him hell again with Hennie's 'conniption fits' and

Marvin's meddling. They were upset because of Roberta's sudden departure and had questions. They knew something was up when the matter of the London apartment was dropped so suddenly. Hell, Roberta was too much like them to give up that easily.

Marvin and Hennie had taken to drinking lately. The video episodes had taken their toll on them and their marriage. They rarely spent much time together and saw each other only in passing at The Peabody. Marvin was careful, ever so careful, at least in managing the affairs of the team. Spring training was coming up and deals were being made for players. Harmon Vance was always watching.

Marvin spent his time barhopping, but staying clear of Beale Street and its environs afraid that John would find out. He was alone now, having been stripped of his Friday night rendezvous with Lucy and sought refuge in the bottle.

Hennie and Lucy had become close, real close. Where she had been a Frigidaire with Marvin, she had found a friend extraordinaire in her firebrand accomplice Lucy. They spent many hours together taking up the slack in Marvin's absence. Hennie didn't care where he went. Their marriage was basically over.

Lamont and Harmon met Ophelia at the Memphis hangar, curiously without John. Ophelia wondered how and when she would approach John with her questions. She could figure no way to independently confirm or refute what Miguel had told her. She would have to just go head-on with John and ask him. Then, she would rely on her instincts. Only then would she know how to react.

"Where are we going, Harmon? We missed the turn on Beale. I love to ride down that street," Ophelia asked as the limo made its way straight down Riverfront Drive and past Beale.

"We're going just up the street here, Ophelia. I want you to see something," Harmon told her as she was now leaning toward the river side of the car.

The limousine pulled up at a brick building with the name 'Thompson' faintly visible on the riverfront side. She knew this was the old Thompson Building John's brother had bought many years ago, but she had never been inside it.

John was waiting in front in his wheelchair. Lamont smiled at Ophelia as he opened the door. David Muggs was with John.

"Come here, girl. I've got something to show you!" barked John as she hugged and kissed him.

The entire group got into the elevator in a lobby that bore evidence of newly completed construction and fresh paint. Ophelia realized that since she had known John Henry Thompson, she never had to wait long for a surprise event to occur. Although John had earlier given her a clue as to what was about to happen, she wasn't prepared for what she was to see and feel.

The elevator opened directly into the sixth floor of the old Thompson Building, into what used to be Gordon and John's offices. But instead of offices, the entire floor was now a luxurious townhouse replete with a river view that extended the length of the building.

"This is all for you, girl. Hell, you've got a better view of the river than I do at The Peabody!" John exclaimed as he waved his usual approval over the site.

It was spectacular and complete. Furnished much like John's penthouse with leather furniture and lots of wood paneling, the finishing touch was one of the old stadium seats from the Ballpark at Memphis, the ones John saved before he renovated the field. And Ophelia was for once, again, almost speechless.

"Mr. Thompson, I don't know what to say!" she yelled.
As Lamont poured champagne, filling all their glasses for a toast,

Ophelia did not realize she had tears streaming down her face. As they toured the three-bedroom townhouse, John told everyone where the old offices used to be, including the one at the southern corner where John's was so briefly those forty years ago.

As Ophelia just looked around in awe John told her, "I sat here for a total of two days before I figured out I needed to go out on my own girl! Right, Lamont?"

"I remember, John. Can you believe he'd rather have been down at the old Union Hotel with me, Ophelia?" Lamont said, smiling as he always did when John included him in one of the stories of the good old days.

"Yes, I can Lamont. I'd like to think I would have done the same thing," Ophelia said as she hugged John, Lamont and Harmon in a group hug.

"Well, come on downstairs. I've got something else to show you," John said as Lamont refilled everyone's glass.

The old elevator seemed to take an eternity to get to the ground floor. Ophelia's mind was awash with regret of having met with Miguel Hernandez. She almost could not look John in the eye, afraid that he would sense what she now thought to be betrayal. As she rolled John out into the foyer he pointed to the front door.

"You need something to get around Memphis in while you're here, girl."

She could only see one thing – a forest green, shiny Mercedes-Benz E-Class sitting right outside the front door. Muggs had brought it around and Lamont stepped outside and opened the driver's side door.

"It's one of those new ones they're putting out now, just the right size for Memphis. Take it for a spin. We'll go back up to the townhouse and wait for you!" John commanded.

Ophelia couldn't believe it. She drove up and down the river and felt on top of the world. The events of the last few days were a million miles away. Her fears of John's involvement in Ramon Hernandez's death evaporated as did her checking to see if she was being followed, 'protected' as John would say of the presence of David Mugg's Range Rover not far behind.

She pulled back up to the townhouse with all kinds of questions and expecting no answers. Sure, John had said she would need, no, that he *would get* her a place and a car since she had moved to Memphis. But this was fairytale land.

David Muggs got out of the Range Rover and followed Ophelia into the elevator, her feet hardly touching the floor.

"David, did he find out about our ordeal with Roberta? I mean this is incredible."

"No, he genuinely cares about you Ophelia. He's just trying to make the people he loves happy. Hell, he gave me that Range Rover out there!" Muggs said as they rode up the elevator.

"Please, just live here, drive the car - make the old man happy. He wants you to have all this. And I hope you know; it's yours, not a loan, not temporary!"

As the door opened to find the gang back looking out at the Mississippi, Ophelia said, "Mr. Thompson, this is too much. I can't accept all this!"

"You've earned it – and you're going to earn it. Anyone that can handle Danny Carson, Marvin and that damned Henrietta the way you do! I need you here and happy!"

Ophelia shot Muggs a look acknowledging their secret encounter with Roberta. If John only knew.

They finished the champagne and listened to John's stories about the old days in Memphis. This was definitely not the day to talk with John about Miguel.

Chapter Twenty-Two

California, Here We Come

"How do you feel about California, girl?" John asked Ophelia, forever catching her off guard now.

"The land of fruits and nuts? A nice place to visit, well, you know the rest," Ophelia conveyed, knowing all too well John would get her meaning.

"That's pretty good! Let's go out and have a look around. We need to make sure it hasn't changed any!" John told her.

John had received a call from an old friend, one he had kept at a distance but at the same time close at hand. Truman Forsythe was living his dream, mostly courtesy of John Henry Thompson and the seed money that John had given him since the 1950's to get through law school, the Attorney General's office and his long term service as the state's Republican Governor.

John always thought Truman would make a good President, if only he was a little more ruthless, willing to grab power at any cost. But Truman was actually one of the good guys. He was living his dream on 'the left coast' as John called the more liberal side of America, even though Truman was about as conservative as you could get.

Truman was good at building partnerships, coalitions that include the diverse strata of Californians that ran the gamut from Hollywood liberals to migrant farm workers. He had become a legend there – fighter pilot hero from Korea, superstar lawyer and political genius – and member of John's Class of 1946. A controversy never darkened his door.

Forsythe had asked John personally for a meeting, something he had never done before. John, for his part always wanting to stay in the shadows, content with working through his straw men, acquiesced and agreed to come out on the '404' jet for a few days. 'What the hell', John thought. Since the stroke, he was starting to enjoy life more every day.

The flight out gave John plenty of time to fill Ophelia in on Truman. She knew about Truman, everyone in America did. He was a rising star. It had even been rumored that he would go up against Danny Carson, his classmate at The Point for the big show campaign.

Harmon Vance, Lamont Boone and David Muggs made the trip too. Harmon hadn't seen much of Truman since The Point. It would be a reunion of sorts, he thought.

John had agreed to meet in Laguna Niguel south of Los Angeles where he kept a suite at another of his favorite Ritz hotels, the Ritz-Carlton at Laguna Niguel. It had a splendid view of the Pacific being on a bluff over 150 feet above the ocean. Located halfway between Los Angeles and San Diego, it allowed John the flexibility to fly into or out of either city, freeing the gang up to travel wherever they wanted.

John told Lamont to take the limousine up the Pacific Coast Highway. He loved the view and the smell of the ocean air. John never was much one for traffic of any kind, much less the nightmare of Interstate 5. Any chance he had, he preferred the small, less-traveled roads, anything to remind him of home, even if he was a world away from it.

Truman was already at The Ritz and had taken a suite in

someone else's name, wanting no one to know he was in town. He had even left his usual entourage of Governor's Security men at Sacramento, preferring to travel with his personal assistant, Justin Thornton, an old friend from his time in Korea.

Truman called John's suite the minute John and the gang arrived. Harmon was taking the calls and the two chatted briefly about graduation day at The Point and the fact that it had been forty years since that momentous event.

At the end of the call, Harmon told John that Truman wanted to meet alone. John would set the rules and told Harmon to invite Truman up to the penthouse. Harmon would stay for now.

Truman Forsythe was probably the best guy, the best all-round guy out of the Class of '46. He was a legal scholar, a good husband and father, a bona fide war hero fighter jock and had done wonders for California. Good looking and personable, he was the perfect Presidential candidate. John wondered why he hadn't run.

Truman hadn't seen John in about six years, much less since the illness. He was prepared for how much he had changed and didn't skip a beat as he gave John a big hug. He shook Harmon's hand, understanding that John had made the decision that Harmon would stay for the meeting. Ophelia and Lamont had excused themselves before Truman arrived and had gone out onto the balcony to watch the sea.

"John, how are you holding up? You look strong," Truman said in earnest. He knew John was a fighter, never one to give in to illness or any other opponent.

"I'll be okay, Truman. This has just made me that much meaner and determined to live a full life. I'm enjoying myself more than ever," John said as Harmon nodded.

They talked of the old days at The Point, the three of them putting up with Cadet Sergeant Mark Davis, all of them amazed that Davis had made it to the rank of full General, four stars, and how he was now at the Joint Chief's office in the Pentagon.

"He's not such a bad guy Truman. I helped him get those stars. He's returned the favor many times over, especially when he was in charge of the US Army's Southern Command in Panama."

Truman didn't dare ask what that meant. He had read with interest what had happened to Ramon Hernandez.

Truman made John acutely aware of his deep-seated appreciation of John's help throughout the years. He knew that without John's support after he left the Air Force, he would not have been able to make it this far. Sure, Truman had the intellect and everything else it took to get to the top, but John's money and contacts, his synergy, helped get Truman get there quicker and easier.

Truman understood that without John's monetary support for those many struggling years, Truman may not have been the effective 'King of California' as *Time Magazine* had named him the year before. And John knew his appreciation was sincere. Truman was *not* a Danny Carson.

"Truman, you know back in the early fifties when you came to me wanting some help, I didn't hesitate to give it to you. You're a good man, one of the best people I know, a real public servant. For the life of me, you must be. Otherwise you could be a really wealthy man. What can I do for you? You name it," John said.

"John, it's hard for me to say this, to ask for your help," Truman started.

Harmon sensed he needed to give John the option of having him leave the room. Truman was a good man and he thought it might be humiliating for him to have to ask whatever he wanted of John in Harmon's presence.

"John, I'll go and check on Ophelia and Lamont," Harmon offered.

"You do that Harmon – and fix us all a Black Jack while you're out there. I sense a toast in the making."

Truman took a breath and waited for Harmon to leave the room.

"Thanks, John. I'll be brief. You know my goal in life, the one I told you I had since I was at The Point?" Truman started.

"You don't have to say another word, Truman. You'd make a fine Chief Justice of the US Supreme Court! When's Warren Burger leaving?" John asked to Truman's relief.

Truman let forth an audible sigh. He went on to explain, very confidentially he said, that Warren Burger had told him he would retire within the year, but wanted to wait until the new President was elected in order to give the man the chance to nominate his own Chief Justice, hopefully Burger's friend, Truman. He wanted John to use his influence over Danny Carson, if elected President, to nominate Truman – if John could get him to do it.

"He'll be elected, Truman. I'm behind him. Besides, you may be able to do me a favor some day. Don't worry about it. You're in!"

Just then, as if on cue, as if not to give Truman a chance to respond to John's comment, his caveat on the nomination, his conditions; Harmon Vance entered from the balcony and handed them both drinks.

"Let's toast to it, Truman. Here's to our success!" crowed John as he leaned from his wheelchair to Truman.

Hell, Truman Forsythe didn't even drink. As a sign of agreement, of respect, he simply took the glass and met John's half way. Harmon just smiled as they cemented the deal. He knew what Truman wanted. He knew what John wanted. Harmon was again amazed at John Henry Thompson and how far they all had come since The Point.

⚜ ⚜ ⚜

John brought Ophelia and Lamont into the penthouse and introduced them to Truman before he left. John knew Truman would not want to be seen in public, preferring this meeting to be secret that day and forever. John had known why Truman wanted to see him, it could only have been that one thing Truman didn't have, the only office he hadn't risen to since that meeting in Memphis so many years ago.

And John knew he had gotten his return from his investment. Beyond Truman being good for California all these years, he could do better work on The Court, especially as Chief Justice, John thought. A select few people would know just how Truman got there, indeed how he had made it so far. That was alright with John.

John was tired and everyone could see it. They had dinner on the balcony of the penthouse and watched the sunset as everyone had Black Jacks and Cubanos. Ophelia had come to like cigars herself and generally would enjoy one with the rest of the gang now.

Truman had instinctively liked Ophelia. He thought her to be a real person and found no surprise in the fact that John had befriended her. A quick study of human behavior like John, it was comforting to Truman when he watched Ophelia and John laugh and talk. John deserved a good friend, he thought.

Harmon and Ophelia would let John turn in early, leaving Lamont at the penthouse to look out for him. Since Ophelia had never been to this part of Southern California, John had asked Harmon to take her on a tour of all the art galleries that night. It would be a good opportunity to ask Harmon a few questions.

Ophelia loved art – Impressionist, Old Masters, even California art. She had even recognized a Joseph Kleitsch painting at John's penthouse in Memphis. John had thought that pretty sharp for a girl from Franklin, Georgia.

Harmon and Ophelia walked arm-in-arm looking through the

galleries that lined the Pacific Coast Highway in Laguna Niguel. Harmon liked art too, but really wanted to get a feel for Ophelia's mood since she had been to see her parents.

"Ophelia, you know John really thinks a lot of you. That's the reason he gave you that apartment and Mercedes. He wants you to be happy – and to stay in Memphis," he said, waiting to gauge her reaction.

"I'm very happy, Harmon. And, you know, I wanted to let you know how much I appreciate you staying with Mr. Thompson after his illness. He depends on you and Lamont so much. I know you'd probably rather take some time off. You all mean a lot to him."

Harmon thought for a minute and chose his words carefully. He trusted Ophelia and wanted her to know she was truly one of the gang now.

"Ophelia, let me tell you something about John. He is one of the kindest people you will ever know. But he's been through a lot. Since this illness I believe all he wants to do is enjoy life – and you're a big part of that. So am I. And I intend to do everything I can for him. We've been through a lot together," Harmon told her softly. "He helped me many years ago when I needed it the most. I would do anything for him."

"So would I," Ophelia said.

With that, they had both put into words, knowing where each of them stood. They shared the commitment to John for a lifetime. Harmon had been there for many years. Ophelia felt like she had too. Harmon had sensed she would be a team player since the first time he had met her.

But more than that, Harmon knew Ophelia was good for John, in a sense keeping him alive and happy. He knew she had been through a life-changing experience signing on to the John Henry Thompson team. She even handled the pains in the ass that were

Marvin and Hennie. Not everyone could do that. Most people would have broken and run at the attacks, the problems with Roberta. She was John's go-getter alright. She would be okay.

"Harmon, I do have one question you may be able to help me with."

"Ask away. What's on your mind, Ophelia?"

"That thing with Ramon Hernandez and his son Miguel. Tell me about why Miguel thinks John had something to do with his death."

Harmon stopped to light another cigar, to collect his thoughts. He sensed that now was the time to tell Ophelia what she needed to know, the story according to Harmon, the truth. And he was grateful she had not asked John first.

"Ophelia, Ramon Hernandez was not a good man. He came from a long line of tyrants, of men who ruled with an iron fist."
As they continued strolling, Harmon's expression was enhanced by the cigar's fire and smoke as though he were telling a campfire story. And Ophelia was hanging on to every word.

"You see, we had all been at The Point together – John, Ramon, Danny, Truman and me, even Jerry Slater from Missouri."

Ophelia didn't interject that she knew every fact so far. She just listened, content that she was hearing a story, *any* story that may answer the questions, the only questions she had concerning John.

"After we all split up and went our separate ways, Ramon came to power in Nicaragua when his brother died under what were some pretty suspicious circumstances. His brother was no good either. He stole from the people, built up a fortune, pretty much was a tyrant. All the while, Danny Carson was making a name for himself in US politics, eventually on the Senate Foreign Relations Committee. And then comes Ramon. In many ways, he was even worse than his brother."

Ophelia began to fear for the worst, that John did cause Ramon's death to help Danny Carson.

"When Danny declared his candidacy, his biggest problem, and biggest chance for stardom, was Ramon Hernandez in Nicaragua. The country had gotten so bad that the US was worried that the Soviets would make it a puppet regime. Enter our John Henry Thompson. He was the only person that could influence Ramon, to get him to calm down his rhetoric. I mean, John helped Ramon maintain power through John's holdings in the country. You met Mr. Fuentes in New York, right?" Harmon asked her, making sure she was getting the linkage.

Ophelia just nodded her head as she wondered where this explanation was going.

But Harmon was to stop short of telling Ophelia everything, of the meeting at the Marietta Tower with Danny when the deal was made, of just how much Danny Carson owed John.

"Ophelia, all we did was to convince Ramon that he was to be overthrown – for his own good, before someone killed him and maybe even his family. We told him that things were getting so out of hand that he and his family were in grave danger. His response was to take his own life, thinking his son Miguel would take over. We just made sure Miguel didn't. We were all afraid it would just be business as usual. John didn't have anything to do with Ramon's death. Ramon did what he finally thought he should to protect Miguel, he killed himself with an overdose of pills."

Harmon paused before he delivered the last line he would need to satisfy Ophelia.

"But Danny Carson thinks John actually *had* Ramon killed – and he knows he owes him forever!" Harmon said definitively.

"You see, John's plantation, hell, Nicaragua itself is the one project left undone in John's life. He loves the place and wants the whole country to be like his plantation. I think you'll love it too. I believe John is counting on it, Ophelia."

Ophelia let a wry smile creep over her face. Now she knew what she had needed to know.

Chapter Twenty-Three

The Marvin and Hennie Show Redux

John knew it was time to get Ophelia back on the road. He felt that he and his gang should get back to Memphis and check in on the 'Marvin and Hennie Show', as he now called the continuing exploits of his son and daughter-in-law. David Muggs had reported the events of late, of Marvin and his barhopping around Memphis and how Hennie and Lucy had become close friends. The video surveillance was too risky now since the episodes of lust had been exposed. Muggs had to be content with reports from his spies at The Peabody and around Memphis to keep him abreast of their activities.

John was only concerned that the businesses, the ball team and property developments may be damaged due to Marvin and Hennie's antics. For John's part, he didn't care what they did otherwise, or so he thought.

Muggs reported that Hennie was unusually busy, taking up the slack when Marvin was out on his jaunts. And it appeared she was doing it all with Lucy right by her side.

"It's curious to me, David. See if you can tell what's going on. I want to make sure this Lucy girl is not trying to take Hennie for a ride. Lucy may be blackmailing her," John told Muggs. He wanted David to do a little video surveillance on his own.

It wouldn't be a difficult task. Since the incident with Marvin and Lucy, Hennie appeared to be letting her hair down. She was to be seen nightly with Lucy on, of all places, Beale Street, right down the road at Bumble's Billiards. They would shoot pool, drink beer and belly laugh at events of the day at The Peabody and about Marvin.

When John received David's first reports his curiosity peaked. He was upset that Hennie was laying out the business of The Peabody and The Thompson Group on Beale Street.

"Hell, David, find out what they're doing. I want to get this done with once and for all so I can get some peace of mind!" John commanded.

John was tiring of the business end of his life. He knew he would never be fully recovered from the stroke and was more determined than ever to have fun, travel as best he could and spend time with his friends, especially with Ophelia when she wasn't out with the Carson expedition.

"We'll get on them 24/7, Mr. Thompson. Something's going on here," David promised. And there was.

Muggs got his break on a Friday night, the night Lucy formerly had reserved for her rendezvous with Marvin. As usual, Hennie and Lucy spent a couple of hours at Bumbles right there with the 'little people' as Hennie used to call them, the plain good old folks that flocked to Beale Street to party. They left together in Hennie's Mercedes and ended up at Lucy's condominium on the river.

Lucy was making good money by putting up with Marvin and Hennie. She could afford the riverfront condo in a prime location near the river bridge, not far from where Ophelia now hung her hat.

Muggs couldn't believe what he saw. As he would tell John later, right there 'in front of God and everybody', he told John, Hennie planted a 'lip-lock' on Lucy as they went inside. Hennie's old Frigidaire sexual demeanor had become a blast furnace.

Hennie stayed into the night. Muggs called in additional surveillance, people Hennie or Lucy wouldn't know from The Peabody. It was clear from their reports that Hennie had jumped that great divide. Where she had been putting on a show in her bedroom with Lucy to shock and infuriate Marvin, as Marvin would put it, she had obviously come to like a little 'dark meat' herself.

"David, you'd better see what Marvin's up to," John told Muggs the next day. "This has turned into a damned three-ring circus around here!"

Marvin, so far, was just getting drunk. His humiliation at the hands of Harmon Vance at the hospital and then Hennie in the Lucy sexcapade had clearly ruined him. Muggs and his men had an easy chore following Marvin from bar to bar in an ever-widening ring away from downtown Memphis. That is, until he hit the Airways Boulevard area where he landed at Tiffany's Strip Club. That's when, as John aptly put it later, 'the shit hit the fan'.

Marvin had hit rock bottom. Muggs's men delivered a sordid report that had Marvin tipping the girls $100 bills in their g-strings while gulping down cheap champagne at a ridiculous $200 a bottle. It only got worse.

The professional working girls sensed an easy mark with the winner taking Marvin home with them. Marvin even let them drive his Mercedes. Still worse was the final report to John.

"Mr. Thompson, you've got to excuse me when I say this," Muggs started as John just cringed, "but you ain't going to believe this shit!"

Muggs gave John the blow-by-blow of how the night started, progressed through the $5,000 tab night at Tiffany's, and then just told John straightaway.

"And Mr. Thompson, well I don't know how to tell it."

"Damned, David. What'd he do, kill somebody?" John said

demanding to know the rest.

"Well, no. But the damned 'woman' he went home with was a damned man dressed like a woman. But she, or he, was damned good-looking!" Muggs told him now gasping for breath at the events of Marvin's 'lost weekend'.

John had suffered enough. He called Harmon Vance and Lamont Boone in.

"David, thanks for all your work. As you know, it goes without saying that this is very confidential," John told Muggs who nodded and left the room.

"Harmon, get Marvin and that damned Henrietta in here. It's time for a talk."

✤ ✤ ✤

"You two are the worst excuses for human beings that exist in this city, hell probably the state of Tennessee," John started as he met with the two in his office, alone.

"Now, I'm responsible for bringing you into the world Marvin, and into this business. You are responsible for bringing this woman into my world. But *I* am responsible for this business and for the Thompson name being attached to it. And, you two are not going to shame it by tear-assing all over Memphis with your fly down and dress up around your shoulders," John boomed as his eyes darted back and forth between Marvin and Hennie.

Marvin and Hennie's eyes did not rise from floor level. Both of them started crying uncontrollably, a fact that did nothing to subdue the tone or content of John's sermon. John thought later that it was as if a Sunday school teacher had just caught the two of them smoking 'rabbit tobacco' out behind the church when they were kids. They had been caught – again. And again it was their own undoing captured by John Henry Thompson. Would they ever learn?

"I want you both to know, that until the day I die I will make sure that your every moves are watched, recorded and reported to me. If you ever, *ever*, embarrass me like this again, I will disinherit you both and give all *this* to St. Jude's Hospital!"

At that last word Marvin and Hennie's eyes shot up to John's. For once, he had their attention.

"And now, I will be traveling, secure in the knowledge that you two will be good. Or am I harboring a misconception here?" Marvin and Hennie gasped a collective, "No sir!"

As bad as they were, they would be good from now on – as long as John was alive.

✦ ✦ ✦

John told Harmon just enough to let him know there was to be no expense spared in watching these two. He wasn't going to disinherit Marvin, but Marvin sure as hell didn't know that. There was lots of activity going on with the ball club, in Atlanta and the ever-growing business in Memphis. But John had made all the money he wanted to make.

Harmon assured John that all would be taken care of in Memphis. It would necessarily require another layer of trusted straw men, they both agreed, to ensure that no matter what Marvin and Hennie did, the business would survive and prosper. It would be John's legacy.

John was ready to head back to Miami and the warmer climates where he could enjoy his yacht and make short visits to Tobacco

Road. Harmon and Lamont would be with him until Ophelia could get back from the campaign.

Ophelia was rejuvenated from the California trip. Harmon's explanation of Ramon Hernandez and his death, the lack of John's direct involvement in it and the answers she had for Miguel put her at ease. The fact that Danny Carson owed such a debt comforted and emboldened her too.

Ophelia began to spend more time in Washington, DC as Carson balanced his obligations as a sitting Senator with those of a Presidential candidate. It was becoming harder to do with the campaign and fundraising heating up. His opponent, only recently decided, since the Democrats until then had been fighting among themselves, was a liberal Governor from Illinois, Luke Spearman.

Spearman had a lot of baggage. A war protestor during his college days during the Vietnam era, he didn't play to the Cold War, anti-communists that dominated American politics at the time. He had long hair and was starting to grow a beard, just as he had received the nomination. Ophelia thought that was funny.

The consensus opinion was that it was Danny's race to lose. That is, as long as he didn't make some stupid mistake. John always believed what old Senator Hugo Moore said about a 'shoo-in' type of candidate. "As long as he doesn't get caught in bed with a live boy or a dead woman, he'll win."

It was that kind of certainty.

Ophelia's suite was at The Mayflower Hotel on Connecticut Avenue just blocks away from the White House. The largest luxury hotel in DC, it was the watering hole for the big wigs, politicos and big-time journalists that covered the White House and the campaign. Corky Benedict had a suite there too and would meet Ophelia when she arrived.

Corky was enjoying his role as John's spy in the Carson

campaign. It hadn't taken Harmon and John long to convince him that John could do much more for him than Danny Carson ever could. Corky was smart enough to see who made people like Danny, Truman Forsythe in California and Jerry Slater in Missouri.

And he wanted to end up just like one of them.

One of the primary reasons John had gone after Corky was to learn more about Danny Carson's girlfriend, his paramour that could destroy his candidacy, and John's investment – something that could ruin 'the plan'.

"It's his press secretary, Ophelia. Emily Wright," Corky told Ophelia.

"Well, that's pretty high cotton! She's gorgeous, articulate and rich!" Ophelia shot back as they huddled at a corner table of the Mayflower Hotel lounge.

Emily had been a prime-time news correspondent for one of the networks for some time. She had been the beat girl for Capitol Hill and had extraordinary access to members of Congress. 'Gee', Ophelia thought, 'I can guess how she did it now'.

Still, it surprised everyone when she resigned her high-dollar news job to take on the task of being Danny's press secretary for the campaign. And Corky was the only person that knew the truth. He arranged the rendezvous times and places for the two. Although infrequent, they occurred at Danny's suite during the very early morning hours. Corky just made sure no one was around, or could get inside the suite.

Since Danny had been assigned Secret Service protection the job had become problematic since someone now had to tell them to back off and give Danny some space. Corky suspected the Service knew what was going on, but true to the nature of their jobs they kept whatever secrets they may have known.

It was time Ophelia had a talk with Danny. Corky was her

open line to him and all she had to do was send a message that she wanted a meeting. Danny had no idea Corky was, as John put it, 'playing both sides against the middle' and that Corky was leading him into harm's way.

That was the reason Ophelia was in Washington, DC. Danny was doing his Senatorial time that week and Corky would have no problem setting a meeting. It would take place on her turf at The Mayflower Hotel. It was familiar ground to her and removed the possibility of Danny setting up any sort of surveillance in her suite.

The meeting would happen that night.

Ophelia was certainly more confident now due to what she learned from Harmon Vance in California. She was going to take the initiative here and make her status as John's straw man clear to Danny. After all, this was her chance to get a piece of the future President for herself. In that concern, she had decided that she should make herself available to John in his efforts to reform Nicaragua as well.

Danny came alone as far as Ophelia could tell. He arrived at precisely 7:00 PM, just as Corky said he would.

"Ophelia, it's good to see you again. How's John?" Danny asked immediately, showing genuine concern.

"He's getting better every day. We've been doing a little traveling – and talking about you Danny. We're a little concerned."

Ophelia wisely used the collective 'we' when speaking of John and his involvement in the campaign. John had told her everything about Corky, of his first meeting, Corky's 'conversion' to being a straw man for John, all of it.

Danny quickly became uncomfortable. He knew his only weakness was Emily Wright. And it wouldn't surprise him if John Henry Thompson knew all about it.

"What's on your mind, Ophelia?" Danny asked, immediately

betraying his acceptance of Ophelia's status as John's stand-in.

"What's wrong?" he asked, never realizing the obvious, coy answer that would demand from Ophelia.

"It's what's Wright, but wrong – and it's spelled W-r-i-g-h-t, Danny. You've got a problem, the one that makes her money with her good looks and her mouth," Ophelia said coolly, staring the future President down as if he were a delinquent schoolboy. "And we've got to fix this immediately. John would want it that way."

The cool, debonair Danny Carson dissolved in front of Ophelia's eyes. He yanked at his $200 Hermes necktie as if it had suddenly turned into a noose and leapt from his seat. The clean and sober Danny needed a drink and Ophelia knew it. And she was ready. She already had one poured.

"Here Danny, have a Black Jack and water - we need to talk." Ophelia knew *exactly* what she wanted out of Danny Carson, and she wouldn't even have to use up John's favor to demand it. She realized that straw men get perks too. And she had a ready-made story to lay on Danny like a new suit from Marx's Men Store.

"Don't worry Danny, we can make all this go away. Miss Wright is a team player. You can still keep her around, even take her into the White House as your press secretary," she started as Danny gulped the Black Jack down.

"Don't even tell her that anyone knows. We'll break it to her gently," she said as Danny sat back down, at the same time somehow feeling trapped and calmed at the news.

"It's just something that happened," Danny said, invoking the age-old excuse of the straying spouse caught with his hand in the cookie jar.

"This will ruin me if anyone finds out!"

"It's over. Don't worry about it. Consider it a favor. But from now, until after the first Tuesday in November, keep your dick in your pants!" she said, invoking a phrase that her fellow Georgian would recognize as his last chance.

Danny snapped to attention as he did when Cadet Sergeant Mark Davis had just entered the room some forty years ago. He straightened his tie and looked for some sign that it was time for him to leave, if Ophelia was done with him.

Ophelia wasn't.

"By the way Danny, I have an intense interest in Nicaragua and its politics. I plan on spending a lot of time there at John's plantation and I think I'd like to be involved in seeing the country progress, in helping its people. I may even like a diplomatic post down there someday – the ambassadorship," she shot back to an interested and nodding Carson.

"You just let me know when. I'll take care of it. I've always been interested in getting good people involved in government, always interested Ophelia," he said as he backed toward the door in retreat, escape.

"I'll let you know. Just remember what we talked about Danny. I'll let John know you're okay," she said as he made his exit.

Ophelia would later remember hearing a "yes ma'am" coming from Danny's mouth as he closed the door.

"Did you get all that, David?" Ophelia said to the two-way mirror Muggs had installed in the suite.

Muggs stepped out from the adjoining room laughing, video camera in hand.

"I'm sorry Ophelia, but is *that* what's going to be leading the Free World?" he asked.

"No, your boss will be."

Chapter Twenty-Four

Back in Miami

John was anxious to learn how Danny Carson took the news that his secret was out. Harmon Vance and Lamont Boone had gone down to Miami with John to The Ritz at South Beach to get some sun with him on the boat.

Ophelia couldn't wait to get back out on the boat John had named for her. She didn't like spending too much time in DC, afraid that she may turn into 'one of them', her phrase for the horrible politicos that inhabited the capital city.

"Well, how'd he take it Ophelia? Did he take it like a man?" John asked her as she fixed herself a Black Jack on the aft deck of *The Ophelia.*

David Muggs just chuckled, stealing Ophelia's fire before she could tell John how Danny had come apart.

"Let's just say Danny Carson is walking the straight and narrow now. You could have knocked him over with a feather, Mr. Thompson. I don't think we have anything else to worry about from now on," she said as she gave John a hug. "As you're fond to say, 'you can stick a fork into him, he's done', Mr. Thompson."

John and the group laughed as *The Ophelia* headed out to open water. They could relax now.

John, Harmon and Lamont had been talking before Ophelia had arrived, and they had something to tell her. Harmon and Lamont had made the painful decision to retire from the Thompson Group, the ball team, Atlanta and Beale Street. John took the news in stride. He knew it was coming.

But he worried that Ophelia would be upset, feeling the gang she had come to know and trust was breaking up for good. He didn't want her to think that anything would change between them, that she somehow wouldn't have the backup she depended on all these months past.

"Girl, you know things change. Nothing's forever," John started as Ophelia feared the worst. She immediately had noticed that John looked weaker, but thought it was just the sun and ocean, from being back on the boat so soon.

"Are you okay," she asked as she searched Harmon and Lamont for an answer. Both of them looked away toward the horizon, increasing her fears that John's health had taken a turn for the worst.

"I'm about as well as can be expected considering the fact that Harmon and Lamont are deserting me," John said in a whimsical way so as to let Ophelia know he was happy for them. "But don't worry girl, I couldn't run them off forever if I tried."

Ophelia immediately hugged Harmon and Lamont and began to cry. She felt like she was losing members of her family, and in a way she was. The two of them had taken her in, reassured her of her position with John and made her feel at home. She would always be in touch, they were friends for life, she knew. But she was used to having them around every day. They were part of her new family.

"I'm going to stay down here in Miami, Ophelia. We only stayed around to help you get on your feet. It's obvious you're on stable ground," Harmon said as Ophelia gave him one of her trademark 'sister kisses'.

"Lamont, what are you going to do?" she asked as Lamont let

a tear slip. He had become attached to Ophelia and knew what she meant to his childhood friend.

"I'm going back to Slabtown, Ophelia, at least for a while. I'm going to build a community center so those kids can have a head start coming up. Heck, John was my head start, and I'm gonna' name it in his honor. Then, I'll probably spend time with my wife, Grace, down here in Miami with old Harmon."

Ophelia gave him another hug saying, "I'm going to come down and fish and go to Kesterson's store for lunch. You know Mr. Thompson will want to come down often. I know I'll see a lot of you, Lamont."

"There's someone I want you to meet, Ophelia," Lamont said as he waved toward the cabin of the yacht.

A young black man about thirty years old, looking curiously a lot like Lamont walked onto the deck and shook Ophelia's hand.

"My name's Arthur Boone, Miss Hartwell," he said looking directly into Ophelia's eyes while extending a firm hand.

"Lamont, you can't deny this one. He's darn sure your son," she said as Lamont laughed.

"Ophelia, Arthur here's going to be taking care of me from now on. I've known him since he was born at Baptist Hospital in Memphis. He's a fine man – and you can trust him," John said in that tone Ophelia knew so well, one of firmness and finality.

That would be good enough for her. Lamont Boone had Arthur running his share of the show at the Beale Street properties, the ball team, the shares John had rewarded him with over the years. Arthur was a team player, John would say. And he could keep the secrets.

"A toast!" John said. "To new beginnings and good friends! I treasure them both. That's what life is all about!"

⚜ ⚜ ⚜

Ophelia could see that John was getting tired and weaker. She felt that he had come back from the illness too quickly, had traveled too far and too often. While she had Harmon Vance as good counsel, she would try and get a handle on how he felt John was doing.

"Ophelia, all I can tell you is this. I've known John Henry Thompson for forty years, been all around the world with him. He's like a brother to me," Harmon said firmly.

"And he's going to do *exactly* what he wants to do, come hell or high water. He's his own man," he said, not exactly the detailed information and advice Ophelia wanted to hear.

"But, be sure in this. John loves you and trusts you. So do Lamont and I. We wouldn't be leaving if we didn't. Just take good care of him, and remember, we're just a phone call away," Harmon added for effect, making clear Ophelia had their confidence.

As they returned to the marina Ophelia had time to think, to digest all the day's momentous events on the boat. She should have seen it coming. With the advent of the new straw men being put in place to watch Hennie and Marvin back in Memphis, John was increasingly distancing himself from the operations of the business. She had to realize that she too was part of that, handling the political liaisons with Danny Carson, one of John's biggest prizes.

It all made sense now. John would be really retired, content in the money he had made, the properties he owned and the events he had put in motion with Danny Carson, Truman Forsythe and Jerry Slater in Missouri. Whatever else that had to be done – all of it would be on her now.

✤ ✤ ✤

John seemed to be more anxious to get off the boat than usual. Arthur was now wheeling him instead of Lamont. It looked like he

234

had been there all along. The two joked and laughed, looking at the pretty girls that were starting to emerge around South Beach now that the weather was getting warmer.

Harmon and Lamont bid them all goodbye at the hotel. They had brought their families down for a little boat time. They would make great use of the yacht now that they were retired, really retired too, like John.

But Arthur would always excuse himself after wheeling John into his penthouse, at least while there was other company present. Ophelia knew that although Arthur could be trusted, no one could ever rise to the level of trust earned by and bestowed upon Lamont Boone. He had been there from the start.

"Girl, things are going to be different from now on. I know I've said it before, but I really believe I can take it easy now," John said as Ophelia made a couple of mojitos in Corky's honor.

"You know, I want you to finish out this campaign, such as it is. That communist Luke Spearman doesn't stand a chance against Danny. That is, as long as you think Danny's changed his evil ways," John said as he smiled and sipped the mojito.

"He'll be fine, Mr. Thompson. I don't think we'll need to watch him as closely now. I wonder what possessed him to do such a stupid thing with that Emily Wright?" she asked, somehow knowing John had an answer.

"Does the name Hennie mean anything to you? Yeah, poor bastard married himself a Hennie Thompson in that beauty queen he latched onto after The Point. Hell, Harmon and Lamont were the only ones that married sane women!" John explained.

Ophelia laughed that Southern laugh, the one that came from deep down, one she couldn't contain, the kind that makes your eyes water.

"Well, let me take that back. Jerry Slater married well, a lawyer named Sara from St. Louis. She's no beauty queen, but she's got some sense. You'll get to meet her," John added.

Ophelia was puzzled, something she should have expected by then. John always had surprises up his sleeve. As if scripted, there was a knock on the penthouse door. Ophelia opened it to find a man she didn't immediately recognize. John rolled his chair to her side.

"Speak of the devil – Ophelia I want you to meet one of my old friends, Jerry Slater," John shouted.

Just as Jerry extended his hand it hit Ophelia that she had never met him, that he was a mysterious piece of the puzzle that was John's life and connections, his synergy.

"It's great to meet you! I've read a lot about you. And I've been down to that riverfront you developed in St. Louis," Ophelia said.

"It's good to meet you, Ophelia. I've heard a lot of good things about you. And that riverfront deal, I was just copying off old John here," Jerry said patting John on the shoulder.

Slater made his way inside. A casual visit, no a planned meeting at least, Ophelia thought.

Jerry hugged John in his chair. Slater was a toned-down version of Danny Carson, polite, amiable, a nice looking man but kind of unassuming. He wasn't the hard charger that Danny was.

Then John pulled another blindside on Ophelia.

"Jerry here's going to be our next Vice President!" John boomed his best Hugo Moore impression.

Once again, Ophelia was caught off guard, really off guard, floored, disappointed that she hadn't figured this out for herself.

She was still stammering as she asked, "Vice President? What about, I mean," is all she could get out before John interjected.

"Danny's going to make the announcement tomorrow. It's the Class of '46 to the rescue!" John added as he puffed on a Cubano.

Jerry was smiling. Ophelia immediately recognized that he was content to still be the front man, the straw man for John.

Ophelia just gave him a hug. She knew she would see a lot of him from now on throughout the campaign, and she appreciated the private introduction that would cement her relationship with the entire White House-to-be, and her future.

As they toasted what seemed to be Jerry's de facto ascension from the Missouri Governor's office to national politics, Ophelia didn't know what to expect next. Could Elvis walk thought the door now, she wondered?

The irony was that the one member of the Class of '46 that the public knew least would have the most power, would trump the players whose names everybody knew. It was just then that the words John lived by hit home for Ophelia – power, synergy, might makes right.

And it wasn't over yet. She would live by those words now.

Chapter Twenty-Five

The Real Miguel

Ophelia was ready for Miguel's call. She and John had been back in Memphis only one day when she received a call from a white male voice telling her that Miguel was in Memphis. It was like he knew when she had returned.

Ophelia had pre-planned the meeting well. Ophelia told the caller to tell Miguel to meet her that night on the Arkansas side of the Mississippi River at the Southland Greyhound dog-racing track, section three at eight o'clock. The drive over the bridge would provide Ophelia with the ability to detect any surveillance that may be on her that night, including any from David Muggs.

It would be crowded at the park and many Latinos would be there. There was a large Latino population in Eastern Arkansas and she thought that Miguel would not stand out in the crowd as much.

Ophelia made her way out of The Peabody having told Muggs that she was turning in early. She wouldn't be going out tonight, she said. Just in case, Ophelia drove the route twice, over the river and back to make sure David hadn't put one of his men she didn't know on her that night.

The Southland Track was abuzz with activity. The races went off every thirty minutes and the pace was fast. There were people from Arkansas, Mississippi and Missouri as well as Tennessee there. It was a hot spot for gamblers intent on betting on the dogs.

Miguel was standing at the entrance to section three just as Ophelia had ordered. She didn't know, but she suspected that whoever had called her for Miguel may be watching too. She motioned for him to follow her to change the location of the meeting so she could check for any surveillance. She was still suspicious. She stopped at the end of the betting gallery and waved Miguel over.

"Miguel, Mr. Thompson did send word to your father that his presidency was in trouble. That people in power here wanted him out – and that you and your family were in danger. Whatever happened after that, he had nothing to do with it," she told him.

Miguel listened intently. He knew there would be a follow-up.

"Miguel, I believe your father committed suicide."

Miguel just hung his head and Ophelia watched him closely to gauge his reaction. From what she had seen at their first meeting in Birmingham, she couldn't imagine that this explanation would placate him. For whatever reason, based on some evidence, he had been so sure his father had been murdered.

"That's what I was afraid you would say," he said as his eyes welled up with tears.

Ophelia sensed they needed to leave the park. Since he was clearly no longer antagonistic, she thought it safe to walk outside.

"I believe I was being used by my father's friends to get them into power. I have since found out that they knew all along my father took his own life. They just wanted to use me to protest the current government, to overthrow the President, Hector Gonzales. I was wrong about Mr. Thompson. He was my father's friend," Miguel said.

Ophelia resisted the urge to hug Miguel but gave in as he began to sob harder than ever. As she held him, she felt that she was somehow, however strangely, developing a rapport with him. She felt for his loss, maybe the first tangible aftershock of one of John's political maneuvers. She determined then and there that she would help him.

"Call me tomorrow at the number I gave you. I'll take the call personally," she told Miguel as he wiped his eyes.

"And by the way. Who else knows about this?"

"Don't worry, it was just some guy I paid $20 to make the call," he said, for the first time drying up and revealing a hint of a smile.

⚜ ⚜ ⚜

Ophelia didn't dare tell Miguel about Danny Carson, her plans, nothing that would give away what she or John might have in mind for Nicaragua. Miguel now seemed pacified, neutralized as a threat to Danny Carson and the campaign. She could do more good for Miguel later after the election. First things first, she thought.

Ophelia didn't want to get in over her head with Miguel, in her newfound relationship with Danny Carson, until she talked with John. She had stuck her neck out doing what she had done. She didn't really even know what John might already know about Miguel and what she had been doing. John's man David Muggs was a sharp operator. She had seen him in action.

"Mr. Thompson, when I met with Danny Carson the subject of Nicaragua came up. I think I might like to do some diplomatic work, maybe at an embassy after the campaign, and, well, I mentioned it to him. I hope you don't mind," Ophelia said as she broached the subject, perhaps not too subtly the next day at The Peabody.

John paused, not always a good sign for things to come. It

wasn't dark yet, but it was cocktail hour somewhere, John must have thought as he asked Ophelia to pour him a Black Jack.

"I'll tell you this girl. Danny Carson owes me a big favor, I know you're aware of that," John started, being careful in what he said. As he lit a Cubano he looked at Ophelia with his business face on.

"You be careful with Danny. He won't lie to you, but make sure you get a firm commitment from him," John said as Ophelia listened intently.

"And by the way, Harmon told me about the questions you had about Ramon's death. That's pretty clever, girl. You go ahead and use that with Danny whatever way you can. You're a go-getter," John said to Ophelia who was openly relieved.

"Since you're interested in Nicaragua so much, I want you to go down with Muggs and check out my operation. I've got a nice place down there. It's a tobacco plantation that I imagine Marvin and Hennie will sell when I'm gone. They hate the place," John said as he frowned at the sound of their names.

"I'd love to, Mr. Thompson. I'll let you know when I can get a break from Danny," she said, trying to imagine the place.

"You make your future wherever you can. I'm not always going to be around, Ophelia. You could find worse places than Nicaragua. I love the place and I want to see it change. You'll see what I mean. And I know you'll do the right thing girl," he said to a somewhat puzzled Ophelia. John rarely talked in riddles but this was one of the occasions where she did not fully understand his meaning. She would soon.

Ophelia almost felt as if she had dodged a bullet in asking Harmon about Ramon. She knew she was taking a calculated risk in dealing with Miguel too. But in this exchange with John she gained some reassurance that he knew she had to take steps to make sure she would be okay after John was gone, to be her own person. She knew John wouldn't want it any other way.

"I know you're doing a good job keeping up with Danny. You'll have to spend more time with him for the rest of the year. The campaign's going to pick up speed this summer and I want you to check in with me every day," John told her as she nodded.

"In the meantime, take a day or two and get some rest here in Memphis. I'm going to have a few friends over tonight and I want you to meet them, old Mitch Ferguson and his wife Betty. They're quite the characters," John said as they went out onto the balcony.

Mitch Ferguson was an old corporate executive with Federal Express and helped grow the company in the late 1970's to over $1 billion in revenue before he retired. John had met him through the company's founder Fred Smith, an old military man himself.

At 68, Mitch was a little older than John and had actually made his money in cotton, farming out his operation and rarely visiting the fields outside Memphis. The scion of an old Southern family that hadn't lost everything during the War of Northern Aggression, he had married Betty ten years before after a first marriage went awry. Betty was a Southern Belle extraordinaire with a genuine Southern drawl to match. Naturally pretty, she made all the Memphis cocktail parties, formal balls, and pretty much every social event on the calendar – a calendar she kept in her purse.

Mitch wasn't as enthusiastic about the social scene as Betty. He stayed away from it all thinking it too pretentious; 'Bugtussle chic' as he would call it with all these small town Memphians pretending they were big city elegant sophisticates who gathered to blow smoke up each other's ass.

Mitch had been all over the world, first with FedEx, then as a world traveler bent on drinking and womanizing his way around the globe. These rich people in Memphis were boring to him. Like

John, he was comfortable around real people who enjoyed a stiff drink and a cigar.

Mitch and Betty were frequent visitors to the penthouse at The Peabody. John would call often to check up on Mitch who had health problems of his own with a heart attack a few years ago. It was a special treat for Betty to be invited into John's inner sanctum for a dinner on the balcony.

"Ophelia, you won't find a finer, more humble man in Memphis than Mitch Ferguson," John said as he introduced him that night.

Almost as an afterthought he said, "And this is his wife Betty."

Ophelia liked them both instantly, for different reasons. Mitch was an engaging character still very much an attractive man at over six feet tall and had retained his chiseled military looks.

She could tell that when around friends who knew that he wasn't trying to impress them, he would share old war stories and tales of his travels. In that way, he was much like John, powerful but subdued.

Betty adored Mitch and was along for the ride. It seemed as if she'd always had someone on her arm since she came to Memphis from Arkansas. Ophelia thought her to be a kind bon vivant who loved to be around people, to drink and 'talk their ears off' as she would say. They were quite a couple – and very political.

John had thought it was time Ophelia met them, to make some local political and social contacts since she was living at her own penthouse on the river now. Mitch and Betty were the two best people in Memphis to accomplish that goal, Mitch, with his down-to-earth connections among old-money Memphians, and Betty who knew everyone of every political and social stripe. Naturally, Marvin and Hennie despised them and felt them to be a threat, stealing John's time and attention – and maybe his money, they thought.

Betty and Mitch felt at home with Ophelia. They could see that John was very close to her and that was enough for them. The spring was leading to a summer that could be unbearably hot in Memphis. It was a good time to enjoy another dinner on the balcony of John's penthouse.

"Ophelia's quite a political and social animal too," John summarily announced to Betty, "just like you." John wasn't pulling any punches and got straight to the point.

"I think she'd like to be shown around the Memphis that you know."

Betty jumped at the chance. She loved nothing better than educating someone special in all things Memphis. She laid out a schedule before the night was over that included all the black-tie dinners, teas, local fundraisers whether charitable or political, and any event of note for Ophelia – right from the resources she carried in her purse.

"I'm going to be on the road off and on with the Danny Carson campaign, Betty. I'm helping coordinate fundraisers among other things," Ophelia told her as she quickly came up with an inconspicuous description for her role with Danny. Somehow she knew that 'John's straw man' wouldn't be appropriate, even though Betty and Mitch would certainly know what that meant.

That's all Betty needed to hear. She was a talker and could barely contain her enthusiasm. She was able to shift gears from campaign to campaign as easily as she could from person to person. John liked that part of her. She was a go-getter in a different sort of way, a manner that he knew could be of use to Ophelia and himself in broadening Ophelia's contacts in Memphis.

As Betty fine-tuned her list and inundated Ophelia with names and places she would take her, who she would introduce her to, John and Mitch just looked at each other and smiled. She was a piece of work.

Ophelia would have a friend for life in Betty. The fact that Ophelia was a close friend of John's was reason enough for Betty, but the fact that Ophelia was interested, no, *involved* in the Danny Carson campaign was icing on the cake for her. She would have had a stroke if she had known how involved Ophelia really was.

"Sounds great Betty. As soon as I get back into Memphis from the campaign, I'll give you a call," Ophelia promised as she gathered her many notes about what Betty was planning.

✤ ✤ ✤

Ophelia would barely have time to meet with Miguel before heading back out on the '404' jet to meet Danny's next important campaign stop. She had felt she was already spread pretty thinly as it was. Now with Harmon and Lamont gone, she would be even busier.

Ophelia highly anticipated the call at her new office in The Peabody. She couldn't forget the look on Miguel's face at the greyhound track when she told him how his father died. Nor could she forget the hug they shared. It was the first hug she had felt in a long time that wasn't the kind that 'just friends' share. She felt she was becoming emotionally involved in the Nicaraguan matter, and that made her afraid.

She didn't have to wait long for the call. Miguel telephoned at 8:00 AM on her personal line.

"Ophelia, I hope you don't mind if I call you Ophelia, do you?" Miguel asked sheepishly.

Ophelia had made up her mind that until she could meet with Miguel again personally, before she could know more about him, she would be brief and to the point with him.

"No, of course not. Listen, I need to go out of town for a while. Do you know where Mr. Thompson's estate is outside of Managua?" she asked Miguel who didn't immediately answer.

"Yes, of course I do. My family and I would spend time there every year. It's fabulous. I have so many good memories of that place," he said, obviously moved at the thought of the place.

"Well, I'm going to be there sometime soon. Can you get back to Nicaragua okay? How can I get in touch with you?" she asked.

Miguel gave her a series of telephone numbers in Nicaragua. Between them, someone would be able to get a message to Miguel. She was to leave the same message with each person to make sure he was reached.

Things had changed somewhat for the good since Ramon's father died, at least at John's plantation, but the place could still be dangerous. Miguel would certainly be watched while he was in Nicaragua, but he knew he would be safe if he made it to John's estate. His association with John and Ophelia would make it safe to go there from now on. That is, until people knew the truth.

"Good. I will telephone the numbers before I leave the country. I have a plan," she said.

Ophelia was learning her lessons from John well. She had a real good plan. She had no clue that she was only a part of John's plan – *the* plan. As long as Danny Carson was elected President.

Chapter Twenty-Six

Reunion

Ophelia was now part of Danny Carson's official team and all the major stops were on Ophelia's agenda. Corky was introducing her to the right people, movers and shakers in the cities and towns where Carson would stop. She was working like there was no tomorrow, raising money and making contacts and helping coordinate events.

Danny wasn't taking anything for granted either. His speeches were more organized, comprehensive. And the message was being parsed, making sure he wasn't promising everyone the world. Even though Luke Spearman had a liberal streak that glowed in the dark, Danny was playing it safe, in more ways than one.

As Corky Benedict had reported, Carson had a long talk of his own with Emily Wright and gave her one of those John Henry Thompson 'how the cow ate the cabbage' speeches. Corky was even present when it happened. There would be no more fooling around – at least until after the election where he could manage his indiscretions within the secure confines of the White House.

Emily took it in stride. She had been assured that her place as the future White House press secretary was secure. Corky had discovered that Emily had slept her way to the top of the network news as well and had shared that information with Danny before their meeting with Emily. It made Danny feel a little better. After all, as far as anyone knew, it was his first affair.

Danny had taken his talk with Ophelia to heart. He had also taken a call from John, one that Ophelia knew nothing about. John had, in his country manner, dropped a little more than a hint that he would be pleased if Ophelia took a more visible role in the campaign – and afterward in a Carson administration. John was careful not to let Danny get the impression that this would be the favor that Danny should grant him in return for 'silencing' Ramon Hernandez. Danny got the message.

"Ophelia, I wish you would get out front more, you know, make a few talks, get together with some of my contributors as my stand-in. It would really help the campaign, and it would get you some exposure," Danny told her as they talked one day on the campaign bus.

Ophelia had just rejoined Carson and had figured John must have called him. She could always tell when John had motivated someone. They had that spark in their eye, an eagerness in their voice that only John could inspire.

She was already doing what Danny asked. This was just a formal request, just so she knew he would be indebted to her, solidifying their connection now and after the race was over.

"Well, I'd love to," as she slightly batted her eyes in a style reminiscent of Betty Ferguson's true Southern Belle effect. Always the quick study, she had learned it on John's balcony that night back in Memphis when she met Mitch and Betty.

"Excellent! Corky will go over the schedule with you. Let me know how it's going, would you? I'm trying to be two places at once nowadays," Danny chirped, secure in his standing with John now, as confident in the race as he had never been.

Ophelia, and by extension, John was confident too. She would feel secure enough now to strike out on her own with Corky and make the fundraising circuit to give talks with the 'high-rollers' as

John called them, raising money in all parts of the country.

Ophelia wasn't surprised when she recognized many of the names as being people who had season tickets to The Memphis Blues games and to the World Series, courtesy of John. There was a nexus between New York, Miami, Los Angeles, Missouri and back to Tennessee. She saw evidence of Harmon Vance's influence in Chicago too. It was a remarkable insight into the connections John, Harmon, Jerry Slater, Truman Forsythe and Danny Carson had put together over the years since The Point. It was that synergy borne of the fraternity of West Point men. Partners, if not friends, for life.

There was even evidence of the ghost of Ramon Hernandez in the campaign in the Latinos forces that turned out for Danny Carson. Since he had claimed the throne of human rights leader for all Central Americans after Ramon's timely exit, the Latino community rushed to champion his candidacy. The Cuban exile block was even behind him. If only they knew the whole truth, she thought.

Ophelia was a natural born public speaker, whether or not the group numbered 10 or 100 people. Her folksy charm translated well with elitist politicos or common people who just wanted to learn more about Danny. Many told her she should seek public office herself. She was a lot easier on the eyes than Danny.

And she was the natural vehicle to trumpet Danny's successes on the foreign policy front too. It gave her an opportunity to brag on how the situation in Central America had made a turn for the good under Danny's leadership on the Senate Foreign Relations Committee – to position herself for the political post she, and John, had in mind.

Ophelia had been schooled well by John in his methodology of synergy, building strategic alliances and planning for the future. By the time summer had arrived she was ready to make the sojourn back to Memphis to brief John.

She had been in contact via telephone every day and had developed a long distance bond with Arthur Boone. He had settled comfortably into the role of being John's caretaker and was his constant companion. But it was time to see John in person.

✤ ✤ ✤

"I hear you've been making quite an impact out on the campaign circuit. I like that, girl," John said as Ophelia came down the stairway of the '404' jet.

It was early morning but John had Arthur drive him out to the hangar at the Memphis airport. He missed Ophelia terribly but didn't want to show it. He wanted to let her spread her wings a bit while the Carson campaign was in full bloom. He also wanted her to further one of his grand plans, one that she didn't as yet fully understand.

Ophelia couldn't contain her glee in seeing John again. She hugged him until it hurt and smothered him with 'sister kisses'.

"Mr. Thompson, it's so exciting out there. The people, the message, I'm really beginning to get into it. But I'd rather be here with you!" she cried as Arthur helped John into the limo.

"How's Danny? Is he staying straight?" John asked knowing that Corky was at Carson's side. "From what Corky tells me, he's focused with his eye on the prize."

"I don't think we have anything to worry about, Mr. Thompson. Like you say, it's his race to lose," she said as David Muggs nodded and smiled.

David had missed Ophelia too. He had been allowed to let Ophelia travel on her own since the Miguel situation had been defused. His spies at The Peabody had enough to do making sure the Marvin and Hennie Show didn't erupt again. And he was ready to take her to Managua as soon as John gave the go-ahead.

"Betty Ferguson has been calling your office every day wondering when you would be back Ophelia. She's heard about the upcoming Carson fundraiser here in Memphis. She's going to have a stroke if you don't call her," John told Ophelia.

"Give her a call. I think she has a couple of things on that calendar of hers you might be interested in, or that you might tolerate."

As the limo made the customary path right down Beale Street John's thoughts, then Ophelia's memories of Beale Street were vivid.

"I miss Lamont the most," John said as they passed The Boogie Woogie. "I can't believe it has been so long, forty years ago since I started all this."

And the street was busy. Even in the early morning Beale Street was open for business. Summer had brought with it baseball again. The Blues were doing well and John missed doing the hands-on work with the team.

Marvin and Hennie had their shoulders to the wheel of the team and The Thompson Group business, continuously being watched by John's surrogates in the organization. They were being careful to the point of paranoia, fearful their next misstep would lead to the threatened disinheritance.

"Mr. Thompson, I've got a great idea," Ophelia said as her eyes lit up, one of the expressions in her emotional repertoire that John loved the most.

"*If* you feel up to it, let's go down to The Boogie Woogie tonight!" she squealed. "Just for a little while!"

"You know what girl, that's just what I need!" John exclaimed as Arthur nodded vigorously.

Ophelia knew that John had been getting tired more easily, more quickly than even just a few months ago. Arthur had been telling her that he seemed to be wasting away now that his gang had left the nest, reminiscing more and more.

Lamont or Harmon would call every day from Miami asking John to come down, to take out *The Ophelia* with them and do some fishing. But John was not getting around well. He was drinking a little too much and smoking too many cigars, not that anyone but Arthur noticed, except for the doctors.

John had become fond of 'shooing them away' as he would tell Ophelia during their daily telephone chats. His speech wasn't getting any better and he found himself relying more and more on the wheelchair. It was a vicious cycle that fostered his physical weakness. Mental anguish followed as John knew he was becoming a shell of his old dynamic 'go-getter' self.

John would get his now-customary nap that afternoon as Ophelia made plans. Arthur had told her that since she had been on the campaign, John would not allow him to roll him over to Beale. He preferred to just drive slowly down the street and admire the tourists that flocked to Bumbles Billiards, the Boogie and Porky's. John would gulp the smells and sounds and have Arthur just make block after block. John missed it all.

They had been driving down to Slabtown too, but John would not even get out at Sister's house. She would get in the Range Rover and ride down the old highway just slowing down at Kesterson's store. He didn't even want to fish in the creek where they had caught so many fish. It was sad. It was decline for sure, Arthur thought.

John had become even more philanthropic. The old West Tennessee State Teachers College at Memphis where his teachers from boyhood graduated had become a full-fledged university now, Memphis State University they named it. John had built them a new gymnasium and endowed a chair in business along with a new business college building. Fittingly, they named the business school in honor of him.

John was even sharing his now enormous collection of art. What had started as a small collection of well-known American artists, including the California artists Ophelia had seen, it had turned into one of the most eclectic repositories of art in the South. The works were now couched within the John Henry Thompson Foundation for the Arts and were exhibited all over Memphis for everyone to see and enjoy.

"Mr. Thompson, are you sure you feel up to this," Ophelia asked as they made their way into the limo for the two block ride to the Boogie Woogie Café. "I don't want you to get too tired."

"Hell, I've been in that penthouse too long. I don't get to see you that much. Yes, let's go have a good time!" John bellowed, somehow his energy boosted and a healthy color coming to his face.

The Boogie Woogie looked quiet, even for a Tuesday night. John first noticed that the tunes were missing, the ever-present sound of a horn, maybe the drums. No, that wasn't it at all. There was no music – and the place was dark.

"Girl, I'm afraid we came at a slow time!" John said in amazement. He had never seen the Boogie this quiet and he worried that something was wrong.

"Surprise!" was all John could hear as they rolled him into the Boogie Woogie. The place went from gloomy dark to brilliant white lights as 300 people screamed 'happy birthday' to their old friend John Henry Thompson.

"What in the hell? I'd forgotten it was my birthday!" John boomed, sounding every bit the Hugo Moore now, newly invigorated and sitting up ramrod straight.

Lamont Boone, Harmon Vance and their families, they all were there. And John was in his element. Immediately, an enormous birthday cake was brought out. Aglow with dozens of little candles, Ophelia placed it briefly on his lap as flashes from cameras snapped amid the applause.

As John smiled, the widest he had smiled in weeks he told Ophelia, "Girl, I'm going to strangle you! How did you keep this a secret?"

"To tell you the truth Mr. Thompson, knowing you, I figured you probably already knew about it!" she yelled over the applause that seemed to go on forever.

Immediately, Lamont, Harmon and Ophelia stepped in and blew out the candles to a number with John. John looked toward the bandstand as '*Happy Birthday*' was kicked off by a voice he knew from long, and not so long ago. A photograph Ophelia would treasure forever was snapped of the gang around John and the cake.

B. B. King sang the birthday wishes that night. Ophelia had planned the event well. Lamont and Harmon had flown up from Miami on their own so as not to alert John through the usual channels. She had stealthed it well. She learned her lessons from John and put them to good use. John was happy.

"Mr. Thompson, I've got a surprise for you! A few other people want to wish you happy birthday!" Ophelia said as the crowd parted to reveal a large projection screen. A button was pushed and a tape rolled.

The images that appeared were familiar and surprising to John at once.

"John, this is Cadet Sergeant Mark Davis! Snap to attention!"

It was his old nemesis and friend from long ago. The man he had helped get the four stars he wore on his Army dress uniform these days.

"John, I just wanted to tell you happy birthday. We've both come a long way since The Point! God bless you! You're a fine American!" General Davis screamed in his best Cadet Sergeant firing range voice.

Just for good measure, and cryptic humor, Davis added as he stared into the camera as if straining to see through the screen, "Cadet Vance, is that you standing by John? I just wanted to finally tell you, I know you got the best of me that day at the firing range!" he said as he turned away and walked from the microphone, one obviously set up at the Pentagon.

John and Harmon burst into laughter as everyone else looked puzzled. The rest of the crowd certainly didn't get the joke of how Harmon had trumped Davis at The Point that day he shot John's target. Some things were best left secret, they thought.

Davis turned and saluted giving an "at ease" for effect. John and Harmon loved it. Davis wasn't such a jerk after all. John was right in helping him get those stars.

There was a slight pause on the screen before the tape continued. Just as John and the revelers thought the show was over, Danny Carson and Jerry Slater appeared on the screen.

"Happy birthday!" they both chimed in unison. "We wish you the best John!"

As if on cue they echoed General Davis with "You're a fine American! God bless you John Henry Thompson!"

'A fine American'. John could think of no better epitaph.

Chapter Twenty-Seven

Lake Nicaragua – Twin Volcanoes

John was worn out from the night at the Boogie Woogie. But he was happy. He needed to see his friends, his gang and the party at the club was just the right venue. Ophelia had done well and for once surprised John instead of the other way around. She wished she could spend more time with him instead of going to Nicaragua, but she wanted to know and see more. Still, it was almost as if John wanted her to go as much as she did. Indeed it was all part of another plan, the grand plan.

Ophelia and John talked about the trip to Nicaragua, that it would be a good time to see the operation while the campaign was going well. Ophelia was anxious to see Miguel again, perhaps for reasons she did not want to admit. She was concerned for him and wanted to help him. But she felt a strange connection to him, a sense that he had been wronged, that he really wanted more than to understand what had happened to his father. She believed he wanted to find out what had happened to his country.

"I'll have Julio Feuntes meet you at the airport in Managua," John told Ophelia and David Muggs. "If you need anything at all, he can handle it. He's a good man."

David had been to the tobacco estate many times. It was a relatively short trip in the '404' jet to Managua and the boat ride to the island where the estate was located was even shorter.

John had acquired the estate after Ramon Hernandez came to

power not long after the Beale Street Revival had taken off, and he loved the place. It was like being a million miles away from the hustle and bustle of his heyday. He had fallen in love with the people too, and they adored him like a benevolent king.

"Ometepe is absolutely enchanting girl! I wish I were able to go with you," John said as his eyes widened. Ophelia could see he was imagining being there with her. He would leave it to Julio and David to show her around the estate and acquaint her with the country.

"It's paradise on earth, girl. The views, the smells, it's so exotic, like something from a fairy tale. You'll love it!" he told her as she tried to get her imagination to run wild, to envision such a place.

Such a place was a volcanic island called Ometepe in Lake Nicaragua, one of the largest lakes in the world and the most recognizable place on the Nicaraguan map. Ometepe drew its name form the Aztec words for 'two hills', emblematic of the twin volcanoes that one could see from any part of the island.

The volcanoes were named Concepcion and Maderas and the last eruption of either of them to speak of was in 1957. That little event caused John to think twice about the project. He went forward anyway and planted tobacco in the rich volcanic ash. The place thrived.

"Now you watch those howler monkeys down there. They'll bite the shit out of you if you try to pet them!" John joked.

He didn't want to see her leave but knew she had to go. Ophelia wasn't someone he could keep on a leash. He had brought her into this world of John Henry Thompson, but he would let her lead her own life. There was much of his life that she did not know. Ometepe was just one more part of it she needed to learn and experience, especially if she had what John thought was on her mind.

✿ ✿ ✿

Ophelia had only known what John had told her, what she had read about Nicaragua – and what she had seen on the news. Nicaragua had a history of violence, drugs and dictators, she knew that much. She was prepared for all that and whatever Miguel had to share with her. But even though John had told her much about the island, she wasn't prepared for what she was to see.

The trip down to Central America was almost directly straight south from Memphis. John used to just say he was 'going south' whenever he visited the estate. Everyone knew what he meant, and where to find him.

Julio Fuentes met the '404' jet at the Managua airport in the estate limousine. Ophelia immediately noticed the Range Rover right behind the limo complete with Latinos carrying AK-47 assault rifles. And they were obviously trying to be conspicuous about it.

"Ophelia, welcome to Nicaragua. Bienvenidos!" Julio said as he hugged Ophelia, then shook David Muggs's hand.

One of the Latinos handed David a chopped down version of the assault rifle. Ophelia wondered if she would get one too as they appeared to be standard issue.

"Did you enjoy West Point? I know John was going to drive you up there," Julio said, remembering the night he first met Ophelia at Peter Luger's Steakhouse in New York City.

Ophelia recounted the midnight visit in every detail, how she had seen the football field, John's old barracks, all the time being chaperoned by the Commandant of Cadets.

"Ah yes, I miss The Point myself!" he told Ophelia who was unaware that he was one of the military gang himself. "I graduated a *few* years before John," Julio laughed as he stroked his gray hair.

It figured, she thought. Just one more person John could trust, one he could entrust with her safety. Until now she didn't know much about Julio. She had never been around him more than for a dinner in New York and then didn't have much of a conversation with him. Now it all made sense. It fit. Everything John did had a structure, a purpose – there was always a well-oiled machine of a plan.

Julio had his men load all the bags into the Range Rover for the 50-mile trip to the little port of Rivas where the group would take a cruise down Lake Nicaragua to the island. It was hot and muggy and Ophelia thought she could have waited until a cooler month to visit, had it not been for Miguel and the campaign. She wanted to know all she could, as soon as she could know it.

The cruise on the lake was unlike anything Ophelia had ever seen. What looked to Ophelia to be a ferry boat spirited them away from the mainland for the two-hour journey through the lake, making their way around some of the over 300 little islands, 'Las Isletas' Julio called them, that lay in the 3200 square mile lake. It was beautiful, unlike anything Ophelia had ever seen. And there were hardly any other boats, any people. It seemed to be at the edge of the earth.

Green parrots were swirling along the coast as the twin peaks of Ometepe Island came into view. The island was massive at 150 square miles and looked to be actually two islands with the volcanic islands joined by a narrow isthmus. It looked like something out of the *King Kong* movie with Ophelia halfway expecting to be met by Fay Wray at the dock.

The ship arrived at the port of Moyogalpa where yachts and fishing vessels came up the San Juan River from as far as the Caribbean Sea - and as far as Miami.

To Ophelia's amazement, there standing on the pier were Lamont and Harmon, all the way from Miami on *The Ophelia*.

"Ahoy there, don't I know that woman from Memphis, Tennessee?" Harmon shouted.

John thought Ophelia and Muggs may get a little homesick and had arranged for *The Ophelia* to be ferried down to Lake Nicaragua from Miami. Harmon and Lamont had flown into Managua the night before and were waiting at the harbor with the yacht. Although she had planned on some time alone with Miguel, she was undoubtedly glad to see them. She knew she would love this place, King Kong or not.

⚜ ⚜ ⚜

It was a new adventure for Ophelia and all the gang was there to begin it with her, all except John. It felt strange to be enjoying the fruits of his labor without him. Harmon and Lamont knew Ophelia missed him. They could sense it as she gave them both hugs at the dock and saw it in her eyes as they boarded the Range Rover for the short ride to the estate. Although they would be with her there, this was very much a journey she would take on her own.

Ophelia was overpowered by the sights of the tropical forests and pasture grass, the smells of guava and fragrant plumeria flowers as they drove and talked about the island, the estate and the tobacco John grew, some of the finest cigar filler tobacco in the world.

John's plantation lay at the foot of the 3,800 feet high Maderas volcano. The mountain, shrouded in clouds from about half way up and to the summit, was an eerie sight to Ophelia. The tobacco fields were beautiful, unlike any she had seen in the Carolinas so close to back home. It had a rough-hewn look to it. It was like that Fantasy Island from television, unreal and magical. 'You were right Mr. Thompson', she thought. 'This *is* paradise'.

The estate was a working one, not a tourist trap or gentleman's plantation. Julio showed Ophelia the fields as Harmon and Lamont retreated to their suites inside the adobe main house that boasted eight bedrooms and a separate guesthouse where Ophelia would sleep. There were workers everywhere weeding and tending to the tobacco. Julio showed her how it was all done. She gained a new appreciation for a good cigar.

There were also the ever-present security guards with their AK rifles at the ready. Muggs seemed to trust them implicitly. At once, Ophelia felt at peace but in a dangerous place.

Ophelia couldn't wait to use the telephone, first to call John and then Miguel. The modern conveniences inside the house brought her briefly back to reality and allowed her to gather herself enough to talk with John back in Memphis.

"Mr. Thompson, you never cease to amaze me!" Ophelia gasped as John laughed uncontrollably.

"You didn't think I'd let you get lonesome down there did you? Lamont and Harmon love that old barn they call an estate," John said. "Plus, they can smoke all the cigars they want!"

"I hear those monkeys you told me about! I know why they call them 'howlers' now!" Ophelia said as the howler monkeys screamed their spooky rant in the background. "They're everywhere down here – and the birds and flowers, all of it, it's beautiful!"

"You just have a good time. David and Julio will take good care of you down there. It's my little heaven on earth," John said.

'Heaven on earth' Ophelia thought. With all the misery the country had suffered through in the past, how could this place be so beautiful? But, it was. She instantly became attached to the place and took to roaming through the tobacco fields that very first day. She smelled the amazing varieties of flowers and looked on amused as the howler monkeys chased after the startling green parrots that seemed to be everywhere.

Still, she sensed a tension in the air that could not be overcome by the vastness and natural beauty of the island. She made up her mind to learn everything she could about the estate, the island, the country. This was a place she thought she could call home someday.

"What do you think of John's little Central American hideaway, Ophelia?" Julio asked with a smile.

"I love it with all my heart, Julio. I can see why Mr. Thompson loves to come down here," she said as she suddenly realized John might never make it back due to his health.

Her naturally twinkling eyes dimmed as she thought to go ahead and ask Julio about the darker side of the country.

"Julio, why is there all this security? Is it not safe here?"
Julio's tone changed as well. He looked away from Ophelia and waved his hand toward the mountain.

"All this beauty, these mountains, this land, it has always been fought for, disputed among peoples for thousands of years. Come, I want to show you something," Julio said as he motioned for the Range Rover – and the security team.

Julio took the Range Rover as far up the mountain slope as it could go before the rocky ground forced them to strike out on foot.

"This place was home to an ancient people called the Nahuatl. They came here hoping it to be a place of refuge from the Aztecs up north," Julio told Ophelia.

"Look at those rocks. Those images were carved more than 3,000 years ago," he said as he pointed to three large boulders engraved with large spiral carvings. Halfway up the slope he pointed out rocks with intimate images of men and women, and of hunters chasing game.

"It's all right here. Nothing much has changed, Ophelia; art, sex and man's struggle for survival. And that is what is still happening in this country. Some people want the power to take it all for themselves and they're driving the others away, into poverty and desperation," Julio told her as Ophelia struggled for the hidden meaning in his words.

"Are you saying there is tyranny here? That this government is still oppressing the people?" Ophelia asked.

"I'm just saying the people are looking for something new. Nothing has changed for them since the Aztecs, the Spanish conquerors, the dictators. They're still poor, afraid of the drug bandits and their land still has not been returned to them from the Ramon Hernandez days. They're still trying to get away from the Aztecs, if you will," Julio told her. "But, in the midst of it all, John has made this plantation a refuge for the people."

Ophelia wasn't one to miss a metaphor, whether it was one of John's home-cooked ones or an ancient one from Julio. She knew now that the people weren't happy with Ramon Hernandez's replacement. They wanted change. And in this country, change inevitably came at the muzzle of a rifle.

"John has made this island a refuge for people who want to work, to own their own land. To be sure, he owns all that you see, but as a partner. He gives the people 10% of everything the plantation produces. If they stay on here, they get land and he buys their crop. And they're safe here," Julio said with deep emotion.

'Damnation', Ophelia thought. John had created a sort of Beale Street Revival right here in the middle of the jungles of Central America, the 10% ownership, enabling the people – every component part of his, their, success. She wondered if it could be done for the rest of the country – so did John.

Chapter Twenty-Eight

Nicaragua According to Miguel

Harmon and Lamont wanted to show Ophelia as much of the estate and the mountain as they could. But one could live a lifetime in, around and on top of these two volcanoes and never see it all. But she just had to see the San Ramon waterfall and the lagoon at the summit of the dormant volcano Maderas, straight up from the estate.

"The locals say this land is inhabited by magical fairies, Ophelia," Julio told her as they made their way up the mountain, as much a climb as it was a hike.

"They're all sorts of supernatural beings here, they say," Julio gasped as he pulled himself up to the edge of the lagoon.

Where the volcano's crater lay, there was a large lake shrouded in mist. It looked like a place not of the earth, Ophelia would admit. Harmon, still fit as ever from the days at The Point, was taking the hike in stride. Lamont was another story.

"Lamont, are you okay?" Harmon asked as Lamont slumped onto a rock, terribly out of breath.

"I feel like I'm back behind that plow at Slabtown, Harmon. It didn't used to be this hard for me to climb this old rock," Lamont gasped. "I guess I'm getting old."

And Ophelia was getting worried about Lamont. She insisted they leave and start back down, concerned that they had been a too-gracious host, showing her the mountain in such muggy weather. They weren't spring chickens either, she thought. The climb might be too much for them.

Lamont seemed to recover pretty well by the time they reached the foot of the mountain. The Range Rovers were waiting and took them back to the house for a breather. But Ophelia wanted to learn more about the estate and the people who lived there.

The workers all lived in homes that were modest by American standards, but palatial compared to the dwellings of their fellow countrymen. Ophelia took Julio with her as an interpreter and guide. He introduced her as 'Mr. John's woman' a moniker that induced giggles from many of the people. They loved Mr. John and missed him very much.

There was a small school for the children, a small Catholic church and even an entertainment center. These weren't migrant workers, these were residents of the tobacco plantation community. Ophelia would think of them often. She would have a new appreciation for cigars too, one borne of the workers and craftsmen that put their lives into this work. It was hard, but honorable work. John had given them careers of sorts, the best they could hope for in their country.

The gang would enjoy Nicaraguan beefsteaks and Black Jack that night sitting on the terrace of the estate with mosquito netting all around. John had not told Ophelia about the mosquitoes. They were ever-present as their continuous hum could be heard through the night. Still, it was an enchanting place, a world away from Memphis and John. Sitting there, they all missed them both.

⚜ ⚜ ⚜

Ophelia called all the numbers Miguel had given her. She left the same message just as instructed. Ophelia had made the decision that to 'hide in plain sight' would be the easiest way to talk with Miguel. The security at the estate left Muggs relaxed and not worrying about watching Ophelia. She could come and go as she pleased among the workers, in the fields or on the mountain. Miguel could mix and mingle with the workers and go unnoticed, especially if Muggs was not around. Muggs knew Miguel's face.

"Come to the estate and be at the end of the tobacco road at five o'clock tomorrow," was her message. Simple, complete and oddly reminiscent of the Tobacco Road Club back in Miami, the night club where Miguel first successfully got his message to Ophelia.

She would be leaving the island with the others in two days after a short cruise on *The Ophelia*. It was now or never, she thought. Miguel had visited the estate with his father many times as a boy. Ophelia knew he could find exactly where she had instructed him to go, but she worried if he would be afraid to come so close to a place he might now fear so much.

Ophelia told Muggs she wanted to mix with the workers in the fields that day, to learn more about them and the land. Muggs didn't think anything of it. He was relaxed and certain that the security guards were as good as one could get. Julio had personally recruited all of them. They could be trusted.

Every day was a muggy one on the island. The workers didn't seem to mind and were probably used to it. It was their way of life. Ophelia loved to be among them. Sure, there was the language barrier but they were just like the laborers back home, the ones she and John would see in the cotton fields. It was hard work. But Ophelia could smile when she saw them. John was lifting them up, sharing in the profits, in the land. Synergy, it was about the people. Some things never change, she thought.

And finally there was Miguel, there at the end of the tobacco road. He was puttering around like a shiftless worker, pretending like he knew what he was doing in the fields. Even Ophelia knew he had never worked in the fields a day in his life.

"Miguel, let's take a walk," Ophelia said as she walked past him. "We need to talk quickly."

Ophelia had planned carefully. She led Miguel to a place just behind a tobacco barn by the fields, making sure no one followed. As they reached a shed Miguel grabbed Ophelia by both arms and kissed her hard, so hard she couldn't break away, so she didn't want to struggle. It would be futile, she thought. And she also thought that she was starting to enjoy it. This was the first non 'sister kiss' she had in a long time.

Miguel slowly released her and Ophelia's adrenaline kicked in. She stepped back slapped him so hard she thought that surely the security guards would think it was a gunshot.

"What in the hell? You enjoyed that, I know you did!" Miguel screamed through a whisper, making sure not to alarm anyone.

"You didn't know I would, damn it! We don't take such things for granted where I come from," Ophelia shot back.

"Where *I* come from, we don't have the luxury of wasting time when we care for someone. I care for you – because I know you care for me. You are taking a big chance just meeting with me. I know you want to help me, help us, my country!"

Ophelia knew he was right. She wasn't there just because she was curious, because she just wanted to know more. She did care. She shared what John believed, in enabling people, in making people's lives better.

She leaned toward him and he leaned toward her. She returned the kiss, ever so briefly, but she returned it with the same passion just the same. This was going to get complicated, she thought.

Miguel wanted more.

"No, Miguel, no. It won't be safe here until Mr. Thompson is behind whatever we do. He has to know everything. But you have to tell me everything first. It's the only way I can get anything done. Without him, I'm, we're powerless," she pleaded.

"I'll tell you everything I know. It will take time, but when I am done you will see that my father's death was not a good thing," Miguel said as he backed away from Ophelia.

"But he was not doing this country right, I know that, and we are heading down an even darker path now. My father was planning on resigning and I was to succeed him. I wanted to give the land back to the people. We were never given that chance. He thought that I would be killed. That's why he took his life," he told her.

Miguel went on to tell Ophelia that there was a movement to unseat the sitting President, Hector Gonzalez, formerly a supporter of his father. But the rebels were not organized, had no money, and did not want to use force – unless they had to do so. They needed help. They couldn't even be considered rebels and they really didn't want to be. They were the political opposition.

They needed John Henry Thompson and, or, a sitting US President to win. Danny Carson didn't care what happened to his people as long as there was no killing, no bad news coming across the newswire. But there would be bad news. They would do what they had to do to reclaim their country.

Miguel also admitted that his father was indeed a strongman, a bully and held onto power at all costs. John had provided him the money to do so, but never took part in the oppression of the people. John had taken care of the estate workers and rarely ventured out into the country off the island. He had his own little world, sheltered from the reality that was Nicaragua under Ramon Hernandez.

Ophelia looked into Miguel's eyes. She believed him. She

was starting to believe in him, which she felt was inherently more dangerous.

Ophelia turned to leave when Miguel grabbed her arm, hard this time.

"Ophelia, I know you are the only person that can help us," he said as he pointed to the Maderas volcano, still shrouded in clouds.

"This country is just like that mountain. It will explode again some day. It's not a question of if, but when. But we can control the damage and we must act soon. I cannot be responsible for what happens unless we act fast!"

"I'll do what I can. But I will not go behind Mr. Thompson's back. You don't know him like I do," she said with such a resolve that Miguel believed every word.

"You stay here and do what you can. I will call you at the telephone numbers you gave me as soon as I talk with him," she said as Miguel's head drooped.

Ophelia reached to him and held up his chin. "I'll help you Miguel. I have seen why you love this country. I feel like I do too."

She gave him what she realized was a mixture of one of her sister kisses and a real one, one like they had shared before. It would have to suffice for now.

"You need to leave now, Miguel. The next time we meet, I hope we will not have this secrecy to deal with," she said as Miguel backed away.

"God bless you. I will think of you every day Ophelia," he whispered as he backed onto the tobacco road.

Ophelia would think of him too.

✤ ✤ ✤

"What do you think of my country," Julio asked Ophelia as the gang drove the Range Rover to Moyogalpa harbor. "Do you think you would like to return some day?"

"It's enchanting, Julio. It's beautifully mysterious. That's probably the best way I can describe it," Ophelia said as she scanned the countryside as if she might see Miguel's face one more time before she left.

"It is all that Ophelia, and more. I hope you will come back," Julio said.

Julio knew more than he told. He was much closer to John than Ophelia knew too. He had been John's straw man in Nicaragua for many years. Once a hard-line Ramon Hernandez man, he had mellowed over the years since he was now comfortable, wealthy and more compassionate, mostly because of John's influence. He wanted the best for the people and he knew John was too ill to come back, to exert his influence and to bring the people forward. He also was an integral part of 'the plan'. And whether she knew it or not by now, so was Ophelia.

Ophelia would have been angry had she known that Julio Fuentes was Miguel's uncle. Ramon had married Julio's sister, a fact known to Harmon and Lamont but never shared with Ophelia.

Julio had never trusted Ramon, in reality, he despised him. Julio had found refuge in running John's plantation for him, hosting Ramon and his family in their retreats from Managua when Ramon wanted to get away from the capital city. He could confide in Julio. After all, he was a fellow West Point man.

Julio had delivered the message to Ramon when Harmon Vance called after the meeting with Danny Carson in Atlanta. He knew Ramon was going to commit suicide. Ramon knew Miguel would be killed if he tried to succeed him in office. Ramon's power had deteriorated to the point that his presidency was about to end anyway, through whatever means. Julio promised Ramon that he would take care of Miguel and do all he could to right the wrongs, the pain Ramon had inflicted on the country.

"We need more people like you here, Ophelia. Please promise me you will return," Julio said, almost pleading.

"I can promise you I will be back. I love this place," she said as Julio hung on every word.

And Julio knew that Ophelia would come back for Miguel too. He knew that part of the gleam in her eyes was for Miguel. He also knew that Miguel had met her at the plantation – Julio was the person that made sure they could be alone. It would be some time before Ophelia became aware that the plan included Julio.

Harmon and Lamont were listening intently. They had spent much more time there than had Ophelia. They loved it too but realized there was much work to be done. They had seen the political strife, the social unrest and the poverty that had been rampant over the years. Even from the relatively safe and rich standpoint of the island, there was no missing the real truths of the country.

"This place can get under your skin, Ophelia. It's addictive, it will draw you back more and more if you let it," Harmon said as the ferry pulled away from the dock.

He sensed something powerful was going on in her head. It didn't surprise him that she had a keen interest in the country. Ever since the night in Laguna Niguel when he told her the story of Ramon's death, he knew she wouldn't be satisfied until she had seen this place herself, to learn on her own. That was the two-edged sword of Ophelia Hartwell, he knew. She was a team player, but she always wanted to know more. He sensed that Ophelia had become entangled in the web of beauty and politics of Nicaragua and could not, would not, remove herself from this place. John was counting on that.

She would have many more questions for John, to be sure. But after this journey she felt she not only had answers but an understanding of what had happened here, and what she wanted to see happen next, and it all involved Miguel. He would be the focal point for her plan of action.

But she could not, would not, do it without John.

Chapter Twenty-Nine

The Great Commission

Ophelia had a lot of time to think on the flight back to Memphis. She at first drifted off to sleep but quickly was awakened from dreams of what she had just seen and heard. The estate, the people, the smells never left her senses. She was still at Lake Nicaragua in her mind, where she had left Miguel behind the tobacco barn on the tobacco road.

It all seemed surreal. Until this trip, Nicaragua had been an almost abstract distraction with Miguel being the only tangible in the mix. Now all of it was so real. And she had fallen in love with it all.

Ophelia had realized that John had built a paradise, but a flawed one. But it could be fixed, she thought. It may take a lifetime, but such a place just might be worth it, the people would be worth it all. Neither she nor Miguel possessed the power or resources to do it all. It would take synergy beyond her wildest dreams to pull it off.

Lamont was still suffering from the effects of the climb on Maderas and Ophelia was worried, feeling more than a little responsible for his fatigue. He fell fast asleep as they made their way to join John for a brief visit before Harmon and Lamont returned to Miami and continued retirement. Harmon was alert and watching Ophelia.

"Ophelia, I can see you have a lot on your mind. I'll just say a couple of things more and then I'll shut up and let you sleep," Harmon told her.

"John loves the plantation, the people there, everything except the government, the conditions under which the other people live, the ones outside the plantation he can't help."

Ophelia sensed an opportunity to find out more. The fact that John seemingly had not done more through his West Point classmate Ramon Hernandez had always bothered her, especially since she now knew more than ever.

"You see, Ramon was not the kind of person to take orders, even at The Point. They only let him in because of his brother, to pacify him and to try and control him. Now *his brother* was a tyrant, a power hungry tyrant!" Harmon explained.

"But John could never get through to Ramon, that if you just treated people right, shared in the profits, that he could stay in power forever, or as long as he wanted. Ramon always wanted all of it for himself. It was his undoing," he explained.

Ophelia had read of the terror that Ramon's brother had been before he died and Ramon came to power. It seemed that it was the way of the world in Central America, banana republics, she thought. But that was much before her time and before she knew more and had a vested interest.

"John did all he could through Ramon. Finally Ramon relented, allowing John to essentially have his own little kingdom in Lake Nicaragua. John hoped it would serve as a model for the rest of the country, to inspire democracy, to inspire Ramon. It didn't work," Harmon said, frustrated as if he was trying to explain one of John's few failures in life, in kingmaking.

"Instead, Ramon used it as his private refuge when things became too politically hot in Managua. John played host and tolerated Ramon, but things got worse and Ramon and John saw less and less of each other as Ramon became more unpredictable. He caused a lot of problems, Ophelia. He had to go."

Ophelia for once was getting more, the information that made her more comfortable with John's involvement, of what he had and hadn't done, and why. As she learned more facts, circumstances, she had a better idea of how John's involvement in Nicaragua played out, why he never visited anymore, never trumpeted it as one of his projects, one of the incubators that produced another success story.

"But what about Ramon's son, Miguel?" she asked, almost too quickly, hesitating at the name, afraid that she would give herself away.

"He's a wild card, Ophelia. No one knows what he's going to do. John always liked him, though. Every time he would come to the estate they would have long talks about living in America. John brought him to Memphis several times. He's not like his father. He's a good man, I believe. I haven't seen him in some time."

"Thank you, Harmon. I do love that place and I sensed Mr. Thompson did as well. I see a future there, for those people, one better than they have now. I just don't know how to make it happen, Harmon," she said as Harmon listened intently.

"Talk with John, Ophelia. Together, you might be surprised what you can do."

Ophelia couldn't sleep. Her mind was ablaze with all the 'what ifs' about Miguel and Nicaragua. Her mind wandered back to Franklin, Georgia and wondered how Mom and Pop would feel if they had any clue where she was, where she had been. They would worry themselves sick at the thought of her jetting here and there. She was sure they didn't even know where Nicaragua was, much less who was President or how the people lived. Somehow though, she thought they would care.

Ophelia also thought it strange that for once Harmon didn't

know everything, but knew he wouldn't have disapproved of what she was doing. He would only have cautioned her to be careful and to seek John's approval. And that's just what Ophelia was going to do next.

⚜ ⚜ ⚜

Harmon and Lamont wanted to see John before they returned to Miami and the whole group headed for The Peabody as soon as the '404' jet touched down in Memphis. The trip seemed longer without John there. The gang wasn't complete without him.

Lamont loved the limo ride through Beale Street. He would have the window down waving at complete strangers, but everyone waved at everyone else on Beale Street. At least that hadn't changed.

"Look over there, Harmon. Porky's is getting a new sign. What's that all about? No one told me. What's wrong with the old sign?" Lamont asked in a panic.

"Don't worry Lamont, Arthur told me they're just getting a bigger one, something about not being able to see the old one from outer space. Sounds crazy to me. As much as we'd like them to stay the same Lamont, things are changing around here," Harmon lamented as they drove on to The Peabody.

Ophelia realized the same thing. As much as John and the others wished that the gang could stay together, that Beale Street would never change, the more change was inevitable. John had changed it and his small part of Nicaragua forty years ago and they were still changing. With the advent of Danny Carson, Truman Forsythe and Jerry Slater, the political landscape had changed as well. John had caused it all. But it all started right here.

Just then, Ophelia realized that change was exactly what she wanted to talk with John about that day. But Ophelia needed, as much as wanted to see him. She had so much to say and had been deliberating on how to say it all.

She knew she had to get back to Danny Carson's campaign. It would be just a few months more and it would all be over. There seemed to be so little time and change was upon them. One was either to be an agent of change, or simply just changed by one. She was a go-getter. She would do the changing.

✠ ✠ ✠

"How did you like my little paradise, girl?" John asked as he took an unusually strong hug from Ophelia.

She was delighted to see him. Since she learned so much from visiting the estate, the country, she felt like she had seen a whole new side of John. The Lake Nicaragua estate was vintage John alright; compassionate, caring, but at the same time calculating, a well done plan, another operation.

"I fell in love with it!" she gushed, being more than a little emotionally revealing, she would realize.

"I believe she's thinking about moving down there for goodness sake," Harmon added. He had sensed her enthusiasm ever since he saw her arrive on the ferry. She had been drinking in the sights, smells and sounds like no one he had ever seen before.

"It's just the same, John. They all miss you too. The estate misses you," Harmon told him, patting him on the back and rolling John onto the balcony.

Ophelia knew how much the people in Nicaragua missed him now. In the glances the people gave her, the awkward ones that led

277

to smiles and respectful interaction, Ophelia saw that as the people realized she was 'Mr. John's woman', their attitudes changed. They missed John terribly and hoped that she would be his surrogate, his straw man who would continue the tradition of support and give them hope for the future.

'John's straw man in Nicaragua'- that's exactly what Ophelia thought she should be. That's where she wanted to go and what she should do. She had never had a goal so admirable, so lofty. At the same time, she realized, a goal that would become so self-satisfying, and until she met John, one so seemingly unattainable.

"I may just want to do that, Mr. Thompson, move down there that is. I love the people and I can tell they love you too. You never told me about all the things you have done for that place," she said.

"Girl, there's a *lot* of work left to do down there. I just wish I was up to it!"

"Let's all have dinner tonight here on the balcony, Harmon. I miss those nights we would just sit here and hear the echoes of the music from Beale Street. I miss you and Lamont," John said as he looked toward the Mississippi from his chair.

"But Lamont, I'll tell you this, your son Arthur has been a great companion to me. In him, I have a big piece of you!"

Harmon and Lamont felt a terrible sense of abandonment in leaving John for Miami and retirement. They both moved toward him at the window of the penthouse. They sensed that John had recovered as much as he ever would from the stroke and heart attack. It was good to be back at John's home, but they knew they could never really go home again. It would never be the same.

Ophelia watched the three of them silhouetted against the setting sun and the Mississippi. She wished she had a photograph of them at just that instant. It would not be how she would want to remember them, she preferred the 'kick ass and take names' John and his gang she first met in Atlanta. But this was the reality of it all now.

The steaks, cigars and even the Black Jack Daniels whiskey didn't taste the same that night. John wasn't telling his usual stories of Beale Street and the old days. He appeared tired and the realization that John had not been out of The Peabody since she left on her trip, caused Ophelia to worry even more.

Harmon and Lamont were still tired from the trip and left for the night taking suites at The Peabody. They all hugged, something Ophelia had never witnessed before. She for once saw them as getting old, as retirees, not as go-getters anymore.

Harmon and Lamont were to leave the next day for Miami to rejoin their families. It was their new home, but they hated leaving John. But they knew he was in good hands with Ophelia and Arthur, and then just Arthur as Ophelia would leave again soon.

At least Marvin and Hennie were not as much of a problem nowadays, nor were they the help as they should have been to John. They just existed, running the ball team and handling the day-to-day operations under the watchful eyes of John's surrogates.

Ophelia would learn from Arthur that John hadn't even been to a baseball game since she had left. He didn't even seem to care who got the coveted seasons tickets he used to cherish and hand out like political plums. It didn't seem to bother him that The Blues wouldn't make The Series this year either.

Ophelia thought that as much as she didn't want to worry, or tire out John, she had to talk with him about her future, their future. Unfortunately, that included Nicaragua, the campaign – and finally Miguel.

"Mr. Thompson, I need to talk with you about something very serious and dear to me," she started.

The balcony felt like the right place. Harmon and the others were gone. Arthur had gone downstairs and David Muggs was at Rita's desk outside, his post when the office was shut down and after hours. It would be their only time alone before she went back to her own penthouse on the Mississippi and then off to the Danny Carson show again.

She had John's attention, and he knew it was coming. Even in his declining health, John was a people person, intuitive, and still possessed deductive reasoning skills far beyond those of most men – and good intelligence from the field.

"Girl, I hope you know I'm not getting any better. I want what's best for you. Do you want that plantation? If you do, it's yours!" John told her.

"Or do you just want to save them, those wonderful people down there?" he said as he turned his chair away from the river. "I can do one with the stroke of a pen, but you'll have to do the other. I don't have enough left in me to do both, girl."

Once again, John had caught Ophelia off guard. Just when she thought him to be weak, possibly vulnerable or not wanting to engage in conversation, he took the initiative and was a step ahead – always thinking.

"And don't be angry with Julio, but he tells me you're in love with that boy!"

As Ophelia was prone to say, 'once in a great once in a while' she might be caught speechless. This was one of those times.

There was what she would say later a great 'pregnant pause' as she caught her breath. John knew everything – and it shouldn't have surprised her.

"Now just listen to me, Ophelia. If you play your cards right, you can finish what I started down there," John said as Ophelia slumped into the nearest chair knowing she should just shut up and listen.

"You're a smart, good-looking girl, that'll take you a ways, but not all the way. Stick to Danny Carson like white on rice and we'll get this done!" he commanded, now gaining strength in his voice again, almost reaching Hugo Moore decibels. "So much of this depends on you!"

She slipped and let out, "But Mr. Thompson, how can we...?"

"Enough! Let me handle the details. Do as I say, and you have a good chance at this. Until you actually made this trip down there, until you convinced yourself to go all the way, I would have given you a 1 in 3 chance. You're on a roll now! It's all about synergy, the people, hell, it's always been about all that!" John boomed.

Synergy, the people. Absolutely right.

Chapter Thirty

Southern Politics

Ophelia hadn't called Betty Ferguson yet. She knew John wanted her to and the only Memphis fundraiser for Danny Carson during the campaign was coming up. Betty would have a cow if Ophelia didn't invite her. It would be a good time for her to cut her teeth, as John would say, on good old hometown politics, Memphis style.

"Well, I declare, I surely would like to accompany you to the fundraiser," Betty drawled her authentic Southern accent when Ophelia called the next day. "I wondered what had happened to you, Ophelia. I thought maybe one of these Memphis wild men had kidnapped you," Betty gasped, always prone to dramatics.

The Danny Carson campaign was coming to town and Ophelia would be front and center with Corky Benedict in organizing the event. It would be good for Ophelia to see him again. She felt like it had been an eternity since she had been to a fundraiser. The Nicaragua trip had put a lot of space between her and the real world.

"Betty, we need to make sure we have a big turnout. The campaign people have been working on this for some time and I've been out of town, so I need your help," she told an eager Betty Ferguson. That's all Betty had to hear.

The woman was a human social dynamo. If the event hadn't been held outdoors at Mud Island, Ophelia might have been worried that Betty had invited too many people. Betty burned up her Rolodex getting her fellow Memphis socialites mobilized. Every invitee was to invite one more person, each at $500 a head. Betty would raise $100,000 on her own. What synergy, Ophelia thought.

John himself had built the amusement park, museum and parks of Mud Island a few years earlier on the river at the foot of the Mississippi River Bridge, the 'new' one old Hugo Moore had built after his nephew Billy was killed running off the old one. It was a venue for concerts and had banquet facilities right on the river, perfect for a nighttime fundraiser.

And it was the perfect place for Betty Ferguson to put on a show, mint juleps, hoop skirts and all. The riverfront was certainly a beautiful place. The Mississippi hadn't changed much since the days when Hugo Moore's grandfather had crossed it during the 'not-so-Civil War' as Betty would put it. She could give walking historical tours with the best of the Mud Island tour guides. She would be needed as there were many Yankees coming into town, and it wouldn't be the New York Yankees.

"I swear Ophelia, I haven't seen this many Yankees since Reconstruction," she told Ophelia on Fundraiser Eve. "The Peabody's full of them!"

Betty was meeting Ophelia at The Peabody bar for a recap of her efforts. It had been some time since Ophelia was able to relax at the old Art Deco bar with its high, decorated ceilings and ornate woodwork. Even though the campaign atmosphere was hectic and John was resting upstairs, the bar had a comforting effect on her.

"Betty, I want you to meet Corky Benedict. He's Danny's campaign coordinator, and he's a good friend of mine," Ophelia said as she introduced Corky. "He's running the show," she said, much to Corky's delight.

Corky had been working very hard and it showed. With Ophelia on leave in Nicaragua and making speeches raising money, his job was that much harder. Being responsible for keeping Danny out of trouble and then reporting to John was a full time job. The actual campaign work was piled on top of all that.

"Betty, I've heard so much about you," he said doing his best to give a Southern gentleman's bow from the waist. "Thank you so much for all your hard work! Danny is very appreciative. He would like to meet you!"

You could have knocked Betty over with a feather. To meet Danny Carson, the next President of the United States would be a highlight in her life. She could talk about that forever!

"Well Mr. Benedict, aren't you the charmer?" she cooed. "I'd certainly love to *receive* Mr. Carson."

Corky didn't know exactly what that meant, but he was sure it was in a Southern vernacular that Ophelia could translate later.

Corky and Ophelia ordered Black Jacks as usual with only a passing thought at a mojito. Betty actually had a mint julep. They had done well for Danny Carson.

✤ ✤ ✤

Mud Island was lit up like a Christmas tree in the summer night. Betty was in her element as she flitted from table to table making sure everyone's glass was full. She was a great Southern hostess. And Ophelia was watching and taking mental notes. Every friend of John's was there and had ponied up big money just to sit at Danny's table.

John had even thought about trying to make it down to the river for the event. Instead, he borrowed Ophelia's riverfront townhouse and was watching out the window. With a pair of binoculars, he and Arthur had a bird's eye view of Danny's grand entrance that night. Mitch had joined them to see his wife in action too.

Danny had arrived by pickup truck driven by a local cotton grower who made sure he still had a little mud left on the mud flaps. It made Danny look more like one of the guys, a commoner who would fit in with the catfish and hushpuppie crowd.

Corky was by his side as they made a beeline for Ophelia - and Betty.

"So, you are my new best supporter here in Memphis, Mrs. Ferguson!" Danny barked as Betty melted. "Ophelia, where have you been keeping this woman all this time?"

"Why Mr. Carson, I do believe you're making me blush. Shame on you!" Betty gasped as she stifled a Southern curtsy. "I've been a fan of yours for years," she said as she strained the vowels as best she could to maximize her true Southern drawl.

"Well, I just hope we see more of you. May I call you Betty?" Danny asked as he actually kissed her outstretched hand.

Corky just rolled his eyes as Ophelia let a giggle slip. All that was missing was Rhett Butler to play to Betty's Scarlet. 'It was a hoot' as Ophelia would later tell John, who with Mitch, could fill in the dialog from their perch in Ophelia's townhouse.

"Damned Mitch, that Danny's good!" John yelled as they slapped their knees with delight.

"Yeah, and Betty's Scarlet is pretty dead-on too, John. That's my girl!" Mitch told him, admiring his Southern Belle from afar.

There was a Memphis Blues band, enough fried chicken, fried catfish and hushpuppies to feed the Russian army that night. Everything was fried including the twinkies. It was a mass heart attack waiting to happen.

Danny Carson had prepared a speech appropriate for the Memphis crowd. He even invoked the ghost of Senator Hugo Moore as he motioned toward the bridge Hugo had secured, the one that opened up the way for Arkansas cotton to be ginned and loaded onto Gordon Thompson's barges on the Mississippi over forty years ago.

Danny could make even old Hugo sound like the 'Great Emancipator' rather than the 'Great Manipulator' that he really was. John would have had another stroke if he had heard all that bullshit. Ophelia would tell John only that Danny had made a 'silk purse out of a sow's ear' that night talking about Hugo. It was good theater, she thought.

Danny stayed an unusually long time. He even danced the Tennessee waltz with Ophelia. Everyone, including the society writers and photographers from the *Commercial Appeal* newspaper noticed it too.

Danny would claim his front-page time on the next day's newspaper with that shot of him and Ophelia. It would serve to confirm Ophelia's place as a mover and a shaker on the Memphis political and social scene. Another John Henry Thompson plan that came together quite well. Betty Ferguson was aglow.

⚜ ⚜ ⚜

"Girl, you beat anything I've ever seen! That reminded me of the old soirees out at old Hugo Moore's place. You and Betty did well!" John said as he gave Ophelia and Betty a hug.

Betty and Ophelia had joined John and the others back at her penthouse after the night was over.

"Betty, I'm so proud of you!" Mitch told her as he hugged her too. "What did you think of Danny Carson?"

286

"Mitch, you are my number one beau, but I must say that he is a danged good lookin' man!" He's a charmer!" Betty gasped as she fanned herself.

"I believe he just might win that race!" she said as she mixed some mint juleps for all of them.

"A toast!" John boomed as his Hugo Moore voice had returned. "To Danny Carson and Hugo Moore! Long live politicians and the people that make them!"

They toasted the night away as they looked down on the cleanup crews scurrying along Mud Island to pick up the debris from the event.

John pointed down on the scene and declared, "But somebody's always got to clean up their mess, don't they?"

Ophelia and everyone else just smiled.

✣ ✣ ✣

John would take Danny Carson's call the next day at The Peabody penthouse. Danny had flown out right after the Memphis fundraiser to make another event in Chicago, right in Luke Spearman's back yard.

"John, I want to thank you for all you've done for me. That Ophelia and Betty Ferguson really put on a show for us last night. Please let them know how grateful I am John," Danny told John in his most sincere voice. "I'm really working hard out here."

"You can tell her yourself, Danny. She'll be out there working for you every day from now on. She'll make you a good hand if you let her, and I know you will," John said with more of a command form in his voice. "You're going to win this thing, Danny."

"Keep in touch with me – and let me know if you need anything, and I mean *anything*, Danny!" John told him forcefully. And John meant it.

"I am eternally grateful, John. I'll be in touch."

Danny was on a roll and it was all down hill as he inched toward that first Tuesday in November. Ophelia would be returning to her schedule the next day after spending time with John. He needed to send her off in style and had arranged a quick reception at The Peabody with Betty and Mitch in attendance.

The mezzanine level of The Peabody was the perfect place. David Muggs had arranged to have the floor locked out on the elevators and only the people John had invited were allowed up for the event.

Arthur wheeled John down with Ophelia in tow. Many of the same faces from John's birthday party graced the crowd, all close friends of John. Marvin and Hennie, now on their best behavior, and medication, were even allowed to join the group. The Blues band from the Boogie Woogie was there as John gave a toast to Ophelia, his 'right arm' he said.

One could almost hear Marvin and Hennie's teeth grind over the applause. It would be the sendoff Ophelia needed, the shot in the arm that would keep her going while she spent the rest of the campaign away from John.

It was John's way of openly endorsing, almost crowning Ophelia with his public approval. If Memphis didn't realize it after the fundraiser, they would certainly know it now. After the events of the last two days, Ophelia was a force to be contended with in her own right.

It was almost a goodbye, Ophelia realized and for a second the thought of asking John if she could stay instead of heading back on the road crossed her mind. But she knew she owed it to John to go back to work. She never lost sight of the fact that she was an employee as well as a trusted friend and confidante.

It would be lonely. Corky and Carson would be in different parts of the country most of the time. She would only meet with them at the bigger events. Ophelia even invited Betty to join her for a few events that were arranged in the Southern states. It would free up Mitch to spend more time with John while she was gone and Betty loved it. She jumped at the chance. She would fit right in.

It was just a cocktail reception, something where John wouldn't get too tired. Mitch and Betty went back upstairs with John and Ophelia after it was over for cigars and Black Jacks.

"Betty, I hope you have as much luck out on that campaign as you did here in Memphis. With that $100,000 you raised, it put Danny's take over half a million, and that's just from right here in Memphis," John told her. It was the best compliment he had ever given her.

"I'll give it my best John. I think it's exciting!" Betty told him, as enthusiastic as a schoolgirl.

Mitch and Betty said goodbye to give Ophelia and John some time alone. They knew she would be leaving the next morning.

"This will all be over soon, girl. This campaign will be something you'll remember all your life. And the things that will come out of it will change your world forever," John told her as he looked at the river from the balcony.

There was a sadness in his voice. It was almost as if John were signing off, resigning from the world. And he had more words that gave Ophelia an indication of it.

"I remember years ago when Senator Moore ran for office. Hell, he never had an opponent, but he ran like the devil was after him," John said as he smiled a wide grin. "Now *he* was a politician!"

"Tell me about him Mr. Thompson. Danny Carson mentioned him at the fundraiser," she said as she knelt down beside John's chair.

"He was all about power, Ophelia. All he wanted was more money, land and people he could control. He never understood that you have to enable people, share in the profits, build people up, and not tear them down. He tried to control me, and he did, for a while."

Ophelia could see the memories flooding back into John's mind. She could also see they were painful but satisfying at the same time.

"The best thing I ever did was to get him to sell me his interest in this ball team before he died. He lived one year more, that was it. I had more money than he did before I was thirty years old. It killed his soul," John told her with a bit of regret, maybe bitterness in his voice. John paused a full minute before he spoke again.

"Hold out your hand girl," he said to her as he extended a fist toward her.

Ophelia held her hand open, palm up, into which John dropped a ring, his West Point ring.

"I haven't worn this since the day that old man died. That's all he cared about at first, the fact that I had come back here to work after graduating from the Academy. I want you to have it. Put it on a necklace and wear it for me. It'll remind you of me every day. Hell, it's so damned heavy, it'll have to!"

Ophelia started to cry, like she hadn't cried since she was a child. She felt intensely sad, grateful, lonely and afraid all at once. Her life of hardship, strife, struggle and happiness all washed through her mind. She loved this man. He was a father, friend and benefactor all rolled into one. She didn't want to leave. They sat there for hours and enjoyed the river, not talking at all. She felt at home with him.

Chapter Thirty-One

A Plan – *The* Plan

"Meet me in Miami at the club, Tobacco Road, the place where you slipped me the note. I will be there next Wednesday at seven o'clock," Ophelia told the message handlers via telephone.

Ophelia was excited that she had John's blessing to move forward, although cautiously and without totally telling him what she would be doing with Miguel. She couldn't wait to see him, buoy his spirits and make some sort of plans to help him and the country she had fallen in love with on her visit.

The campaign seemed to be getting on a faster track, the election being just two months away. Ophelia felt a sense of urgency, to be everywhere with everyone at once. She wanted to be with Miguel, make plans and be at every fundraiser she could. She also needed to be with Danny whenever possible, but it was an impossible schedule to keep. She would need some help.

"I declare, I've never been on a jet like this!" Betty Ferguson told Ophelia as they sped toward Miami. "This is comfortable, to say the least!"

Betty had jumped at the chance to make another campaign event. She could keep Ophelia company and would be an asset at the fundraisers; in a strange way, she may keep Ophelia sane. It couldn't hurt, Ophelia thought.

David Muggs had been told to let Ophelia have a little freedom.

John now felt more secure that she would not be in any danger from Miguel Hernandez. Muggs would still sweep the rooms for any electronic bugs as everyone wanted to play it safe until Danny was elected.

And it would be good to see Harmon and Lamont again so soon after the Lake Nicaragua trip. Although they missed John and Memphis, they were enjoying retirement, spending their days out on *The Ophelia* cruising out on Biscayne Bay. Ophelia wanted to take Betty over to meet them and show her around the boat before their next event in two days.

"I can't think of anything more flattering than having a boat named for you, Ophelia," Betty chirped as she was lead onto *The Ophelia*. "I've heard so much about this yacht from John."

Harmon and Lamont had their wives with them for the first time in many trips on the boat. Ophelia gave hugs all around as Betty reacquainted herself with the others. It had been some time since she had seen them at one of her soirees in Memphis. It was like old home week out in the ocean.

"Lamont, are you feeling okay since the trip?" Ophelia asked. Lamont still seemed tired and sluggish. Ophelia knew he missed John and the life he had in Memphis, but this was something else.

"I can't seem to get any energy back, Ophelia. To be honest, I don't believe I've ever recovered from that climb," Lamont almost gasped. "I guess maybe it's the sun. I believe I'll stay inside the cabin today."

Betty loved any new nice place, plain and simple. One could see she was making mental notes for the stories she would tell her socialites back in Memphis. Younger than Mitch, she still looked good in her swimsuit at age 51.

Ophelia made a ship-to-shore telephone call to John to check on him. He and Arthur were just sitting in the penthouse at The

Peabody, he said. He wanted Ophelia to have fun and work hard at the same time. Somehow he knew he wouldn't have to worry about that. Just call when she could, he told her.

That night Ophelia looked for a sign that Miguel was back in Miami. She had John's penthouse at The Ritz South Beach to share with Betty. It was plenty of space to share but Betty was always one to want to talk all the time. Ophelia had made up a few fictitious meetings she told Betty she would have to make ensuring she could get time alone with Miguel when he called.

As Ophelia and Betty watched the sea from the penthouse balcony they both noticed two men standing near the pier in the distance. They appeared to be arguing loudly and it struck Ophelia that they looked familiar.

She was sure it was Miguel Hernandez and Julio Fuentes. But they weren't arguing, they were laughing and hugging. They both seemed to realize that Ophelia and Betty were watching them as they fell silent at the same time, taking care not to fix their gaze on the two women at the hotel.

Ophelia made an excuse to go downstairs leaving Betty with the penthouse to herself.

"Betty, I'm going to have to run an errand for about an hour. Why don't you order us up some champagne and steaks? We'll have a 'girl's night in' tonight!"

As Ophelia made her way out to the dock she made sure Betty wasn't still watching. It was Miguel and Julio as she thought.

"Julio, what are you doing here?" she asked, sure that John would pop out in his wheelchair, or maybe Muggs with his electronic black box.

"Let's go inside my suite, Ophelia," Julio said. "We need to talk."

✠ ✠ ✠

Ophelia was beginning to wonder when the surprises would end, or if they ever would. It seemed that every time she turned a corner in her life now there was an event that turned everything upside down.

"Ophelia, I have known Miguel all his life, since my sister gave birth to him I should say," Julio said as if he had just been caught in a lie, the half-truth he had allowed Ophelia to believe.

"Miguel is my nephew. I wish I could have told you earlier. I just thought it wasn't time."

Miguel was hanging his head as well. He knew that he didn't need any roadblocks to Ophelia helping him, in caring for him. But he thought it time he had Julio meet with them both. It was time to plan.

"I think I need a drink," Ophelia said as she sat in the nearest chair in Julio's suite. She looked around the room making sure no one else was there. Not to her surprise, she saw a familiar black box in a chair next to a bedroom door.

As she took the Black Jack Daniels she yelled, "Come on out David! We might as well have everyone out in the open!" It was one of the few mistakes Muggs would make.

As Muggs came out of the bedroom Ophelia knew it was time to assert some authority, to set the record straight.

"Now you guys know more than I do, and I don't like it one damned bit," she said coolly as she took a big swig of her drink.

"But right here and now, all that is about to change."

Miguel had yet to speak a word, Muggs was clearly at a loss and Julio looked like the only person who had anything to add.

"Ophelia, first of all I want to tell you that we have John's full confidence. He is letting you take the lead in getting something done for our country, for Miguel," Julio said, now recovering from his embarrassment at the deception – and at being caught.

294

"We had to be careful, and…" he tried to say as Ophelia waved him to a halt.

"If you people don't trust me by now, then we have a problem," Ophelia said as she fixed her attention on Miguel. "If we've finally gotten that issue out of the way, can we talk now?"

And they talked straight for an hour until Ophelia remembered she had Betty upstairs waiting, wishing at that point she hadn't brought her to Miami. The best they could do was to clear the air, that Julio was who he was, that Muggs was in on the game, however Ophelia would decide she wanted to play it from now on. And she made it clear that was the way it would be.

"No more of this cloak and dagger bullshit guys!" she said very matter-of-factly. "I've got a lot of work to do from here on. Miguel, forget about Wednesday night and call me at the penthouse at midnight tonight." Ophelia was not happy with any of them.

They had made it clear to her that Harmon and Lamont knew nothing of what they may have in mind, what their plans might be. Ophelia felt good about that. Lamont was clearly not taking retirement well and Harmon didn't seem to be up for this sort of thing anymore either. It would be just Miguel, Julio and Muggs, the 'new gang' of sorts formed of a mutual concern and drive for change – and on following orders from John, she realized as well.

The new gang would have much work ahead of them, but no one but Ophelia could act now.

Betty had the champagne and steaks all laid out nicely. They enjoyed the night at The Ritz, content to stay at the penthouse and enjoy the view. The fundraiser would be the next night, just enough time for Ophelia to do whatever with Miguel, get back to Memphis for a night with John and then back out onto the road. But Ophelia's mind was anywhere but in that hotel suite.

"Ophelia, I appreciate you inviting me down here. This place is lovely," Betty said as they enjoyed the Moet-Chandon and T-bones.

"Mitch and I have never been down here to John's penthouse."

"I appreciate you Betty and I needed some company on this trip. It can get a little lonely on these trips and I miss Mr. Thompson. He's quite a man," Ophelia said. Betty knew how much she adored him, how close they had become. She let it go at that. Betty was becoming a good friend, someone Ophelia could count on.

Betty, with all her energy and spunk was still one to turn in early. By ten o'clock she was ready for bed. That was fortunate for Ophelia who wanted to have a long talk with Miguel – by telephone.

Straight up at midnight, he called. He knew she was upset.

"I'm so sorry about Julio. He demanded that I not tell you about him being my uncle, Ophelia. It wasn't my fault," he tried to explain.

Ophelia wouldn't have any of it. If there was one thing she would not, could not tolerate, it was being lied to by someone she was doing her best to trust.

"If you ever lie to me or hold back anything like this again, I'll never have anything to do with you! Let's get that straight right now," she said, trying her best to hold her voice down even though she was on the private line and far from where Betty might hear her.

"If I am to help you, really help you, I have to be able to trust you, Miguel."

"You can, Ophelia. The fact that I swore to Julio that I would not tell you has torn me apart. I want to see so you badly it is about to drive me insane. Please see me," he pleaded.

Ophelia thought twice before she said what she was about to

say, then decided to go ahead and go for it.

"It's midnight, Miguel, but I'll meet you at the Tobacco Road for a drink."

After what obviously was a stunned silence Miguel simply said, "I'm on my way!"

✠ ✠ ✠

Even at the late hour the place was hopping. The doorman recognized Ophelia as she stepped out of her cab. As soon as he could clear the way, he escorted her to the usual table.

Ophelia looked around to see Miguel in the same place she had seen him the night he passed the note, at the back near the restrooms. She just looked at him for the longest. He looked tired and worried. His life since the death of his father had been an ongoing ordeal, a hell on earth for him.

Ophelia ordered a mojito and all the while thought of Corky who was somewhere out on the road with Danny. Miguel stayed where he was, just waiting for a sign from Ophelia. She would drink the cocktail before she motioned for him to follow her out the door. As fond as she was of the place, there were too many people there for her to feel comfortable being seen with Miguel. The stakes were higher now and she didn't know who all the players were, ones that might be on the other side.

Ophelia just started walking. The scene was lit with pastel neon, abuzz with people out on the town, looking for fun that was the swinging 1980's in Miami. Miguel was following. Ophelia didn't stop and meet him for all the reasons that made sense, the danger, and the conflicting emotions of anger, compassion and distrust. But her wants and needs finally won out. She ducked into a diner, one of those that looked like it belonged in a 1950's movie and sat down to order coffee. She looked over her shoulder and motioned a waiting Miguel inside.

As Miguel sat down in the booth across from her he looked even more tired than a few minutes ago at Tobacco Road.

"I'm sorry, Ophelia. Please forgive me, but I thought I was doing the right thing. I promise, I will never keep anything from you again. I care for you deeply. I wish we were back in Nicaragua, alone."

Ophelia took Miguel's outstretched hand and held it tightly. As she pulled it toward her chest it met with the hard lump of John's ring on her necklace beneath her blouse. It was as if she had just solidified another significant bond, one made through John.

"Maybe someday if we're lucky, we may just do that. For now, be strong. And you need to trust me, Miguel. I want this to work too!"

"Now let's get you something to eat," Ophelia said, feeling that he looked emaciated and in need of a good meal.

They talked for the first time about little things, where they grew up and how Miguel had lived a privileged life, he said, with his father the ruler of a country. And it had all now gone to hell with his mother and sisters living near the plantation on the island in Lake Nicaragua. Julio had done all he could but was afraid that they could not be seen in public for fear of retribution from the new government, Hector Gonzalez's regime.

Ophelia shared who she was, where she'd been, who she had become. It was the first time she had done so with a man, romantically at least, in a long time. Her last involvement with a man had not ended well, his marriage having just before ending in divorce leaving him exhausted mentally and physically.

In Miguel, she sensed a renewed hope for a lasting romantic

relationship. It was comforting to her, the way Miguel listened and asked questions about her Mom and Pop. He would love to see this Franklin, Georgia, he told her.

Conversation brought them closer together. They communicated on a level like never before. Just as Miguel moved from his seat across from Ophelia to be next to her, to kiss her, Ophelia's eyes widened as she saw David Muggs burst into the diner.

His eyes were filled with tears as he sobbed, "Somehow I knew I would find you down here. We've got to go. Lamont Boone is dead."

Chapter Thirty-Two

A Family Break-Up

Ophelia remembered an old proverb about death, the one that said that good men must die, but that death cannot kill their names. She knew Lamont Boone would live on through his son Arthur, John's new Man Friday. But Lamont could never be replaced and everyone that had ever met him knew that was a fact.

It was an excruciatingly long, hard ride back home in the '404' jet. John had sounded inconsolable on the telephone and Ophelia felt awful that she was not there with him when Lamont died. Harmon was almost as bad, crying the entire flight to Memphis. She wished that Miguel were there now to comfort her and wondered when fate would stop intervening in their meetings, if not their affairs.

John had sent a separate jet for Lamont's body to be accompanied by his family back to Memphis and then Slabtown.

"Do we know what happened Harmon, how he died?" Ophelia asked as Harmon stared out the window.

"His wife said he woke up in the middle of the night with chest pain. She called an ambulance and then me. We live very close to each other, Ophelia. I beat the ambulance there, but he was already gone. It was a massive heart attack," Harmon said, barely able to form the words he used, refusing to use the word 'dead'.

Ophelia felt terrible about the day in Nicaragua when they climbed the mountain. Harmon assured her that wasn't the cause or even the beginning of his decline. It turned out that Lamont had been suffering from heart disease for many years, a fact known to only a few people.

As the '404' jet landed at the Memphis airport Ophelia could see the black limousine was already there. Arthur Boone was there with John in his wheelchair. They had dark glasses on and both looked disheveled and worn out. It had obviously been a long night for them.

Ophelia bounded down the jet ramp and into John's outstretched arms. She grabbed Arthur and hugged him tightly. Harmon joined them all and they cried for what seemed like a long time, saying nothing. It wasn't lost on them all that their gang was back together again with Arthur standing in for his father. It was the deepest pain any of them had suffered in many, many years.

"Mr. Thompson, I'm so sorry. What can I do?" Ophelia cried.

"Girl, you can just wait here with me for Lamont. I want to be here for his last ride out to Slabtown," John said. Ophelia, Harmon and Arthur nodded.

Arthur helped John back into the limo as Harmon and Ophelia took their usual seats. Each of them looked at where Lamont would have been, his empty seat right across from John where he had been for forty years.

John drifted into what seemed to be an almost unconscious recitation of his relationship and history with Lamont. As the limo idled John recalled the first day he met Lamont. As best he could remember it was when the entire Boone family walked by the Thompson home out in Slabtown, the time John's father pointed out to Gordon and him that "there but for the grace of God go you", that lesson about there being people out in the world more poor than them.

"Daddy was wrong, girl. Lamont was always one of the richest people I ever met. He was a good man and a fine friend. I've been so blessed in this life with many things. But my greatest gifts have been my friends. If you can find ones like Lamont and this man here, you're set for life," John cried as he laid his hand on Harmon's knee.

Ophelia hadn't prayed in a long time. Along with her prayer for Lamont, she prayed for just what John had said - friends for life.

The second Thompson jet landed a full three hours after Ophelia, Harmon and David had met John. It taxied up to the limo as Arthur got John's wheelchair out and helped him into it. Lamont's wife, Grace, got off first and hugged them all. Ophelia hadn't really gotten to know her but knew that she and Lamont had been together for nearly forty years, ever since they hit it big on the Beale Street Revival with John.

It was the big jet, the only one capable of bringing back Lamont's body in the plain wooden casket, the kind he had always said he wanted to be buried in. Lamont had been that way, not flashy, just practical, plain country folk by nature. The funeral home hearse had just arrived and John climbed in with Grace telling the gang he wanted to ride to Slabtown with Lamont one more time.

What followed was what Lamont would have wanted. It was a celebration of life, not of death, but of that good name Lamont had made for himself. All of Slabtown turned out at the John Henry Thompson Community Center Lamont had built there with some of his money he had earned with John. As many white people as blacks turned out to honor the person, the name of Lamont Boone. They even re-christened the center The Lamont Boone and John Henry Thompson Community Center. John made sure they listed Lamont's name first.

And John gave them a check for $1 million in Lamont's honor. No one but the Boone's ever knew it, but he gave another $1 million to Grace and Arthur that weekend. It was only money now to John. What better use than to honor Lamont and maybe, just maybe help ease the pain of his family. But it wasn't as if they needed it, unknown to most folks in those parts, Lamont had salted away a cool $30 million on his own, following John's investing lead all those years.

"Mr. Thompson, I just want you to know, I want to stay on with you," Arthur said after the service. "My father would want it that way."

As Arthur and his mother hugged John, the people just flocked to John seated in his chair near the casket. Two of Slabtown's greatest had come home that day, one of them to stay now forever.

✠ ✠ ✠

It was the death in John's family that he dreaded the most. He had known of Lamont's heart problems and had encouraged him to retire many years ago. He felt perhaps the most guilt of anyone that Lamont had died. He had known that Harmon and Lamont had stayed on with him just out of loyalty, friendship and to try and take care of him. Now that Lamont was gone, so had a piece of John, a big piece that had always been with him since the days behind the mule team. John was inconsolable.

As the limo returned by the route they had all taken so many times, by the river, down Beale Street and up to the back of The Peabody, John didn't say a word. He might have been expected to point at the back door of the Boogie Woogie Café where he and Lamont had snuck out with drinks in hand that night they planned the Revival forty years ago.

Or of the old Union Hotel that Lamont bought outright with his first bonus from John twenty years ago, his first act being to preserve that old Room 404 in John's honor.

But John seemed not to even notice when they had arrived at The Peabody. Harmon had to tell him they were home.

"I'm going to spend some time with John here in Memphis at the hotel Ophelia. I'm more worried about John than ever," Harmon told her as Arthur wheeled John into the lobby. "Let's talk tomorrow."

Ophelia felt that John needed to be alone. She held the West Point ring close to her as she was driven to her townhouse on the river. She needed time alone too, she thought. She just sat alone looking out at the Mississippi wondering where she would end up in life. The Memphis she knew seemed to be crumbling with John's decline in health, Lamont's death, her heart moving far south with Miguel and Lake Nicaragua.

Ophelia was being torn between John, Miguel and the campaign work she knew John wanted her to do first. And she knew why he wanted it so much for her. He knew that her future hinged on the outcome of the race, on what Danny could do for her, who she would be after John was gone. But the real conflict was that she just wanted to be with John, her friend who had brought her up out of obscurity in Atlanta, just another real estate agent with no clear goals or dreams.

Ophelia didn't sleep much that night. She had made up her mind to tell John that she would give it all up to spend her time with him. She would leave the campaign, stay in Memphis instead of 'tear-assing', as John would say, all over the country helping him make the king of all political kings, to help make his greatest straw man ever.

The next morning as Ophelia drove the Mercedes John had given her to The Peabody, she believed she must make that offer to John. As she entered The Peabody she caught a glimpse of Marvin who actually smiled at her. It wasn't a friendly, smile it was one of those 'you're days are numbered' smiles.

As if on cue, David Muggs followed her into the elevator and gave her a hug. He was a legacy at the hotel too, Ophelia remembered. Old Rufus Muggs, John's friend from the old days at the hotel, the head porter and David's father had died long ago.

And then, there as she got off the elevator was Arthur, only a day after his father's funeral, he was right there with John, then Rita, the legacy of a secretary.

It struck her just then that this was the season of change for John but his friends' legacies lived on. *That's* what John wanted her to do – live on and leave a piece of his legacy, one of doing good for the people using his power, synergy – in spite of Marvin or Hennie.

She couldn't ask him to let her stay. She owed it to John to continue to do his work – and be his straw man. Ophelia, in that short time from the lobby to the penthouse of The Peabody, realized that she would be selfish to ask John to let her stay. It was John's will that she go back out into the world – and complete his plan.

"Mr. Thompson, how are you feeling?" Ophelia asked as she hugged him on the penthouse balcony.

"I'll be okay, girl. Just don't you worry about me."

It was as if John had anticipated her offer to stay with him. Before she could utter the words she had already made up her mind not to say, John spoke quickly.

"You just get back out there and get this thing done with Danny Carson," he said as he turned his wheelchair around so he could look straight into Ophelia's eyes.

"Don't you realize *everything* depends on Danny winning?

I'll be okay here, you just go out there and make sure your dreams come true," he told her, almost pushing her away.

Prophetically John added, "I'm not going to be here forever."

❖ ❖ ❖

Betty Ferguson had stayed on in Miami and attended the fundraiser in Ophelia's absence. Corky Benedict had heard of Lamont's death and told Danny who called John with words of condolence. Ophelia had to catch up with the two of them in Los Angeles. She would stay close to them throughout the rest of the campaign just as John wanted.

Truman Forsythe had called John too. He didn't know Lamont well but knew that he was close to John and that it must have affected him greatly. Truman told John he was using all of his organization he had built over the years in California as he climbed the political ladder to get out the money and votes for Danny.

At the California fundraiser, Danny Carson, Presidential nominee, and two of the nation's Governors, Truman Forsythe and Jerry Slater looked good together on the podium that night. The charming Senator from Georgia sandwiched between the popular former fighter jock Governor of California and the good-guy Governor from Missouri. It made great newspaper copy and fundraising easy. Former West Point classmates gave over $200,000 all by themselves. It was the Class of '46 at its best, that is, if John could have been there.

❖ ❖ ❖

Betty Ferguson joined Ophelia at the next stop in St. Louis too. Jerry Slater was a smart choice for Danny's running mate. He had emulated John's success on Beale Street with his own Mississippi River riverfront revival – after John loaned him the money. Jerry had made an old riverfront business area into one of St. Louis's most vibrant tourist attractions.

Laclede's Landing, as it was called, was named for the 18th century French explorer who set up a trading post there while exploring the wilderness. Laclede was, ironically, the same explorer for whom General Pershing's home town Laclede, Missouri was named.

Ophelia thought it looked eerily like Beale Street with its clubs, festivals and Blues music. But unlike John, Jerry didn't own it all, or even most of it. He was just content with doing all the development work and then flipping the properties, satisfied with being financially set so he could run for public office.

And Missouri liked their Governor. They hadn't had anyone associated with the White House since Harry Truman and were satisfied that Jerry would occupy only the number two spot. By association, they loved Danny Carson who was taking Jerry with him all the way to the top.

Jerry's people put on a great party. Ophelia missed John all the more as she felt the sensations of Beale Street at Laclede's Landing. Betty loved it too and had called some of her friends in Memphis to make the short trip over to St. Louis. They even dipped into their pockets again to help Danny.

Danny was warming up to Ophelia as he realized her people skills on the campaign more than offset his thoughts of her being a constant reminder of the hold John had on him. Ophelia was spending more time at the front table with him too, and more people were starting to notice. With each event she was moving closer to being accepted and validating her claim, or future one.

After the St. Louis event it came time for Betty to return to Memphis since the next stop would be in Yankeeland Chicago. Ophelia had asked her to be her lifeline to John, her stand-in while she was on the road. She promised Ophelia she would fill John in on everything even though Ophelia talked with him every night. Betty had become a close and trusted friend despite her sometimes overblown Southern idiosyncrasies.

Danny had already been to Chicago and fed off the Harmon Vance contacts there, the ones left over from the Vance Industries days and afterwards when Harmon joined John.

But Carson wanted to slam Luke Spearman again where it hurt the most, his hometown. Luke had tried to woo the vote with the left wing that kept trying to tell him to shave the beard, act more conservative and overall not to be himself if he wanted to have any chance to win.

Luke wouldn't have any of it. He preferred to spend time on the 'left coast' as John still called it with Hollywood celebs like Warren Beatty and Robert Redford. Ophelia honestly thought Luke knew he wasn't going to win and instead was trying to set himself up for a movie career. She believed what John had told her. Luke was all 'style over substance', all show and no go. He sure as hell wasn't a team player or a go-getter by John's definition.

"Mr. Thompson, you just wouldn't believe the support Danny has up here where Luke's been Governor for eight years! It's phenomenal," she told John on her nightly telephone call from Chicago.

But it all made sense. Luke had made all the wrong moves, particularly in Chicago. He had opposed the revitalization of the North Loop and had even fought against state money going to save the old Chicago Theater. It had just been saved from ruin, partly due to an endowment from Harmon Vance and his family. Danny and Ophelia attended one of the live performances there while in Chicago.

"Mr. Thompson, I even went to see that new talk show everyone's screaming about, that lady from Kosciusko, Mississippi, Oprah Winfrey! She's hot!" Ophelia told him one night. Oprah had received national attention less than a year before when her show was syndicated nationwide.

"She's a go-getter alright, Ophelia. She grew up not far from Memphis! You need to watch her, girl! She'll make some news," John said doing his best to draw enough strength to boom like old Hugo Moore. John was always one to spot talent.

Betty and Mitch were keeping John company now and Harmon was staying on until the campaign was over, all doing their best to keep John strong and in good spirits. It was tough duty seeing their friend decline even further in health and spirit, especially when Ophelia was not there.

"It's all over but the shouting," John would say as the first Tuesday after the first Monday in November approached. And there would be much shouting indeed.

Chapter Thirty-Three

The President-Elect

Ophelia had done her job well. Danny Carson and Jerry Slater were on the road to the White House. Luke Spearman was still somewhere in California with no message and very few friends, even among the Democrats. He had thoroughly embarrassed the party to the point of just about being disowned by them.

Ophelia was able to make it back to Memphis to vote and see John. But she wasn't prepared for what she was about to see.

David Muggs met her at the Memphis airport as the '404' jet rolled into the hangar. She should have known something was up when John was not there to see her.

"Where's Mr. Thompson?" she asked David before her feet hit the tarmac. "What's wrong?" she now demanded.

"Ophelia, he's not feeling that well," was all David could say, not at all satisfying her. "He wants to see you."

Of course he did, Ophelia thought. What an odd statement to make. She had finished out the campaign just as he asked of her, as he wanted. She did as he asked only when she realized it was his will, the fulfillment of his grand plan through her, for her.

Immediately she thought that perhaps John was upset with her. She searched her memory for anything that had happened since she left to rejoin the campaign. It wasn't that. John must be more ill than she knew. She thought about asking Muggs, but didn't want to put him in the position of having to lie to her, or at worst, for her to be mad at him for not having called her and told about his condition.

The weather was still tolerable in Memphis even though it was already November. Ophelia's first clue that something was wrong came when she did not see John on the balcony of the penthouse as they arrived at The Peabody.

As she made her way to the elevator and then up to the penthouse she saw no familiar faces, no one that might give her word, even a clue as to what was happening. John wanted to see her, was all Muggs had said.

Secretary Rita was not looking well and it should have been an indication to Ophelia of things to come. As she entered the penthouse the first, the only thing she saw was a hospital bed, one of those tricked-out kinds with all the bells and whistles. And there lay John, pale as the sheet he was propped up on.

"Come here, girl. It's been too long," John said faintly.

Ophelia had that 'fight or flight' feeling John had told her about. At first she wanted to flee, just not face the fact that John was bedridden now, sicker than before. Then she had the overwhelming urge to fight back tears and be strong, to follow through with being John's best friend and companion, and to do whatever she could for her friend.

"Mr. Thompson, have you just taken to the bed now, a man of leisure?" Ophelia quipped, trying hard to make John feel at ease with her discomfort of the shock and awe of seeing John like this, of having been kept in the dark.

Then she just hugged him and let loose the tears. She was sorry that she wasn't as strong as John hoped she would be. But at that moment she didn't care. This was *her* John, the man that had changed her life forever. And now he was confined to this penthouse that had been converted into what amounted to a plush hospital room with monitors, nurses and doctors there in place of his friends and leather chairs. Even the baseball stadium seats were gone.

John had suffered another heart attack, albeit a milder one that put him on his course of descent into what now was a sedentary state of being. And try as she might, Ophelia was mad, hot as hell at Harmon, at least at Harmon for not telling her to come home. To hell with Danny Carson and the campaign. She should have been told, she thought.

"For the life of me Harmon, first Lamont and now this heart attack, why didn't you let me know?" she pleaded, knowing the answer.

"He forbade me to say a single solitary word, Ophelia. He wants you to finish what he, what you started," Harmon said as he, for some reason, stared down at his West Point ring.

The *point* wasn't lost on Ophelia, the symbolism, the fact that John had never made it to the army, but that he had made it out of Slabtown, conquered Memphis and the world. John couldn't finish it himself. And Ophelia knew she would have to go back out, away from John and see it through – and she had to leave now. It was Election Day.

✤ ✤ ✤

John was asleep, he slept most of the time now, when she left on the '404' jet to Atlanta. It was that proverbial, every four-year exercise in the American Constitution, Election Day, and John wanted Ophelia there in Atlanta with Danny. She had taken John his absentee ballot and they both voted before she left Memphis.

Corky met her at the jet and had a limo waiting to take her to the Ritz-Carlton downtown. It had been a long time since she had been to John's suite there and any victory celebrated there that night would be bittersweet and hollow at best. Ophelia told Corky what she could, what she thought she should about John's condition. She said only that he was weak and had taken to the bed most of the time, not the whole story. John didn't want Danny to know. He refused to be perceived as being in a position of weakness.

The Ritz was Danny's election-watch headquarters and the place was abuzz with news cameras, supporters of all sorts, big money people and folks fresh from the Underground and already boozed up. It was going to be a night of celebration for sure.

Danny was not seeing anyone. Holed up in his suite half the size of John's penthouse, he had however asked Corky to bring Ophelia by to see him. The Secret Service man at the front door recognized her as a 'full access' person and let her in.

"Danny, it's the night we've all been waiting for!" Ophelia said, never showing any sign of the great stress she was under concerning John. "How do you feel about it?"

"It's way too early to know right now, Ophelia. The polls don't close in California for two hours. But the exit polls show we should have it won!" he said, barely able to contain himself. "I can't believe this is going to happen!"

No one else was in the room so maybe that was why Danny gave her a hug. She hugged him back, sensed a new closeness to him, closer than they had become even after all the time on the campaign. She was actually happy for him, even though she knew he was a jerk. Again, after all, he was a politician first and foremost.

"I'll never forget all that you and John have done for me," Danny said stating the obvious. "I've had calls from all over bragging on your work. Just tell me what you want."

Ophelia knew that she already had, he knew it too, so she left it at that. She would wait for John's cue. He was still well enough to run this show.

Corky and Ophelia spent the election night watching returns in the penthouse. But she had already made arrangements for a party of her own. She had called Mom and Pop and sent a limo over to Franklin, Georgia to pick them up. She even invited Charles Waller, her old commercial real estate boss telling him to bring the guys from the office where she used to work. Corky would get to see Ophelia in action around her family and old friends. It was time to celebrate.

Mom and Pop didn't know what to think. They had been to Atlanta many times but never to the Ritz-Carlton. Pop just wanted to watch the news on television, Mom just wanted to cook. It was the only election party that night with cornbread as the main hors d'oeuvre.

As the television news networks were prone to do then, two of them called the election as being a big win for Danny before California and the West Coast had even finished voting. Luke Spearman went on television and called for some sort of 're-vote' crying foul, even though he could have won the entire Pacific time zone and still have not been elected. It was pitiful, Ophelia thought.

Mom and Pop were already asleep by the time it was ready to go downstairs to the ballroom to meet Danny and his wife. The place was full of people even though they had been screened by the Secret Service. There were balloons already falling from the ceiling, people with noisemakers, it was chaos.

And out came Danny and Jerry, first with their wives and then the campaign gang, the close ones, Ophelia, Corky, just the select few. John was watching it all on television back at The Peabody with Harmon Vance and Arthur Boone.

"I just wish your daddy had lived to see this, Arthur," John

314

said as he stroked Arthur's arm. "Harmon, we did it!" John gasped as Harmon handed him a Black Jack and Cubano. To hell with it, they agreed, John was going to celebrate.

Ophelia was finally in the limelight, but it was not blinding as she thought it might be, there was no warm glow. It was all dark without John. As soon as Danny gave his acceptance speech she made a beeline to the nearest telephone to call John.

"Can you believe it, Mr. Thompson? Danny Carson is going to be the next President!" she squealed like a little girl.

"I know. He's already called me to thank me for all your help! See, you did the hard work, girl! Now you stay down there as long as you like, enjoy yourself," John told her, hoping she would want to come home to him.

"Please let me come back, Mr. Thompson. I want to be with you!"

"Then come home tomorrow, you've done well. You're a fine American!"

⚜ ⚜ ⚜

Ophelia saw Mom and Pop off the next morning, determined to get back to John as soon as possible.

"Ophelia, I swear before God, I could hear that ruckus all the way upstairs last night," Pop told her. "I got up and told those 'secret people', or whatever you call'em to see if they could hold it down," he said as he got into the limo for the short ride back to Franklin.

Ophelia was glad she called them. She wanted to share the night with them, a once in a lifetime event they might enjoy, or at least talk about for a few years back in Franklin. Mom loved it and everyone loved her cornbread. Corky thought they were great and had asked Ophelia where she had been keeping them. They would have been great campaigners.

'A fine American' she thought as the jet roared toward Memphis and home, back home with John. This time Harmon was there to meet her on the tarmac. He told her that his condition hadn't changed much. He was still mostly in the bed, giving orders and making sure she was okay. He was elated at the news of Danny's election and it had seemed to give him enough strength to smoke a cigar and take another drink – though only after they had run the doctors off.

"Mr. Thompson, you look great! I love you!" Ophelia chirped as she leaned over the bed to hug him.

"I love you too, girl. They tell me I'd better rest for a while. I guess I might ought to take their advice. Stay here with me now. At least until we get that man sworn into office. I want you to be there for me," he said as he drifted off to sleep.

Ophelia was still holding his hand as she looked at Harmon who had a tear in his eye. She stayed there all night, waking up to see if he was okay even though the doctors said he should sleep through the night. She wanted to make up for lost time and didn't even think about going to the river townhouse for the night. She wanted to stay until he awoke, to make sure they would talk again. There was so much to say.

✤ ✤ ✤

Ophelia didn't tell John, but she never left The Peabody after the election until the inaugural in January. She promised him she would attend the inauguration at the Capitol with Corky and Harmon and then for the inaugural ball, even though the glitz, glamour and power of the campaign, the Presidency didn't seem real, attractive or desirable anymore.

She took a suite at the hotel and never let the stares from Marvin and Hennie bother her. Harmon, David Muggs and Arthur were there to comfort them both when John took his protracted naps that seemed to get longer and longer each day. He was lucid, made conversation about the estate on Lake Nicaragua and occasionally let his mind drift back to Beale Street, Senator Moore and always, always, Lamont.

Christmas that year was particularly difficult for them both. Marvin and Hennie had to see John while Ophelia was there. John refused to make her leave the room. John's eldest son Hank brought his children too. He had begun to see more and more of his father now that he was sick, sicker than before. And John wished many times that Hank had stayed to run the business, not that the ball team and all the property mattered that much anymore.

Ophelia took note that John didn't talk that much about baseball anymore. It was all about the people now. Effie had been brought up from Slabtown to see him. She only made things worse as she was prone to break down and talk about death all the time and where they all would be buried. Ophelia thought it kind of creepy, but it never seemed to bother John.

John began to shower Ophelia with gifts, a Presidential Rolex, his 90% ownership of the Boogie Woogie. It was as if he were putting his affairs in order while he could still see the pleasure people would get out of the things, the money he had accumulated. He just wanted to see people happy. He even gave Harmon the yacht after Ophelia had told him she didn't think she could go out on it anymore without him or Lamont being there.

Ophelia had given John a cane with a solid gold handle, one he had admired in a Neiman-Marcus catalog. It was one of those awfully priced items like jet airplanes they make only one of and

317

then send out in the catalog for everyone to drool over, knowing full well they can't buy them. John actually used it to get around the penthouse as best he could.

They all celebrated New Year's as John seemed to gather some strength from Danny's upcoming inaugural. He demanded that Ophelia still attend with Harmon and to represent him well. It was like he wouldn't believe Danny's election was true unless she was there to confirm it.

And then it was time to leave. Ophelia didn't want to let go. Harmon had to lead her away as John was in the midst of one of his prolonged naps that day. As she leaned over him to give him a kiss, his West Point ring fell from under her blouse and onto his chest. John awoke to feel the kiss and return it.

"You're a go-getter, girl. Now go out there and get'em. Show the world," he whispered. The he fell back into his deep sleep.

Chapter Thirty-Four

The New Regime

Ophelia, Harmon and Betty boarded the '404' jet to Washington, DC just one day before the inauguration. Ophelia wanted to get up to DC and return as soon as she could so she could be with John. He had insisted that she make the swearing in and the ball, then she could come home to him. Mitch was keeping him company. He thought it was that important.

The inaugural ball they would attend after the inauguration was for the Georgia and Missouri followers of the new President and Vice President. It would be held at the Washington Hilton at Dupont Circle where the new gang would spend the night. The city was crowded, packed with people who wanted to get a look at history in the making.

Corky Benedict met them at Washington National Airport in a limousine to whisk them away to the Capitol where Danny and Jerry were already preparing themselves to be installed as President and Vice President. It was a miracle that Corky could get the group there in time to have them up on the upper stage where Jerry and Danny would be during the swearing in before it all kicked off.

There wasn't a minute to spare as the ceremony started promptly at 11:30 AM. The senior members of Congress, Danny and Jerry with their families were front and center along with Chief Justice Warren Burger. Ophelia, Harmon and Betty were bundled up against the weather three rows behind them. Everyone was freezing and it appeared they all wanted to get it over with as soon as they could.

Everything was being broadcast worldwide to a live audience. Ophelia knew that she and the gang would be in the field of view throughout the entire ceremony. She had a prearranged signal to John, pulling on the West Point ring through her blouse, so she could send a message that she was thinking about him. John saw it all back in his bed in Memphis and smiled.

After all the preliminaries, it was time for the actual oaths to be taken, Jerry first being sworn in by the Speaker of the House and then Danny. It was smooth as silk, except for when Chief Justice Burger leaned over to Danny and whispered to him that he would be retiring in one month. Danny turned and shot a look at Truman Forsythe seated just behind Ophelia. They suspected what that look meant – and what Burger must have just told Danny.

A huge luncheon was planned just after the inauguration at Statuary Hall inside the Capitol. It was a beautiful setting with its dozens of marble statues of American luminaries of history. Danny was fond of the statue of Alexander Hamilton Stephens, the Vice President of the Confederacy. He was a Georgia-born United States Senator like him, one who had been refused his place after the War because Georgia had not yet been re-admitted to the Union.

Jerry Slater was admiring the statue of Thomas Hart Benton, his hero from boyhood, a US Senator from Missouri first elected in 1820, serving 30 years. His opposition to slavery cost him his Senate seat.

Ophelia admired all the statues and wondered if one of John would someday stand there. If people ever figured out how much he had molded and shaped the destinies of so many leaders like the ones that had just been sworn in, she was sure he would be there.

It was time to see Danny and Jerry up close for the first time since they had assumed office. The closest Ophelia had been to them was during the ceremony outside when Danny kept shooting glances their way. Ophelia had planned well for the moment. Along with Harmon and Betty, she had brought along a friend, one for whom she had obtained a security clearance through Corky.

"Mr. President, I would like for you to meet Miguel Hernandez. I believe you knew his father," Ophelia said to an unusually cool, seemingly not surprised President Danny Carson.

Perhaps to everyone's surprise except Vice President Jerry Slater and Ophelia herself, Danny grabbed both of Miguel's hands and shook them vigorously. Ophelia made sure there was a photographer there to capture the moment for posterity.

"I knew your father at The Point," Danny whispered, leaning toward Miguel. "He was a brave man."

A curious way to characterize someone Danny believed he had removed from office, by whatever means necessary such a short time ago. Miguel kept his cool.

"President Carson, I hope we will be seeing much of each other in the future," Miguel said with a coy smile. Ophelia just looked on.

Danny gave Harmon and Betty a big hug and thanked them for all they had done. Danny told Harmon how much he had enjoyed the renovated theater back in Chicago and reminisced with Betty about the soiree in Memphis. Then he asked about John.

"Is he okay? I wish he could have been here," Danny told Ophelia.

"He's just fine. This weather would not have been good for him, Mr. President. He'd like to send his congratulations though.

Maybe a telephone call would be in order," Ophelia *told* Danny more than recommended.

"Definitely. I'll call him tonight," Danny said as he gave her another hug. "Can we talk just a minute, Ophelia?" he asked as he led her away from Miguel and the others to behind one of the massive marble statues.

It was an odd and uncomfortable scene. A newly elected President of the United States having to ask what in the hell was going on here. Danny knew he would be approached, but he thought that he would actually make it into the White House down the street before it happened.

"Ophelia, what is Miguel doing here!?" Danny demanded.
Just then Jerry Slater, Vice President Jerry Slater, touched Danny's arm to let him know he was there.

"I invited him, Danny," Jerry said. "We'll talk about it later. Let's just get back to the luncheon."

Ophelia's eyes never left Danny's fixed stare. And Danny's never left her's. The 'game was on' in earnest now.

✤ ✤ ✤

The Washington Hilton wasn't the most glamorous venue for one of the many inaugural balls that would take place that night. Danny, Jerry and their wives would make them all though, it was part of their first duties as President and Vice President. But this was the important one.

Everyone who was anyone from the former candidates' home states was there. It was a mixture of Laclede's Landing with St. Louis Jazz music and Underground Atlanta revelry, a party like none other. Hometown boys, West Pointers made good, and everyone expected great things. Many expected great favors.

Danny Carson felt like a man trapped in a cage. "You did

what?" he snapped at Jerry back stage before they made their grand entrance that night.

"That's right Danny," Jerry stated flatly. "I met with Ophelia and John in Miami the night before you announced my acceptance of your offer to be your running mate. I know everything. You need to just do what's right."

'Might does make right after all' John had told Danny when the new President called him just minutes before.

Danny slumped into the nearest chair and stared at the floor. Not even one day had passed and he felt neutered, a man without a country to run. He was already paying for the sins of his compromised rise to the highest office in the land where he thought he would be king of the world. He realized once and forever that he was nothing but a glorified straw man. But he was still the newly-elected President of the United States. He could be defiant now, he thought.

"You tell Ophelia Hartwell that I'll nominate her for the ambassadorship to Nicaragua, but that little bastard Miguel has got to go!" he barked as he shot up from the chair, almost bursting out onto the stage before the introductory 'Hail To The Chief' music had even started. He left Jerry standing there just shaking his head.

It was strange. It was as if Danny was the only person who didn't know, or didn't care what his place was in all this, this grand plan of John Henry Thompson's. Jerry Slater knew. A good man, content to do good things as second in command, he knew his place and remembered how he got there. In time, he would get his shot at the top, he thought.

Corky Benedict knew exactly where the power was. He saw that a long time ago and had been an obedient servant, 'pulling on the same rope' as John would say for the greater good and Danny Carson's election.

Even Emily Wright who Danny thought was 'true-loving' him as John had put it, who had dropped Danny like a hot potato sexually – but not politically. She would dutifully, and opportunistically take her place as White House press secretary.

Ophelia, Harmon and Betty were having the time of their lives, oblivious to what was happening back stage. John had bought Ophelia a David Emanuel dress flown in from London. She had admired Emanuel's fashions Princess Diana was wearing at the time and looked every bit the Belle of the Ball in her ivory silk, pure taffeta gown.

But Betty stole the show with the Georgia crowd. She had chosen a red dress almost identical to the one Rhett Butler had forced Scarlett to wear to Ashley Wilkes's birthday party in *Gone With The Wind*. The Atlanta crowd recognized it immediately and Betty became the envy of the native Georgians, much to Betty's delight.

Danny was anxious to get out on stage and get it over with, to spend his first night in the White House. The orchestra struck up 'Hail To The Chief' and out strode Danny and Jerry with their wives in tow. Danny was smiling the toothy perpetual smile he always sported, but he was searching the crowd for Ophelia Hartwell.

It became more awkward as Danny addressed the crowd, thanking everyone for their hard work and support, promising to be the best President he could be. It was obvious he didn't see Ophelia and Corky standing right in front of and below him. And Ophelia had Miguel on her arm.

It was hide in plain sight for Miguel now, for better or worse. As the waltz music started, just as Danny and his wife made their first dance turn, he finally spotted them both. Even with the silly smile on his face Ophelia could read the Georgia 'go to hell' look Danny gave them both.

Harmon and Corky saw it and Danny saw them. He saw Harmon's West Point ring too. From his vantage point above Ophelia he saw another one, the one hanging on the necklace down Ophelia's gown. He knew for sure it was John's and that it was a symbol of her power now.

✤ ✤ ✤

"There's no turning back now, Miguel," she told him as they strolled along the reflecting pool near the Lincoln Memorial that night. The party had become too crowded and Ophelia only wanted to stay until Danny and Jerry had left. She had made her point. Harmon and Corky were there and Ophelia felt safe. It was getting late.

"I'm ready, Ophelia. I've been ready since long before my father died. I knew his regime would come to a bad end, but I still believe he didn't have to die. I guess it was inevitable," Miguel sighed as he looked up at the statue of Lincoln.

As Miguel stared at Lincoln, mesmerized, Ophelia could see the dreams in his eyes, ones of freedom and prosperity for the Nicaraguan people.

"Do you mind if we go back to the hotel, Harmon," Ophelia asked. "It's been a long day and I'd like to get an early start before getting back to Memphis."

They took the limo for a turn down Pennsylvania Avenue first, down by the White House where they slowed almost to a stop.

"It's going to be interesting, Ophelia. Nothing will ever be the same now," Harmon remarked. "It's a new regime." Regime was the word for the night.

"I wouldn't have it any other way," Ophelia shot back as

Miguel nodded.

At the Washington Hilton the party was still going on. Betty Ferguson was winding down having danced all night long, taking down names and numbers and checking her calendar for dates to invite her new friends over to Memphis for cocktails with her and Mitch.

Danny and Jerry were long gone even though this party was the last on their list.

"Let's all go up to my suite," Ophelia said as they left the ballroom.

Ophelia had made arrangements for cocktails and hors d'oeuvres to be served around eleven o'clock as a sort of reception for Miguel. She had the largest room available at the hotel and was determined to make the best out of her short time in Washington, DC. She had invited all the big money people from Georgia and Missouri to the suite.

Betty was in on the plan. She naturally invited all her new friends she had made that night, especially the ones she had identified with the right connections Miguel would need to legitimize himself on the American political scene.

Miguel was introduced to everyone as a human rights activist from Managua. In effect, that's what he was and it was surely how Ophelia sought to have him portrayed to his new friends and to the world.

Miguel was articulate and naturally knowledgeable about the subject. He wooed the ladies with his Latino good looks and convivial nature. He got his points across, how the current government was repressive, not in touch with the people. No one in the room even knew who President Hector Gonzalez was, much less that he had replaced Miguel's father as the de facto dictator of the country. For that matter, most of the people couldn't find Nicaragua on the map.

But it sounded good and they were political animals always looking for the next dogfight. They had never been around someone with such charisma who was championing a cause new to them, and one obviously near and dear to Ophelia Hartwell. If it was good enough for her, it was good enough for them. Some even started to break out their checkbooks thinking it was another fundraiser, that maybe the cycle had started all over again. It was that good.

But Ophelia's aim was to only start making introductions, to get Miguel's name out into the circle of friends of the new President. Pretty soon, she thought, Miguel would be the new favorite kid on the block, and by extension, someone Danny Carson could not deny.

But it was already after midnight and the party was just about pooped, as Ophelia would say. Harmon, Corky and Betty had bidden goodbye after all the rest and now it was just Miguel and Ophelia, alone. As Miguel reached the door he kissed Ophelia gently and opened the door to leave. Ophelia grabbed his arm and pulled him back. Time was wasting. This time, he was staying the night.

Chapter Thirty-Five

Growing Pains

"I saw you pulling on that ring girl, sending me that message on the television! Did you have fun up there in DC? How'd Danny do?" John asked Ophelia. He was excited she was back and was, much to her pleasure, back in his wheelchair, but weak. The hospital bed was still in the room and reminded her that he was still not well.

"Mr. Thompson, he put on a good show. And you should have seen Betty, I mean Scarlett O'Hara, she was a hit too!" she said as he she gave him a kiss.

"Sit down and tell me everything. Damned, I wish I had been there!" John said as reached for a Cubano.

Ophelia told him every detail, every word Danny spoke, the inaugural, the luncheon at Statuary Hall, everything. John had seen the inaugural address on television with Mitch. He thought Danny did a good job, Danny was always articulate, a well polished speaker.

And he also saw Chief Justice Burger lean over to Danny after he swore him in.

"Did I see Burger give Danny a damned kiss?" he laughed.

"No, he said something to him, although I don't know what. But Danny immediately shot a look a few rows back at Truman Forsythe," Ophelia explained.

John smiled. He knew what that meant.

"Well, Danny called me that night after the inauguration. He said he had talked to you and Harmon and that he had asked about me. I appreciated the call. Maybe he'll do right after all. I know we're going to need to stay in touch with Jerry, I mean *Vice President Slater*," he smiled. "Here's the number where you can reach him anytime. Just keep me posted and watch yourself girl."

John was always one to tell Ophelia to be careful. He was feeling like talking and she thought she would try and get a few more stories out of him, about the old days. It always seemed to do him good to talk.

"Mr. Thompson, do you really feel like these people would do anything to hurt me? I would be amazed if they did," she said leaning on his arm.

"Some people, *some people,* will do anything to get ahead. Don' think they won't," he said with a gasp. "Let me tell you what happened right here in Memphis, how it affected me personally. It's not a pretty story and I've never told it to anyone else. I hope you don't either."

As Ophelia shook her head vigorously she took a seat beside John.

"There was this young man named Royce Phelan. He was a little older than me, about my brother Gordon's age," he started. Ophelia had never heard the name.

"Old Hugo Moore, the Senator, he pegged Royce as one of his potential go-getters, and well, Royce knew the Senator through Hugo's nephew, Billy. Billy and Royce were close, University of Tennessee alums and Billy was the only real family Hugo had to his name. Billy was in line to get everything after Hugo died," John almost whispered now.

"But Royce, well I knew Royce only a little, let's just say I saw him around town when I was building up all this," John said as he motioned out the window toward Beale Street.

"You never knew my brother Gordon, but he was a lot like Royce, he would have done damned near *anything* to be as successful as I have been. But, he didn't have any people skills, girl. He wanted it all handed to him or he would take it, just like Hugo."

Ophelia remembered that Harmon Vance had told her that Gordon and John had a 'parting of the ways' as John put it many years ago. She was about to learn why.

"Well, my brother and I fell out long ago when he told me something he shouldn't have," John lamented.

He told the rest of the story only to make a point. Seems Gordon knew that Royce Phelan really started the great race to make a million dollars forty years ago by running his best friend Billy Moore's car off the river bridge – with a drunk Billy in it.

"He thought he would have it all, be Hugo's heir-apparent after he killed Billy. But in the end, all he did was stick a gun in his mouth," John whispered.

"Are there people out there that would kill your ass for the almighty dollar, for power? You damned well better believe there are. And the stakes now are much higher than seeing who gets Hugo Moore's money, girl!"

The point wasn't lost on Ophelia. As her hands shook, she poured them both a Black Jack.

⚜ ⚜ ⚜

Ophelia called Miguel daily now. He was back in Miami waiting for word from her, what to do, when to do it. It had been three weeks since the inaugural and Ophelia was staying in Memphis close to John. It buoyed his spirits and consequently his health. She was staying at her townhouse now and helping run the big show of The Memphis Blues, the media work, the press releases on new player acquisitions and interview requests.

Ophelia and Betty made the social scene in Memphis and even over to Nashville. Betty had contacts all over Tennessee, Chattanooga, Knoxville, everywhere. Ophelia was getting an education about Tennessee politics from border to border.

Ophelia would leave on the '404' jet to travel to Atlanta with Betty to stay in touch with the new friends they had made, but they would always return to Memphis the same day. She was maximizing her time with John.

On returning to Memphis and The Peabody offices one day she saw a message she had received from the White House Office of Presidential Personnel. It was a ream of paper requesting personal and business information about her, basically concerning everywhere she had been and everything she had ever done. It was about an appointment as Ambassador to Nicaragua.

"Mr. Thompson, I thought they would at least telephone me first!" she said, as she couldn't contain herself. She had taken the packet directly to John.

"I'm sorry girl, Jerry Slater called me the other day. I wanted it to be a surprise. I guess they're still working out the kinks up there," he said as he gave her a hug and a kiss. "Congratulations girl, you'll be a shoo-in at the Senate hearings," he gushed.

Senate hearings. Ophelia hadn't thought about that. Her mind immediately went to Miguel. Would he be an issue? Then she thought of the Lake Nicaragua plantation.

"Mr. Thompson, what should I say?" she wondered aloud.

"You don't worry about it. You're going to take this paperwork up there tomorrow and see Jerry. It'll all be taken care of. Don't worry about it," he tried to convince her. Ominously he said, "Danny will do the right thing!"

It was always the right thing according to John Henry Thompson. She knew she would have to spend at least one night in DC and made arrangements to leave early. She thought she should keep her distance from Miguel until it was all confirmed, a process that she thought might take some time.

⚜ ⚜ ⚜

Some Vice Presidents are shoved into the Old Executive Office Building digs, Jerry Slater was right in the West Wing with Danny. By John's design of course, Jerry was involved in all the daily briefings and in every decision the new administration was making.

Jerry greeted her as the Secret Service escorted her to his office.

"Ophelia, it's wonderful to see you! Thank you so much for coming to the inaugural. How's John?" he asked warmly.

"He's okay. He sends his regards, Mr. Vice President," as he hugged her and motioned for her to have a seat across from his desk.

"None of that, Ophelia. In here, it's Jerry, please," he said. She was comforted and felt out of place at the same time. She was worried about Miguel and the impact he might have on the hearings. She wondered if she had been too bold in bringing him to DC on inaugural day. She decided to follow Jerry's lead.

"Now listen, everything's taken care of here. Danny, of course, doesn't like it, but the hearings will go smoothly. Just put on a good face and keep your cool. It'll be okay," he said, much to her relief.

"Now, let's go see Danny," he blurted – much to her surprise. Jerry led Ophelia around the hall to the Oval Office. She had never been there and was indeed not prepared to see Danny Carson, President Danny Carson again so soon.

It was just like in the movies, the huge desk, the flags, and Gilbert Stuart's portrait of George Washington on the wall, the stunning rug with the Presidential seal. It all sent chills down Ophelia's spine like she thought it would. It was magnificent.

"Come around here and have a seat," Jerry said as he motioned Ophelia to sit behind the President's desk – in the President's chair. She naturally hesitated, but went ahead anyway.

"Don't worry, Danny won't be here for a few minutes!" Jerry said.

Wouldn't you know it? The instant she sat down, just as the photographer Jerry had called in snapped her picture, Danny walked in the room.

"Well, I see you have designs on my office," Danny laughed as he strode very Presidentially over to Ophelia.

"I'm sorry, Mr. President!" she yelled as she shot up from the chair. "Jerry, I mean Mr. Vice, I mean, Mr…." she blurted out.

Danny and Jerry, even the photographer laughed loudly as Danny walked around the desk and gave her a hug. They made her feel at home, unusual coming from Danny after the events of inaugural day, she thought.

She stayed fifteen minutes, a lifetime for her knowing that Danny's schedule must be a nightmare. He assured her everything would be okay during her confirmation hearings, that it would be 'smooth sailing' for her. It was almost too good to be true.

"We have a friend named Julio Fuentes down in Nicaragua," Danny said as Ophelia perked up. "He's a West Point man like Jerry, John and me. I believe you've met him, haven't you?"

Caught totally off guard, Ophelia resisted the temptation to lie. Why would they care if she had been to the plantation and met Julio? She trusted that if it were a roadblock to her nomination, to her confirmation, that John would have foreseen it.

"Yes, I do know him. A fine man," she said firmly.

"Good," Danny said. "Listen to him. He'll tell you everything you need to say. Jerry will fill you in further."

And that was it. After the photographer was brought back in for a few photographs with Danny and Jerry, she was handed a press release with a photograph of her and Danny already on it, a print from the inauguration day luncheon at Statuary Hall.

"Let me know if you need anything, Ophelia. Let's stay in touch," Danny said as he hugged her again. Danny had a plan, he thought.

Jerry was taking Ophelia under his wing and she knew how and why. A long time ago John had made sure Jerry would be in the White House with Danny for just such an event. Jerry was even feeding Ophelia dinner that night.

✤ ✤ ✤

Sara Slater was a Harvard trained lawyer who had done very well in St. Louis. She divided her time between the capital, Jefferson City, and her offices not far from Laclede's Landing in St. Louis. She was as smart as Danny's wife was pretty and a great asset to Jerry.

Ophelia didn't know her as well as she did Jerry since Sara had spent so much time apart from him on the campaign doing her own thing. She was a natural campaigner in her own right. There was even talk that maybe she was the one who should be in the office next to Danny instead of her husband. That fact never bothered Jerry. She didn't have someone like John backing her all the way.

"Ophelia, welcome to our new home. It's still a mess. We're using our own furniture and I'm afraid it's taking a while to get settled in," she said politely.

Ophelia felt comfortable, if not a little guarded around Sara. She didn't know how much Sara knew, a feeling she would have around many of the new people she was going to meet in government. Jerry would assure her that it should be the other way around. The people that worked for her should be the ones worried about being uncomfortable. She would be in charge.

The Slaters had taken up residence at Number One Naval Observatory Circle, the official residence of the Vice President since 1974. It was a white 19th Century house over on Massachusetts Avenue just down the hill from the Naval Observatory.

It was more than just a dinner. Jerry used the occasion to brief Ophelia on the 'problem' with Danny. The new President was adamant that Miguel Hernandez would never hold any position of power in the Nicaraguan government. To force the issue would be a problem, he thought. But he would do whatever Ophelia, and John wanted done.

Jerry's best advice was to get Ophelia confirmed first, then worry about all the details of changing the world.

"One step at a time, Ophelia," Jerry said carefully, and in front of Sara. Ophelia had to think by now that Sara knew the story. She felt as if she could speak openly.

"Jerry, all I know is to trust what Mr. Thompson tells me. Why is the President so opposed to Miguel?" she asked.

"It's not Miguel per se, Ophelia. It's the fact that he is his father's son. It's a 'sins of the father' situation, I'm afraid. You know, like in Leviticus, the book of Kings, the Bible?" Jerry explained.

Ophelia wasn't as up on her Bible as she might have been but she got the meaning.

"So it's all because Danny, the President, hated Miguel's father, because he wanted him removed so he could claim credit and launch his campaign?" she asked. "And that's it?"

Jerry looked at Sara and said simply, "I'm afraid so. You see, Ramon was an embarrassment, especially being a classmate of ours at The Point. Listen, let's give it some time. We'll work on it."

Damned right she would.

Chapter Thirty-Six

Confirmation

Ophelia wondered aloud why Danny Carson had brought Julio Fuentes into the discussion. He was to be her briefing contact on all things Nicaraguan before her confirmation hearings were to begin. They were to meet at the Ritz in Miami with Harmon Vance leaving Memphis and John to make it more comfortable for her. She would call Miguel to meet her there as well.

John was still in his wheelchair at The Peabody when Ophelia called to let him know about the meeting with the President and Vice President. She was excited while still slightly intimidated at the meeting, the prospects of the confirmation and the work that had to be done to prepare her for the Senate hearings.

"Mr. Thompson, I hope I'm up to all this. I've never been through anything like this before," she told him by telephone as the '404' jet sped toward Miami.

"Just listen to Julio, girl. He knows what you need to say. It'll be a cake walk," John told her in his casual, stress-free way. "Harmon will be there to help you."

Harmon would be a great comfort to her. However, he was a constant reminder that the old gang had been broken up, that John was back in Memphis while she was trying to move forward in her career, to make her and Miguel's life better. She was torn between all that and wanting to be back in Memphis with John. But there

337

was no time to waste and she needed the preparation, time she knew she would not get if she went back to Memphis.

Julio and Miguel were already there at the Ritz when she arrived. David Muggs was with Harmon and they would arrive later that day. Miguel and Ophelia had time to walk the harbor before the others were ready to get down to business, time to wonder what would happen if she were to be confirmed as Danny Carson's ambassador to Miguel's country.

"Ophelia, I don't want to be a liability to you, not now, not when you have a chance to do something good for my country, for my family. I don't need to be here," he said as she stopped beside *The Ophelia* docked in the harbor.

"What do you mean? How can I do anything you want without your input, your guidance?" she asked, puzzled as to how she might form a plan without him there.

"Just listen to Julio. We must leave each other now. It's the only way," he said, giving her a slight kiss as he pulled away from her.

Ophelia fell silent as he walked toward a car parked a block away. A man was standing there with the rear door open, obviously waiting for Miguel all the time. Ophelia started to follow but instead followed her instincts and said nothing. She had learned by now that there had to be a plan, some well-constructed scheme to save all this between her and Miguel. John and too many others knew how important he was to her.

As Miguel reached the car he turned and waved to Ophelia. He was going back to Lake Nicaragua.

⚜⚜⚜

"Why did Miguel leave, Julio? How can I know what issues to bring up in the hearings if I don't have him as my guide? What's going on?" she asked as Julio drew on his Cubano he had lit.

"Miguel will be at the plantation where he will be safe, Ophelia. We don't need him to be in the mix right now. Danny hates him, no, a better description is that he is afraid of him. He represents everything Danny thought he fixed in Nicaragua, instability, cronyism – all of it," he said as he sat next to Ophelia.

"I have a plan, but I need you to follow it to the letter or none of this will happen, none of it. Trust me," he said as he looked deep into her eyes.

Ophelia had no choice. Julio, John, Miguel, even Jerry Slater had given her no other choice. All the people she trusted since she had met John Henry Thompson seemed to know what to do. But as always, she did not know the whole plan and understood by now that it was for her own good that she didn't.

Julio had a ream of notes for her to absorb. The information ran the gamut from the topography of the country to its political history, focusing on the most recent 'troubles' under Ramon Hernandez. That was the touchy part. She had to tread lightly on the issue of Ramon. And there could be no mention of Miguel. To do so would incur the wrath of Danny Carson's friends on the Senate committee.

Harmon and David Muggs arrived that night to help her and shepherd her through the mounds of papers. Harmon had experience on Capitol Hill helping John's politicos get positions in government over the years. He would drill Ophelia until midnight every night in a question and answer format making sure she knew everything there was to know about the country and the people.

On the subject of politics, she was to offer nothing to the Senators, until asked. Then she was to say only that the people should be free, Julio told her. They should be free to make their own decisions on who should run the country and on the issues of commerce. People should be able to own land and prosper from it.

It was just like John had promised the people who had helped him make the Beale Street Revival come true so many years ago. Just like he had told old Hugo Moore. It's not all about making more money, it's about the people. Even as John was amassing a fortune around the world, in real estate, in oil and gas, in a hundred different ventures, he never forgot about the people he dealt with.

That was the reason he kept his enemies close to him too. Better to have them near and watch them than far away and wondering what they were doing. It was even more important in politics, John would say. You make and break a politician, he thought. Better to make them and have them on your side. Truman and Jerry were big political prizes and were already on his side. But Danny, the biggest prize of all, would still need a little convincing. He was the keystone and stumbling block to getting this plan to succeed. There would have to be some sacrifices made.

❖ ❖ ❖

Danny had named an unusually large number of potential appointees already and the confirmation process was moving along swiftly. He had received over 60% of the popular vote and was already becoming a popular President too. Having served in the Senate, he didn't have much opposition in getting his nominees confirmed there. His former colleagues preferred instead to curry favor with the new President by moving the candidates through with a dog and pony show made up of mutual admiration speeches.

Ophelia had come highly recommended. The contacts she had made on the campaign circuit had served her well. With the telephone calls and letters coming in from John's friends daily, Ophelia seemed to be a shoo-in for immediate confirmation.

David Muggs would make the trip to Washington, DC with her but could not be at the hearing. It would be an 'up and back' trip with them returning to Memphis the same day she testified.

The Hart Senate Office Building was the site for Ophelia's hearing. She was nervous and was all alone, no one could be there that might tie her back to Julio, not even Harmon. Jerry Slater had sent Corky Benedict to sit behind her as the administration's representative. It was comforting to have Corky there, even though she knew she would have to form her own answers and opinions, Corky was now Danny's Chief of Staff and would be a continuous reminder to the Senators that she had Danny's endorsement.

She was technically a Tennessean now, but that apparently didn't mean anything to Democratic Senator Hubert Montgomery, the heir to Hugo Moore's seat. He had campaigned on freeing the state from the political machine Hugo had built, for equal rights and breaking the shackles people like Moore had bound the little people with all those years. He wasn't a bad Senator, he just like to grandstand, be the 'people's Senator', as he styled himself.

John had not helped Montgomery get elected. He took no sides when half of Tennessee tried to take Hugo's place as Tennessee's political boss. John knew those days were over for Memphis and Tennessee. People had their fill of characters like Hugo Moore and were determined to never let anyone get that much power again, at least not in politics. John preferred to let them all fight it out. He didn't 'have a dog in that fight' he would say.

Montgomery was shrewd to realize all that and instead promised to stand up for the guy on the street and campaigned openly on an anti-corruption platform, an indirect anti-Hugo campaign of sorts, and it worked for him. And he had lived up to his promises. He was the devil's advocate on the committee and would ask questions of the Pope if he would ever be nominated for anything.

Montgomery was only powerful in the sense that he was one of only one hundred in the upper body of Congress. His refusal of political action committee money had made him somewhat of a pariah in the Senate making the rest of the bunch look like they could be bought. It also made him less effective as a legislator and was counterproductive for him. He should have taken the money, John would think. Politicians were always bought and sold, he would say. Just look at Danny Carson.

Ophelia answered all the questions easily. She had done her homework, shared her knowledge of the country, her love of the people and places she had seen. It was all very convincing. But Senator Montgomery had a few questions of his own.

"Miss Hartwell," he started. "You work for John Henry Thompson in The Memphis Blues baseball organization, don't you?" he asked as Ophelia leaned toward the microphone.

"Yes, I do. I handle media affairs and scheduling for Mr. Thompson among other things such as real estate development," she told him.

Ophelia thought that was a pretty good summary of her duties. But Montgomery wanted to know more.

"Did you happen to know Ramon Hernandez, the late President of Nicaragua?" he asked catching Ophelia by surprise.

For a second she thought he had asked her about Miguel and she immediately wondered if she should defy the oath she had taken to tell the truth. But he had asked about Miguel's father, a person she had never met. Ophelia would choose her words carefully.

"No sir. I never met Ramon Hernandez," was all she would reply.

Montgomery seemed perplexed – and angry.

"Miss Hartwell, I want to remind you that you are under oath," he said as he leaned toward her, peering over the top of his glasses. "So, you mean to tell me that you have no allegiance to Ramon Hernandez!"

Ophelia thought quickly. She had never met Hernandez and she didn't support or agree with the way he ran the country either. She could answer truthfully that she had no allegiance to him or his ideas. Miguel even agreed that his father was a tyrant. That was the reason he was trying to change things. But she knew she could not put herself into a box, paint herself into a corner. She would have to leave room for her eventual support of Ramon's son.

"I have no allegiance to Ramon Hernandez or any of his ideas. In my view, he was not a good President," she said.

Ophelia almost added that the current President, Hector Gonzalez, was not a good President either. But that could wait.

✣ ✣ ✣

"You did it, girl!" John said as he hugged and kissed her.

Ophelia had taken the '404' jet directly back to Memphis after the hearings were recessed. Hubert Montgomery's question was the last for her and it left a bad taste in her mouth. She wondered if Montgomery had gotten his information a little skewed, if he had meant to ask her about Miguel instead of his father. She thought twice about asking John but found it wise to wait until he broached the subject. She knew it must have been part of a plan. Nothing like that was ever left to chance and certainly wouldn't be in such a high stakes game they were in now, the Big Show of politics.

"You know that damned Hubert Montgomery has been a pain in the ass ever since old Hugo died. At least in Hugo, you knew what to expect," John said as he lit a cigar. John had slowed down a bit, but Ophelia sensed that he was getting even weaker.

"But, I finally got through to him, girl. Seems he wants me to invest in doing some development along the Cumberland River over in Nashville. I told him to go to hell," John said as he puffed on the Cubano.

Ophelia was learning just one more thing about John, that he was miserably tired of it all. He had all the money that he or ten generations to follow could spend. But he knew an opportunity when he saw one and wasn't about to waste it.

"That was six months ago. He wasn't going to get any money out of it. It was just the fact that Nashville needed some sprucing up, his hometown, you know. Last week I called him and told him to get with Marvin, that he would handle all the details. Marvin would cut him a check. Seems like it worked out okay for you!" John said, laughing a coarse, coughing laugh.

"But Mr. Thompson, you heard how he was grilling me on Ramon. I mean, why did he give me all that grief if he was grateful to you now? It scared the shit out of me!" she squealed, still not getting the hidden meaning.

"Girl, he did exactly what he was supposed to do. He inoculated you against anyone ever accusing you of being a supporter of Ramon Hernandez. The question had to be asked, the issue put out of the way. If he hadn't asked you, one of Danny's friends would have. You needed to say the words that you had never even met Ramon, and you did it," John said flatly. John even complimented Montgomery's bit of acting skill to annunciate the point of Ophelia not ever meeting Ramon. "Didn't know he had it in him," John would say.

John had just one more politician under his belt, one that had eluded him for many years. It was another small coup to add to

344

his victories of synergy and power. And it all came at just the right time.

Through Hubert Montgomery Ophelia had plausible deniability. She had told the world that she came into the embassy in Managua with no allegiance to, no admiration for, Ramon Hernandez. She had not mentioned Miguel or Hector Gonzalez - there was plenty of time for that.

Chapter Thirty-Seven

Managua – The Other Nicaragua

Ophelia couldn't wait to see Miguel, but she tried as best she could to reign in her excitement, her passion for him and Nicaragua. Her nomination had been sent to the full Senate with a unanimous recommendation from the committee. The Senate followed through and Ophelia's nomination was confirmed. No one who voted that day had any idea what was going on in Ophelia and Miguel's minds or hearts, or what was about to happen.

Ophelia hated to leave John who obviously wasn't taking it as easy as she would have liked. He was still making deals with people like Hubert Montgomery and everything he did seemed designed to further her career. She had terrible feelings of guilt as she sat on the US State Department jet heading to Managua.

Ophelia knew that she must be received by the Nicaraguan President to present her diplomatic credentials. She had prepared herself well for the hearings but this was another ordeal in itself. Hector Gonzalez had picked up right where Ramon Hernandez left off. The safe harbor of Ometepe Island and John's tobacco plantation belied the economic and social strife that was the rest of the country.

Gonzalez knew full well who the United States was sending to his country. He also knew that Ramon had killed himself to protect his family from any harm that may come through him being overthrown. He felt no allegiance was owed to the United States, John Henry Thompson or anyone lese. He was his own man, in charge and would do anything to maintain his stranglehold on the country.

Ophelia met the staff at the American Embassy on Carretera Sur, or South Highway, in Managua. It was a side of Nicaragua she had never seen. Managua, a city of almost one million people was not in good shape, especially since Hector Gonzalez had done nothing to extend any aid to the poorest of the people who struggled just to find enough to eat.

The embassy was not much better than the rest of the city. The previous embassy had been destroyed by an earthquake in 1972, an event that left the majority of downtown reduced to rubble. It sparked a movement toward the outskirts of the city from which the downtown area never really recovered. The results were that businesses and government buildings were scattered all over the city making it hard to get around effectively.

Ophelia was replacing Michael Threlkeld, a do-nothing drunk and political crony who spent most of his time sailing on nearby Lake Managua, preferring the calm of the lake to the reality of the political and civil unrest that lay just outside the embassy doors. And Ophelia didn't like him.

There was one career service employee she could trust, Steven Goldberg, a man John had known from Atlanta. She was told he was not an appointee but a civil servant who would stay on board no matter who was appointed ambassador.

Steven had even been down to John's Ometepe tobacco plantation where he would take his family as a getaway from the drudgery of Managua. Steven had in turn helped John in the embassy as a go-between, ferrying messages to Ramon and his government. It was through Steven and his contacts with Ramon that John was allowed to operate the plantation and give the workers a new life.

Ophelia was treading in dangerous waters in the diplomatic corps and welcomed his help. John said she could trust him and that was good enough for her. Goldberg would introduce her to Threlkeld and stay with her for the briefing he was supposed to provide.

"So you're the new ambassador, huh? I stayed on down here until you got here to fill you in on just what a shithole you're moving into in Managua," he started as Ophelia listened calmly.

"You have no clue, do you?" he asked smugly.

Ophelia made her way around to behind the desk in the ambassador's office and sat down. She looked at him squarely and asked, "And what have you done to better this place, to advance the interests of the Nicaraguan people and the United States?"

"The people? Hell woman, most of these people don't even know who the President of Nicaragua is, much less of the United States. They're just concerned where they're going to get their next meal. I've heard about you, and I can see right now you think you're going to change the world. You're a crusader, aren't you?" he asked as he poured a martini, obviously not his first.

"But let me tell you one thing," he said as he took a gulp of gin. "As long as Hector Gonzalez is in office, you'll get nothing done here!"

With that, Threlkeld walked toward the door. As he opened it, he turned and threw in as an almost afterthought, "To hell with the briefing, it wouldn't have helped you anyway." Threlkeld walked outside, grabbed his briefcase and had a car take him to the airport. He was done.

Goldberg just shook his head. He was glad Threlkeld was gone. But Ophelia was a wild card, an unknown in the diplomatic circles and he wasn't sure if she was just another political crony or serious about Nicaraguan relations.

"Miss Hartwell, Madame Ambassador, I'm sorry for that. He's been pretty bitter since he was given this post instead of France. He was just in it for the prestige. He came to hate Nicaragua pretty quickly," Goldberg explained. "He's really not such a bad guy," he told a not-so-convinced Ophelia.

"What was that comment about hearing about me? What did he mean by that?" Ophelia asked Goldberg. She could see that he was hesitant to make any negative comment about Threlkeld. He was, after all, a career employee there to assist the ambassador, any ambassador, and not to take sides. Ophelia knew she would have to make him feel at ease.

"Listen Steven, I like you and we have a mutual friend in John Henry Thompson," she told him as his face brightened. "I'm going to need your help and discretion. We've got a lot of work to do here and I mean to do it well. Can I count on you?"

"I want what's best for the United States, Miss Hartwell. However we can get to that, count me in," he said, much to Ophelia's pleasure. "Threlkeld told me that you were a crusader, as he put, that you wanted to change the world down here, just like he said before. That's all," he told a somewhat disappointed Ophelia. But there was more.

"But, he was right Miss Hartwell. As long as Hector Gonzalez is President, Nicaragua is in trouble."

⚜ ⚜ ⚜

The embassy employees, everyone except the Marines who guarded the compound were housed outside the embassy in commercial housing. Ophelia's quarters were nothing to write home about either. She only used the secure telephones at the embassy and never said anything she didn't mind anyone hearing on her telephone at her quarters. Goldberg had convinced her that the Gonzalez government had the telephones at the housing tapped just as Ramon Hernandez did.

She had telephoned John after she settled in and told him how much different Managua was from the plantation and beauty of the island. He had warned her not to expect too much.

Steven Goldberg and the embassy staff had one week to bring Ophelia up to speed before her meeting with President Gonzalez. She would be seeing classified documents that would tell quite a story of what had been happening in Nicaragua for many years, the corruption, the killing and the efforts to place a progressive pro-American President in office. Someone had been doing something after all.

John had told her a lot, but even he did not know everything the United States government had been doing. Under the cover of USIA, the United States Information Agency, the US had been fomenting revolution with the peasants throughout the country. Just as the movement was going full force, Ramon Hernandez died and a political free-for-all ensued. The result was Hector Gonzalez, a man in many ways worse than Ramon Hernandez. And there was intelligence that Gonzalez was talking with the Russians.

"He's all about the money, Miss Hartwell," Goldberg explained. "And the drugs. He has a pretty healthy cocaine appetite himself."

"What are we doing to unseat him? What about the USIA efforts?" she asked Goldberg as she scanned through the documents.

"We've had to start all over," Goldberg told her, never mentioning Miguel Hernandez. Miguel's name never came up during the briefings, a fact that Ophelia found curious and unsettling.

350

It didn't stand to reason that the embassy did not know about him and his activities. She had to find out more and Steven Goldberg was the only one she knew to trust.

The embassy wasn't bugged, but Ophelia didn't want even the embassy employees to overhear anything she might say to him regarding Miguel. She asked Goldberg to take her on a driving tour around Managua, just so she could get a sense of the place, hoping all the while that she might see some redeeming qualities about the city.

"Miss Hartwell, I'd love to, but we'd have to take Marine escort vehicles. It can be rough out there."

"Fine. Let's go," she said to an amused Goldberg. He liked her spunk and style. Had he been familiar with the phrase, he would have thought her a 'go-getter' as John would say. But he was first a prudent man and chose a crack crew of Marines to man the cars in front of and behind their car. Hector Gonzalez must know by now she was in Managua and he wasn't taking any chances.

The people of Managua knew the US cars when they came by. The black Dodge sedans stuck out like a sore thumb as they made their way through the cobblestone streets off the ring road in Managua. Behind the near-black, tinted windows of the guard cars the Marines were armed to the teeth with M-16 automatic rifles and geared up for any fight that might come their way.

Ophelia and Goldberg were alone in the middle vehicle and Ophelia wanted to talk. It would be her preferred venue for conversation with the only man she knew she could trust to tell her the truth, and to give sound advice.

"Steven, I want you to call me Ophelia when it's just you and me, no Miss Hartwell or Madame Ambassador. I'm just a country girl from Franklin, Georgia," she told Steven, an order that put him at ease. As it always happened with everyone, Steven had liked

Ophelia from the minute he met her. She was like a breath of fresh air in the stale embassy in Managua.

"Thank you, Ophelia, I appreciate that. And you're right. It needs to be Madame Ambassador around the embassy. It's for your own good. By the time Threlkeld had left, the staff had lost all respect for him. They're still watching to see how you're going to handle this job. I can tell you that they like you already," he said making Ophelia feel at ease now.

"I want to ask you a question, but I have to know that what I say to you will remain in the strictest confidence. It's like the State Department briefing people told me, it's in the interest of national security," she said as Steven drove the streets, being careful not to hit the stray dogs and children that were everywhere.

He was surprised to be having such a conversation with her. In the four years Threlkeld had been on the post they had never even discussed a national security issue. It was a first for him and he relished the opportunity.

Ophelia decided to start with a question rather than revealing her alliance with Miguel. She wanted to see what Steven knew first, what allegiances of his own he might have.

"What can you tell me about Miguel Hernandez?" she asked. Steven pulled over to the side of the road. The escort vehicles obliged and kept their positions as Steven told Ophelia his story. And Ophelia was about to get more than she bargained for.

"Ophelia, you were wise to take these precautions today. I know of your relationship with Miguel Hernandez. Although I do work as a Diplomatic Assistant to the Ambassador, it is also a perfect cover for my true work as Station Chief here for the Central Intelligence Agency, a role only you will know about," he said flatly, now in a new business tone that Ophelia had not heard until now.

Ophelia wasn't totally surprised. She had been told she would receive a briefing from Agency employees when the time was right, that they would reveal themselves to her and tell her what she needed to know. The Agency had an active presence for many years with the unrest and threat of undue Soviet influence and shared the same concerns that then-Senator Danny Carson had when he launched his campaign for President.

"Well, I was wondering who was running the show down here," Ophelia laughed a nervous laugh. "Now, can you tell me what I need to know?"

Steven went on to tell Ophelia that there was a fledgling, loosely knit opposition movement against Hector Gonzalez. Miguel was not the leader, in fact, as far as they knew, there was no leader as such. The Agency was trying to help them all they could, but Gonzalez was too strong, the movement too weak to do much good.

In essence, Steven hadn't told Ophelia much more than she already had learned from Miguel. There must be some way to unseat Hector, she thought, but what?

He only had to offer a little more in, "We have a plan Ophelia."

As they turned onto the main highway out of Managua Ophelia knew even more now that Steven was the trusted hand she had hoped for in Nicaragua. But she also knew that he had bosses at CIA back in Langley, Virginia that called his shots. He would be good for information, but any plan of action, particularly one she may devise had to be part of *their* plan. She thought that even John's tentacles did not reach that far, did not influence decisions there. But she was wrong again. There indeed was a plan.

Ophelia got an eyeful that day. The farther they drove outside Managua, the worse the people looked, the poorer, and the more pathetic they seemed. Children were picking through garbage cans and drinking muddy water from potholes. Only now did she fully understand and sympathize with Miguel. Something had to be done very soon.

Chapter Thirty-Eight

Something Had to Be Done

Ophelia hadn't even met Hector Gonzalez yet and she hated him, hated him as much as Miguel or any of the poor and dying people in Nicaragua might. But she had to be a diplomat, keep her cool, 'lay behind that log' John told her in one of her many telephone calls. 'Strike when the time is right', he would say.

John sounded okay on the telephone. Still too weak to travel, he was sending Harmon Vance down to take a look at the plantation and wanted Ophelia to make it out onto the island to see him. She would make it a point, she told him, she hadn't seen Miguel since she had assumed her post and could talk with him only briefly on the embassy telephone.

She trusted that the phones weren't being monitored by Gonzalez's secret police, but had lingering doubts that maybe Steven Goldberg and his Agency people might be listening in just in case there was a mole in the embassy, maybe one of the Nicaraguan nationals who worked there. Goldberg assured her that her calls were confidential, but still seemed to act as if he knew what was going on everywhere, all the time. It was, after all, his job.

Goldberg would be accompanying Ophelia to the Presidential Palace for the introduction to Hector Gonzalez. That fact made Ophelia feel much more comfortable, knowing that the man by her side knew just about everything, about her and Gonzalez, and that he was on her side.

The Palace was opulent and stood in stark contrast to the poverty that started just blocks away and continued on throughout the country. There were guards everywhere armed with AK-47 assault rifles backed up by armored personnel carriers and even tanks. The place was a fortress and Ophelia thought a tyrant like Hector needed all the security he could get.

Steven had told Ophelia that there was nothing to worry about. Although relations between the United States and Nicaragua were not on the best footing, Hector would be insane to try anything against the US Ambassador.

Hector kept them waiting over an hour, an obvious snub and gesture toward his ultimate power. He could do anything to anyone he wanted. But it only made Ophelia mad.

"Bienvenidos," Hector told Ophelia as he took her hand to kiss it, an odd gesture from a tyrant, Ophelia thought.

Steven had told Ophelia that Hector spoke fluent English but their intelligence on the man noted that he refused to speak to Americans in their native tongue, a sort of backhanded slap in the face and open insult at the same time.

Hector was dressed in a silly looking military uniform that he wore when meeting foreign dignitaries. He thought it a further message to all that met him, reminding them of his status as commander-in-chief of the hated armed forces. It was adorned with ribbons and medals, most of which he had awarded himself since his rise to power.

"Hello, Mr. President, I'm Ophelia Hartwell, the new United States Ambassador to your country," she said as she retracted her hand, much to the consternation of Gonzalez. She then presented her outstretched hand for a regular, firm handshake. Hector paused, but then smiled a shallow smile and shook Ophelia's hand. It was a stroke of genius that served to show Hector that he was meeting a formidable foe, no cheeky blonde know-nothing from Hicksvlle.

Through an interpreter, Hector told Ophelia and Steven that he hoped for continued 'good relations' with the United States. Ophelia felt insulted and came back with a well-planned response phrased in a question.

"When will you start giving your people basic human rights, food, and the chance to determine their own destiny? Until that happens, we will never have what you like to call 'good relations'," Ophelia snapped back quickly.

Even though Goldberg had counted on her firmness, it was even bolder than Steven had hoped for.

"This meeting is over!" Hector said, and this time in English and directly to Ophelia. He turned on his heel to leave the room, never even making it to the photo opportunity that was supposed to take place. He was pissed off and it showed. Just what they needed, Steven thought, a pissed off crazy as hell dictator, mad at the United States.

Ophelia was supposed to be conveying the foreign policy of her President. She had crossed the line and had made demands of a President, albeit a bad one, of a sovereign state.

Ophelia shocked Hector with, "Y tambien, eres un puerco!" calling him a pig in *his* language as he abruptly left them standing in the room. She wanted to give him a dose of his own medicine, in his own tongue.

As Steven and Ophelia were being led out of the office, Ophelia made the comment loud enough for Hector's interpreter to hear, "He looked like a Mexican Field General in that silly outfit."

Hector was not amused.

⚜ ⚜ ⚜

Ophelia had made one hell of a first impression, but at least Hector knew that he was being put on notice, she was no Michael Threlkeld, content to fiddle or sail Lake Managua while Rome burned. She was going to do something, she cared about the country and knew that the United States had done nothing to change it for the people, no pressure, or economic sanctions, no political maneuvering that might benefit the Nicaraguan people and ensure the national security of the United States.

The country had only 'traded one tyrant for another' as John put it. It was the main reason John supported Danny Carson, why Jerry Slater was in on everything, with Julio Fuentes waiting in the wings. Why she was there. And why Steven Goldberg had to move up his plans now.

Steven Goldberg was amazed. "Ophelia, you are the only person walking around alive that has ever gotten by with calling Hector Gonzalez a pig – in any language!"

Within the week, Ophelia and Steven were on their way to Ometepe and the plantation to see Harmon and Miguel. She had no idea how quickly things would happen. She was now traveling on a US Army helicopter with a sense of urgency, no more leisurely cruise on Lake Nicaragua watching the parrots and sightseeing. It was all business now, even with Miguel.

Ophelia had put the fear of God in Hector Gonzalez. He had never been talked to like that before. He got the message that she would not sit idly by and allow her adopted country to sink further into decline. He knew she would do something to help the Nicaraguan people and thus shore up the national security interests of the United States. Gonzalez was on the move as well and it served to quicken the pace of change.

Steven Goldberg realized it as well. The Agency intelligence told him that Hector was girding himself for a challenge, for a possible coup, even though he knew there was no organized resistance. Hector was paranoid anyway, but Ophelia's visit had gotten his attention.

Ophelia wished with all her might that John could be there. She was flying solo now, she thought, out on her own with no co-pilot except for Steven Goldberg and the entire United States government behind her. Still, she would have traded all that for the simple presence of John Henry Thompson. He would know what to do.

She had called John from the embassy over her secure line before the trip. He seemed very tired and almost gasped his words. Arthur Boone had told her that he wasn't sleeping well and that he had taken to his bed refusing to get into the wheelchair.

"Girl, are you watching yourself down there? Now you be careful at that plantation. You stay there until it's all over. You go show the world, girl. Just show the world what you're made of," he said not allowing her to say much at all, much less ask for clarification to wait for *what?* He seemed almost delirious.

"I love you, girl," he would say.

"I love you too, Mr. Thompson. I love you too."

⚜ ⚜ ⚜

The Army Jet Ranger helicopter hovered just near the tobacco road where Ophelia and Miguel shared their first kiss. She saw him standing there and knew that both of them must have been thinking about that day, how so much had changed and how they both were out in the open now, pulling on the same rope of change.

Harmon Vance was standing right beside Miguel and Ophelia

thought it strange to see them both together. It was all coming together. But where was Julio? He had been at her side for the briefings just like Jerry Slater said he would be. He should be running the show she thought. For some reason she was deathly worried that something had gone wrong.

It seemed like an eternity for the Jet Ranger to touch down. She had no clue that a US Army ground team was scanning the jungle to make sure there was no threat present before they landed. The game was on in earnest now and Ophelia had forced Hectors' hand, something John, Jerry Slater and Julio knew would happen. And time was wasting.

Ophelia resisted the urge to hug Miguel and Harmon. She was a diplomat now and, as silly as it seemed to her, she wanted to appear to be more dignified as a dignitary ought to be, she thought. Instead, she gave a slight peck of a kiss to each of them as they walked to the estate house. Ophelia looked up at the volcano Maderas and thought of Lamont, wishing that he was there too. It would be the old gang back at it again. Those were the good old days. But she had what she wanted now. It was time for action and she finally had the people around her that could make it all happen – through John.

Ophelia thought this would be just a retreat to see Harmon. What she saw was the entire embassy staff at the plantation. Everyone, except for the Marines, was in the chapel John had built. Something was going on here, something she had no clue was to happen. And she had started it all in motion.

"Where's Julio," she asked instinctively with no immediate answer.

Looking at Miguel she demanded, "Where's your uncle, Miguel?"

"He's dying today Ophelia, Madame Ambassador," he

whispered. "He's dying for his country," he said, sobbing now.

Ophelia turned and looked for answers in the eyes of Steven and Harmon, anyone. There were none. Miguel would have to explain. He took her by the arm and tried his best to calmly tell Ophelia what was to happen that day, of how Julio Fuentes was to meet with President Hector Gonzalez on the ferry out in Lake Nicaragua, alone with Hector and his vast security staff and advisers.

Miguel told Ophelia that Julio was the de facto leader of the resistance. Jerry Slater knew it, Steven Goldberg now knew it – but President Danny Carson had no clue that the former West Pointer had anything to do with overthrowing Hector Gonzalez. He would never have had Ophelia meet with him had he known. And he certainly didn't know that Julio had less than six months to live, brain cancer, inoperable.

Everyone wheeled when they heard the explosion, a deafening roar that came from beyond the jungle, somewhere out in the vast lake. A Hellfire missile fired from a US Army Blackhawk UH-60 helicopter was all it took. Everyone on board the ferry, Hector, his staff, Julio, all of them were killed instantly.

Ophelia turned to Miguel who was now crying openly. A woman who she knew must be Julio's wife was holding her head in her hands. Miguel moved to her and tried to console her. "He did it for us," is all he could tell his aunt.

Steven walked to the chapel and told the embassy employees that they would be at the plantation for some time, until *it* was all over. Until it was safe to go back.

"Until *what* is over?" Ophelia demanded, now taking Steven by the arm and away from the group. "Until *what* is over, damn it!" she demanded.

"Ophelia, you jump-started all this. We weren't ready, *they* weren't ready to move on Hector just yet," Goldberg said as he motioned to Miguel who was now standing with a group of men, all carrying weapons. Ophelia recognized some of them from her first trip to the island. She thought they were just security people before. She now knew that they were armed resistance fighters, ones who sought to overthrow Hector Gonzalez, to change their world.

Ophelia's mind was ablaze with clarity now. The plantation was a staging ground, a headquarters, Miguel a guerilla, Julio a leader, all unknown to Hector Gonzalez, but known to and facilitated by John Henry Thompson. She realized that John had been pissed off for a long time. She was the final spark to start the explosion of real revolution, of change. And although the point was lost on everyone else but her, Ophelia knew that John had counted on her going to Nicaragua and putting Hector Gonzalez on notice. John was literally calling the shots.

Some people would have felt used, some sort of a puppet. Ophelia knew what straw men were though, and she knew she had been one for a long time. John knew what she wanted too, Miguel, a free country, and that she didn't mind being a pawn in his chess game. She knew she was the Queen to his King and that he had allowed her to move in any direction she chose – with a little coaching.

But she still couldn't imagine where all this was going. Steven explained the explosion, that it was people dying, that Julio was sacrificing his life by luring Hector into the lake on the ferry with a promise to betray Miguel and Ophelia. He could have their heads on a plate, Julio had told Hector.

Miguel and the armed men boarded the helicopter for places unknown to Ophelia, but she suspected Managua. But there was one more thing that *had* to happen for this grand plan to come into its fruition. And it all centered around John. He had to make his move now.

Chapter Thirty-Nine

Good News, Bad News

The news of Hector Gonzalez's death did not take long to make it to Washington, DC and into the White House - and Danny Carson was livid. The reports, the confidential reports, were shocking to say the least, impeachable offenses he thought. Danny had given the Joint Chiefs of Staff the okay to conduct war games in the western Gulf of Mexico. The request came from none other than the now-*Chairman* of the Joint Chief's, his old West Point comrade General Mark Davis.

"How in the goddamned hell can a Blackhawk helicopter fly out of the Gulf of Mexico up the San Juan River and sink a ferry in Lake Nicaragua thinking it to be a practice target ship?" he demanded as General Davis and Vice President Jerry Slater sat in the Oval Office.

"Mr. President, no one but you and I and a very few others know of this mistake. I suggest we think about our response," Davis told Danny coolly.

"Mistake hell! This is an impeachable offense, no a criminal violation of international law, goddamn it!" he bellowed, throwing an ashtray at the wall, barely missing the Washington portrait.

Davis didn't miss a beat as he looked straight at Vice President Jerry Slater when he said, "But Mr. President, *you authorized* this exercise."

Jerry just smiled as Danny wheeled around and pointed his finger in Jerry Slater's face.

"No, *you* are the one that brought this seemingly innocuous *exercise* bullshit to me Jerry. What in the hell were you thinking?" the President demanded.

The fact that Jerry and Mark Davis were smiling at each other wasn't missed by Danny. As incredible as it may seem to him, he knew now that this was no accident. And it served as perfect proof that he was not running the show. Danny slumped behind his massive desk and clasped his hands over his face.

"Why?" was all he could come up with in the face of it all.

General Davis stood up and said simply, "Mr. President, I'm afraid we're obliged now to send in our troops to secure our embassy and ensure order. I have already evacuated our embassy employees to a place of safety – John Henry Thompson's estate."

At the instant Davis uttered John's name, Danny sprang to his feet and began a tirade that 'would have done old Khrushchev proud' as John would say.

"That son-of-a-bitch is behind this! You bastards set me up! I'll crucify you for this, every goddamned one of you!" Danny barked.

Just as Danny was marching to the door to get the Secret Service agents into the room, Jerry Slater walked to the telephone and dialed it.

"Danny, before you open that door, I think you need to talk to someone. If you don't, you won't even be in this office by this time next week." Slater said coolly.

Danny somehow knew not to take another step. As he turned, he saw Slater dialing a number he knew too well, one that started with area code 901 – Memphis, Tennessee.

"Hold on just a minute John, he's right here," Slater said as he held out the phone to a still-frozen President Danny Carson.

Danny had the look of a corpse on his face. There was no visible color anywhere under his skin. Indeed he was dead inside when he slowly walked to the telephone and snatched it from his Vice President's hand.

Danny's mouth was so dry he had to call up enough saliva to form the word 'hello' to a waiting John.

"Danny old boy, you're in a world of hurt right now. I thought I'd just give you a ring and call up that favor. Just do what Jerry and Mark tell you today and we'll be even!" John said very matter-of-factly.

For effect John added, "Hang on just a minute, Danny, and let me turn down the noise on this tape recording of that day we met in Atlanta, the one my man David Muggs made from the other room. No, wait a minute, this is the one of you and Ophelia in the room that day you promised her the diplomatic spot. You remember, don't you? The night she told you to stop seeing that cute little press secretary," John said.

John felt the business of unmaking kings a little depressing and even tiring. He was done.

"Gotta' go now Danny, I'm feeling really tired." With that, John simply hung up the telephone.

Danny couldn't speak. He didn't speak. He simply held the telephone in his hand. Jerry had to put it back on the receiver.

General Mark Davis stood and asked, "Should I go ahead and give the order to secure Managua, Mr. President?"

Jerry just looked at Danny, Danny simply nodded his head and sat down.

"And by the way, Mr. President," General Davis said. "A West Point graduate was killed on that ferry today - our friend Julio Fuentes. I believe our best story will be that he was your emissary, trying to discuss peace with Hector and that he had Julio killed. We intervened – and the rest, well, it'll follow quite smoothly, I think. Hell, Mr. President, you'll come out a hero on all this," he said as he smiled at Jerry and dialed the Pentagon.

As Danny's head snapped up to look at Davis, it was clear that this king John had made had no clothes on now. Danny would wear his Presidential suit just three more years and never run for office again. He was a ruined man and would leave office after just one term.

⚜ ⚜ ⚜

Nicaragua was like a drill for the combined forces of the United States. Already primed for battle with the 'exercise' General Mark Davis had begun, air, sea and land forces made easy work of mopping up the rest of Hector Gonzalez's remaining forces in Nicaragua. The hardliners were all on the ferry and were killed. What had been expected to be a party cruise on Lake Nicaragua had turned into their funeral pyre.

At the plantation, Steven Goldberg had been kept abreast of the invasion. There was cautious celebration and uncertainty. Where were Miguel and his men? Ophelia paced the floor of the plantation and tried her best to telephone John. She couldn't get through. No one had any telephone service. The only means of communication was by radio and then only for official purposes, the network being reserved for the operation.

Steven had set up a command post inside the plantation and was in contact with the military planners and tactical teams that had been inserted into the country. Some had even arrived at the plantation much to the delight of the embassy employees and the workers who felt they had just been liberated.

In fact, they had been rid of the tyrant they all detested. But they had false hope before. Ophelia would do her best to make sure this opportunity was not lost. Steven had told her that there was minimal loss of life in Managua where a few of Gonzalez's die-hard supporters had holed up in the Presidential Palace. That's where Miguel was, fighting to get inside.

Ophelia demanded that Steven take her back to Managua.

"How can I expect these people to respect me, to believe in me if all they see is me here, cowering at this plantation? I have to get back there and do all I can, Steven. Take me back now," she told him.

Somehow he knew that refusal was out of the question. She was technically the boss and he would have to obey her orders and order a helicopter into the plantation. Three Blackhawks were summoned to fly escort to the Jet Ranger that had by this time returned from the run to Managua, and Ophelia and Steven got on board.

Harmon Vance promised Ophelia he would keep trying to get John on the telephone and tell him they were okay. He also said that he would lie and tell John that she was okay. Harmon did his best to talk her out of leaving the security of the plantation. John would know by now what had happened and be worried sick about their safety. And he wasn't about to tell John that Ophelia had turned into a warrior.

It wasn't long before they could see smoke coming from Managua from the Jet Ranger. The embassy looked secure so Ophelia ordered the helicopter to take a pass over the Presidential Palace. She wanted to see where Miguel was and what the scene looked like. But it was there that her diplomatic status was trumped by the military orders the pilot received. They were to land immediately at the Managua airport and wait for further instructions. The Palace was too hot to make a flyover.

As the helicopters landed, Steven did his best to convince Ophelia to stay put, to wait out the gunfire and then make her way, with cover, to the Palace. But there were American troops everywhere. Many were going downtown and Ophelia wanted a ride, that's all – no special privileges, no private escort.

"Major, I am Ambassador Hartwell," Ophelia told the highest-ranking officer she could find, Major Janny Biaz, a young go-getter who spoke fluent Spanish. "Do you know who General Mark Davis is, the Chairman of the Joint Chiefs?" she asked with a bluff she hoped would work.

"I have talked with him personally and he has given me permission to go directly to the Presidential Palace downtown. This might be right up your alley. Will you take me?" she asked, not ordered, the young Major.

The young man didn't have to be asked twice. He saw the West Point ring now dangling through Ophelia's disheveled blouse and knew that she must be telling the truth. He had been in the Army for twelve long years now and couldn't wait to get into the shit anyway. He took two platoons from the 101st Airborne and some vehicles and took off toward the Palace. If he wasn't court-martialed, it would make for a great story to tell his grandkids, and it may be the only war story he would get throughout his career.

The streets were deserted. The Managuans didn't know who would be their next leader, tyrant or not, they really didn't care. All they wanted was to escape this coup, or whatever it was, with their lives and some food. They were used to all this by now.

By the time they made it to the Palace the shooting had stopped. There were dead bodies everywhere, mostly of Gonzalez's followers.

Then Ophelia heard a voice, a familiar one. As she looked up to the balcony of the Presidential Palace she saw Miguel. He was blood-stained, but alive and screaming in Spanish through a loud speaker to a group of citizens gathered below. She just stood there and looked at him.

She now saw Miguel in a new light, the one he was basking in on that balcony. She could also see something else she had never seen before and she knew immediately what it was. It was a shiny West Point ring, Class of 1946 on a necklace around Miguel's neck. It was his father Ramon's, one he had put around his neck that day, a sign of respect and of how things could have been, how they were to be.

Miguel was a sight to behold. He was already preaching freedom to his people, of liberation and prosperity. Finally, he saw Ophelia and nodded. They would see much of each other from now on. The country was secure. Another John Henry Thompson plan coming together quite nicely, she thought. A hell of a lot more exotic than anything she had seen before, but in the end, she knew it was the same old concepts. It was all about the people, enabling them through power, synergy, might making right. They had done the right thing here.

⚜ ⚜ ⚜

Ophelia and her mini-army found the American embassy in pristine shape, as was most of Managua. It turned out that Ophelia's little outburst at her meeting with Gonzalez, the one that sparked Hector's paranoid response and early action in the 'exercise', actually benefited the invasion, taking Gonzalez and his troops by total surprise.

Harmon and the embassy staff were there by now. The staff's

families were even starting to return to the commercial housing with armed escorts until the threat of any residual resistance was snuffed out. It was a one-day wonder, an invasion and almost bloodless coup, except where Hector's forces were concerned. It was a well-planned operation.

Harmon Vance did not look well.

"Did you get in touch with Mr. Thompson, Harmon?" she asked. Harmon didn't answer. He just slumped into a chair in Ophelia's office.

"Can I have a drink, Ophelia? I'm going to need one," he gasped.

"John is dead."

Ophelia dropped the decanter and fell to her knees. She didn't cry. She didn't say a word. Harmon knew to keep his place, not to try and comfort her. It would take some time for it to sink in. She just stared out into the courtyard wishing with all her might she had never been to Nicaragua, that she was in his penthouse suite with him every minute of every hour since he fell ill.

But this was all part of John's plan, Miguel, the plantation, his will - and she knew it. He would not have had it any other way. John was dead. The king was dead – long live the king. The kingmaker was gone.

✤ ✤ ✤

John had hung up the telephone after his conversation with Danny Carson and died. His chores on earth were done. Arthur Boone saw it all. It seemed fitting that he was the man who was with John when he died, the son of John's best and oldest friend, Lamont Boone.

Ophelia would leave immediately with Harmon and return to Memphis. Steven Goldberg could handle things indefinitely, if need be. Her job could wait, a triumphal return to Nicaragua seeming somehow not so victorious. A huge price had been paid for it all, for what she, Miguel, Julio and John had wanted.

Danny Carson would have the perfect excuse not to attend the funeral. After all he had an invasion to take credit for, one that the whole world celebrated as a great accomplishment, an extension of American might making right, a real foreign policy coup for the little people just like Danny wanted back before the campaign.

Jerry Slater and General Mark Davis knew the truth, but they let Danny take all the credit. They knew he was on his way out. They were going to the real hero's funeral in Memphis.

Harmon and his wife would stay with Ophelia at her penthouse on the river. Betty and Mitch would come by and offer their condolences. They wouldn't see each other much after that day. It seemed that when someone like John is the glue that keeps people together, when they're gone, it's just never the same again.

Only a select few were invited to the 'private memorial service' Marvin and Hennie had arranged. Harmon was there. He would have been there whether he was invited or not. Marvin still had that West Point imprint on his face from Harmon's ring. He knew not to leave Harmon out of the service.

John had left an explicit will leaving his money and possessions to charities, Marvin and Hank, all of it except ten million dollars each to Arthur Boone and Harmon Vance. He left Ophelia the plantation in Nicaragua and $100 million. Ophelia cried for an entire day. She was flabbergasted.

John also directed that he be buried at Slabtown with no fanfare – right next to Lamont Boone. Ophelia didn't even get to tell him goodbye. Marvin and Hennie wouldn't hear of it. She was out now.

Ophelia went to The Peabody to collect her things the day after the funeral. She was to meet Betty and Mitch at The Peabody lounge one more time. She was selling the townhouse and would make Nicaragua her home, for now just the embassy and the plantation, tomorrow, who knew?

As she entered the lobby of the hotel she ran head on into Marvin. He gave her an icy cold stare and asked bluntly, "What are *you* doing here?"

She loudly answered, "Seeing my friends you sorry son-of-a-bitch! Now get the hell out of my way!"

She shoved Marvin's whispy little body aside and proceeded to her table with Betty and Mitch who were laughing out loud at Marvin, along with the rest of the hotel and the world.

Ophelia saved her tongue-in-cheek wrath for Hennie. Just before she left Memphis she sent Hennie a note telling her how much she appreciated "being allowed to take part in the Memphis miracle" that was John Henry Thompson. Hennie never responded.

Ophelia left Memphis and never looked back. Without John Henry Thompson there, it was an empty place to her. She would never go back. Her grieving for John took on a different manifestation, not just crying at a funeral like the rest. She would grieve for him the rest of her life.

Epilogue

Show The World, Girl

"Are you doing okay, girl? Are you alright?" John asked. He was dressed in his best suit and standing upright, tall with vim and vigor, right on Beale Street. Then Ophelia woke up.

It surprised no one that John Henry Thompson was dead, least of all Ophelia Hartwell. He had done in one lifetime what millions of men put together could never do. And he was a good man. He gave the Ophelia Hartwells of the world a chance. He built up people and institutions and tore down the users of the world making them his straw men, in the end, to do good things for good people. Good men didn't have to hog the limelight, but they could be the man behind the curtain.

Jerry Slater was content with his role in doing good things through a flawed man. Truman Forsythe only wanted to be the Chief Justice of the United States Supreme Court and he did John proud when he was appointed to the Court, serving honorably for the rest of his years. Corky Benedict kept calling Ophelia urging her to take a more active role in politics. He wanted her to run for public office herself.

Marvin and Hennie turned into shells of their already vacuous selves. They spent money like water, founding little mutual admiration societies like a private harbor and a club on the Mississippi with membership by invitation only. It was a joke that everyone got but them. They had all the friends money could buy now.

Miguel became a star. His countrymen loved him, somehow morphing the US-led invasion into a revolution started by Miguel, all by himself. He and Ophelia would deliver. The country came to be more like John's little kingdom on Lake Nicaragua. The people deserved it, John thought. It was his last grand plan he wanted to see through. Then he died. He had done his work.

Ophelia would be a bigger star someday too, if she wanted. Danny Carson would serve out his one and only term. A new ambassador would come to Nicaragua, one appointed by the next President. Unlike Michael Threlkeld before her, Ophelia would stay around for the briefing, one that really wasn't necessary. Everyone knew about the Nicaraguan miracle. But then, not everyone knew the whole story, that a kingmaker had made it all happen.

As Miguel and Ophelia listened to the howler monkeys at the plantation one night, Ophelia thought she heard John and Lamont's voices. They were talking about the old days, about Beale Street, the cigars, the Black Jack and the pitiful Marvin and Hennie show. But it was just the wind and her imagination, the dream that was her life with the gang. Ophelia wondered what lay in store for her. 'Show the world girl', she could hear John whispering. She might just call Corky Benedict and give that a try